A Winter Wedding at Bletchley Park

MOLLY GREEN

Published by AVON
A division of HarperCollins*Publishers* Ltd
1 London Bridge Street
London SE1 9GF

www.harpercollins.co.uk

HarperCollins*Publishers*
1st Floor, Watermarque Building, Ringsend Road
Dublin 4, Ireland

A Paperback Original 2022
1

First published in Great Britain by HarperCollins*Publishers* 2022

A catalogue copy of this book is available from the British Library.

ISBN: 978-0-00-847990-9

This novel is a work of fiction. References to real people, events or localities
are intended only to provide a sense of authenticity, and are used fictitiously.
All other characters and incidents portrayed in it are the work of
the author's imagination.

Typeset in Minion Pro, 11/14pt by
Palimpsest Book Production Limited, Falkirk, Stirlingshire
Printed and bound in the UK using 100% renewable electricity at
CPI Group (UK) Ltd

MIX
Paper | Supporting
responsible forestry
FSC™ C007454

This book is produced from independently certified FSC™ paper to ensure
responsible forest management.

For more information visit: www.harpercollins.co.uk/green

MOLLY GREEN has travelled the world, unpacking her suitcase in a score of different countries which often became her new place of work. On returning to England, she set up an estate agency business which she ran and expanded for twenty-five years. Eventually, she sold her business to give herself time and space to pursue her dream to write novels. She recently moved to a village near Lewes in East Sussex and is still ably assisted with her writing by her white rescued cat, Dougie.

To all the men and women who worked in the 'enigma' that was Bletchley Park. It's been widely acknowledged that the codebreakers brought about the ending of the war by approximately two years, thereby saving thousands of lives. The work, especially that performed by the women and girls, was mundane and tiring, the constant changing shifts causing havoc with their health. What's more, they were rarely told any details about any event they'd played a part in, nor how vital their work was in the war effort, but now their secret is out we can thank them profusely for what they uncomplainingly achieved.

It's also been officially recognised that the geniuses of Bletchley Park created the world's first electronic digital computer, the forerunner to our modern computers, namely, Colossus. At appointed times a facsimile of Colossus can be seen in fascinating action at Bletchley Park in the National Museum of Computing in Block H. In fact, I highly recommend a visit to the Park to appreciate in fuller detail the huge variety of work which was carried out in this most secret location. The few dozen clever and talented people who began on this experimental work at the beginning of the war became 10,000 by Victory in Europe Day, perfectly chiming with a comment once made by Hitler that the Enigma would never be broken because you would need to employ 10,000 people to do it!

Before . . .

Near Norwich, Norfolk
23rd January 1936

Rosemary Frost stood impatiently while her mother adjusted the white satin wedding dress she'd drastically altered from the one her friend's daughter – at least three sizes larger – had worn for her own wedding ten years before. To Rosie's eyes, the way her mother had not only taken it in, but also brought it up to date, made it look brand-new. Rosie glanced at her wrist where her watch, the most beautiful thing she'd ever owned – that is, until she'd looked at herself in the mirror and seen the transformation the dress had made – told her that in half an hour she and Dad would be walking down the aisle towards the boy she loved with her whole heart and soul. She still couldn't believe she'd managed to persuade her parents to allow her to marry Hugo. She might only be seventeen, but she knew her own mind and she would never change it.

What would he be thinking right this minute? Would he be nervous? No, she didn't think so. She'd always admired his confidence. His perfect understanding of what to do in any situation. Maybe that came from being older. Last month he'd even gone with her to her parents and asked her father for his daughter's hand in the old-fashioned way. At first Dad had been knocked for six, though he'd managed not to be rude. But his pinched nostrils gave him away. She grinned at the memory, though at the time she'd quaked. He'd immediately said no, she was far too young.

'Do you have *your* parents' permission?' he'd demanded of Hugo, when the four of them were crammed together in the parlour.

Hugo flushed. 'I'll be twenty-one in January . . . when we plan to marry,' he added, 'so I won't need it.'

'Hmm.' Her father's mouth was a grim line. 'That means *they* don't approve neither.' He lit a cigarette and Rosie bit her lower lip as she waited for him to say something . . . anything that would mean she could marry Hugo.

'If you both feel the same after two more years, your mother and I will reconsider.' He looked at Hugo. 'Then at least you'll have had some experience in your father's business and will be able to support Rosie.'

After Hugo had gone home, thoroughly dejected, she tackled her mother on her own. If she could get her on her side, Dad might be persuaded.

'It'll be one less mouth for you to feed, Mum,' she said. 'And Hugo's so generous with his money. Look what he's bought me.'

She'd hidden the watch for a few days. Hugo had told her it was a special design called Art Deco and that the casing and chain-link strap were solid silver. Where the number '6' should be was a tiny second hand in its own little patterned border of coloured glass. She'd loved it immediately.

'I'll keep it specially for our wedding day as it's too beautiful to wear for every day.'

'Don't think that,' Hugo laughed. 'It's for you to wear now

and enjoy it.' He took the watch from her. 'Here, let me put it on for you.'

Once it was on her slim wrist she admired it even more. Kissing him, she said:

'I'll always wear it – always.'

'Keep it on, and don't take it off until I give you one with diamonds the next time,' he'd chuckled. 'Then you can put this one in the back of the drawer.'

She'd vehemently shaken her head.

'No, don't, Hugo. I don't ever want another one. I love this one.'

A few days later Rosie had rolled up the sleeve of her new jumper she'd knitted from a bag of wool her mother had brought home from one of the ladies at the Women's Institute, and held out her wrist for her approval.

'This would have cost a great deal of money,' her mother said, as she bent close to examine the watch. 'You shouldn't be acceptin' expensive presents from a boy at your age. We in't brought you up like that. I shall speak to Dad and he'll say you have to give it back. It gives Hugo the wrong impression of you.'

'Mum, you might as well know it, but he's asked me to *marry* him. And I've said yes.'

Her mother drew back in horror. 'You're *seventeen*, Rosie. You've got your life in front of you.'

'My life is with Hugo. We're in love and we're going to marry, whatever you and Dad say. We don't want to wait. We'll go to Gretna Green if we have to.'

She hadn't meant to blurt out the last bit. Her mother's mouth dropped open.

'You wouldn't.'

'Yes, we would.'

'You'd bring shame on the family. That we couldn't afford to give you a proper wedding.' Her mother's eyes suddenly hardened. 'Are you expectin', Rosie?'

'Course I'm not.'

'Are you sure?'

'Yes, I'm sure.'

Her mother shook her head.

'I should have told you the facts of life when you started your monthlies – not to let a boy near you until you were married. It's easy to get carried away and—'

'Mum, I *know*. And I'm not.'

'But you let him go all the way.'

Rosie was silent.

'How could you, Rosie?' Her mother's expression was grim. 'We in't brought you up to let boys have their wicked way with you.'

'Not *boys*, Mum. Just one, who's not wicked. He happens to love me – and I love *him*.' She blew out her cheeks. 'Honestly, Mum, Hugo wants to *help* the family if you'll let him, not bring any trouble. As I keep telling you, he's really generous—'

'Dad and I wouldn't dream of accepting handouts from the Garfields,' her mother cut in. 'Your dad's got far too much pride.'

'You sound as though you really dislike them.'

'That's hardly fair. We've only met them once on Hugo's birthday when he took us all out to that expensive restaurant.'

'I only had to see your faces to know what you were thinking. And that was a whole year ago.' She appealed to her mother. 'We haven't changed our minds, Mum. We still love each other and want to be together.'

Her mother sighed. 'We don't have anything in common

4

with them. They're in a class far above us. That's what worries Dad – that Hugo's taken advantage of you when you're so—'

'Y-o-o-o-u-ng.' Rosie dragged out the last word.

'Don't be cheeky, Rosemary.'

Her mother only called her Rosemary when she was really cross. Rosie bit her lip.

'Mum, we don't want to run away to Gretna Green, but we will if—'

Her mother put the palm of her hand up.

'That's enough,' she said. 'I don't want to hear no more about that.'

Rosie got up from her chair in the kitchen and planted a kiss on her mother's cheek.

'Please, Mum, will you talk to Dad? But about us getting married, not about the watch.'

After several days, when Rosie had gained dark circles under her eyes through lack of sleep, her father had eventually, though reluctantly, said yes, he would allow the marriage to take place, but he couldn't be hypocritical and go so far as to give her his blessing.

She didn't care two hoots about his blessing. It would have been nice but it wouldn't make any difference – the outcome was the same. She would go down the aisle in a beautiful white dress which she and her mother would make, and the boy who made her heart sing whenever she set eyes on him, and whom she adored more than anyone else in the world, would be waiting for her.

And finally the day was here – the day they would be joined together as man and wife. Mrs Hugo Garfield. She hugged herself.

'Keep still, love,' her mother said, positioning the veil and digging a kirby grip into Rosie's scalp, making her squeal.

'Ouch, Mum. That hurt.' She twisted her neck to look round at her mother. 'You're not so worried now, are you, Mum, about Hugo?'

Shirley Frost glanced at her.

'I suppose he's genuine enough, but your dad's still got reservations.' She paused. 'That's partly your fault, love. You've kept Hugo under wraps. You've never even said how you met him. I wouldn't've thought he'd mix with our sort.'

Rosie flushed. 'I met him at the Samson where my friends and I went dancing every Saturday night. He was the first boy to ask me to dance.' She smiled at the memory. 'I just hope once we're married Dad will accept him.' She looked at her mother directly. 'Hugo's a lovely man, Mum. I wouldn't be marrying him if he wasn't.'

Shirley Frost sighed. 'I just hope one day you won't regret it. We had great hopes for you after you won the scholarship to go to grammar school – the only one in the family. And studying for your School Certificate. With your brains you'd have gone on to university and won a degree. You could've been a teacher. That's what you've always set your heart on. Teachin' the older kids mathematics. Your dad and I would have been so proud . . .' she trailed off wistfully.

It was true. Rosie had voiced it more than once to her parents. And she was sure she'd be happy in such a vocation instilling enthusiasm in the children by making the subject come alive. But since she'd begun to learn Italian with Signorina Bonetti, her dream was to visit Italy – the culture, the history, the language. And Hugo, who also spoke Italian – it was one of the things that had drawn them together – had promised to take her.

'I'm not just going to stay at home while Hugo goes out to work. I'd go potty. No, Hugo's encouraging me to continue my studies.'

'It won't be the same, love,' her mother said. 'And next thing you know it will be babies. And then you really *will* be tied to the house.'

Like you are, Mum, with all of us.

Not that she'd dream of saying it aloud. She only knew that babies weren't going to get a look in – not for ages anyway. Hugo planned they would have a few years of fun before settling down to a family. He wanted to take her to the Continent, forever describing the museums of Paris, the cathedral in Milan, the natural light in Venice that artists loved to capture, the music in Vienna, as well as places she'd never heard of. Rosie felt a frisson of excitement. She couldn't wait to absorb it all. It was a good thing Hugo's family were well off. If it was left to hers, they wouldn't be going further than Norwich. But even that would be heaven – so long as Hugo was by her side.

She'd wanted only a small wedding, and although Hugo's mother had tried to take over with the guest list, Rosie had firmly put her foot down. A crowd of strangers whom she'd never set eyes on before, showing off their finery and making her parents feel inferior, was the last thing she wanted. Since then, Hugo had mentioned his parents wouldn't be attending. That was fine as far as she was concerned. But how did Hugo feel?

'Is it going to make things difficult for you at home?' she'd said, worried.

Hugo caught her in his arms and kissed her.

'Quite honestly, I'm relieved. I don't know most of them either. It's a pity about Mother as she doesn't get out much, but I wouldn't care if it was only the two of us with two witnesses. So I'll leave it to you. I'll have two or three friends and that's it.'

'What about your brother?'

'Lance? He's still in India. I doubt if he'll be able to get leave.'

'Do you two get along?'

Rosie realised as she asked the question how little she knew her husband-to-be. Well, there'd be plenty of time for them both to get to know one another once they were married. She couldn't help the tingle of anticipation.

'Yes, he's a decent bloke but wouldn't go into the family business – so it was a big disappointment for my father. I'm now the one expected to take over one day, but as I'm the younger son, it wasn't what he had in mind. Lance is only too glad to be out of it and Father's never forgiven him.'

What a horrible man. Poor Hugo.

Hugo kissed the tip of her nose.

'No need to concern yourself about all that, darling,' he'd said. 'Just the usual stuff between family.'

Hugo had ordered two motorcars for the wedding day – one for her parents and her little brother, six-year-old Roddy, and one for Rosie and her two younger sisters, fourteen-year-old Heather and twelve-year-old Ivy, the bridesmaids. The first motor disappeared down the road and when Rosie was making a final check in the dressing-table mirror there was a knock at the front door.

'That'll be ours, I expect,' Rosie said. 'Heather, go down and tell the driver we'll be five minutes, and see if it's stopped raining.'

'Why am I always the one that has to—?'

'Heather, please don't argue on my wedding day.'

Heather curled her lip and disappeared.

'Rosie, I've made you something as a surprise,' Ivy said, holding out a posy of roses and pansies, her glasses slipping down her nose in her excitement.

'Oh, Ivy, it's lovely . . . and you really made this?'

'Yes. I'm sorry they're only paper but—'

'I love them,' Rosie swiftly kissed her sister, 'because you made them specially for me.' She examined the delicate flowers closely. 'You know, Ivy, you're really talented.'

'I'm not that good,' Ivy said, her eyes lowered. 'And Heather says it's a waste of time if I don't sell them to make money.' She looked at Rosie. 'She even said I should charge *you*!'

'Really?'

Heather was becoming a problem, Rosie thought. She'd have to have a word with her. Poor Ivy was becoming stifled under Heather's catty opinions.

'Just because she's two years older than you she's not always right, you know,' Rosie added. 'Anyway, love, tell me if I look all right.'

Rosie gave a twirl for her sister, the ankle-length skirt lifting to her mid-calf as she did.

'You look beautiful, but you always do.' Her sister gave Rosie an admiring look. 'Especially with your lovely red hair. I wish mine was that colour.'

Rosie glanced at Ivy's two forlorn-looking brown pigtails. 'Maybe, but you might not like all the names I've been called at school like "Carrot Top" and "Ginger". I forced myself to ignore them, but they still hurt.' She gazed fondly at her sister. 'And you, Ivy, are lovely just as you are, and the kindest person. Never forget that.' Rosie looked towards the door. 'Now where on earth has Heather got to?'

At that moment Heather burst through the door.

'It's still raining,' she announced.

Almost as if she's pleased.

'And the driver said we better be going right *now*.' Heather stuck out her hand waving an envelope. 'Oh, and the telegram boy's been.'

'Keep it for now. I'll look at it later. It'll just be another good luck message.' Rosie grabbed the little posy and made for the door. 'Come on, you two, or we'll be late.'

Twenty minutes later at St Stephen's, one of the oldest churches in Norwich, Rosie and Ivy climbed from the wedding car with the help of the driver but somehow Heather caught her foot as she followed, promptly falling into the muddy grass.

'Now look what you've done to your best coat,' Rosie admonished. 'You're going to look a right mess, and everyone will stare at you.'

Heather glared as Hugo's best man, William, came running over and helped her up.

Rosie brushed her sister down. Oh, if only she could just get this all over with. All she wanted was to say her vows, take a quick look-in at the reception in the church hall for appearances' sake, and then go off on her honeymoon to Rome with her darling Hugo. But William was looking worried.

'Is something wrong, William?'

'Just that Hugo's not here yet.'

Rosie's eyes flew wide. 'What?'

'He's probably just been delayed.'

'But he's never late,' Rosie said, alarm making her voice rise. 'Oh, William, do you think he's had an accident?'

'I shouldn't think so. I'm sure he'll turn up any minute.'

The vicar and her father appeared at the church entrance, then hurried towards her.

'What the devil's happenin'?' Her father's face was grim.

'We don't know, Dad.' Rosie heard her voice crack.

'I have a funeral to go to after the service.' The vicar put his hand up to his dog collar. 'I can wait another quarter of an hour – that's all.'

'Come on, you two, we'll go and wait inside,' their father told Rosie's sisters.

The next fifteen minutes dragged. Then twenty. Something terrible must have happened and he couldn't let her know. He was in an ambulance at this very moment. Nausea rose in the back of her throat as she imagined a lifeless body on a stretcher.

Oh, Hugo. Where are you?

Every time Rosie heard the purr of an engine she thought it must be Hugo. Eventually, the vicar went back inside the church, warning her that he couldn't wait any longer.

And then it dawned on her. Hugo wasn't coming. He'd jilted her. But it wasn't possible. He loved her. And she loved him – with all her heart. But there was no other explanation. If there had been, someone would have got a message to her. Even his awful parents. Oh, how could she face everyone? The humiliation. Angry tears trickled down her cheeks.

'He's changed his mind – I know he has.'

'No, not Hugo,' William said. 'He adores you.'

She shook her head. 'I bet it's his parents. His horrible father. He's tried everything to break us up.' She swallowed hard. 'You'll have to go inside – tell them the wedding's off.'

She screwed up her eyes. 'I can't face them,' she added, her voice faltering.

'I can't leave you like this.' He looked at her, his face pinched with worry. 'I'm beginning to wonder if we're jumping to conclusions. Maybe there *has* been some sort of accident . . .' He trailed off.

'This was his *wedding day*,' she flung at him. 'Even one of his hateful parents would surely have let me know.'

She dropped down onto one of the churchyard benches and wrapped her arms round her bowed head. A few people were already leaving the church but she took no notice. She stared at the graveyard, not seeing it through the blur of tears. William put his hand on her shaking shoulders, talking gently to her, but his soothing words had the opposite effect. She shot up and looked him in the eye.

'Please go, William. But don't you dare tell him I was crying,' she flashed. 'Tell him I'm glad he changed his mind. I wouldn't marry him if he was the last man on earth. I hope he rots in hell!'

PART ONE

Chapter One

Rosie entered the parlour, normally only used by her parents or on special occasions. Her father's *Daily Mirror* was tucked under her arm, as she carefully carried her cup of tea. She sank into his armchair, dead tired, having been on her feet all day. How much longer could she bear this relentless routine? The tea-break chatter from her fellow workers, usually about boys, clothes and the scarcity of both, only occasionally broken by the sobbing of someone who'd just lost a friend or relative in action. She scolded herself for being so intolerant as she thought back on the day.

'Did you hear the latest, Rosie?' Gloria had said while their team was eating lunch.

'What's that?'

'We won't be able to add a bit of nonsense to our under-clothes,' Gloria answered with disbelief. 'Everything's got to be under the new Utility Clothing Scheme from now on. Bad enough to have clothes rationed, let alone haberdashery. A bit of lace here and there is the only thing that keeps my Sid interested in you know what.'

Several girls giggled. The edges of Rosie's mouth barely lifted.

15

'You all right, duck?' Martha, an older woman in her usual brightly coloured turban, asked.

'Bit of a headache,' Rosie said. 'It'll go.'

But it wouldn't. It would remain with her for the rest of the day.

The others threw her sympathetic looks, then continued their conversations until the bell rang for everyone to resume work.

I hate living like this, Rosie thought as she packed boxes of Caley's chocolates ready to be put on the delivery lorries. She'd asked many times if she could work in Accounts. But Mr Lane always turned her down, even when they'd had a couple of vacancies these past two years when one of the bookkeepers and an apprentice accountant both left to join the Army. When she'd tackled him as to why he refused to transfer her, Mr Lane had answered that she was only bound to get married and then he'd have to train someone else.

Fat chance of that, Rosie now thought bitterly as she took a sip of her tea. The war was dragging on. Only days ago the Japanese had attacked the US port of Pearl Harbor in Hawaii, but as far as Prime Minister Winston Churchill was concerned, he was jubilant; he'd got his dearest wish. The following day the Americans retaliated and now Britain had a powerful ally and would no longer fight alone.

When would this horror end? It was all very well remaining cheerful here in Norfolk, but Norfolk folk hadn't faced the merciless bombing that London and Liverpool people had. Those cities were far away but it would surely only be a matter of time until the Luftwaffe picked on Norwich. The beautiful cathedral, the castle, the medieval buildings. She closed her eyes for a few seconds, trying to imagine the destruction. It was an awful thought. Even worse was the constant discussion of invasion. It was enough to freeze the blood in your veins. She bent her head to read the main headlines in the newspaper.

All Single Women Must Go To War

New Parliamentary Act decrees by Spring all single women and childless widows between 20 and 30 must join the armed forces, work in industry, or join the Land Army, unless in a reserved occupation.

It went on to state what the reserved occupations were, such as teaching and nursing.

Rosie bit her lip and the pulse of her headache became more insistent. She was twenty-three. High time she did something definite to help in the war effort. But where did she stand? Her parents would never let her join the WRNS, which she'd longed to do ever since war broke out. It would take her away from home and her mother needed all the help she could get looking after the two young ones, Roddy and Poppy. But surely her two sisters, now twenty and eighteen, were old enough to pull their weight.

For goodness' sake, Ivy is already a year older than I was when I thought I was getting married.

But she mustn't be unfair to Ivy, who was a munitions worker at Lawrence and Scott's. Rosie knew only too well that factory work was physically exhausting. But Heather was in for a shock when *she'd* be conscripted in the autumn because a salesgirl wasn't considered a reserved occupation. Rosie couldn't help smiling at the thought of Heather toeing the line. Then her smile faded. Mum would argue they were both at work all day so couldn't help with all the cooking and washing for seven people, seeming to forget her eldest daughter was also working all day, too.

With a sigh Rosie stood and left the newspaper on the chiffonier in the parlour. She'd known conscription for women was bound to happen. And it was right. Women *should* play their part as much as the men. But the only way she could obey the new act was to continue the lie she'd been keeping up for some time now. And no doubt the guilt would only worsen. But even that thought couldn't stop her heart fluttering that this might just be the opportunity she'd been longing for.

As she went upstairs to change out of her overalls, she made up her mind to speak to her parents right away.

'Rosie, where are you?' her mother called up the stairs.

'In the bedroom, Mum.' Rosie looked round the room she shared with Heather and Ivy. Heather, as usual, had thrown her belongings on every conceivable surface including the floor, her excuse being that the single wardrobe allocated for the three of them simply wasn't big enough. Scattered on an old desk serving as a dressing table was a hairbrush tangled with all three shades of hair, and Heather and Ivy's few toiletries. Rosie was always careful to hide her own precious pot of Pond's cold cream and Amami shampoo, but even though she'd labelled them 'RF' and hidden them in different places every few days, Heather always found them. She sighed. The room was a permanent mess.

'It's hard for you being squashed in with Heather and Ivy.' Her mother glanced at the bed the girls shared, next to Rosie's single one. 'You should have your own home by now, let alone a bedroom to yourself.'

Don't bring that up again, Mum. It was six years ago.

Rosie swallowed. It might be six years, but it didn't make her feel any less bitter.

Her mother sent her an anxious look.

'I'm sorry, dear. That was rather tactless.'

Before she could answer, Rosie heard the back door open.

'Shirl? Where are you?' a voice shouted in the distance.

'Oh, that's your dad home already.'

Shirley Frost hurried downstairs, and after a moment of hesitation, Rosie followed. Her mother gestured towards the back kitchen door. 'I'd better put the kettle on as he'll be wantin' a cup of tea.'

Her father was outside holding on to the doorframe of the scullery with one hand, the other tugging at his fireman's boot.

'You're early,' Rosie said. 'It's freezing out there. Come into the kitchen and I'll help you get that boot off.'

He looked up. She felt a pang when she saw the lines of exhaustion on his face, enhanced by streaks of filth. His eyes were bloodshot and expressionless, as though the life had been sucked out of him.

'What's happened?' Rosie asked, dreading the answer when he sat at the kitchen table and finally pulled off one boot.

'There's been a bad fire over at one of the warehouses. Weren't even a bomb this time. Some twerp didn't stub his fag out. One of the lads died and another went off to the hospital in an ambulance with bad burns. I don't know if he's goin' to make it, poor sod.' He let out a long breath. 'We've bin goin' non-stop. No tea break, no nothin', so when a few of the lads on the next shift turned up early, the boss sent us home.' He grunted as he yanked the second boot. It didn't budge.

Rosie grimaced at the news. But the others would soon be home from school. This might be her only chance to talk to her parents in private. While her mother made the tea, Rosie managed after a tussle to free her father's other boot.

'I can see why it was difficult to pull off,' she said. 'Your ankles are really swollen.'

'I'm not surprised. The braddy boots don't fit right and even if I had the money to get another pair, they're almost impossible to come by these days.'

It was true. Clothes rationing had started in June, and it took too many coupons for shoes and boots that were scarce anyway. Even if you found a pair in one of the shops, they were often the wrong size. The children wore one another's cast-offs and her mother constantly worried their feet would be ruined in years to come. But with a large family to provide for, and only her father's modest wages, her mother had struggled to make ends meet all the years before her daughters went out to work.

Rosie shut her eyes, trying to block out the reason why the money had to stretch further than it ought. She swallowed hard. When Poppy was born she'd promised she'd be completely responsible for the baby until she was old enough to go to school. Poppy, just turned five, had started in September and at that point Rosie had gone to Caley's so she could properly contribute to the household. But now with this latest news . . .

'I think I'll go in the front room and read the paper,' her father broke into her thoughts. 'Can you bring my tea in, Rosie?'

Rosie went back to the kitchen. Her mother poured a mug of tea and added two teaspoons of sugar.

'You should cut him down to one,' Rosie said, 'now sugar's rationed.'

'Oh, he has mine,' her mother said. 'I gave it up in tea last month.'

'You're getting thin,' Rosie observed. 'You shouldn't keep giving Dad your rations. I see you doing it,' she added as her mother opened her mouth to reply. 'And not only Dad, but you give yours up to Roddy as well.'

'He's a growin' lad,' her mother said mildly. 'Besides, I've probably had a bite you in't seen.' She gave Rosie a wan smile. 'Anyway, you'd better take his tea in before it get cold.'

'Mum, I need to talk to you and Dad about something serious.'

'I'm trying to get supper, love,' her mother said. 'Can it wait?'

'No, it can't.'

'Why don't you have a word with Dad first?'

Rosie sighed and picked up the mug.

'Just the job.' Her father took his tea and nodded for her to take the other armchair. 'We don't often find time for a chat, do we, girl?'

'I thought you liked to be quiet and read your paper.'

'I do. But now you're here—' He broke off to swallow some tea, then glanced at the front page. 'Well, well, conscription is to be compulsory for girls and widows without kids,' he said without looking up, 'and you're in the right age bracket.' He stroked his chin and looked directly at her. 'I gather you've seen this.' She nodded. 'I doubt they'll make workin' in a chocolate factory a reserve occupation with a war on, even though we like a square or two ourselves when you bring home the odd bar.' He smiled but it quickly faded as though he'd thought of something. 'Mind you, I don't see you knucklin' down to the discipline.'

'I would if I thought it was helping the war effort,' Rosie protested.

He grunted. 'Your mother won't be able to cope on her own. She needs you.'

'I've been thinking about it.' Rosie paused. 'Heather and Ivy are adults so Mum won't have to look after them. Heather always moans that she's tired after a day on her feet in Woolies and leaves me to help Mum when I come home, but I've worked just as hard in that blasted factory all day. She'll just have to buck up and give Mum some help with Roddy and Poppy. Ivy helps when she can, but her boss gets his pound of flesh. And whatever I earned I'd send Mum most of it, as I do now.' She looked across at her father who was rolling a cigarette. 'I'm sure we could work something out. And I've thought about which of the services I'd like to join – it's the WRNS.'

'You can forget that. The Navy is the snobby one. They want the cream of the crop – which we're most definitely not.' He looked her directly in the eye. 'No, my girl, it'll be the ATS for you.'

'I don't want the Army,' Rosie protested. 'I love the sea. When we used to go to Aunt Dot's I loved watching the waves when there was a storm and—'

'You're living in cloud cuckoo land,' her father interrupted. 'Women aren't allowed to serve on ships.'

'I know, but if it's abroad, you'd have to get there on a ship,' Rosie argued, then lowered her tone. 'Anyway, much as I want to see the world, I know it's not practical now.'

Her father struck a match to his cigarette, puffing furiously to get it alight.

'Your mother's getting too thin.'

So her father *had* noticed.

'I was going to talk to you about that, Dad. Do you realise she gives you half her rations most days, and if she knows you've eaten well at the canteen she'll give it to Roddy.'

Her father's jaw dropped. 'I didn't know that.'

'Well, you do now, so can you keep an eye on *her* plate?'

'Yes, but don't nag.' He shook his head. 'Braddy war and braddy Jerry.' He paused. 'Mind you, they must see their

22

own people are gettin' killed and cut to pieces as well. For what? An Austrian maniac who don't care tuppence for them, only his own vanity to conquer the world. Well, he's got another think comin' if he thinks we'll let Blighty go in a hurry.'

Their relationship wasn't the easiest. Try as she might, she'd never wholly forgiven him for his threat all those years ago. Rosie swallowed hard. There was no doubt Dad was a brave man. He never complained about his job, even on that terrible night when there was a raid of high explosive bombs on Colman's mustard factory. Five young women had been killed. Several mills had burnt to cinders. There'd been three huge fires roaring and at the same time one of the water mains broke and a warehouse fell into the river just where he and the other firemen were drawing out the water. To cap it all, the ambulances hadn't been able to get down the main roads to pick up the injured as they were blocked by the bomb damage.

Things had quietened down a little since, but you never knew when a raid would start. Her mother was permanently on edge, bracing herself for the next tragedy to occur.

'I was thinking that if I *did* join up, I might get a better wage which would help the family.' She hesitated. 'As you say, with the conscription news I'll be called up anyway by one of the forces – most likely the ATS – and sent too far away to come home every day, so I'd rather make my own decision.' She hesitated.

Should she . . .

Before she could stop herself, she blurted, 'Unless I tell them the truth. Then they can't make me.'

She felt a hollowness in her stomach. It would be a wrench to leave the family if she did become a Wren. Roddy was becoming more independent by the day, but it was Poppy

23

she worried about most of all. Poppy needed constant attention and understanding. Rosie gulped. She was a beautiful child with bright red hair, just like her own, and eyes that had turned from blue when she was first born to the colour of grass – exactly the same colour as Hugo's, Rosie thought, not for the first time. It was hard for her with the others so much older and she didn't seem to make friends very easily at school. She was thankful that Caley's allowed her to come in an hour early and leave in time for her to go to the school and meet Poppy. But the little girl was nearly always on her own, waiting forlornly at the school gates.

Her father began to cough. 'There's nothin' wrong with the Army,' he said finally. 'It would give you some good life skills. Maybe drivin' an ambulance like your Aunt Dot in the Great War, though I in't sure she's tellin' the truth. But I know girls are doin' that sort of thing this time. Even learnin' to strip down engines and change tyres.' His tone was almost disbelieving.

'There's no reason why Aunt Dot's fibbing,' Rosie said. 'And a girl can learn about engines just as any boy can, if that's what she wants. There's had to be a war for us to have the same opportunities as the men. But I can't see me doing that.'

'Well, most often it pays to think things through carefully. You're no longer that starry-eyed seventeen-year-old, thinkin' you could rule the world.'

'You don't need to remind me,' she said, feeling the nausea that had suddenly returned. 'I'm well aware of how stupid I was.'

'You were too young and got carried away. But *he* –' anger coated his words, and she knew he couldn't bring himself to say Hugo's name '– was old enough to know better. I'll never forgive him. But at least you now have the experience to know that you can't always trust people. They let you down when you least expect it. Mark my words.' He gave her a rueful smile. 'Now where's my little poppet?'

Rosie glanced at her watch – the one Hugo had given her. She'd told herself it was practical to keep it as she could never have afforded to buy one of her own, but she knew deep down she couldn't bear to part with it. It was all she had to remind her that Hugo had once loved her.

'I'd better go and pick her up.'

'I'd come with you if I weren't so braddy tired.' He stubbed his cigarette in the upturned lid of a tin and gave a deep yawn.

'I'd stay where you are, Dad.' Time alone with Poppy was far too precious. 'Take advantage of a quiet house for once and have a nap. It won't stay like it for long.'

Chapter Two

Rosie hurried to Poppy's school, wanting to be at the gates before Poppy came out. She hated to see the child's worried look on her face when she couldn't immediately spot her. Ah, there she was – on her own, as usual. She waved and called out. Poppy broke into a beaming smile and raced over. Rosie's heart somersaulted as she bent down and the little girl threw her arms round her.

'Mosey, Mosey, I wanted it to be you to meet me.'

Rosie's heart turned over at the serious little face looking up at her.

'What did you do today?' It was her standard question as she and Poppy began to walk home.

'I forget.'

'You can't already have forgotten. You've only just left.'

Poppy's mouth turned down. 'I read my book.'

'Good. What else did you do?'

'Nothing.'

'Did you play with your friends.'

'I don't have any friends.'

'Of course you do.' Rosie gave her an encouraging smile.

'I don't. Nobody talks to me.'

'What about the teacher?'

Poppy was silent. Then she said, 'Sometimes Miss Andrews asks me a question.'

'Do you answer it correctly?'

'I don't answer. I don't say anything any more. I always know the answer and then the others are horrible to me. I *hate* it. And I hate school.'

Rosie felt the stirring of anger.

'Doesn't Miss Andrews tell the others off?'

'They don't do it when she's there. They do it when no one's looking. They're nasty.'

They were bullying her. Rosie bit her lip hard. She'd have to talk to her mother. Decide what to do. They couldn't let such behaviour continue.

'They can't all be nasty, darling.'

'You don't believe me.' Poppy looked up at Rosie, her eyes bright with tears.

'Yes, I do, and I'm going to do something about it,' Rosie answered.

Contented, Poppy put her hand in Rosie's and the two of them walked home, Poppy skipping and hopping, seeming, to her relief, to have forgotten about the nasty children.

It wasn't possible for Rosie to talk to her mother that evening about the bullying. Heather and Ivy were squabbling over Ivy having borrowed one of Heather's jumpers without asking permission, and Roddy rudely telling them to for goodness' sake shut up about the bloody jumper.

'It is not for you to tell anyone to shut up,' their father cut in, his brows knitted. 'And you will immediately apologise to your sisters for swearin'. You will then go to your room. I will not have you or anyone under this roof use that word. Do you hear, Roddy?'

27

'Yes.'

'Yes, what?'

'Yes, *Dad*.' Roddy jumped up and slammed the door behind him. Rosie heard him thump up the stairs.

Poppy began to cry. Shirley scooped her up.

'You're tired, my love.' She turned to Rosie. 'Can you get her ready for bed while I clear up the kitchen, dear?'

'Why don't you go and sit in the parlour with Dad for a change while Heather and Ivy clear up the kitchen,' Rosie said, thinking it would give him the opportunity to speak to her mother, and ignoring Heather's scowl.

'Good idea.' Her father glanced at his wife. 'Come on, Shirl. You've done enough for the day.'

Mildly protesting, Shirley muttered to no one, 'If you're sure.'

In her parents' room which Poppy shared, Rosie read the child a story about a little girl who meets a wicked witch, only the witch turns out to be good in the end. She'd read the story to Poppy many times and after a couple of pages she had an idea.

'Why don't you read it to *me* for a change?'

Poppy beamed and took hold of the book. She had been reading for quite some time before it occurred to Rosie that she hadn't turned a page.

'Let me see that book a minute,' she said, taking it from Poppy's small hands.

She leafed through it and realised the child had memorised several pages. The pages were taken up with a smatter of illustrations, but still, it was quite a feat. But could Poppy actually read? Well, she wouldn't test her this evening as the little girl was patently tired, but she'd take her to the library at the first chance and let her choose a fresh book, then see how she got on.

She tucked Poppy up and kissed her on her forehead.

'Goodnight, darling.'

'G'night, Mosey.' The child looked up. 'Is Mummy coming to say goodnight?'

For a brief moment Rosie closed her eyes.

'She will. Maybe a bit later. You'll probably be asleep.'

'No, I won't. I'll wait 'til she comes up. I won't let myself go to sleep 'til she's been to kiss me goodnight.'

Rosie couldn't help smiling. Poppy was her own person – no doubt about it.

Since the war started, the Lazar House library in Sprowston had become much busier. It seemed people, especially mothers at home, needed to escape in novels to shut out the horrors for an hour or two at a time. Today, after Rosie had helped Poppy choose a book and taken a couple for herself, she checked the rack of various leaflets on joining the Army or the Air Force or the Navy. She rifled through them again. Not one leaflet represented the women's forces except to be a Land Girl. Rosie shuddered. That was the last thing she'd want to do.

Her hand firmly holding Poppy's while they waited in a queue to have their books stamped, Rosie sighed at the five people ahead of her. She must try to curb her impatience but there was only one assistant to ask for any help. Finally, it was her turn. The elderly lady behind the counter caught her eye and smiled.

'Well, if it isn't Miss Frost. We haven't seen you for a while.'

'I know. I've been busy lately. But I wanted to bring Poppy so she could choose a book. She seems to know the ones at home off by heart.'

Miss Perriman smiled. 'They do it to fool you into thinking they're a good reader when really they're memorising,' she said.

'I *am* a good reader,' Poppy piped up.

'I'm sure you are, dear,' Miss Perriman said. 'But it's always nice to read a new story.'

She stamped the three books. Rosie was aware of more people joining the queue. Her question would hold them up. But it was her only opportunity. She lowered her voice.

'Miss Perriman, I'm considering joining the WRNS but there aren't any leaflets so I don't know how to apply.'

'We're waiting for them to come in . . . oh, I might have an old one in the drawer.' She disappeared behind the counter for a few moments, then popped up with a triumphant expression, and pushed a creased leaflet towards Rosie. 'There you are, dear. This should do for now. But you do realise it's the elite force. A question of who you know. The right connections. Maybe your father . . .' She raised her eyebrows questioningly.

I once knew someone with such connections.

Rosie swallowed hard. She glanced at the folded paper with the words: 'Women's Royal Naval Service' and underneath, 'Join the Wrens and free a man for the fleet'. She automatically tucked the leaflet in her bag, though applying didn't now seem very hopeful. She felt a hand on her arm.

'Did I hear right about your wanting to become a Wren, my dear?'

Rosie swung round to face a well-dressed woman in a smart cream coat with brown hat and matching handbag and smiling crimson lips.

'Yes, but I keep coming up against a blank wall.'

'Hmm. Maybe I can help.'

'Move along. We haven't got all day,' a man from the back of the queue called. 'Some of us have to work.'

'Shhhh!' Miss Perriman sent him a frosty look. 'No talking in the library unless absolutely necessary.'

'We can't talk here,' the woman said in a low tone. 'Wait for me next door in the café. I'll be along as soon as I get my books stamped.'

'Thank you.' Rosie looked down at Poppy. 'Shall we have tea with the nice lady?'

Poppy nodded. 'Then can we go home?'

'Of course we can.' Rosie turned to the woman. 'We'll see you in a few minutes then.'

By the time she and Poppy had been shown a table in the café and removed their coats, the woman in the cream coat appeared. She picked up the menu and glanced at Rosie.

'Will it be tea for you, my dear?'

'Yes, please.'

'And what's your name?' the woman addressed Poppy.

'Poppy Frost. What's your name?'

'That's rude to ask,' Rosie said quickly.

'But the lady asked mine,' Poppy argued.

'Poppy's not being rude at all.' The woman smiled at the little girl. 'And you have a very pretty name.' She extended her hand to Rosie. 'Claire Edgerton.'

'Rosemary Frost.' Rosie shook her hand.

Mrs Edgerton looked up as a waitress approached the table. 'A pot of tea for two, please, and the little girl will have . . . ?'

'Orangeade,' Poppy piped.

'What do you say?' Rosie said sternly.

'Ple-ea-se.'

When the waitress scuttled off, Mrs Edgerton said, 'The library assistant was unfortunately right. To get into the WRNS is usually reserved for debutantes – you know, *gels* who've been to finishing schools, or have fathers in the Royal Navy who can put in a word. Mind you, it won't be a bed of roses if you get in. ' Her stare was unwavering. 'How serious are you, Miss Frost, about becoming a Wren?'

31

'Very. I want to do my bit in the war and I've not been able to until now as I've had to work close to home to help Mum look after the young ones. She isn't in the best of health.' She looked at the smiling woman and added, 'I've always loved the sea so being a Wren seems a natural choice.'

'And now there's conscription for women.' She glanced at Poppy. 'Though it shouldn't affect you, my dear, as you have a child.'

'Oh, no.' Heat rushed to Rosie's cheeks. 'Poppy's my baby sister.'

'I'm not a baby.' Poppy's green eyes flashed. 'I'm five.'

'Quite the young lady,' Mrs Edgerton smiled, then turned to Rosie. 'I'm sorry, I hadn't realised. So you're free to go?'

'Yes,' Rosie gulped. 'And I'd rather make my own decision than someone make it for me.'

'I don't blame you.' Mrs Edgerton glanced at Poppy and said in an undertone, 'Who will look after Poppy, as your mother's not very well?'

'I have two grown-up sisters, so they're perfectly capable of helping Mum now with Poppy.'

'I don't want you to go away.' Poppy's eyes filled with tears.

'I'm not going anywhere yet, darling, but wherever I go I'll come home often.' She looked across the table at Mrs Edgerton. 'You mentioned you might be able to help me.'

'I have a nephew who does something at Whitehall – I'm not sure exactly what. I think it's all a bit secret. I think if he met you he'd put in a word.'

'Really?' Rosie felt a glow of something close to hope.

The waitress set a tray of tea and a glass of orangeade on the table.

'Will that be all, madam?' she said, addressing Mrs Edgerton who nodded.

'Thank you, miss.' Mrs Edgerton glanced at Rosie. 'Shall I be mother?'

'Please.' Rosie felt the same impatience Poppy always did when someone interrupted something she deemed important.

When they were sipping their tea and Poppy was looking around, a straw in her rosebud mouth to drink her orangeade, Mrs Edgerton said:

'His name is John Palmer and he's coming over for supper on Friday.' She looked directly at Rosie. 'In fact, my dear, why don't you join us?'

Chapter Three

Rosie stared inside the dark interior of the wardrobe. Although the three of them had few clothes, they all had to be crammed into the small space. What on earth was she going to wear? She hadn't got any clothes for such an occasion and there'd been no time to make anything.

In the end she decided upon her faithful straight black skirt she'd made at the start of the war and a blouse she'd bought in a summer jumble sale. It was a silky material with a cream background splashed with brightly coloured flowers, with short puff sleeves. It wasn't really appropriate for the dead of winter, but it would pass for supper at Mrs Edgerton's. She daren't think too much about meeting some strange man who worked at Whitehall. If she did, she'd be overcome with nerves and not turn up after all.

She shook herself. She was being ridiculous. He was just a man and might possibly be able to help her get out of the factory and do something to use her brain for once. She knew she wasn't like the other girls she worked with whose main interests were boys and make-up. But how could she say such a thing to Mr Palmer without being horribly disloyal to them? After all, they put in a good day's work every day, the same as she did.

Rosie had only mentioned to her mother she was meeting

a friend for supper. It hadn't seemed like a lie as Mrs Edgerton had certainly been friendly. And if John Palmer didn't like her or didn't think she had the right background and education, there would be no need. And even if that wasn't the case, there was no guarantee that any good word put into the right ear would open a magical door. No, she'd have to be patient and only tell her parents if anything positive transpired. But since she'd studied the leaflet she was more convinced than ever that it was the WRNS she wanted to join as several of the categories that had caught her attention had specifically stated: *Mathematics essential.*

Rosie tucked the blouse into her skirt and glanced into the small mirror on the wall above the wash basin. She grinned at the way the bright blouse clashed with her red hair, then took the top off the precious tube of scarlet lipstick her workmates had given her on her birthday two years ago. But the stick was no more. It was completely flat to the rim. She knew there'd been a little left so one of her sisters had been using it. But not Ivy. The tube had Heather's fingerprints all over it. Rosie grimaced. Using her little finger she managed to dab some onto her mouth. It would have to do.

'Bye, Mum,' she called as she took her only winter coat off the hook in the hall.

'Have a nice time, dear. Mind you don't miss that last bus.'

'I won't.'

Rosie slammed the door behind her and made for the bus stop.

'I'm on the Wroxham Road,' Claire had told her. 'Catch the 40 and ask for The Old Vicarage – one stop before the Broads. I live one house beyond it with a yellow front door.'

Rosie put her arm out for the number 40 and squeezed between two large women and a young lad on a side seat.

'Toight,' the conductor said, warning Rosie to hold on tightly as the bus jerked forward.

She soon found herself walking up the drive to the rambling Victorian house where a black motorcar was parked. Was it John Palmer's? She took a deep breath and walked up the steps. No sooner had she pressed the bell than the door opened to reveal a tall fair-haired man, looking to be a few years older than herself, wearing a broad smile.

'Do come in,' he said, stepping aside in the wide hall. 'You must be Rosemary. I'm sorry, I didn't catch your last name when my aunt told me you were coming.'

'Rosemary Frost.' She looked at him and added, 'And you must be Mr Palmer.'

'Call me John,' he said, extending his hand. 'Pretty name.' He grinned. 'Yours, not mine.' She smiled and briefly shook his hand. He closed the door behind her. 'May I take your coat?'

Feeling a little awkward she unbuttoned her coat and removed her hat, handing them to him. He carefully hung them on the coat stand.

'Come this way,' he said. 'Claire, my aunt, is talking to Cook. If you sit yourself down in the drawing room –' he opened a door to a room large enough to take several of her rooms at home '– I'll tell her you're here.' He disappeared.

She barely had time to decide which would be the more appropriate seat, finally deciding on a small armchair, when John Palmer breezed in.

'She won't be a mo,' he said, opening one of the cupboards in an alcove at the side of the fireplace. 'And I'm to offer you a drink. What would you like?'

Rosie felt a warmth creep up her neck. No one had ever asked her this question. She stared at him, angry with herself that she just didn't know how to answer him.

'Would you like me to surprise you?' John Palmer said, seeming to read her mind.

'Oh, yes, please.'

She heard the squeak as he unscrewed a bottle and the soft glugging as he poured some sort of liquid into a glass. Then a splash from another bottle. He picked up a third and allowed a few drops into the glass. Finally there was a tinkle of ice cubes and the sound of stirring. It all seemed very complicated but she supposed he knew what he was doing. Seconds later he handed her the glass.

'Tell me what you think.'

She took a swallow, more than she'd intended. A bitter-sweet warmth ran down her throat.

'Mmm. It's delicious. What's in it?' Then she flushed, wondering if he'd think her naïve.

His eyes twinkled. 'It's mainly brandy with orange liqueur and a dash of bitters. It should have a slice of lemon but they're not easy to come by these days.' He looked at her as she raised the glass to her lips again. 'Take it slowly if you're not used to it. It's such a nice drink one sometimes has more than one should, forgetting it's pretty strong.'

Rosie's flush deepened as she set the glass on a table by the side of her chair, wishing Mrs Edgerton would make an appearance.

'I understand you're thinking of joining the WRNS,' John Palmer said, taking a seat opposite her by the fire, 'but can't find a way in.' He paused. 'My aunt seems to think I might be of some help.'

'Yes,' Rosie said, relieved they could get down to the reason why she was here. 'She mentioned you work in Whitehall.'

'Hmm.' John leaned back in his chair and gazed thoughtfully at her. 'Why don't you start by telling me about yourself.' He proceeded to light a pipe.

She'd keep it as short as possible.

'I have both my parents, and three sisters and one brother. The two older girls go to work – the two younger ones are at school.' She was about to move on to her education when he said:

'What does your father do?'

'He's a fireman in the city.'

John Palmer nodded. 'Norwich is where the first German bomb fell in Norfolk last year.'

'I know, but how did you?'

'Now we're at war, Claire keeps me posted as to what's happening in Norfolk,' he said. 'It's where most of my family comes from.' He paused. 'I need to know she's safe. She's more like a mother to me than my own mother.'

Rosie thought she noticed a glimmer of regret in his clear grey eyes.

'Where did you go to school?' he asked.

'I won a scholarship and went to Blyth Grammar School.'

'What did you like most?'

'Italian and mathematics,' she responded instantly. 'I enjoy both.'

She noticed a slight lifting of John Palmer's eyebrows.

'Hmm. Mathematics could be extremely useful. Possibly Italian as well, though I didn't think it was taught in many grammar schools. It's usually German and French.'

'Italian wasn't officially on our curriculum either. But we had a wonderful history teacher called Signorina Bonetti. Her father was an Italian prisoner of war in the Great War, so we learnt a lot of Italian history. Her great love was the Renaissance and Italian composers, especially Puccini. She'd sometimes play a record for us after school. The other girls didn't like opera so there was only a handful of us and we got to know her well. She'd speak to us in Italian and I found myself easily picking up the words. I was supposed to learn French but I asked if I could learn Italian instead.' She hesitated, her eyes directed to John. 'Oh, you don't want to hear all this.'

'Oh, yes, I do,' John said, leaning forward. 'So what did she say?'

'She said she'd ask the headmistress. And Miss Ayles agreed.' Rosie smiled. 'I loved the sound of the language, but I also liked trying something different from the other girls.'

'Ah, an independent thinker.'

She felt a warmth to her cheeks. 'Perhaps. It turned out to be the right choice for me as I passed with distinction.'

'Well done.' He paused. 'Have you spoken it since leaving school?'

She wondered why he was asking.

'Yes. Miss Bonetti . . . well, she's married now but I still call her that . . . we arranged to meet one evening a week and only speak Italian. We've kept it up all these years and talk about every subject under the sun, though it's been more difficult since the Italians are now the enemy.'

She wouldn't say that going to see her old Italian teacher had been her Wednesday evening lifeline all these years and how scathing her father had been.

'You're wastin' your time. Better if you learnt German because if Hitler gets his way, that's what we'll all end up speakin".'

'How good are you?' John asked, breaking into her thoughts.

'Miss Bonetti says I'm almost fluent.' Rosie didn't bother to disguise a note of pride. 'She said I should go on to university and study Italian literature.'

'It sounds as though you didn't go.'

'No, I didn't, which was a pity as I would have been the first in the family.'

'What about future plans? Do you have a boyfriend . . . or fiancé?' His eyes flicked to her hands.

She shook her head, a little resentful that he was questioning her so closely. But she supposed he needed some background to know if she'd be a suitable candidate to become a Wren and not be rushing into marriage six months later.

'No.' She tried to keep her voice neutral though she felt her stomach churning again.

'Usually, to get into the WRNS you have to have connections,' John said, puffing on his pipe. 'That's why I asked about your father's work.'

There it was again. Rosie curbed a sudden flash of temper. Not having the right connections had been the reason why she'd lost Hugo. His parents had never approved of the match and she was sure it had been something to do with them that Hugo had changed his mind – and jilted her.

Now, under John Palmer's curious gaze, she was swept back into the humiliating memory. She pictured herself so happy, getting ready on her big day, thinking Hugo would be feeling the same. She started to feel dizzy. This was how it always affected her. She put a hand to her forehead and shut her eyes tightly.

'Rosemary,' John Palmer broke into the storm going on inside her, 'are you all right?'

She forced her eyes to focus – to come back to this beautiful room.

'Rosemary . . .' John put his pipe down and leapt up. 'You've gone very pale. Are you ill?'

She shook her head. 'No.' She swallowed hard, fighting the tears.

'There *is* something. You're crying. What is it?'

He looked so kind, so concerned, so very normal, that

for an instant she wanted to blurt out the whole miserable story.

'Don't tell me if you don't want to. But at least take my handkerchief.'

He whipped a spotless white handkerchief out of his pocket and she dabbed her eyes.

'I'll wash it and give it back to your aunt,' she said, feeling awkward as she dropped it into her handbag.

'Keep it,' he said. 'Here, finish your drink.' He handed her the glass.

She took a sip or two. She mustn't do this. Break down at something that should be a distant memory that could no longer hurt her. She took another sip and put the glass on the table.

'Are you feeling better?'

'Yes . . . thank you.'

'I was worried I'd upset you when I asked about your father. I must have sounded awfully rude, as though your future depended on him, but I wasn't meaning to be. I hope you know that.'

'I do, but it doesn't seem fair to be held back by a situation I can't help. Not to measure up because of my background.' She lifted her chin. 'We're working-class people but I don't think that's anything to be ashamed of. My dad is honest as the day and extremely brave.'

'He'd have to be if he's a fireman,' John said. 'Bloody dangerous job, excuse my French. Not everyone would choose it.' He looked at her. 'You're right about people's backgrounds. It's the person that's important. And never let anyone tell you different.'

She didn't know how to answer and was relieved when she heard a knock at the door. A maid put her head round the opening.

'I'm to say that supper's ready,' she said, then vanished.

John jumped to his feet and offered his hand, but Rosie was out of her chair before any contact. She was furious with herself for breaking down in front of a complete stranger, especially one she'd badly wanted to impress. Whatever must he think of her?

'We'll talk some more later, but for now I imagine we're both hungry.' His eyes fell to her glass. 'I'll bring your glass in for you, though knowing my aunt, there'll be a decent wine on the table.' He grinned and she mustered a slight smile in return as he guided her into the dining room.

'Good evening, Rosemary,' Claire Edgerton said with a welcoming smile. 'Forgive me for not greeting you but I know John wanted to speak to you privately.' She turned to her nephew when they were seated. 'Pour the wine, dear.' She looked at Rosie and laughed. 'I hope he approves.'

'It's not for me to judge,' John said, grinning broadly. 'I'm grateful for anything, especially with the war.'

Mrs Edgerton smiled back, then turned to Rosie.

'He knows I keep a reasonable cellar,' she said. 'I think you'll like this. It's a decent Burgundy which will go very well with the chicken.'

Enticing smells emanated from the covered dishes and soon Rosie was tasting her first coq au vin.

'How is it, my dear?' Mrs Edgerton said.

'Delicious.' And it was. She'd never eaten anything like it.

Mrs Edgerton kept the conversation light and general and Rosie was thankful there was no more questioning that made her feel uncomfortable. Not that John made her feel uncomfortable. No, it wasn't that. She could tell he was a decent, upright man, and that his aunt adored him by the way she was smiling back at him. But Rosie was terrified her secret would be out before she knew it, blighting her chances of

42

becoming a Wren. At all costs she must stay alert and be on her best behaviour. She took a sip of the smooth Burgundy and listened to the flow of conversation which mainly went over her head. After a couple of minutes Mrs Edgerton turned to her.

'Sorry about that, my dear,' she said. 'We were catching up on people you don't know, which was extremely rude but we haven't spent much time together lately.' She gave Rosie an encouraging smile. 'You and I didn't have much chance to talk the other day, but I got the impression you were serious about joining the WRNS so that's why I thought my nephew might be able to put in a word.' She looked at him. 'Do you think you can, John, dear?'

Did he hesitate?

'Oh, please don't think you have to,' Rosie said, quickly. 'You can hardly recommend me on such a brief meeting.'

'My aunt's an extremely good judge of character.' He smiled at Rosie as he took a swallow of wine. 'I believe she told you I work with one of the commanders at Whitehall. I think there could be a role for you, and your Italian might well come in handy.'

'I'd have thought they'd want German.'

He shook his head. 'There are far fewer Italian speakers so that might count as a real plus. We might not hear so much about them, but unfortunately the Italians are very much the enemy.'

There could be a role for you. A flicker of hope curled through Rosie. To travel. It would be a dream come true. Then she came back to earth. Her mother needed her. Poppy needed her. She couldn't desert them.

'Would I be sent abroad?'

'It's possible,' John said, 'though you can always state your preferences.'

'I'd love to go abroad, but for the moment I'm hoping I wouldn't have to live too far away from my family.'

'There are plenty of places in Britain where we have Wrens,' he said. 'Even in Norfolk.'

Rosie drained the rest of her glass. 'That sounds a million times more exciting than Caley's chocolate factory,' she said, then felt the heat rush up her neck. She hadn't meant to say anything about the actual work she did. They might not think a factory worker would be considered suitable.

As though John read her mind, he said, 'If I can organise an interview for you, it might be a good idea not to mention factories. It might scupper your chances.' Rosie's lips tightened. 'Sorry, Rosemary, but as you already know, that's the way it works in this world.'

'Yes, I know,' Rosie said bitterly. 'In my own case, where any career is concerned, it seems I was dropped off at the wrong doorstep.'

Chapter Four

John Palmer changed subjects as he talked about books and gave no further indication that he was concerned about her upbringing. His aunt encouraged Rosie to have a second helping of the delicious chicken dish, seeming to take everything in her stride and not judge her. But that was because they were nice people, Rosie told herself. Someone high up who might interview her for the women's Navy could have a completely different attitude. Lost in her thoughts, she started when John leant over to top up her glass.

'Just half,' she said, but John simply grinned, and as he filled it told her it would do her good to relax.

It was such a treat to talk to two adults she didn't know but felt comfortable with, without the constant bickering and interruptions of her sisters and brother. She felt a little disloyal thinking this, but she loved the fact that the rusty gears in her brain seemed to be working again. She'd missed school when she'd left. She'd loved studying and had soon realised her parents had been right when they'd wanted her to go to university. What an opportunity she'd missed. Rosie bit her lip, then pulled herself round to the present. If she had, there'd be no Poppy. And Poppy was her world. She raised her fresh drink to her lips.

'I propose a toast,' John said, lifting his glass and smiling broadly. 'To Rosemary Frost. May she fulfil her dreams with the help of her two new friends.'

'I'll second that,' Mrs Edgerton said, with an identical smile to her nephew's.

'You're very kind,' Rosie said, taking a bigger gulp than she'd intended.

After a pause in a conversation when John was asking her what kind of books she read, Mrs Edgerton remarked, 'I think we'd better open another bottle.'

'Not for me, thanks,' John said.

'Please don't for me.' Rosie hoped she hadn't sounded presumptuous. 'It must be getting late and I'm not used to wine.' She glanced at her watch and tried to work out the time, but the numbers were fuzzy. She blinked, trying to refocus. 'I think my watch must have stopped.'

'Ten-thirty-three,' John told her.

She gave an intake of breath. 'Oh, my goodness, the last bus goes at ten to eleven. I've just got time . . .' She shot up from the table, then had to put a hand out to steady herself. Her head was swimming. It must be the wine.

Pull yourself together, for heaven's sake.

'There's no need to rush,' John said. 'Just take your time. I came up from London by car. I can take you home.'

'But you've got a long drive back to London.'

'He's staying the night, my dear,' Claire put in, 'so you've no need to worry.'

'I don't want to put you to any trouble—' Rosie began.

'No arguments, please. It's no trouble at all, but if you'd rather go right now then we will.' He got to his feet.

'Can you fetch Rosemary's hat and coat, dear?' Claire said.

'Of course.' He disappeared.

'I've had a wonderful evening,' Rosie said. 'Thank you so much for asking me, Mrs Edgerton.'

'Oh, please call me Claire.' She kissed Rosie's cheek. 'I'm so glad we met in the library. I think it was meant to be.'

'I'm glad too,' Rosie said fervently as John returned and helped her on with her coat.

Did his hands linger a second or two on her shoulders? No, of course not. It was only her pure imagination. She wasn't in her right mind with the novelty of such stimulating company, the delicious food and that equally delicious wine.

'And I'm sure John will be able to do something for you.' Claire sent a mock-stern look to her nephew.

'I promise to do everything I can,' he said, smiling at his aunt as he opened the front door.

Rosie stumbled on the last step and from behind John grabbed her.

'Steady on, Rosemary.' He kept hold of her arm.

Furious with herself for not being more disciplined where the wine was concerned, she allowed him to lead her to the same black motorcar she'd noticed when she'd arrived.

Once John had settled her, and not daring to look at him, she closed her eyes, letting her head rest on the back of the seat. Had she blown her chances? Would he think her a stupid girl who couldn't even handle a couple of glasses of wine, therefore couldn't be trusted to do any job, let alone an important one? She opened her eyes and gave him a surreptitious look. He caught her eye and grinned.

'Are you okay, Rosemary?'

'I am now I'm sitting down, but the wine must have gone to my head. I'm not usually like this.'

'My fault,' he said breezily. 'I shouldn't have topped you up.'

'And I should have realised what it was doing to me.'

'Take a couple of aspirin when you get home and you'll

be right as rain in the morning,' he said cheerfully. 'Meanwhile, close your eyes and have a nap.'

But she couldn't relax. Just being in his motorcar, the smell of the leather seats brought back painful memories. Hugo had had a snazzy sports car and loved taking her for a spin, as he called it. He'd been a fast driver but it had suited her adventurous spirit. She'd had to stifle that feeling all these years – now, here was a stark reminder that once again she was stepping out of line, trying to live above her station. She blinked as the tears threatened, then brushed a lone tear away with the back of her woollen glove.

John glanced at her but said nothing as he drove, taking only minutes on the empty road until he came to the Brickmaker's pub, where Rosie directed him the rest of the way to King's Avenue, which sounded far grander than the row of terraced cottages suggested.

'We're here.' She pointed to one of them, no different in appearance to all the others.

'Right-o.' He turned off the ignition key and turned towards her.

What was he about to do?

She didn't want him to kiss her. Or for him to feel he had to.

As if he read her thoughts, he said, 'Don't worry, Rosemary. I'm not going to make a pass at you. And I don't condemn you for getting a bit tiddly. We all do it when we're young. Some of us still do when we're older.' He gave her a rueful smile. 'I think you're an intelligent young woman with a charming personality and I shall be having a word with my boss about you.' He opened his door and hopped out to open hers.

'I see you're number twenty-seven King's Avenue,' he said as Rosie stood outside her gate awkwardly facing him. 'I'll easily remember that as I'm twenty-seven myself,' he chuckled. 'I'll drop you a line. It might be a few days, but I'll tell you the outcome either way.'

'Thank you.' Her head had begun to swim again.

'Take some deep breaths.' He waited while she did. 'All right?'

'Yes,' she said. 'I'm all right.'

'I enjoyed the evening . . . *very* much.'

'I did, too.' It was difficult to see his expression in the dark.

'Goodnight, Rosemary. It's a bit early but I wish you and the family a Merry Christmas.' He bent and gave her the merest brush of his lips on her cheek, then went back to his car.

She put her key in the door but there was no sound of the engine. She opened the door and stepped inside the hall. Only then did she hear his car drive away. What a very nice man he was to have made sure she was safely inside.

The house was in its usual darkness at this time of the night. Her parents made a thing of going to bed by ten o'clock and if Rosie ever went out, which was rare, she had to abide by the same rules. It must be well after eleven by now. Trembling with nerves, but thankful she could creep upstairs without disturbing anyone and being questioned, she was on the first tread when her father's voice called from the parlour.

'Rosemary.'

Sighing at his use of her full name which meant trouble, she pushed the door to. His voice came from the direction of his armchair but if he hadn't spoken he could have been anyone in the pitch black.

He switched a small side light on.

'You're late, my girl.'

She kept her distance. The last thing she needed was for him to accuse her of being tipsy. 'Sorry, Dad. I didn't realise the time.'

'Your mother won't go to sleep until she knows you're home. And you know the rules. In by ten.' He peered at her. 'Who's this friend anyway?' His voice was coated with suspicion.

'Mrs Edgerton. I met her in the library.' Rosie hesitated. Should she tell him more? Yes, perhaps she should drop John in subtly. 'Her nephew was there, too.'

She could almost see her father's ears prick up. 'Oh, yes. Who's he, then?'

'His name is John Palmer.'

'Was that him just now in the motor I heard?'

'Yes, he kindly gave me a lift.'

'He should be away fightin' for King and country.'

'He's in the Navy,' Rosie said, heaving a sigh. 'He's a lieutenant and works in Whitehall. His aunt asked him if he'd put in a word for me to join the WRNS.'

He frowned. 'Oh.'

'You don't sound very pleased.'

Her father looked across at her. 'Have you told him about Poppy?'

'Course I haven't.' She swallowed hard. 'I don't go around telling people. I promised not to, if you remember.'

'Because if anyone found out—'

'They're not going to,' Rosie cut in. 'But I must start living again, Dad. Meeting other people. I think I've paid the price and been punished long enough. Six years of staying at home and helping Mum with taking in sewing and looking after the others, and now at that blasted factory—'

'You brought this on yourself, don't forget.'

'How *could* I forget?' she snapped, reaching out to steady herself on the back of her mother's armchair.

She closed her eyes and the full horror swept over her, making her dizzy as she clung to the armchair and replayed that awful scene when she was just seventeen . . .

Crying herself to sleep every night, she'd put off telling her parents for as long as she dared, but her mother would soon notice. She couldn't leave it a moment longer. But her mother had beaten her to it.

'Did I hear you bein' sick this mornin', Rosemary?'

'Yes.'

She stared at Rosie. 'You know what that means, don't you?'

'Yes.' Rosie's voice was a whisper.

'I don't know what your dad's goin' to say.'

Her father had exploded.

'This in't how we brought you up,' he said, his face alive with rage. 'And you have another think comin' if you imagine we're goin' to welcome some bastard kid in the house.'

Shockwaves pounded through her.

'Are you saying you're putting me out? Me and my baby?' She stood there defiant, but inside she was trembling from head to foot. 'You'll be the grandparents. Surely that means something to you.'

Her father shook his head.

'I'm afraid not, Rosemary. We've got enough mouths to feed and we don't need another one.' His frown deepened. 'So if you want to stay under my roof you'll have it adopted.'

'I'm *not* going to have my baby adopted.' She fought to lower her voice. 'Please, Dad, let me keep it. I'll stay home and look after it. I'll do *anything* – except that.'

'And bring shame to your mother? To the family?' He shook his head. 'No, Rosemary, you'll go to a mother and baby home so the neighbours don't gossip. Then the baby's to be adopted – they arrange all that – and you'll come home and no one will be any the wiser.'

Rosie had rushed upstairs and thrown herself face-down on the bed. Half an hour later her mother entered the room and sat on the bed. She took hold of Rosie's hand.

'You know, Rosie, I in't been feelin' my best lately. I'm tired all the time and that's the truth.'

Rosie shot up, her eyes still filled with tears. 'Oh, Mum, come to think of it, you do look peaky. I'm so sorry – I feel awful. And now I've brought this on you. Shouldn't you go to the doctor's?'

'I've been,' her mother said. 'He said it's normal for women in their forties. He thinks I might have started the change.'

'What's that?'

'When women of my age or a bit older stop havin' their monthlies – then they can't conceive no more – thank the Lord.'

Heat rushed to Rosie's cheeks. She'd never had this kind of conversation with her mother.

Her mother smoothed her apron and heaved a sigh.

'You might not think it, Rosie, but I'm not with your dad about the baby. It would break my heart to know that I could pass a child on the street who could be my grandson or granddaughter and I'd never know – so I've had a think. I won't let the baby be adopted.' She fixed her eyes on Rosie. '*I'll* be the baby's mother.'

Rosie stiffened. 'Whatever do you mean? You can't possibly. You won't show . . . but *I* will.'

'I know that, dear,' her mother said patiently. 'The doctor's told me I need a few weeks' rest, preferably by the sea – that's true – so we'll go to Aunt Dot's.' She looked at Rosie. 'I'm afraid that means you'll have to eventually go to the mother and baby home because we couldn't afford the midwife or a doctor to deliver it at hers.' She paused. 'Anyway, dear, you'll have the baby, I'll meet you at the home when you're able to come out, and we'll come back together on the train . . . but as far as anyone's concerned – including the kids – *I'll* be the baby's mother.'

'How can you if you've started this change?'

'Women often get pregnant then,' Shirley said. 'They don't think they need to take any precautions.'

A bubble of anger burst in Rosie's throat. 'But it'll be *my* baby. *I'm* the mother.'

'Only you, me and Dad will know that.' She stroked Rosie's hair. 'It's the only solution, dear, if you want to keep your baby.' Her forehead creased in thought. 'I'll write a letter to all of them when I'm at Dot's to tell them I'm having another baby – make a joke that it'll be the last one. I don't hold with lying to my children but it can't be helped.'

'They'll have to know the truth one day.'

'Maybe. But not until this has all blown over and they're older.' She paused. 'And one day, God willin', you'll meet someone nice who'll marry you and take the baby on.'

Rosie briefly closed her eyes. How ugly that sounded.

'Dad will never accept my baby in the family. He said so himself.'

Shirley kept her gaze fixed on Rosie. 'I told him I've not asked much of him in all our married life, so he'd better do this for me.'

Rosie's eyes flew wide. It was the first time she'd known her mother to stand up to him. A flicker of hope coursed through her.

'Mind you, he went on a bit, then said how it'll cause me more work but I told him you'd help.'

'What did he say?'

53

'He gave in in the end – I knew he would.' She smiled. 'But you have to promise never to tell a soul. Nor hint. And that go for the children. As far as you're all concerned, you'll have a new baby brother or sister.'

'If I agree to this, the baby will be *my* responsibility,' Rosie said fiercely. 'I'll stay at home and take care of it. Do laundry . . . take in sewing . . . anything to earn some money to pay my share . . . and the baby's.'

And one day I'll tell the whole world the baby's mine, she thought. But she didn't say it.

Five months later, when she could no longer disguise her swollen stomach, Rosie and her mother each took a small cardboard suitcase and boarded a train to Caister-on-Sea with her dear Aunt Dot. Six weeks before the birth Rosie moved into the King's Lynn Mother and Baby Home her father had arranged, rather than the nearest one in Norwich. 'In case someone recognises you,' he'd said.

They worked her until she was exhausted. Every single day with no let-up. She had to scrub floors, clean windows, do piles of washing up, make beds, wash and iron – her stomach forever rolling with the meagre food they dished out. She would have gladly put up with it if they'd been kind. But all she and the other young mothers heard day and night was that they were bad girls bringing shame on their family, not fit to be mothers, and this was their punishment.

Then one day she was sweeping the dormitory where a dozen girls slept when she felt something inside her give way. Liquid was running down the insides of her legs. To her horror she saw a puddle form around her feet. She didn't know what it meant. Luckily, one of the nurses caught sight of it and took her off to bed, telling her that her waters had broken and the baby would soon be born.

But her labour went on for the rest of the day. That evening, exhausted, she finally gave birth, feeling she was being ripped apart as she screamed for her mother who wasn't there. Only one of the nurses who had reprimanded her on several occasions for getting herself into trouble stood by her bed, her mouth in a thin line of disapproval. No mention of the boyfriend's involvement, Rosie thought bitterly.

'If she doesn't soon improve, we'll have to get her into hospital,' she heard the same nurse mutter.

She was too weak to argue that she wouldn't be able to move off the bed.

The next day she felt a little better and was curious to see her baby. And when she looked at the little mite with bright auburn hair and blue eyes, she fell immediately in love with her. Two days later, when she'd struggled back from the bathroom a long way down the corridor, she found her parents bent over the worn-looking cradle. The baby was whimpering. Rosie climbed back into bed and watched as her mother gently picked the baby up and tried to soothe her but she began to howl. Rosie held out her arms to comfort her, but her father mumbled something to her mother, then took the baby and walked round the room jiggling her.

Rosie couldn't stop staring from her bed as her baby opened her eyes to look up at a man who would be known as her new daddy. She blinked back the tears. If only it had all been different. Hugo by her side. Mum and Dad thrilled to be grandparents.

'What's its name?' Her father broke into her thoughts, not taking his eyes off the baby, who'd broken off crying and was looking at him.

'It's not an "it", it's a "*she*",' Rosie snapped. 'I've named her Pauline.'

'That won't do,' he muttered.

'I'm having Pauline,' she protested. 'At least let me give her that one thing.'

Her father gazed down at the baby. For a minute no one spoke. Then without looking at his daughter he said:

'Her birth certificate can say Pauline but she'll be known as Poppy so she don't arouse suspicion by not keepin' to the names of flowers, and she'll be your baby sister from now on.' He looked Rosie in the eye. 'If you keep to your promise, then I promise you she'll be loved just as much as the others.'

And he'd kept true to his word, Rosie admitted. Everything had gone to plan. She'd stayed in the mother and baby home for another fortnight to recuperate – if you could call it that, Rosie remembered with stinging eyes – then she and her mother had come home with Poppy. Poppy quickly had her 'sisters' and 'brother' wrapped round her tiny finger, but it was her father who adored the child. If anything, his love had intensified when Poppy started to talk. Yet the little girl always seemed uncertain. As if she wasn't quite sure of her place in the family. Or was it only Rosie's imagination running wild? Even wishful thinking.

One thing was certain – she was by far Poppy's favourite 'sister'. And for that, Rosie was humbly grateful.

Now, all these years later, Rosie dragged her thoughts back to her father in the front room. He was watching her.

'There was no way you could have looked after the baby on your own,' he said eventually. 'But your secret has to remain one – always.'

'I couldn't have secrets if I ever met someone. And if he really loved me he'd take Poppy as his own.'

Even in the darkness she could see her father's features tighten.

'I can't see many blokes doing that . . . can you?' He paused. 'And even if he did, you'd be scarrin' Poppy for life if you told her the truth. Can you imagine draggin' her away from us to live with someone she don't know but is told she's got to call him "Daddy"? She won't like that, and neither will you when you know how much she loves *me,* who she knows as her *real* daddy.' He looked pointedly at her. 'No, Rosemary, if you love our little poppet as much as you say you do—'

Rosie opened her mouth, but he put his hand up to still her.

'Let me finish. I *know* you love her – there's no doubt. And that's why you'll never tell her. You'll never destroy her world.'

Chapter Five

Her father's words reverberated in Rosie's ears. She couldn't get rid of them. It was as though they were embedded in her brain. She'd gone over and over them. Did it mean she had no future being Poppy's mother? Would someone like John Palmer be the sort who'd never forgive her if he found out she had a child and had kept it from him? She was just using his name as an example because she'd never had a boyfriend in all these years to make a judgement. But it hadn't answered any of her questions.

Just three days later, before going to work, Rosie picked up the post from the mat at the front door. There were a couple of bills and one addressed to her, postmarked Whitehall.

Let it be good news.

She ripped open the envelope and pulled out a sheet of typed paper and a short message, handwritten. She read the handwritten one first.

> *Dear Rosemary,*
>
> *I've spoken to my boss about you. I think he's intrigued! If you're deemed 'suitable' (his word, not mine) he'll pass your name on to the appropriate person who will interview you with a view to your joining the WRNS.*

Before going further can you fill in the form with your particulars and send it back to me right away.

In haste,

John

Her heart beating fast, Rosie skimmed the form, which didn't appear too onerous. As to be expected there was a question about marital status and children. She swallowed hard. She'd kept her secret all this time, she trusted her mother and father implicitly to do their very best for Poppy, but the ache in her heart would never go away unless she could one day tell her child the truth. But according to her father, that was out of the question. Tears sprang to her eyes. She mustn't be selfish. This wasn't about her – it was about her precious daughter. What was best for the child. And for the time being it seemed her father was right. Rosie's mouth tightened. But one day . . . one day, she was determined to claim Poppy as her own.

She'd fill in the form and post it this evening straight from work.

Every day at the factory without hearing anything seemed like a month. The only thing that made it bearable was that she'd discovered Poppy's reading, although shaky, was not as bad as she'd feared, and she spent every possible moment helping her, determined Poppy would inherit her own love of books. And the more Poppy improved the more excited the little girl became.

'And you have such a good memory, poppet,' Rosie said, using her father's pet name, 'that we're going to learn some poetry.'

'What's po-e-try, Mosey?'

'When words in sentences like you read in your books rhyme.'

'What's rhyme?'

'When words sound the same, like "the *cat sat* on the *mat*". "Cat" and "sat" and "mat" sound the same. People called poets make up these poems and you can learn them and say them out loud from memory, just like you do your times tables.'

Was she going too far for a five-year-old? Rosie bit her lip but was rewarded with a beaming smile.

'I'm going to learn one and I'll say it in class.' Then her face clouded. 'No, they won't like it. I'll tell Daddy. *He* will.'

Rosie swallowed. Poppy's 'daddy' always came first in her little world. Yet in a strange way it gave her hope that it might not be such a shock when Poppy was told the truth one day that Mosey wasn't her oldest sister but her *mother*. It wasn't that the child didn't love who she thought of as her mummy, but she'd been a daddy's girl from the day she was born, and the feeling was mutual.

'Yes, he will, darling,' she told Poppy who was dancing round the front room where Rosie had been teaching her. She closed the little girl's book.

Poppy stopped abruptly. 'And one day soon I'll be big enough to write a po-e-try, won't I?'

Rosie smiled from her father's chair. 'One poetry is called a poem. And yes, you'll soon be big enough to write a poem.'

''Cos you learnt me, I'll read it to *you* first, Mosey,' she said, and ran to give her a hug.

The little girl's thin arms wound so tightly around her neck that it took every morsel of effort for Rosie not to burst into tears.

'I shall look forward to it, darling,' she said, the words tangling in her throat. 'I'm sure it will be a wonderful poem.'

'Yes, it will, yes, it will,' Poppy chanted.

Rosie momentarily closed her eyes, thinking of John Palmer and whether he'd been able to talk to his boss. Would she even *be* here by the time Poppy wrote her first poem?

After waiting almost three weeks, when she had almost given up hope, Rosie heard from John again.

Dear Rosemary,
 Sorry it's taken a while since I wrote but my boss was called away for several days. However, he's now seen your details and passed your name on to the powers that be who will ask you to come for an interview. You should be hearing from them very shortly as to a date but I must warn you it might take place in London.
 Let me know when you settle on a date and if you do have to go to London, perhaps we can meet afterwards and you can put me in the picture.
 All the best,
 John

Rosie chewed her lip. It seemed as though she was always waiting.

This time she didn't have long to wait. The following day a typed envelope came for her from an anonymous person at the local recruiting office in Norwich. For a few moments she was disappointed. She'd been quite looking forward to a day out in London, pushing the thought away that it would have been nice to see John Palmer again, but then she felt relief. She would have had to ask her boss at the factory for an advance cash payment to afford the train fare.

She was to present herself at nine-thirty sharp in precisely two days' time. Well, she'd be ready. It would just give her time to tell Mum and Dad.

That evening, after putting Poppy to bed, making sure Roddy was doing his homework, and persuading Heather and Ivy to clear the dishes and wash up, Rosie entered the parlour where her parents were both talking quietly.

'We know what you're about to say,' her father said, taking off his glasses and rubbing his eyes. 'Mum's told me you had a letter from the WRNS this mornin.'

'Yes.' Rosie sat in one of the upright chairs. 'They want to see me the day after tomorrow in Norwich, at the recruiting centre.' She hesitated. 'Are you both all right about this?'

'We've discussed it,' her father said. 'The main thing is – you don't need to worry about Poppy.'

'It's Mum as much as anyone.'

'We decided if you joined up, we'd get a girl in from the village to help a couple of days in the week when the girls are at work. Eve's daughter, Eileen, would be glad of an extra five bob a week.'

'Can you afford her? I might be one less mouth to feed but Eileen will have to eat if she's here all day.'

'There's a war on,' her father said. 'We all have to do our bit for King and country.'

Magdalen Street was a higgledy-piggledy array of shops and houses, with little attempt made to announce it would soon be Christmas Eve. The toyshop window display was meagre – a sad-looking teddy-bear, a grinning clown, a rag doll, a couple of spinning tops, a jigsaw puzzle and ludo set, and what looked like a second-hand train set. The recruitment office at number two was on the corner of the top end in a hefty red-brick Victorian building, standing almost opposite the double-fronted entrance where Heather worked in

Woolworths. As Rosie was early she decided to put her head round the door before her interview. It would be the first time she'd ever seen her sister at work.

Woolworths had a little more of the Christmas spirit with its cotton-wool snow lining the windows and a Father Christmas pulling his cardboard sleigh. There were some small gift ideas such as a torch, a few pieces of cheap jewellery, a packet of handkerchiefs, and some knitting wool, so maybe she'd find a last-minute present for her mother.

She opened the door and looked towards the haberdashery counter. There was Heather, standing behind it with a thoroughly bored expression on her long thin face as a middle-aged woman decided on a pair of scissors. Heather suddenly looked up, her expression hardening as she caught her sister's eye. She silently mouthed, 'Go away' and even from the distance Rosie could see the glint of warning in her sister's eyes, thinking she was being checked on. Rosie merely nodded and walked back to the recruitment office.

Paint was peeling off the windowsills and the front door was faded and mud-splashed from an accumulation of rain and wind. She rang the bell, wondering what might happen between now and when she left the place. The door swiftly opened and an elderly man gestured her in without asking her name. He showed her into a gloomy back room that had been turned into an office, then quietly left. To Rosie's surprise a man and a woman, both impeccably dressed in naval uniform, looking out of place, sat behind a large polished desk which took up almost the whole space of the room. The man nodded and smiled, his pipe still in his mouth, but the woman looked stern with her glasses perched on her nose and her dark hair tightly pulled from her face.

'Miss Rosemary Frost, I presume,' she said.

'Yes,' Rosie replied.

'Take a seat. I'm Chief Wren Baldwin and this is Petty Officer Williams.' She gestured towards the man. 'Please sit.'

Rosie swallowed and sat on the hard wooden chair opposite.

'Now then, we've read your form but we'd like to ask some further questions.'

Rosie stretched her back a little straighter, bracing herself.

'You're twenty-three,' the woman said. 'What have you been doing since leaving school and coming here?'

Rosie took in a breath. 'Mainly looking after the younger children,' she began. 'My mother wasn't in good health so she needed me at home.' This was the excuse she'd decided to use when any employer asked why she hadn't had any previous employment except a year at Caley's.

'So you've had no work experience at all?'

Rosie could feel the woman's eyes boring into her. It would sound pathetic if she said no. It would also be a lie.

'I worked in a factory the last year when the youngest started school.'

'Hmm.' The woman frowned. 'You've had a good education and factory work seems a waste of such an opportunity.'

'How is your mother now?' the man asked.

'She's much stronger, thank you.'

'Most girls are married with children of their own at your age,' the woman persisted. 'What is your position? Have you a serious boyfriend?'

Heart thudding in her ears, Rosie replied, 'No, ma'am.' She was thankful to answer the question truthfully. 'I don't really go out to meet anyone. And most of my friends' brothers whom I used to know joined up as soon as war was declared.'

'Hmm.' The woman fleetingly turned to the man and said

something under her breath, then fixed her gaze back to Rosie. 'So no liabilities whatsoever?'

'None.' Rosie willed the blood not to rush to her face.

'And your parents?'

'They know I'm desperate to do my bit for the war.'

'Why the WRNS?' PO Williams asked.

She told them she'd always had a fascination with ships and the sea.

PO Williams removed his pipe. 'You do realise you wouldn't be serving on any ships.'

'Oh, I do realise that, sir,' Rosie said.

'I hope you're not looking at joining the WRNS with rose-coloured spectacles,' the woman commented.

'Oh, no, ma'am, I'm not at all afraid of hard work. The factory has certainly taught me that. And discipline,' she added for further emphasis. She paused, wondering if this was the appropriate time to put forward her preferences. 'I've read the WRNS leaflet thoroughly and there are a couple of categories where they ask for mathematics skills.'

Petty Officer Williams leaned forward. 'What would they be?'

'Meteorologist and radio mechanic.'

'Hmm. Interesting.' He paused. 'What about a radio operator?'

Rosie hesitated. 'I read that a radio operator might have to work at an isolated station and I'm not sure how I'd cope.' She hesitated. Had saying that just blown her chances? 'I expect that's from being part of a large family.' She gave a nervous smile.

'It sounds as though you might prefer to stay in England near your family rather than go abroad,' the woman said, in a tone as if it wasn't what *they'd* prefer.

'It might be best at present,' Rosie said, wishing she could

65

judge from their serious expressions as to what they thought of her.

'We would need full commitment,' the Chief Wren continued, leaning forward on the desk and studying Rosie.

'Oh, I promise I'd give you that,' Rosie said eagerly.

Another glance passed between the two of them. Finally, the woman said:

'Would you mind leaving the room for a few minutes, Miss Frost. You can take a seat next door. We'll call you back in.'

There was no encouraging smile.

It was all going wrong, Rosie thought, as she thanked them and left the room. All that talk about boyfriends and commitment. She gave a deep sigh as she opened the door next to the office. No one was there. She walked round the room, looking at the shelves of books, noting they were mostly about the armed services in one way or another.

She sat down in a scruffy leather armchair thinking about how she could have answered the questions better. The image of John Palmer popped into her head. He'd been very taken with her knowledge of Italian, as though that would have a positive bearing on whether she'd be accepted as a Wren.

The door opened and the elderly man said they were ready to see her. She got to her feet and followed his shuffling footsteps back to the inner office.

'Take a seat,' the woman said again, gazing at Rosie, her sharp eyes giving no clue as to what was coming next. Then she said, 'We've decided to give you a try.'

It was so completely unexpected, Rosie's heart leapt.

'Oh, thank you, ma'am. I'm really pleased. I promise to do a good job.'

'See that you do,' the woman said, giving a half-smile. 'However, you must first pass a medical, but I should think the work you do at the factory and helping with your younger siblings should be keeping you fit,' she gave Rosie a fixed gaze, 'even though you're rather on the thin side.'

'I've always been healthy,' Rosie put in quickly.

'Good.' The woman nodded. 'We'll arrange for you to take the medical in Norwich, in a few days' time, then as soon as we have the results that you pass as Grade 1 fit, we can officially recruit you.' She gave another half-smile as though her face would crack if she went any further.

'If all goes well, we shall be delighted to have you on board,' PO Williams said, rising from the desk and moving to hold the door open for her. 'In the meantime, Merry Christmas, Miss Frost.'

'Thank you,' Rosie said. 'And Merry Christmas to you, too.'

He didn't attempt to hold back an appreciative smile.

Rosie walked confidently up the steps to the doctor's surgery for her appointment. She stepped into the waiting room and took one of the chairs amongst a dozen or so patients, then opened her book, hoping she wouldn't have to wait too long.

'Rosemary Frost.'

Rosie got to her feet and followed the nurse to a door marked 'Doctor Foulger'. A man of middle height and middle age carried out the medical examination.

'Everything seems to be satisfactory,' he said, as he scribbled some notes.

She knew it would be. She'd never had a day's sickness since she was ten years old with measles.

'Just take your shoes off and jump on the scales.'

When she was ready he ran the balance mechanism and studied her weight, then frowned.

'What is it?'

'The minimum weight to join the WRNS is eight stones and I'm afraid you're under.' He threw her a sympathetic look. 'I'll have to report it.'

'Oh, no,' Rosie said, her eyes wide with appeal. 'I used to be heavier before the war started and now rations have been reduced even further, they're sometimes hard to go round with a large family.' She knew she was sounding desperate but she couldn't stop herself. 'Oh, please don't tell them.'

'I'm sorry, Miss Frost, but I'm obliged to.'

She couldn't – *wouldn't* let her dream fade away. 'It's my only chance,' she told him. 'Oh, can't you do something? Please.'

The doctor hesitated. 'Put your shoes back on,' he said quietly, 'and I'll check I read it correctly the first time.'

Quickly she pushed her feet back into her shoes and stepped onto the weighing machine again. Her heart nearly missed a beat as the doctor bent forward to read it. Then he turned to her and smiled.

'An ounce over, Miss Frost. You've passed your medical. Well done!'

She floated home on a cloud.

Chapter Six

'I'm tired of this damn war,' Heather said.

It was Christmas Eve but there was precious little evidence of it in the Frost family home, Rosie thought, glancing round the dining room. There was no small fir tree in the parlour this year, decorated by her sisters and brother, as there'd been every year before. And although she and her mother had done their best to make the meal special as Dad had to work a 24-hour shift on Christmas Day, the meat pie was only rabbit instead of the usual mutton, turning Rosie's stomach as she envisioned playful rabbits ending up on dinner plates. She had no choice but to get on with it and count herself lucky her mother managed as well as she did.

'You will *not* swear at the table, Heather,' their father admonished. 'Apologise at once.'

'I won't. I'm fed up with it. This is the third hateful Christmas. We haven't even got proper paper chains.' Heather's mouth twisted with exaggerated contempt.

'Yes, we have,' Poppy called out, her fork halfway to her mouth. 'Me and Roddy made them this morning.' She pointed upwards with her fork. 'We made them out of real newspaper and Mosey helped put them up.'

Rosie hid a smile at the 'real newspaper' reference.

Roddy looked up from his plate. 'We shoulda had coloured strips like my friends made,' he grunted, then shoved some more food in his mouth.

'That's what I mean,' Heather whined. 'There's nothing Christmassy in here.'

'Poppy, that's a new tablecloth I put on especially for Christmas,' their mother said, tutting, as she rose from the table to fetch a cloth.

The little girl tried to remove the offending piece of gravy-soaked pie, but her fork clattered to the floor. She burst into tears. Rosie jumped from her seat and put her arms round Poppy's trembling shoulders.

'It's all right, my love. It was an accident.' She stooped to pick up the offending fork. 'I'll wash your fork and you can finish your tea.'

'I don't want any more.'

Rosie bent close to her and whispered, 'Don't say that, poppet, or you'll be sent to bed early. And Father Christmas will want to know why you didn't eat your tea. You have to be a good girl so he fills your stocking.' She paused to let that sink in. Then she added, 'And you need to eat to grow up into a big strong girl.'

Poppy bent her head a few moments, then raised it.

'Like you, Mosey?'

The child looked at her with innocent eyes, once baby-blue but now as green as—

Rosie swallowed hard. 'Yes, darling, just like me.'

'Will you wash my fork?'

'Of course I will.'

Rosie noticed their father studying her. She caught his eye. Immediately, he averted his and resumed eating. It was obviously going to be a difficult Christmas for all of them.

*   *   *

Her father had already left for work when Rosie came into the kitchen just before six on Christmas morning. It was too early to take her mother a cup of tea. She'd make one for herself and take it into the parlour where she could have a bit of peace before they all started talking at once. As she walked into the room, she gave a start of surprise. There, propped against the fireplace, amongst the children's stockings she and Mum had filled late last night, was a fir tree about three feet tall – a beautiful Christmas tree. Who on earth . . . ? She stepped towards the fireplace, then noticed a cardboard box on the table by the window. By the side was a note from her father.

Shirl, I found this box and the tree outside the front door. Must be one of the lads at the station. The kids will be pleased. See you tomorrow. Sid.

At least it will stop Heather from moaning, Rosie thought, as she eyed the tree. Her younger sister often acted more childishly than Roddy. Well, he'd be pleased with the tree. But the one who would be more excited than anyone was her little Poppy.

She sat on a chair at the table and sipped her mug of tea, her eyes on the cardboard box. There was no name on the outside so surely it wouldn't matter if she opened it. She put down her mug and lifted the cardboard flaps, then pulled out a small round item in newspaper and unwrapped it. It was a gleaming red and gold ornament for the tree. And by the look of all the other small packages, also wrapped in newspaper, there were dozens more. Whoever had sent the tree had thoughtfully added a box of decorations. How very kind. She hoped her father would have solved the mystery when he came home tomorrow. If so, they must be sure to thank whoever it was.

Carefully, she laid the bauble back in the box, hoping Mum would let the children decorate the tree on their own, though Heather was bound to take charge. Poor Ivy, she thought. She was so much quieter than the rest and didn't often get a look-in.

After washing and dressing, Rosie went back downstairs to make her mother a cup of tea and start the porridge. Shirley greeted her daughter with a smile.

'What a treat, love.' She shifted up in the bed and Rosie tucked her father's pillow behind her mother's back. 'Stay here a moment. There won't be peace for much longer.' She glanced towards Poppy's small bed.

Just as Rosie was about to perch on the edge of the bed, Poppy awoke and sat up, rubbing her eyes.

'Hello, Mosey,' she beamed. 'Did Father Christmas come in the night?'

'Yes, he did, darling,' Rosie said, going over and ruffling the little girl's auburn curls. 'And it looks as though he's filled your stocking.'

'I want to see it.' Poppy flung her blanket to one side and hopped out of bed. Then as though with an afterthought she turned to Shirley. 'Can I, Mummy?' She looked at Shirley, her eyes anxious.

'Yes, dear. Put your bed jacket on – the one Mosey made you – and go downstairs with her. You can open your stocking before the others come down.'

'I've got a stocking, I've got a stocking,' Poppy chanted over and over.

'Shhhh! Don't wake the others,' Rosie said, putting a finger to her lips.

'Shhhh!' Poppy repeated, her little hand covering her rosebud mouth, then giggling.

It was wonderful to see her acting so normally, Rosie

thought, laughing softly with her. Then a pain stabbed at her. Was she truly ready to leave her darling little girl?

She followed the excited child down the stairs and into the parlour. Then Poppy skidded to a halt as her eyes spotted the tree. She turned to Rosie.

'Why is that tree in the room?'

'It's a Christmas tree,' Rosie said. 'You and your brother and sisters can help decorate it.'

'But Daddy said we can't 'ford one this year.'

'Someone very kind left it for us.'

Poppy's eyes went wide. 'Was it Father Christmas?'

Rosie smiled. 'I think it might have been.'

'Can I dec'rate it now?'

'No, darling. I'm going to make some porridge.'

'Don't want porridge.'

'Yes, you do. Just like The Three Bears. You know how much you love them, and they eat it all the time.'

By the way she was screwing up her eyes, Rosie could tell Poppy was thinking fast.

'If I eat my porridge, can I dec'rate the tree on my own?'

'No, darling. Some of the branches will be too high to reach and you'll need Heather and Ivy and Roddy to help.'

'Will you help, too, Mosey?'

'I will if you want me to.'

'All right. I'll eat my porridge up like the bears.' She kept her eyes on Rosie. 'Then can I open my stocking?'

'I can hear Roddy,' Rosie said, aware of the thumping upstairs, 'so I think it would be nice if we wait for everyone else.' She looked at the animated face of her daughter and swallowed.

'Happy Christmas,' Roddy shouted as he burst into the room, then stopped short, his eyes wide. 'Is that for us?'

'Father Christmas brought it,' Poppy shouted. 'And we're all going to dec'rate it.'

'You're too little,' Roddy said.

'I'm not.' Poppy's eyes filled with tears.

'You are.' He looked at her pointedly. 'And Father Christmas couldn't've brought it 'cos there's no such person.' He went over to the fireplace and pulled his stocking off the mantelpiece.

'It's not true, is it, Mosey?' Poppy said, tears now running down her face. 'Father Christmas comes down the chimney, doesn't he?'

'Roddy's just teasing,' Rosie said, giving her brother a stern shake of her head. 'Why don't you run upstairs and get dressed like a good girl and we'll open our stockings after breakfast when we're all together.' She turned to Roddy. 'And you, Roddy, can put the stocking back where you found it and get dressed too.'

Rosie and the children had almost finished breakfast when the letterbox rattled.

'Postman!' Roddy shouted. 'I'll go.'

He jumped from his seat and moments later appeared with the post.

'They're both for you, Rosie. Is it from your boyfriend?'

'Don't be silly.' She stretched her hand out but Roddy dangled it in front of her.

'It's got a London postmark,' he said. 'He must live in London.'

'Leave off,' Ivy said unexpectedly. 'So what if she's got a boyfriend. It's none of your business.'

'Hand me my letters, Roddy,' Rosie said, 'before I tell Dad to tan your bottom.'

She snatched them from him and glanced at the typed addressed one with a postmark: Whitehall. The other felt like a Christmas card and the address was handwritten. She recognised the writing. Well, she definitely would not open either of them in front of her brother and sisters.

'I'm going to take Mum's breakfast upstairs.' Rosie got to her feet, 'so when you've finished, please clear the table. I'll be back in a few minutes.'

'She wants to read her boyfriend's letter in private,' Roddy said, a huge grin slicing his face.

'Oh, why don't you stick your head in a bucket of water, Roddy,' Heather said, having the last word.

In the bedroom, Rosie sat on the bed and opened the one from Whitehall. She skimmed over it. She'd been accepted! She was to report to Mill Hill, the WRNS basic training depot, on Monday, 19th January 1942. There were a few sparse instructions, but the only thing that mattered was that she'd been accepted. She was finally going to lead an independent life. She brushed aside the thought that this could never have happened if the country hadn't been at war.

As she suspected, the Christmas card with a robin perched on a spade in the snow was from John Palmer.

Happy Christmas, Rosemary, and to your family. I'm wondering if you've heard yet that you've passed. Let me know at above address.

Yours,
John

Rosie put the card back into the envelope. She suddenly knew without doubt who had left the fir tree and the box of Christmas decorations.

PART TWO

Chapter Seven

Leaving Poppy was the worst wrench of all. Rosie sat squashed in a compartment of the train for Liverpool Street in London where she would change to take the Underground to Mill Hill. She took in some deep shuddering breaths as she relived the scene she'd just left.

'Daddy, don't let Mosey go,' Poppy begged, tears streaming down her cheeks, as she pummelled her father as high as she could reach above his knees.

'We have to fight the horrible men, poppet.' Sidney Frost crouched down to smooth the child's hair from her face. 'And Mosey has to help. She's goin' to wear a smart uniform and help the sailors.'

'She's 'posed to help *me*.' Poppy stamped her foot. 'I can only read with Mosey.'

'That's nonsense,' Shirley said, coming into the room. '*I'll* help you until she comes back. We'll learn together. I'll read to you and you can read the next bit to me.'

'It's not the same!' Poppy screamed. 'I want Mosey to help me!'

The child turned to Rosie, who stood transfixed by her

79

outburst. It wasn't one of Poppy's sudden tantrums – this was raw fear, striking Rosie to the core.

As she'd already said her goodbyes to her siblings earlier, she grabbed her suitcase, telling her mother and father to stay home – she couldn't bear to wave them off at the railway station – but when she'd turned round at the top of her street for a final wave before catching the bus, she saw only her father with Poppy clutching on to him, her head buried in his chest, and her screams of utter despair.

Now on the train, Rosie felt an ache in her chest. Heartache – that's what it was.

Come on, Rosie. Mum and Dad will give Poppy so much love she'll hardly know you've gone.

But she knew that wasn't true. There was a special bond between her and Poppy, even if the little girl was fated never to know that her big sister was, in fact, her mother.

Was this the HMS *Pembroke* where she'd been told to report for a fortnight's introductory course? If so, the huge modern building with its bright green copper roof looked less like a ship than anything she could possibly imagine. Rosie's exhausted, stinging eyes – after travelling for nearly five hours with hold-ups and two Underground changes – saw what looked like hundreds of girls, but were probably only eighty or so, milling around, most of them looking as bewildered as herself. She gripped her suitcase even tighter, then gave herself a telling off. This was what she'd longed for – an adventure. Simply to be a young woman with no cares except to concentrate on playing her part in this interminable war. A flutter of excitement took hold of her as she spotted a woman in naval uniform who seemed to be in charge. She let out a slow breath.

'Form an orderly queue,' the uniformed woman ordered, as she walked round several groups who were chattering nineteen to the dozen, 'and proceed *quietly* through the entrance where you will register at the desk. Then make your way to one of the classrooms as instructed, all on the ground floor and clearly marked on the doors.'

Feeling self-conscious Rosie tagged along with four girls who seemed to know one another by the way they were laughing and talking together. One of them turned to her and grinned. She was a tall girl, large-boned, with blonde curls and the most enviable white teeth that shone like pearls.

'Isn't this fun?' she said. When Rosie just smiled, she went on:

'I'm Blanche Saunders – how do you do.' She paused a second. 'This is my dream come true. I've been wanting to join ever since the war started. What about you?'

'Rosemary Frost.' Rosie's smile widened at the girl's enthusiasm. 'I—'

'Get a move on, girls,' the uniformed Wren's strident tones interrupted her. 'We haven't got all day.'

'I'll find out about you later,' Blanche hissed as they were ushered inside.

Rosie was glad to see that Blanche Saunders was in the same room but there was no one else she'd glimpsed outside. She found a desk at the back near Blanche, who sent her a conspiratorial wink. She couldn't help smiling at the girl, who looked as though she could hardly be restrained from her exuberance.

I wish I could be more like her, Rosie thought. It must be being at home for all that while that's made me so serious.

When the room had finally filled, the same woman stood silently in front of the seated class and the chatter immediately died down.

'Good afternoon, girls. I'm Petty Officer Wren Robins.' There was a stifled chortle from one of the girls. PO Wren

Robins frowned as she gazed around the room. 'Until you've finished your two weeks' training, which is your probationary period, you'll be known as Pro-Wrens. You'll be given a bluette overall – boiler suit to you – which you will wear every day, and a medical check. Be warned that this will include a head search for lice.'

There were mutterings of disbelief from several girls, all fashionably dressed, with faces sporting mascaraed lashes and bright lipstick. Rosie hid a grin. No, they wouldn't like someone digging around in their beautifully coiffed hair. It would be insulting, to say the least. However, the petty officer ignored them and carried on.

'Tomorrow you'll be told which section you'll be working in, but for today you will have time to settle in. Any questions during the next two weeks which are to do with anything *other* than your work, please come and see me.' She cocked her head to one side. 'You'll see a booklet of regulations on your desk. Take it with you and be sure to read it carefully now and reread it from time to time to remind yourself.' She glanced round. 'Now, any questions so far?' Before giving anyone time to answer she said, 'No? Right, then bring your luggage and follow me, and I'll show you your sleeping quarters.' She looked at the class again. 'By the way, everything here is described in nautical terms. The bedroom is now a cabin, the kitchen is called a galley, and so on. You'll soon get used to it.'

Rosie's heart immediately lifted at the word 'bedroom'. How wonderful to have her own room after so many years. But it soon fell when she and half the class were shown their cabin, which was in fact a dormitory, and were told it was for fourteen of them.

'I don't know what Mummy and Daddy would say about this,' one girl with shining light-blonde hair styled off her face in a large roll said under her breath to Rosie as Petty Officer Robins was showing the recruits how to make a bed properly using the envelope system at the corners of the sheet and blanket.

'If you've anything to say, Graham, say it so we can all hear.' Petty Officer Robins stood up from her half-kneeling position and threw the girl a glare.

Rosie was glad *she* hadn't given any reply when Gillian Graham had made her innocent remark. It looked as though they'd all have to watch their p's and q's.

'And you finish with this cover.' Petty Officer Robins deftly threw a blue-and-white bedspread over the bed where it fell evenly almost of its own accord. 'Keep the ship's anchor the right way up or the ship will sink,' she said, her lips twitching at the joke, which had probably done the rounds many times.

There were one or two feeble chuckles. Most of the girls looked tired and strained. Rosie turned her head away to smother a yawn.

There were plenty more grumblings in the noisy dining hall that evening, where the meal consisted of a sausage and a bit of yellowing cabbage and two wedges of potato. At the same time Rosie was given a mug of thick cocoa. It made for a strange combination and she couldn't help being amused at some of the other girls' faces, screwed up in disgust. They were obviously used to far superior food – probably even waited on by maids.

But everything about the girls fascinated her, though she tried not to stare. Apparently, several had been debutantes – a world of which Rosie had no knowledge whatsoever. She caught snippets of conversation about finishing schools in Switzerland and Paris and hated having no idea what a finishing school was – but she didn't want to show her ignorance by asking. She supposed it was where upper-crust girls went when they left school. Quickly swallowing the last mouthful, she put her knife and fork together, then realised she was one of the first to finish. The blood flew to her cheeks. They would think she was either greedy or half starved. She'd remember to eat more slowly in future.

The girl sitting on her right put her cutlery down at the same time and turned to her.

'I can't believe you ate all that,' she said.

Rosie noticed she pronounced 'ate' as 'ett'. She glanced at her neighbour's plate. It was hardly touched.

'I haven't eaten since breakfast,' Rosie said truthfully.

'Oh, dear, that's not good.' The girl paused. 'By the way, I'm Lydia Bancroft . . . and you are . . .?'

'Rosemary Frost.' She hesitated. 'I'm pleased to meet you.'

'You, too,' Lydia said immediately. 'What made you want to become a Wren?'

This was where she had to be careful. Rosie kept her tone neutral.

'I've always loved the sea from the first time Dad took us all to Caister-on-Sea where my aunt lives.'

As soon as she said it and Lydia lifted a pencilled eyebrow, Rosie realised she'd made a mistake. She must learn not to give any kind of detail about her life. It was too dangerous.

'Caister-on-Sea? Never heard of it.'

'It's near Great Yarmouth.'

'On the Norfolk coast?'

Rosie nodded.

Oh, how to change the subject. She'll be asking me what I did before I came here, in a minute.

'We had a little pad in Nice we used to go to until the war started,' Lydia went on. She looked at Rosie's crestfallen face. 'Oh, that sounds awful – as though I'm trying to trump

84

Great Yarmouth.' She laughed and patted Rosie's hand. 'Mummy and Daddy never agreed on anything and they left my brother and me with Nanny while they bickered away. So it wasn't all peaches and cream, though we adored Nanny.'

Rosie had no idea how to respond. Thankfully they were interrupted by the same woman who'd served their meal, now holding a large tray. She put a bowl in front of each girl. Lydia looked down at hers and pulled a face.

'Oh, look – would you believe it. Tinned peaches and evaporated milk masquerading as cream!'

Rosie was relieved when supper was over. A couple of girls asked if she'd like to join them in the common room for a cigarette, but she was still worried about being questioned. Best not get too close to anyone, she thought, telling herself she wasn't of their class, so they wouldn't be interested in anything she had to say. Besides, she didn't smoke. For one thing she couldn't afford it, and for another, when she'd tried it a few times, the smoke always caught in her throat, making her cough. Now, she made her excuses and set off for the dormitory, hoping as it was only just gone eight that she'd be the only one there. It would be a good time to look through the regulations booklet and learn about being a Wren.

Breathing a sigh of relief that she was the only girl in the room, Rosie sat on her bunk, fully clothed, the one pillow folded and propped behind her back, and opened the booklet.

There was a handy list of nautical terms she must now use such as 'port' and 'starboard' for left and right, 'going aloft' for going upstairs, and 'decks' instead of floors. She skimmed through several other terms, thinking the concept a little silly when they were plainly on solid ground and not battling the waves, but accepted it all, still thrilled to be here.

Every member will on all occasions endeavour to uphold the honour of the WRNS, she read, *and by the good order and regularity of her conduct prove herself worthy of the Service to which she belongs.*

There was more in this vein. There was to be *no noisy or rowdy behaviour* . . . Rosie had to smile at that one. They should come to visit her family when all her siblings, including herself, were in full throttle. She read on . . . *and no loitering in public especially where men were on duty.*

What on earth did they think the newly recruited were going to get up to? Rosie turned to the next page. The message came across loud and clear that being a Wren was a cut above the Army Territorial Service and the Women's Auxiliary Air Force. How would she fare? For a few moments Rosie wondered if she could adhere to the strict discipline and do a good job. Then she shook herself. Of course she could. She was as good as anyone else. But deep down she remained very uncertain.

The next morning, after donning her bluette overalls, Rosie joined the others ready for the first day's training, called 'square bashing'. At the end of the day Rosie's feet felt as though rats were gnawing at them. She'd marched, saluted, helped to clean their living quarters and scrubbed a flight of stone stairs with cold water and carbolic, and had found it hard to concentrate on the afternoon lectures. She didn't mind hard work at all – she was used to it – but she hadn't expected to be on her hands and knees when she'd first fantasised about becoming a Wren. No doubt this was all part of the discipline, but some of the 'posh girls' (as she silently called them) protested to one another, though no one dared voice their opinion to Petty Officer Robins.

'We're being treated like skivvies,' a girl called Babs said when Rosie came across her in the afternoon, washing the outside windows. 'It'll probably rain tomorrow and that would have cleaned them.' She stretched up, wincing and rubbing her back. 'They gave me this lot to do after I'd already cleaned at least a dozen huge windows inside and out. And I'm frozen. Just look at my hands.' She stuck them out. They were purple with cold. 'This isn't why I joined the Wrens and I'm not at all sure I'm going to stay if this is supposed to be our training.'

'I expect it's to discipline us,' Rosie said. 'See what we're made of. I'm sure we'll be fine when we get through this fortnight.'

To end the day, Rosie lined up with the others to go through the humiliation of having her head examined. Thankfully, the nurse brusquely said, 'Nothing seen, so you may go,' then turned to jot the result in her book and wave to the next girl in the queue.

'I've never been so tired or felt so degraded in my life,' Blanche confided at supper that evening. 'At home, I'm not even expected to fold my nightdress.'

Privately Rosie thought Blanche was terribly spoilt, though she couldn't help liking her. She supposed it wasn't Blanche's fault she'd been brought up so privileged. In a strange way, Rosie began to feel quite pleased she could handle the sorts of jobs they were having thrown at them without making a fuss like so many others.

The daily lectures made a welcome change from the scrubbing and 'galley' duties, hours of marching on the parade ground and learning the special naval salute. Now more used to the routine, Rosie gave each tutor her full attention and meticulously wrote everything down in her notebook. She learned the history of the Navy, how to tie seaman's knots, recognising various badges and ranks, but there was little she could see about what she would be trained for. The most exciting thing was being measured for her uniform, which was promised to arrive by the end of the fortnight's training.

More than a week passed. Rosie began to get impatient, when to her relief one of the Leading Wrens announced the recruits were to be interviewed after breakfast to find out which section they were to work in. Excitement buzzed through her veins as she knocked on the door of the interview room. Inside sat an officer with gold bands on his sleeves which she now knew meant he was a lieutenant.

'Sit down, Wren Frost,' he said as he looked up from his file and smiled. 'This will be brief, but I'd like you to answer a few questions, then you will take some aptitude tests – they're quite short – so we can tell where best to place you.'

She swallowed. She and the girls had been speculating as to the various trades they might be assigned to. No one wanted kitchen duty, and the thought of clerical work in a stuffy office left her cold. Being a driver sounded glamorous but she couldn't drive so maybe something in signals.

The officer asked her a few questions about her family, particularly her father and his job in the fire department, and how she found the training course and what she liked most.

'I enjoyed learning about the history of the Navy,' Rosie said, 'and I feel proud to be part of it, but I'm hoping to be assigned to an active role.'

He nodded. 'That'll be all for now. You may go and join the other recruits in the room next door and someone will be with you soon to supervise the tests.'

'Thank you, sir.'

She quietly left and went next door where there was a

buzz of conversation from roughly twenty new recruits already seated at the individual desks.

'How did you get on with your interview?' one of the girls said when Rosie took a seat next to her.

Before Rosie could answer, an unsmiling, thin-faced man walked in holding a sheaf of papers. The chatter died down as he walked round, leaving a few sheets of papers, face down, on each desk.

'There are three tests,' he continued. 'When I tell you to begin you must fill them out as quickly as possible. You have fifteen minutes on each. Do not start on the next test before I tell you to.' He glanced at the clock. 'You may turn over the first one and begin.'

Rosie's stomach somersaulted. To think these tests were going to decide her future. She *had* to do well. When the officer told her she could start, she turned the first one over with a slightly trembling hand and swiftly cast her eye down the questions and various diagrams. The first one caused her to grin: 'If a hen is placed on the scales and weighs 2lbs 11ozs, how much does it weigh if it stands on one leg?' Immediately she wrote the answer and quickly filled in the others. She'd finished the test well before she heard the man in charge say they could start the next one.

This test consisted of pages of various puzzles involving squares and pyramids and circles that she found trickier to work out, but she managed to finish it. And then it was the final test. She turned the page over and wanted to laugh aloud. This was more like it – convoluted mathematics problems. But beautifully easy to solve. Worried that she'd filled in the answers too quickly she ran her eyes over the questions again. No, she was sure they were all correct.

'Will you all put your pencils down.' His serious expression suddenly broke into a smile. 'We won't keep you waiting as to where we will place you. In the meantime, I've had a message that your uniforms are ready to be collected. You go past all the classrooms and you'll find the door at the far end facing you.'

Rosie joined in the mumbled thanks as she and the other women filed out.

There was nothing more she could do to influence anything. Her fate was in their hands.

Chapter Eight

'Name, please.' The short, stocky older man behind a long table peered at Rosie, now at the head of the queue of chattering girls.

'Wren Frost.'

He studied his list. 'Right. Ratings uniform. Give me your size, and for your shoes.'

She told him and he looked along the shelves and pulled out a bundle, immaculately folded. Rosie took the bundle to the end of the counter. Inside, she found a navy-blue serge double-breasted jacket, matching skirt, three white shirts and black tie, and a cap. Then came everyday shoes and parade shoes.

'Your extras are on the next table,' he said, jerking his head to the right.

'Come for your blackouts and stockings, have you, love?' The thin man with hollow cheeks standing behind the small counter winked.

Rosie frowned. *Blackouts*? What on earth were they?

'Navy-blue knickers to you, darlin'. And some winter-weight black lisle stockin's.' One of the girls ahead of her – Rosie saw it was Blanche – popped the cap on her head, pulled it at a cheeky angle and gave a twirl, giggling to two other recruits who had already collected their uniforms.

'Have I got it on right?' she demanded. 'Hard to tell as there's no mirror.'

'Move along, please,' the man who'd dished out the uniforms called out. 'You can see yourselves in your dormitory. You're not the only ladies I've got to get through by the end of my shift.'

Blanche and several girls nearby smothered their giggles, although for the life of her, Rosie couldn't understand why they were so amused. When they were back in the dormitory, she said:

'What were you all laughing at when that chap made the remark about the ladies?'

'You must have led a sheltered life, Rosemary.' This from a woman maybe in her mid-twenties with a clipped accent. 'Do you honestly mean you don't know?'

'No, I don't – that's why I'm asking,' Rosie replied a little testily.

There was more laughter.

'Go on, you tell her, Deirdre,' another girl called out.

'"More of you ladies to get through" has an unfortunate connotation,' the girl called Deirdre said, grinning.

Rosie felt her cheeks redden. It was the sort of thing she heard every day at Caley's. But on the factory floor she'd never bothered to ask why the women sometimes went into fits of giggles. They'd laugh to see a pudding crawl, was one of her mother's favourite expressions. But now, amongst these girls and women, her new colleagues and far more sophisticated than she was, Rosie wanted to be part of their world.

'I'm sure he didn't mean it, but he made it sound as though he was going to get his leg over all the ladies instead of just handing out their uniforms,' Deirdre said, chuckling, as she stripped down to her lacy cream-coloured brassiere and cami-knickers. 'You surely know what *that* means, don't you, Rosemary?'

Some of the girls sniggered. Rosie nodded and smiled, just to make out she was one of them, but privately it didn't strike her as at all funny. In fact, she thought Deirdre rather crude. Pushing the thought away she laid her uniform on the bed. She gave a surreptitious glance at the other girls who were also now in their underwear and trying on their uniforms, a couple of them pretending to be modelling them. Inwardly, Rosie cringed. She never felt entirely comfortable undressing even in front of her two sisters.

'C'mon, Rosemary, what are you waiting for? Too shy to get undressed? We're all the same, don't you know. You haven't got anything we haven't all seen before.'

Rosie swallowed. If she didn't remove her clothes, the others would think she was a prude and mock her again. Reluctantly, she removed her skirt and blouse and quickly pulled on the uniform. There was only one mirror in the dormitory, so she waited her turn until everyone had admired themselves, although there were a few grumbles that certain items didn't fit correctly.

She tentatively worked her way towards the last three girls, crowding before the mirror. After a couple of minutes they stood aside for her. Rosie stared at her reflection, amazed at the transformation. There was no full-length mirror at home, so this was the first time she'd seen herself from head to toe. And she looked good. She knew it. She was sure she looked better than she'd ever looked before. The cut of the jacket skimmed over the skirt that showed off her shapely legs and though she was taller than average, she looked even more so in the uniform. She gave herself an inward nod of approval, then turned from the mirror.

'My, my, Rosemary,' Lydia said. 'You look absolutely stunning with that fabulous red hair of yours against the navy.'

There were a few murmurs of 'Hear hear'.

'Pity you'll have to tie it back,' Deirdre said with a smirk, fixing her eye on Rosie.

Rosie gave an inward sigh. Oh, well, not everyone was going to like her. At any rate, she needed to be careful about becoming close friends with anyone. That alone could get her into hot water.

After the marching and saluting routine on the parade ground the following morning, when Rosie, together with the other new recruits, proudly wore her uniform for the first time, a Leading Wren told them the results of their aptitude tests were on the notice board. There was a general rush to the board but Rosie hung back. She certainly wasn't going to push her way forward like some of them and then find she hadn't passed. It would be too humiliating for words.

'It looks as though we've all got through,' Babs turned round grinning. 'So it's just a question of finding out what they have in store for us.'

After the others had checked what Babs said was true and had moved away from the board, chatting excitedly to one another, Rosie scanned the list typed in alphabetical order. There it was – Rosemary Frost. Excitement fizzed through her. She'd passed. She'd done it. She would finally make her parents proud.

'Well done that you've all passed,' PO Robins told them later that morning. 'And tomorrow morning I shall see you all, one by one, in my office, to ascertain which section you'll be working in for Special Duties.' PO Robins glanced round. 'Wren Frost?'

Rosie jolted upright.

'Ah, there you are, at the back.' She looked at the sheet of paper. 'Well done on your mathematics paper – you achieved 100 per cent, which is rare, but because no one's perfect we can only award you 99 per cent.'

There were a few chuckles and murmurs of congratulations while Rosie sat, dazed.

PO Robins paused and glanced at her sheaf of papers. 'There are also three vacancies for pre-selection tests for those Wrens we find are the right material for a commission. You will know if you are to sit the tests when we speak to you individually.'

There was an excited buzz amongst the girls. Rosie chewed her bottom lip. Would she be one of the three? She mustn't get her hopes up. Coming from a working-class background, to be picked for training as a commissioned officer would be highly unlikely, though it would be wonderful to be selected. And the increased salary would come in handy for sending home to her family. But whatever the outcome, she'd passed the main test. She was a Wren and she had the uniform to prove it.

The following morning, as Rosie was rinsing her cloth in the basin after cleaning the lavatories, Lydia appeared at the cloakroom door.

'Come on, Rosie. We've all got to meet in the PO's office at eleven sharp to hear where we'll be working. You know what that means in the Navy – five minutes to. They're going in alphabetical order so you're after me.' She gave Rosie an encouraging smile, then disappeared.

Rosie stretched up, her back aching, and rubbed it with her hand. What she wouldn't give for a soak in a hot bath! That was a luxury they'd been offered just once, halfway through their training. They hadn't been allowed to run the taps beyond the mark of red nail varnish that indicated the five inches allotted by war rationing. But she'd still enjoyed it, lying back for a few precious minutes instead of sitting in the tin bath at home, which the whole family used once a week, taking turns who went first.

She washed her hands and tried to tidy her hair with extra kirby grips, using the small tarnished mirror above the sink. Immediately, the thick red strand fell out again. She shoved an extra kirby grip in the offending piece, hoping it would stay, and made her way to the PO's office.

Everyone except a girl called Anne was seated in the small waiting area outside the office. They were unusually silent. Deirdre briefly looked up, unsmiling, when Rosie took a seat next to Lydia, but the others gave her a nervous smile. The door opened and Anne appeared, looking quietly pleased.

'I've been asked to take the pre-selection tests.' There was a murmur of congratulations. 'Thanks,' Anne said, looking at the group. 'Don't worry, everyone. It's not so bad in there – they won't bite.' She looked over at Lydia. 'You're next.'

Lydia rose. 'Wish me luck,' she said under her breath.

'Good luck, Lydia,' Rosie said in a low tone.

Lydia was out in ten minutes. She threw a smile at the group.

'Well, no mention of any tests to become an officer. But they've put me down for Signals which I'm quite happy about.' Her gaze alighted on Rosie. 'You're next.'

'Good luck,' Carole said.

'Thanks.' Rosie got to her feet, knocked and opened the door.

Two people were sitting behind a large desk – one of them Petty Officer Robins, the other a youngish man. Both looked serious. But then this was a serious occasion, Rosie reasoned.

It didn't automatically mean that she was not going to be invited to take the pre-selection tests.

'Chief Petty Officer Rae,' the man said. 'Please sit down.' He took his glasses off and set them on the desk, then regarded her. 'You've passed the three aptitude tests with flying colours,' he said. 'In fact, you've come top in mathematics and very high marks in the other two. That's quite an achievement so I must congratulate you.'

'Thank you, sir.'

'Because of such an exceptional result you would certainly have been chosen as one of the three trainee officers,' he went on, his eyes fixed on her.

Would have been?

She saw him glance at PO Robins, who nodded, her mouth grim. Something was not quite right.

'And I believe you would have made an outstanding officer.'

'I'm sorry, sir,' Rosie said, not at all sure how to answer, 'but it sounds as though this is not what you have in mind for me.'

'I'm afraid it isn't. We've just received some most unwelcome news.'

No, not Poppy. Not something happened to Poppy. Please . . .

She tried to swallow but a lump had already formed in her throat.

'Is it—?' She thought she was going to choke. 'Is it . . . has there been an accident? My family . . .?'

'No, nothing like that,' he said.

Again, that glance between the two of them. What was going on?

'It appears that you haven't told us the truth on your application form before you were accepted into the WRNS,' PO Robins spoke for the first time. 'In fact, we believe you have told us an outright lie.'

Rosie clutched her chair on both sides. This was dreadful. So it *was* about Poppy. She had to hang on to the fact that Poppy was safe. She wasn't ill, she hadn't had an accident, but—

'You have a child,' PO Robins continued. 'She's five years old. Her name is Poppy Pauline Frost.' She stared at Rosie, her expression unrelenting. 'So what do you have to say for yourself, Wren Frost?'

Chapter Nine

Rosie sat like stone on her chair. She couldn't even blink. When she finally did, there was a pain behind her eyes. She *had* to hold herself together. The skin over her knuckles tightened as she gripped the seat of her chair. She must keep control. She would not – must not – let them see the whirlwind going on inside her head.

'Well?' PO Robins slightly tilted her head, waiting for an answer.

There was no point in denying it. But who had told them at Mill Hill? No one here knew. She'd kept her secret from everyone. Her mind rushed hither and thither until she thought she might faint. But she couldn't ask them. She doubted they'd tell her anyway. She had to keep her dignity – for what it was worth.

'Wren Frost?' It was CPO Rae.

'Yes . . . it's true,' Rosie managed. 'I have a daughter called Poppy, who's five years old.'

'So why did you lie on the application form?' he asked quietly.

'Because I've never told anyone, sir. No one knows except my mother and father, so I don't understand . . .' she trailed off. 'I've kept her a secret all these years. Poppy doesn't even know I'm her mother.'

'Does this mean your mother and father have brought her up as their own daughter and that you are, in her eyes, her older sister?' CPO Rae said.

'Yes . . . sir.'

'So the child is illegitimate?'

'Yes.'

'Do you realise what this means?'

Rosie momentarily closed her eyes.

'I'm willing to take whatever punishment you think necessary.'

There was a tangible silence. She waited, sick at heart, dreading the outcome but not believing this was really happening.

'Although you've done extremely well in the tests, because you lied on the application form and have a child out of wedlock, I'm afraid you don't have the moral character required by the WRNS.' PO Robins threw her a look that told Rosie she'd let her down.

Rosie felt sick. Did this mean . . .?

CPO Rae was frowning. 'So I'm afraid it's the end of your career in the WRNS. The rules are very strict.'

No, it couldn't be.

Shock waves travelled through her body. She'd worked so hard this last fortnight, anxious to do everything to the very best of her ability, never moaning about heavy chores that in her view didn't have the remotest link to being a Wren. She was so proud in her uniform to represent such a fine women's service. Surely that one mistake six years ago wasn't going to cost her so dearly. Hadn't she already paid for it? Been punished enough? But she only had to look at their expressions to know there would be no leniency for her. She'd had a child out of wedlock and she'd lied on the application form. In their eyes they had to uphold the rules of the WRNS – what it meant to be a Wren. And lies played no part.

'I'm very sorry it's come to that, sir,' she managed, tears choking in her throat. She stood, her hands on the edge of the desk, needing its support. 'Will that be all?'

The CPO nodded. 'You're dismissed, Miss Frost.'

No more 'Wren Frost' that she'd been so proud to be called. No more smart uniform. No more going off with the others to a special section, ready to learn all she could in order to do her bit for the war effort.

'Thank you, sir . . . ma'am.' Her neck felt too stiff to even look at PO Robins.

She saluted for the last time, then made an about turn just before the first tear rolled down her cheek. Thank God they hadn't seen it. She angrily brushed it away with her fingers and walked from the room, her legs shaking so hard she hardly knew how she managed to put one foot in front of the other. She closed the door quietly behind her. She had to hold herself together in front of the others.

'Goodness, Rosemary, are you all right?' It was Vera Gerard, a curly-haired brunette who had stood, about to go in next. 'You look as though you've had bad news.'

Barely hearing the words, Rosie looked straight ahead, her chin lifted, as she walked between their chairs, feeling the girls' eyes boring into her back as she opened the door to let herself out.

Back in the cabin she flung herself onto the bed and sobbed. How could life be so unfair? She didn't deserve it. She stayed there for several minutes weeping. Finally, she wiped her eyes on the edge of the sheet and pulled herself upright. Her chest still felt it was constricting her breathing, but she ignored it. If that's how they could treat her, she didn't want to be a Wren after all. She'd do something else.

But one thing was certain. She was never going back to Caley's factory.

She tossed her cap on the bed and slowly took off the uniform she'd been so proud of and had looked forward to showing her parents on her first leave. The tunic and skirt, the crisp white shirt, the shoes. She folded everything neatly, swallowing her tears, and quickly dressed in her normal clothes. Then, full of resolve, she removed her suitcase from the top of the cupboard and threw in the rest of her clothes and meagre possessions. A sudden burst of anger at the unfairness of it all made her slam the drawer and cupboard door as she did so. She rinsed her face, splashing cold water onto her eyes, but it did nothing to refresh her.

How could she face Mum and Dad? How could she tell them she'd been thrown out of the service she'd dreamed of belonging to? She pictured her mother's puzzled expression, her father's one of resignation that she'd brought it on herself. Hearing his warning that if anyone found out about Poppy she would be in deep trouble. Well, that had certainly happened. But who had told the WRNS about Poppy? Who hated her enough? And then the terrible realisation swept over her, making her feel lightheaded. Her father adored Poppy. It would be his worst nightmare if she met someone who was willing to take on a five-year-old. He must have been worried sick that she might meet naval men and fall in love with one of them, and then take Poppy with her. Dad would lose the little girl he adored. And the only way to make sure his own daughter came home, so they were all under the same roof again where he could maintain control, was to betray her.

Surely he wouldn't have done that. But if it wasn't him, then who else? It wasn't her mother. She would never do anything to harm her children. Rosie blinked back more tears.

She'd let her family down and she'd let herself down – but almost worse, she'd let John Palmer down. He'd put in a good word for her and someone in the Navy had acted upon it. How was she ever going to explain to him, and still keep Poppy a secret?

A figure appeared in the doorway. It was PO Robins. She came straight over to where Rosie was packing her case.

'I'm really sorry we had to do that.' She looked at Rosie. 'I thought you would go on to have quite a career in the WRNS.'

Rosie bit her lip, not daring to say she wanted to be left alone.

'Do you want to tell me about it?'

Rosie shook her head. 'It won't make any difference.'

'It's just that I'm responsible for you until you leave,' the petty officer persisted. 'Presumably the father knows.'

'No, he doesn't. I told you – no one knows except my parents.'

'Where is the father?'

Rosie drew in a jerky breath. She could feel the blood rushing in her ears as though she were a child on Caister-on-Sea's beach, holding a shell to her ear to hear the sea.

'I don't know.' She bit her lip, desperate not to cry, but it was as though she was suddenly transported to the church again, looking for Hugo, feeling humiliated because he hadn't turned up. 'We were to be married. I was only seventeen.' She gulped. 'H-he jilted me on our w-wedding day. Neither of us knew at the time I was going to have a b-baby. I never knew what happened to him. I never heard from him again.'

'Maybe you should try to find him.' PO Robins' voice was brisk. 'After all, he *is* the father. It doesn't seem quite right that he doesn't know he has a child.'

Rosie swallowed hard. 'I couldn't do that. It's six years ago and I've had to put it all behind me – I just got on with making sure my daughter is loved and cared for.'

Oh, why doesn't the woman go – just leave me to pack up and get out of here?

PO Robins sighed. 'Right then, you can pick up a travel warrant on your way out.'

'Wh-what do I tell the others?'

The woman cleared her throat. 'The best thing is to say there's a family emergency and you're having to go back indefinitely. The other Wrens will all move on from here anyway in a few days' time.'

PO Robins might just as well have added, 'So no one will miss you.'

Rosie turned away so the woman wouldn't see her tears falling and placed her two precious books on top of the few clothes.

'I'll leave you to finish packing then,' PO Robins said. 'Hand your uniform to the quartermaster before you leave.'

Nearly four hours later she stepped off the train at Thorpe Station in Norwich and was grateful not to have long to wait for the bus to Sprowston as the weather had dipped and her coat wasn't thick enough to keep out such cold. Thankfully, only her mother was home.

'How lovely to see you, dear.' She smiled and gave her daughter a kiss. 'How long can you stay?'

'I'm not going back.'

Her mother's forehead creased. 'Oh. Why's that?'

'A misunderstanding.' Rosie hugged her. 'How are you, Mum?'

Her mother gazed at her.

'Something's wrong,' she said. 'I know my own daughter. What's happened? The truth.'

When Rosie hesitated, her mother said, 'Come into the kitchen. I'll put the kettle on.'

'I'll just put my case in the bedroom.'

Upstairs, she looked round the room she shared with her sisters. It was in an even worse state than when she'd left home. They weren't going to be thrilled to have her back with her belongings added to the muddle. Well, they would have to lump it.

In the kitchen her mother measured out one level teaspoon of tea and put it in the heated teapot.

'We'll let that brew,' she said, looking at Rosie with a worried expression.

'Mum, I don't want you to be upset.'

'Why? What have you done?'

Rosie swallowed hard. 'I lied on the application form.'

'About havin' no children?'

'Yes.'

'Your father was worried about that.' She stared at her eldest daughter. 'Are you sayin' they found out?'

'Yes.' Rosie pulled in her top lip, wondering how to continue. Well, Mum had asked for the truth. She took a deep breath. 'Someone's betrayed me. So besides the staff in the home who knew about Poppy – but how would any of them know where I went after I left more than five years ago – there are only three people who knew.' She looked at her mother. 'You, Dad and Aunt Dot. It's definitely not Aunt Dot – she's the one who's never judged me. And remember how kind she was to us, letting us stay with her when I was pregnant. And its definitely not *you*.' Rosie paused. 'I'm sorry, Mum, but that only leaves Dad. He has the strongest motive – to hang on to Poppy. The only way he can do that is to make sure I never meet anyone, which means keeping me from the outside world.'

Chapter Ten

Shirley Frost's eyes widened in horror.

'How can you accuse your own father? He loves you.' Rosie opened her mouth to protest, but her mother rushed on. 'I know he sometimes has a strange way of showin' it – he's the same with me – but as I remember, he didn't try to stop you from joinin' up.'

'Don't you see, Mum, he couldn't very well. I would have been conscripted anyway because in the government's eyes I'm a single woman on their list who's the right age to do her bit for the war effort. And that doesn't mean working in a chocolate factory.'

Her mother was silent.

'But if *he* didn't, who did?' Rosie said. 'I've told no one.'

'And you didn't mention it to those new friends of yours? That woman and her nephew?'

'No, of course not. I've never told a soul.'

'You can ask Dad when he comes home tonight,' her mother said, 'but I think you'll find he didn't do anything of the kind.'

'Well, whoever notified them, it's done now. And I'm in disgrace.' Tears rolled down her cheeks. 'I'll never get a decent job because it'll be on my record.'

Her mother put her arms round her.

'Don't upset yourself, love. Things'll turn out.'

'They won't.' Rosie rounded on her mother. 'I won't be accepted in any of the forces to do my bit. And I can't go back to the factory. I just don't know what to do.'

'Something will turn up, you'll see.'

Rosie shook her head. 'I'll try to get another job in Norwich, but you know, Mum –' she looked at her mother '– I loved being a Wren, even though they had us scrubbing floors and cleaning toilets during our training. It didn't matter. We knew we'd be given something interesting to do after the fortnight. It was all a stupid waste of time.' She burst into sobs.

Her mother glanced at the clock on the shelf above the oven.

'It's nearly time for Poppy to come out of school. Why don't you go and meet her? It will cheer you up . . . Poppy, too. She's been miserable since you've been gone, but at least she's made a proper friend at school. She don't allow anyone to bully Poppy no more.'

Rosie found her handkerchief and blew her nose. She looked at her mother through bloodshot eyes.

'Thank goodness for that.'

'Why don't you go and splash your eyes with cold water,' her mother said. 'You'll feel better.'

Rosie sniffed. 'I'll go and fetch her.' She stood to give her mother a peck on the cheek. 'I'm sorry, Mum, but I'm still not sure about Dad.'

Her mother sighed. 'Don't be late for Poppy,' was all she said.

As soon as Poppy glimpsed Rosie, she sped towards her, then threw her arms around her, screaming at the top of her voice.

'Mosey! You're back. Don't go away ever again.' She stared up at Rosie with solemn eyes. 'Promise.'

'I can't promise, darling, because you know we have to fight the nasty men, but I'll be here as long as I can.'

Thankfully, it seemed to satisfy her, Rosie thought, as Poppy skipped and jumped beside her on the walk home, telling her about her new friend, Julie.

'She's bigger'n me,' Poppy said. 'She's got yellow hair – just like a fairy princess. And she only likes *me*.'

Rosie hid a smile. 'She sounds lovely, poppet. I can't wait to meet her.'

'You will,' Poppy said firmly. 'Mummy says I can invite her for tea soon.'

Rosie swallowed. If only . . . But it was no good following that train of thought. Sighing, she opened the front door to loud voices. Heather, home early, was giving Roddy a telling-off and her brother was yelling back.

Quietly, she crept upstairs. She couldn't take any more upset for the day.

'We just got used to having the room to ourselves,' Heather said when she entered the room and saw her elder sister sitting on her old bed, lost in thought. 'And our own separate beds, I'll have you know.' She stood staring at Rosie. 'How long are you here for?'

Rosie had to admit to herself she'd never felt very close to Heather. She'd always tried to excuse her sister when they were children because Heather was three years younger so they had little in common. But now her sister was twenty, Rosie was startled at Heather's belligerent tone.

'As long as necessary,' Rosie returned coolly. 'And I'd thank you for tidying your things so I have a bit of space on the dressing table.'

'Why should I? You're not here now. No, I'm not moving anything.'

'If you'd just put your things away . . . You have your own drawer.'

'Why are you back so suddenly?' Heather said, narrowing her eyes, as she sat at the offending dressing table and looked at Rosie through the reflection of the mirror.

Rosie's stomach lurched.

'I've packed it in.'

'Oh.' Heather applied what looked like a new lipstick to her sullen-looking lips. 'What's brought that on?'

'Being in the forces wasn't for me, after all.'

Heather turned to face her. 'Really?'

Did Heather know more than she was letting on? She was just about to question Heather when Ivy came through the open door.

'Gosh, you two look very serious,' she said. 'What's up? What have I missed?'

'Ask Rosie,' Heather smirked.

'You've missed nothing,' Rosie said firmly, desperate to hold on to her temper. 'We'd better go downstairs as Mum can do with some help for supper. Ivy, you can lay the table, and Heather . . .' she stared at her sister '. . . *you* can light the fire in the dining room.'

Heather shook her head. 'Sorry, Rosie, you left us and *I've* taken charge with complete approval from Mum and Dad.'

'That's not true, Heather,' Ivy said, smiling gently. She glanced at Rosie. 'She likes to think so, but we don't take any notice of her when she's in one of her bossy moods.'

'Thanks for being on my side, Ivy,' Heather's tone was heavy with sarcasm.

'I'm not taking sides,' Ivy said, her voice steady. 'I just like saying the truth.'

'Little Goody-Two-Shoes,' Heather hissed.

'That's enough, Heather,' Rosie said sharply. 'Mother needs some help so I'm going down to the kitchen, and you, Heather, will light the fire or you'll have Dad to answer to.'

In the morning Rosie woke early and careful not to disturb her sisters went downstairs. She threw on her old coat, and cautiously made her way along the slippery path to the outhouse. Wrinkling her nose at the permanent stink of urine, she was as fast as possible, and was soon back in the chilly house. Tempted for a moment to keep her coat on, she finally put it on one of the row of hooks in the narrow hall and made for the kitchen. Her mouth felt stale and dry. She needed a cup of tea.

As Rosie sat at the small kitchen table sipping her tea, she decided she had to make some kind of plan for her future. And she had to let John Palmer know what had happened. But how much could she – should she – tell him? Nothing? Everything? Whatever would he say? He'd be so embarrassed for having recommended her. But she had to tell him something about why she'd been stripped of her uniform. Oh, this was terrible. She closed her eyes and Claire's face hovered in front of her. That was it! She would tell Claire – and tell her the whole truth. Claire would know how much she should tell her nephew.

I'll write to her today, Rosie thought. She'll have it by tomorrow's post. No, better than that. I won't waste another minute. I'll take the chance she's there and see her this very morning.

'What a lovely surprise.' Claire Edgerton beamed as she gently took Rosie's arm and brought her in. 'You've just caught me. I was about to go into town.'

'Oh, I'm terribly sorry,' Rosie started. 'Please don't let me stop you. I can come another time or—'

'Certainly not. It was nothing important and can wait.' She studied Rosie's face. 'Whereas *you* must have something very important to want to see me. But first I'll put the kettle on. I'm sure you could do with a cup of coffee. Even the maid's left on a day off so we're completely alone.'

It was almost as though Claire was trying to reassure her their conversation would be completely private.

'Come through with me. We can talk while I'm making coffee. I rather like it when there's no one here and I have the kitchen to myself.'

She chatted on as Rosie followed her through the wide hallway and down some steps at the end which led to a good-sized kitchen with a large pine table in the centre with wicker-backed chairs placed around it.

'Sit down, my dear – anywhere.'

She put the kettle on and ten minutes later Rosie was sipping delicious coffee with Claire at the pine table.

'Now, I'll stop talking and listen to you, Rosemary. And anything you tell me will not go beyond these walls.'

'I don't know where to start.' Rosie swallowed.

'At the beginning is always the best.'

'All right.' Rosie took another sip of coffee. 'I've left the WRNS.'

'I thought you had. It was too soon for you to be on leave, and your face tells me something has gone very wrong.'

Rosie drew in her top lip. Oh, how to begin such a shocking story. She looked at Claire who nodded encouragingly.

'I wasn't absolutely truthful on the application form. I put myself down as a single woman – which I am,' she hurriedly added. 'The alternative was a childless widow. And I wasn't a widow.'

111

'But you weren't childless – is that it?' Claire said.

'Yes.' It was almost a whisper.

'You're not the first girl this has happened to,' Claire said. 'I take it you were young.'

'Yes,' Rosie said again. 'Seventeen. But it was nothing like you're thinking. We were going to be married. And not because I was having a baby because at the time neither of us knew. He just never turned up on our wedding day and I've never known the reason why. We loved one another. It wasn't like him to do something so cruel. But his parents were against it from the start. They told him they wouldn't be attending the wedding, so I feel sure they had something to do with it.'

She blinked back the tears. Claire put out her hand to cover Rosie's.

'You poor girl. I'm so sorry. What a dreadful time for you. What did your parents say?'

'At first Dad insisted I put the baby up for adoption. I refused and said I'd leave home and take the baby with me. Then Mum persuaded him to let everyone think Poppy was her last baby, and they would bring her up as their own child, with me as her oldest sister. And that's what they've done. They adore her – especially Dad.' Rosie let her breath escape in a long shuddering sigh. 'I just don't know how to tell John.'

Claire smiled. 'You don't need to worry about him,' she said. 'He's a kind-hearted man. He won't hold it against you, if that's what you're thinking. He'll only be sorry he can't do anything more to help. In fact, I can't see any reason why you need to say anything. You have enough to worry about trying to find another job and he won't even know you're not still in the WRNS. People move around all the time these days.'

'If you're sure . . .' Rosie started. 'I was dreading telling him.'

'Then don't. Just put it behind you. Something else is bound to turn up.'

Chapter Eleven

Back at HMS *Pembroke* in Mill Hill, there was something about the girl that CPO Rae couldn't get out of his mind. It wasn't just her bright head of hair or the hazel eyes, or merely her distress in having to leave, but he'd been impressed by the manner in which she'd maintained her dignity. Such a clever girl, too. She would've gone far. Bloody awful waste. But rules were rules. He relit his pipe and drew several puffs to get it going. He shifted in his chair, all the while staring at her folder. He opened it again and read the updated report PO Robins had given him after she'd spoken to the girl just as she was leaving. The report included details as to why Miss Frost had lied when she'd written on the form that she was single with no children. But she'd been so young when she'd had her child. Hardly more than a child herself. He thought of his own fifteen-year-old daughter, Miranda, and sighed. Rosemary Frost's boyfriend could at least have made an honest woman of her. It was his responsibility as much as hers. What a bounder. There had to be some way . . .

He snatched up the receiver and asked to speak to his CO.

'What's up?' The even tones of Commander Richards came over the wires.

Rae quickly filled in his boss, briefly mentioning the illegitimate baby.

'It's an unfortunate business, sir,' he finished, 'and such a clever girl, too. She's a whizz at maths with a hundred per cent on her test and came second out of about fifty girls in both the other aptitude tests. She studied Italian at school which I daresay could be improved to a higher standard. It seems such a waste for her – and us – not to be able to use her skills for one mistake. I just wondered if we could use her in a different way where her personal history doesn't count in the same way it would if she was in the forces. I know you have quite a bit of influence, sir.'

'Flattery will get you everywhere.' There was a chuckle at the other end. 'All right, Rae, leave it with me. I'll see what I can do.' There was a long pause and CPO Rae was just about to say, 'Thank you, sir,' when his boss said, 'In fact, I've got an idea where this young lady could be most useful, so thanks for passing this on, Rae. I'll keep you posted.'

There was a click of the receiver.

CPO Rae gave a half-smile. If anyone could swing something like this it would be old Richards. Damn nice chap. He picked up the receiver again and pressed a button.

'Diane, be a good girl and bring me a cup of tea.'

Commander Richards picked up the handset and pressed a button.

'Joan, get me Whitehall, please.'

A minute later he was talking to his friend Lieutenant Commander Stephen Ferris. They'd gone through officers' training together and hit it off immediately. They'd always kept in touch since those far-off days.

'Morning, Ferris, old chap – Richards here. Look, I wonder if you could do me a favour. It's about this Wren . . . or rather she *was*. She was dismissed because of a personal matter – a mistake she made when she was a young girl.' He paused. 'You can probably guess. But she's several years older now and wants to do her bit. And apparently she's brilliant at maths and speaks Italian.'

'Maths and Italian, you say?' Stephen Ferris repeated. 'Any German?'

'Not that I know of. But she's an extremely intelligent girl and it seems such a waste not to use her. I'm wondering if you can see a place for her at Whitehall?'

'Not Whitehall,' Ferris answered. 'If she's as good as you say she is, something eminently more suitable springs to mind. I'll get my aide to have a word with her.'

Two days later Rosie received a letter from a Lieutenant Commander Ferris instructing her to report to Whitehall for an interview the following Thursday at 11 a.m.

At ten to eleven, Rosie shifted nervously on the chair outside Lieutenant Commander Ferris's room, her hands clasped tightly together to stop her biting her nails. She'd begun to chew them since that terrible interview with PO Robins and the other one – she couldn't for the life of her think of his name. All she really remembered was the humiliation.

There'd been no explanation as to what today's conversation was to be about. Were they going to bring it all up about Poppy again? She didn't think she could stand it if they did. Were they going to make sure she would never get another job again? She glanced round. This place was far too grand for her to feel comfortable. It had been bad enough trying to find her way round London on the bus. She shouldn't have come. But it wasn't an invitation – more an order.

Rosie's eyes had nearly popped from their sockets when

she'd stepped into the majestic reception hall and a young man in a dark suit had registered her. She couldn't help gazing up at the vaulted ceiling and the magnificent staircase, having never seen anything like them in her life. It was how she imagined the inside of a palace would look. People were coming and going – all knowing exactly where they were and what they were doing. Everyone except her. If only she'd thought to bring a book to read so she'd look less conspicuous in her shabby brown coat – a million miles away from the smart navy-blue uniform she'd worn when she was a Wren.

'Miss Frost, will you please follow me.' A girl's voice interrupted her thoughts.

Rosie stood and followed the girl up the staircase. After a short walk along the corridor the girl stopped and knocked on a door.

'Come in.'

'Sir, Miss Frost for her interview.'

'Thank you, Cecily. Would you bring some coffee for us, please?' John Palmer rose from behind the desk. 'How very nice to see you again, Rosemary.' He put out his hand.

Heat flooded Rosie's cheeks as she barely touched his hand. What bad luck. Oh, why did it have to be him and not some stranger? Then it wouldn't matter so much. Did he know the miserable details of her dismissal from the WRNS? If so, whatever must he think of her?

'I wanted to tell you . . .' she began.

'Difficult when I'm in London and you're presumably back in Norwich. All I know is that you had to leave the WRNS suddenly. I was sorry as I gathered you were all set on the path of a good career, which might well have led to becoming an officer.' He paused. 'Here, let me take your coat and then we can have a proper chat.'

Obediently, she unbuttoned the coat, her hands shaking

117

as she handed it to him. He took it and hung it on the coat rack, then said:

'Have a seat, Rosemary. First of all I'm sorry to surprise you that it's me you're seeing today.'

Questions and possible answers raced through Rosie's head. Trying to keep a semblance of control, she knew her face had reddened with embarrassment as she sat opposite him.

'I thought I was to see Lieutenant Commander Ferris,' she said lamely.

'He was called away unexpectedly, leaving only a brief of the situation.' John Palmer regarded her calmly. 'I'm his aide and will send him a report on this meeting.' He leant forward a little. 'Rosemary, we have to keep this meeting formal, so I'd like you to tell me what happened at Mill House. Please tell me everything. You can trust me that it will be kept in the strictest confidence.'

Rosie briefly shut her eyes. How much should she say? Yes, she trusted him, but what relevance did it have now she'd been pushed out of the WRNS? She opened her eyes to find him staring at her.

'I suspect you've had rather a rough time,' he said when she didn't answer, 'but I need to understand why you were dismissed, so I can assess your suitability for something else. What I *do* know is that it was something personal that can't be changed.'

So Claire hadn't mentioned it. She breathed out.

'I thought leaving the WRNS was the end of the matter,' she managed.

'Not quite.' He paused. 'So please go ahead.'

Rosie told him briefly what she'd said to PO Robins and her boss. John's eyes widened a fraction, though he said nothing.

118

'And that's it,' she finished. 'Poppy has no idea I'm her mother, but we've always been close.' She choked on the last words. 'She's a bright child and quite a character.' She looked him in the eye. 'It's awful that something which happened six years ago is still having a detrimental effect on my life. I don't usually feel sorry for myself . . . ' she swallowed hard '. . . but I loved being a Wren and thinking I had the opportunity to do my bit for the war effort. And I felt terrible that you'd taken the trouble to recommend me in the first place.'

John looked thoughtful for a few moments.

'You know, the Chief Petty Officer who was obliged to turn you out of the WRNS wasn't at all happy to do the deed. He had a word with his colleague who in turn spoke to someone else. He decided you sounded like a bright young woman who could be profitably used in another area of the Foreign Office – but in a civilian role. Something most secret. Until you're accepted, I can't even say where you'd be working, or what you'd be doing, but let's just say it will be to do with Intelligence.' He gazed at her. 'Sorry to be so vague, but would it interest you?'

She hadn't been expecting this. She felt numb, not knowing how to answer. She should feel happy they were prepared to offer her another position where she could use her skills. But she didn't. In her mind she'd still failed at something she'd set her heart on.

'Won't they want to know—?'

'Their main fear is anything leaking out that would undermine their security,' John cut in. 'Such as, are you prone to gossip? Are you a blabbermouth? Does your voice carry in cafés and restaurants and pubs? They're the sort of traits they'd be concerned about.' He leant forward on the desk. 'Look, I'm going to say something that is strictly off the record. If this conversation got out, we'd both be sacked on the spot. So will you be sure to keep it inside these four walls?'

He's taking a huge risk when he hardly knows me.

'Yes, of course.' Her voice was almost a whisper.

'Unfortunately, in normal times your story would put the wind up them and they would look upon you as a security risk,' he continued. 'But these aren't normal times. We've got to beat Jerry using everything and everyone we can. They need to know that any new recruits can act responsibly, work hard and keep a tight lip. But if anyone tries to blackmail you or you come across any rumour or gossip – even a *hint* from someone referring to your past – you must promise to report it immediately to the security officer where you'll be working and he'll deal with it. Do *not* think for a moment that *you* can deal with it. Is that agreed?'

Rosie nodded, her mouth too dry to speak. There was a silence. She swallowed.

'Yes, John, I promise.'

'Good. So back to the formalities. You'll be signing another Official Secrets Act for the new position.'

'If you could only give me *some* idea of the work . . .' she began.

'As they're interested to know you speak Italian, it's probably to do with Italian enemy signals.' He looked at her. 'I think it could be right up your street.'

Rosie's heart beat a little faster.

'Will I be based in London?'

John shook his head. 'No. And the exact whereabouts is kept under wraps until you get there. You won't even be able to tell your family.'

'Then I won't be able to accept it if I don't know where I'll be sent. If something happened to Poppy—'

'If there's an emergency you can always be contacted. So that's not a problem.' He leant forward again. 'I do think it's an excellent chance for you to use your talents and show your mettle.' He paused. 'It would get you out of that factory, for one thing.'

She flinched, knowing he was right.

'Most prospective recruits are not even given the chance to make a decision,' John continued. 'They're simply instructed to carry out the order to turn up wherever needed, so perhaps you should regard this in the same light. You'll be doing your duty – like most other young women now.'

There was a knock at the door and Cecily arrived, carrying a tray. She set out two cups and saucers, a pot of coffee, hot milk and sugar, and a plate of biscuits. He thanked her and she disappeared.

'I forget whether you take sugar,' he said, pouring her a cup.

'Not since the rationing.' She tried to smile but this was serious. She needed time to think. Talk to her father. But what was the point of that? She wouldn't necessarily take his advice. And if word got around about Poppy, she might never again be offered anything interesting where she could use her skills. At least no one could betray her again at a place so secret it didn't even have a proper name. She took a sip of coffee, then drew in a deep breath.

'I'd like to give it a go.'

'Excellent. You'll have an interview with one of the commanding officers as soon as you get there. All I can tell you at the moment is you'll be getting the train to a town in Buckinghamshire.' He passed her an envelope addressed to Miss R. Frost. 'The CO assumed you'd say yes and so this should contain all the information you need. You are strictly under orders not to even mention the town or county to family, friends, boyfriend . . .' he looked at her quizzically, but she didn't flicker an eyelid. '. . . or anyone at all,' he finished. 'And you have to keep the secret of where you're working and what you're doing all the time you are there and probably even beyond the time when the war ends . . . it's so highly confidential.'

'As you now know, I can keep a secret.'

He gave a sympathetic nod.

'I think you'll be able to put your short time in the WRNS behind you once you get stuck into something to keep you occupied.'

'I hope so.' She looked at him. 'May I open the letter?'

'Please do.' He handed her a letter knife.

Rosie bit her lip. Was she being foolhardy? Jumping from the frying pan into the fire? Leaving Poppy to go and work in some secret place? She took a deep breath and slit open the envelope.

The letter was from the Foreign Office. *Dear Miss Frost,* it ran. *You are instructed to report for registration on Monday, 16th February at 19.00 hours.*

Rosie gasped. She looked up to see John watching her.

'They want me in three days,' she said.

'Probably just as well. You won't have time to worry too much about that little daughter of yours, who sounds, if I may say so,' he said with a smile, 'rather like her mother.'

She felt a lump in her throat. It was the first time she'd ever heard anyone truly acknowledge that Poppy belonged to her. Even in the mother and baby home, according to those stern nurses, Poppy was just another illegitimate kid to be adopted as soon as possible. She gave John a brief smile back and read on.

You will alight in a town called Bletchley in Buckinghamshire. Be on the 17.55 from Euston Station and you should arrive in Bletchley just after 19.00 hours. Someone will be there to meet you to take you to your place of work – Station X.

Because of defence security your postal address will be Box III, c/o The Foreign Office. You will sign the Official Secrets Act in an interview at Station X. If anyone questions you, you will say you are a clerk in the War Office.

There was no signature, simply: The Foreign Office. Rosie hadn't realised she'd been holding her breath until she breathed out a long sigh. This certainly sounded intriguing. A shiver of excitement passed over her scalp.

She drank the rest of her coffee, now lukewarm, and suddenly had a thought. Putting her empty cup back on the saucer, she said:

'John, I never thanked you—'

'Thanked me for what?'

'For the Christmas tree and the beautiful decorations.' She looked him directly in the eye. 'It *was* you, wasn't it?' When he hesitated, she said, 'You might as well tell me because I *know* it was.'

He hesitated another moment, before saying, 'All right, yes. But it was nothing anyone else wouldn't do.' He gave her a warm smile.

'It was everything,' Rosie protested. 'You made it feel as though there might still be a little bit of magic in the air. Poppy was beside herself with excitement.'

'I'm delighted. And there's no need to thank me.' He regarded her with a serious expression. 'Rosemary, if you ever need a friend, please let me know.' He jotted down his address and passed her the slip of paper. 'I mean that. You'll get some time off when you've been there a while – and if you feel like coming to London, I'd be delighted to take you out for dinner or a show.'

'Thank you,' she said. 'It's very kind of you.'

John opened his mouth as though about to say something but seemed to change his mind.

But in any spare time they might give her, she knew she would be catching the first train to Norwich . . . and Poppy.

PART THREE

Chapter Twelve

Bletchley Park, Buckinghamshire
February 1942

'Bletchley,' shouted the conductor as he walked through the train, which was slowing down, its brakes screeching. 'This is Bletchley.'

Rosie stood on tiptoe for her case on the overhead luggage rack.

'Here, let me.' A tall soldier in khaki uniform jumped up and with one easy movement he had it down, then slid the compartment door open.

Another soldier in the corridor pulled down the window and felt outside for the door handle. The soldier with the case stepped down and Rosie followed, catching his hand as she stepped onto the platform, bleached white by the full moon nearing the horizon.

'Anyone meeting you, love?' he said.

'Yes.'

'You'll be all right then?'

'Oh, yes. Thanks for your help.'

He nodded and hauled himself onto the train. The station-master slammed the door and blew his whistle. The train moved off.

Rosie watched it fade into the night. It was bitter cold. She turned the collar of her coat up around her neck, wishing she'd worn a thicker scarf. But she hadn't wanted to hurt Ivy's feelings. Her sister had carefully unpicked one of Roddy's scarves that he complained made his neck itchy, and she'd reknitted it and given it to Rosie for a Christmas present.

Hoping whoever was coming to meet her was already here, she picked up her case, but the platform was deserted. No one appeared to have alighted at Bletchley. She made her way towards the waiting room but the shutters were down for the night. She spotted the stationmaster walking towards the entrance of the station.

'Excuse me, but did you notice anyone on the platform who didn't board the train that's just left?'

He shook his head. 'No, miss. Why, is someone meetin' you?'

'Supposed to be.' But all was eerily quiet. She shivered against the cold wind.

'But there was one other young lady who got off,' the stationmaster said, fingering his jaw. 'She wanted to know where the nearest telephone kiosk was. I told her she could use mine in the ticket office where it's warmer – long as it were only a local call – but she said no, it had to be the kiosk outside, which sounds to me like she might be meetin' her bloke and wants to keep him a secret.' He chuckled, making his moustache jump up and down over his thin top lip.

'Which way did she go?'

'Right out of here and the phone box is on the first corner, left-hand side. You can't miss it.' He blew on his hands. 'And good luck, miss, findin' who you're expectin.'

As Rosie hurried towards the kiosk, the door opened and a fair-haired girl in a coat with a fur collar and matching hat stepped out, holding a suitcase and trying to pull up her shoulder bag.

'Oh, hello,' she said. 'Are you going where I'm going?'

Rosie hesitated. She wasn't allowed to mention anything to anyone. Suppose the girl was going somewhere completely different. She looked back at the railway station. She was going to freeze to death anyway if she didn't get in somewhere warm soon. So any threatened punishment wasn't enough to stop her from answering.

'If you're going to Station X—' she began.

'Thank goodness for that.' The girl sounded relieved. 'So am I. They told me to ring from the telephone kiosk and let them know I've arrived. I assumed they'd then send someone, but all they've done is give me instructions on how to get there – by Shanks's pony. *Not* what I was expecting at all.'

Her voice was clipped. Upper class. It reminded Rosie of Hugo's.

'Does it sound far?'

'I don't think so. We go down the main road, turn right, then we come to a country lane. Up the lane until we get to a pair of iron gates where the sentries are there to check us in.' She paused. 'Have you got the letter to show them?'

'Yes. In my bag.'

'We'd better go. For a start we don't know how long the bloody lane is.'

Rosie gave a start to hear the swear word from someone who was so obviously well brought up – and a woman at that! She shrugged. This was no time to make snap judgements. All she could think of was a hot meal and her feet warming by a fire.

'I'm Pamela Perriman-Hale, by the way,' the girl said as they made their way to the main road.

'Rosemary Frost.'

129

'Nice to meet you.' She gave a sidelong glance at Rosie. 'Did they tell you what work you'd be doing?'

'No. Apparently it's all very hush-hush.'

'Do you speak German?' Pamela asked.

'No, Italian. But not recently.'

'I shouldn't worry,' Pamela said airily. 'It'll be like riding a bike.'

'*That* I do know,' Rosie laughed. 'My bicycle is my only form of independence.'

'Good for you.' Pamela stopped. 'Right, here's the main road. Now we turn right and find the lane.'

'Do *you* speak German?' Rosie said, changing her suitcase to her other hand as they started walking again.

'Oh, yes. I'm bilingual. German mother. Dad met her in the last war.' She turned to Rosie. 'I must say, in this weather, they might have sent a car for us. And the moonlight is starting to go.' She looked upwards. 'Oh, I don't believe this – it's starting to snow. And they're making us *walk*. We don't even know how far.'

'Maybe they didn't have anyone available,' Rosie answered, peering ahead through the swirling snowflakes. 'I think I see the lane.'

'Thank God.'

By now Rosie's feet in their stout shoes were numb with cold. She noticed Pamela's feet were encased in a pair of expensive-looking boots. Rosie's mittens, which Ivy had knitted to go with the scarf, weren't nearly warm enough but she couldn't stop to rub them, because Pamela, she was sure, would have simply marched ahead and Rosie was not going to be left on this lonely road on her own if she could help it.

'I bet this is it,' Pamela said. 'Look at all the barbed wire along here. It must be Station X's boundary. It's all very hush-hush and rather exciting.' She paused. 'I wonder what Station X stands for.'

'It could be Station Ten.'

'Oh, well done. I'd not thought of that.' Pamela suddenly stopped. 'Look, there are the iron gates. We should soon come across the sentries.'

No sooner had she spoken than an armed guard appeared from a brick sentry box and opened the gate.

'Good evening, ladies. Your passes, please.'

'We're new,' Pamela said in a firm voice as though talking to a servant, 'so we don't have a pass. But we have a letter to prove who we are.'

She handed over her introduction letter while Rosie fumbled in her coat pockets, heart pounding as they proved empty except for her handkerchief.

'I know I had it here. It must still be in my bag.' She swung her shoulder bag in front and opened it. Thank goodness the letter was on the top. She snatched it out, but not before a hundred snowflakes found their way in. Cursing under her breath in case they'd made the ink run, she handed the paper to the waiting guard.

'Hmm. This signature's well and truly smudged. I shouldn't let you in with this, but as it's such a rotten night . . .' He winked and handed the paper back to Rosie. 'It'll be good enough for you to get your pass.'

'Thank you.' He obviously thought he was being amusing but after a long walk carrying her case she wasn't in the mood. 'Where do we go now?' she asked abruptly.

'Follow the drive up to the Mansion. Someone there will register you.'

By the time she and Pamela had crunched along the gravel drive to what looked in the blackout like the entrance to a sprawling manor house in a band of trees, Rosie's feet were so numb that she couldn't feel any solid ground under them. It was as though she were floating with the snowflakes, now falling faster and thicker. Her whole body inside the skimpy coat was bone-cold. She shivered, praying someone would let them in right this second. The door opened. A tall lanky young man stood there dressed in a coat and scarf and frowning.

'Can we please come in?' Pamela said, pushing forward. 'We're absolutely frozen.' She turned to take Rosie's arm. 'Come on, Rosemary. We can get the niceties over inside.'

'Is it Miss Perriman-Hale and Miss Frost?'

'Yes,' the two women chorused.

'Larry Burton. I was just coming to meet you.'

'Bit late for that,' Pamela said. 'But we'll forgive you if you tell us where we register and where we can get something to eat in the warm.'

The canteen was just outside the iron gates, so they had to traipse back and show their letters again as proof they were to work at the Park. But the canteen emanated warmth, creating a cosy though noisy atmosphere as Rosie and Pamela opened the door. By now it was nearly eight in the evening but there didn't appear to be any let-up in the clattering of knives and forks and the chattering and laughing of men and women, mostly young, in all kinds of dress,. Some of them were in uniform and there were dozens of Wrens scattered throughout the room. Their smart uniforms brought a lump to Rosie's throat. She was surprised to see so many. So she might have been sent here anyway if she'd remained with them. But it was no good harking back. She'd been given another opportunity and this particular job might prove even better.

'There's a table over there with a couple of empty chairs.'

Pamela pointed. 'Let's leave our luggage there to save our spaces.'

Rosie, used to self-service in the factory, quickly filled her tray with a plate of corned beef, mashed potatoes and tinned peas and a small dish of prunes and custard.

'Ugh,' Pamela said, looking down at her own plate. She'd only taken the smallest of portions. 'There wasn't any choice, was there? This looks most unappetising.'

'Whatever it tastes like, I'm really hungry,' Rosie said, picking up her knife and fork. She noticed Pamela had removed her plate and sweet dish from the tray and set them straight onto the table, arranging her cutlery as though she were at a posh dinner. She immediately followed suit. This wasn't like the factory canteen where everyone ate straight off their trays. She made a mental note to watch Pamela in the future, and then was cross with herself. Who was she trying to impress? Pamela obviously came from a privileged background where money was of no concern. As long as she didn't speak with her mouth full, Rosie decided she was as good as anyone else at her table.

'I hope the only reason there's no choice is because it's late and most people have already eaten,' Pamela said in her clear tones. 'But I'd have thought these people would have packed up by now and gone to their billets – not eaten their supper here.'

'They're probably on shift work,' Rosie said.

Pamela opened her eyes wide. 'Really? What makes you say that?'

'Because I . . .' Rosie felt a flush to her cheeks. Well, damn it. She couldn't hide the fact. 'Because I used to work in a factory and we had to do shift work. I imagine this is a similar operation.' Pamela raised a pencilled eyebrow. 'Maybe not packing chocolates as I did,' Rosie added with a grin, 'but more the opposite, unpacking secrets.'

One or two people on her table stared at her. A man in civilian clothes frowned in warning.

'Be careful, young lady,' he said. 'We don't have that sort of conversation anywhere here at the Park.'

Blood flooded to the roots of Rosie's hair. She bit her lip hard. Dear God, she must think before she opened her mouth here. But she hadn't said anything incriminating, surely. She glanced at him.

'Of course,' she said lamely.

He nodded and turned back to the man he'd been talking to.

'Talking of billets,' Pamela said, 'the woman who registered us – Mrs Jones – didn't seem to have any details of where we'll be staying, only that mine is supposed to be in a country house. Well, that would suit me down to the ground, if so. But she didn't even know that much for you.'

'I know.' Rosie tried to push some peas onto her fork, but they kept sliding off. 'Well, we'll find out tomorrow.'

'It sounds as though I'll need a car.' Pamela clicked her tongue. 'I knew I should have driven down.'

Rosie privately thought Pamela was living in cloud cuckoo land. Petrol had been rationed as soon as war broke out, and they were even talking of withdrawing it for private use altogether. She was relieved the country house billet was booked for Pamela and not herself. She didn't want to feel cut off; not only was she used to being around her family but at work she was surrounded by the other factory girls and women. But she did wonder where she was going to end up. Well, she'd know more tomorrow. Mrs Jones had said they could both stay in the main house for the evening and share a room, so for the time being Rosie refused to worry any further.

Chapter Thirteen

Rosie opened her eyes, for a moment wondering where she was. She didn't recognise anything. Not that she could see in the dark, but the whole atmosphere was different. Where were the splutters and snores Heather regularly exuded? And the gentle breathing of Ivy? All was dead quiet. And then she remembered. She was here at this strange mansion called Station X, sharing a room with a girl who had probably never shared a room in her life.

A tingle of excitement ran through her veins. She was here to do important war work. She had no idea what, but then neither did Pamela Perriman-Hale.

She was gasping for a cup of tea. If only she could see the time. There was no use even trying to peer at her watch. And not a bit of good opening the curtains. It would still be dark.

She smothered a yawn, not wanting to wake Pamela, and fumbled for the glass toothbrush holder she'd remembered to fill with water before settling down for the night. Her mouth was horribly dry. Where was the glass? She moved her hand gently in the direction, but to her horror caught it on something which thumped onto the linoleum floor.

Pamela shot up in bed. 'What the devil's going on?'

'That was my glass falling. I'm awfully sorry to have woken you. I just wanted a sip of water. It's so dark in here.'

'What's the time?'

'I don't know. But I need to make sure the glass isn't broken, leaving shards. Do you mind if I put the light on?'

'If you must.' Pamela's voice was almost a groan.

Rosie felt for her slippers and shook each one to be on the safe side before slipping them on and picked her way towards where she hoped the bedroom door was. Thankfully, her hand found the doorknob. The light switch must be nearby. She raised her hand to feel the side of the doorframe. Ah, there it was. She flicked it and the dim light revealed a body shape in the other bed where Pamela had buried herself under the blankets.

Rosie picked up her watch. Twenty minutes to six. No wonder Pamela sounded irritated. They weren't due to report to the administration office until eight to be told about their billets. Work hadn't been mentioned. Even though she'd only just met Pamela, and they were as opposite in their backgrounds as could be, she hoped they might be in the same department. A familiar face would make all the difference.

First things first. She retrieved the glass, which had rolled under the bed, and examined it. As it didn't seem any worse for the accident, she set it back down and fetched a small towel from the sink to wipe up the spilt water. She'd have a wash in the bedroom sink, get dressed and see if the canteen was open for an early breakfast.

Although the previous evening's snow hadn't settled, the cold hit her as soon as she stepped out of the Mansion. Now, in the daylight, she could see a profusion of wooden buildings, and people pouring through the doors or pushing their way in. They must be the Huts. She wondered what conditions were like inside. A hut didn't exactly sound like the cosiest place to work in winter.

Pamela didn't make an appearance for breakfast and Rosie worried that she might have overslept. Back in their room she found her only just throwing back the bedcovers.

'Have you had breakfast already?' Pamela demanded.

'Yes.'

'What was it?'

'Porridge.'

'And . . .?'

'Lumpy. Lukewarm.'

Pamela made a face. 'Ugh! I think I'll skip it.'

'I wouldn't do that, Pamela. I think we're going to need our strength to face whatever the day has in store for us.'

Just before eight, Rosie joined a dozen or so other women, mostly around her own age, clustered outside the Administration Office in the Mansion, talking quietly amongst themselves. Pamela was nowhere in sight. On the dot of eight, a woman with salt-and-pepper hair pulled back in a severe bun emerged from the office.

'Please step inside and form a queue, then it won't take long.'

Twenty minutes later Rosie left the office with her official pass and directions to go to Room 12 for her interview. Feeling a little nervous, she set her chin and strode on until she reached the door and knocked.

'Ah, Miss Frost.' A civilian with a handlebar moustache stood aside for her to enter. 'Do sit down at the table.'

The room was large; it seemed to take for ever to reach a long table covered in an old grey blanket where four men in Army uniform sat. There were several empty seats. She hesitated. Was she supposed to take a certain one? One of the men turned and smiled so she chose the seat next to him.

'Now, Miss Frost, we just need to ask you a few questions so we get an idea of where to place you. But first we need you to sign the Official Secrets Act.'

Unlike when she'd joined the Wrens, the Official Secrets Act involved his reading it out to her, then passing the paperwork for her to sign. She skimmed the document again before she signed and passed it back to the moustached man, who gave it a brief look before putting it into a file.

'We have an extra document at BP,' he said, passing a sheet of paper over to her.

'BP?'

'Bletchley Park.'

'So where is Station X?' Rosie asked.

'Right here. Station X used to be the name of the wireless room in the tower, though that's been moved off the premises. But we kept Station X as a code name to preserve the anonymity of Bletchley Park. Most of us say "BP". No one must know our name or whereabouts or what we do here. It's classed as most secret – and that goes for almost all of the military outside the Park. And you must *never* discuss your work outside your own section. Or to your friends and family or anyone you meet. If you do, it will be considered treason and there will be no leniency whatsoever in the punishment.'

Rosie shivered at these last words. Yet it seemed just the kind of thing she was hoping for. Something to get her teeth into. She looked at the document, which was marked SECRECY. There was a list of five commands and each one began with the words 'DO NOT TALK'. It instructed you what to say if anyone asked where you worked and what work you were doing. You were to say you were a clerk or a shorthand typist doing war work at the Foreign Office and leave it at that. At the end of the paper it said: 'I hereby promise that no word of mine shall betray, however slightly, the great trust placed in me'.

Rosie signed, feeling a flicker of guilt as she remembered the man who'd reprimanded her in the canteen for saying something she would have thought perfectly innocent. She passed the paper back to the interviewer. This time he merely glanced at it as he put it in the same file.

'Good,' he said, turning to her. 'Now let's see how your Italian stands up.' He paused. 'Leslie, can you ask Miss Frost a few questions?'

This was the part she'd been dreading. She swallowed as Leslie, a young man opposite her with a shock of dark hair, some of it falling over his forehead, asked some elementary questions. She answered easily and fluently and breathed an inward sigh of relief. Then he asked more probing questions, and again she was able to respond with little trouble. Thank goodness her memory had always served her well. He nodded his approval and asked her to talk about herself. She began to relax, even using her hands to express herself.

'*Va bene,*' Leslie said smiling. 'Right, give us a minute or two.'

The men put their heads close and muttered. It was obvious they were weighing her up, deciding what she was capable of. After a minute or so when she didn't know where to look and began to shift on her hard seat, the man with the moustache said:

'We're assigning you to work in Hut 4 – in the Naval section. Your Italian is good but not perfect. You'll need some help on the technical vocabulary side. But we should be able to make use of it.' He looked at her. 'You will need some training for whatever they decide to ask you to do. Anyway, we'll put you in the Watch. See how you cope.'

Was he hinting she might be given a more menial task if they thought she wasn't up to the job? Then she scolded herself. There was a war on. It didn't matter what they asked her to do. The important thing was, they thought she could be useful. She'd work her socks off to show them they weren't wrong. And she'd find a way to get her Italian up to scratch.

'What is the Watch exactly, sir?' she asked.

'Oh, the Watch itself covers a multitude of different duties,' he said off-handedly. 'Different rooms concentrate on different tasks. You'll learn as much as you need to know when you're on the job.'

Everything seemed to be cloaked in secrecy. She hugged herself. She couldn't wait to get started.

'Right then, Miss Frost. I think that will be all. Someone will direct you to the Accommodation Office where you'll be given details of your billet. Meanwhile, we'll give you a chance to settle in and report to the Watch in Hut 4 for the four o'clock to midnight shift.'

Good. She was longing to get stuck in.

'Thank you, sir.'

'Right, then. We'll see you at four sharp.'

'Name, please.' A bored-looking young girl glanced up from her typewriter.

'Rosemary Frost.'

The girl flicked through cards in an index box, then pulled one out.

'Oh, yes. This is you. You're billeted in Woburn Abbey.'

Woburn Abbey. It sounded huge.

Rosie's heart beat a little faster as she said, 'How far is it from here?'

'Oh, about ten miles.' The girl wrote the address on a scrap of paper and handed it to her. 'You can make your way there now.'

'How do I get there?'

'There should be a bus soon. It comes right into the Park. You won't be the only one going there.'

Thank goodness, Rosie thought. It sounded like the back of beyond. She wondered if she'd been assigned to the same country house as Pamela. If so, would Pamela be ashamed to be billeted with some stupid girl who was obviously so out of her depth? Then she caught herself.

For goodness' sake, Rosie, what are you thinking? You're not stupid. You've got the same right to be here and live at a posh country house as Pamela or anyone else, or John wouldn't have put your name forward.

But what about if anyone finds out you've been tossed out of the WRNS for having lied? her inner voice whispered.

John said this place doesn't care about those sorts of things. It's what you can do now *– for your country. And he seems to think you can offer something worthwhile.*

She couldn't wait for four o'clock to start her shift in Hut 4 – in the Watch – whatever that turned out to be.

Chapter Fourteen

Still with several hours to go before she started work, Rosie was reading the signposts to see where Hut 4 was located when she heard a familiar voice.

'Rosemary, wait . . .'

She turned to see Pamela a few yards behind.

'Shall we go for a coffee?' she said, slipping her arm through Rosie's.

'That sounds like a good idea – especially as you didn't have any breakfast,' Rosie added. 'Where were you?'

'Having an extra kip. I'm not good first thing but I've been told there's a snack bar in Hut 2 that we're allowed to go to, and apparently they do much better coffee than the stuff you get in the canteen. So shall we give it a whirl?'

Inside Hut 2, the café was buzzing with chatter. It was a small room with a thick fug of smoke.

'I'll get this,' Pamela said. 'You see if you can find a couple of seats.'

Rosie picked her way between the few tables and found one for four with only two Wrens sitting there.

'Do you mind if my friend and I join you?' she asked.

'Be our guests,' one said, turning again to the other girl.

'Here you are,' Pamela said, putting a steaming mug in

front of Rosie. 'I didn't know if you took sugar so I put half a teaspoon in.'

'Thank you.'

Pamela sat next to her. 'Have you got your billet sorted?'

Rosie nodded. 'Yes. Somewhere called Woburn Abbey.'

Pamela's jaw dropped. 'You lucky thing. It's a fabulous country house. But they made a mistake with me. You'll never guess where I've landed.'

'No, where?'

Pamela grimaced. 'In Bletchley, in the local bloody undertaker's house.'

Poor Pamela. It really should have been the other way round.

'Well, at least it ought to be peaceful,' she said with a chuckle.

'I don't suppose you'd care to do a swap,' Pamela said.

'Not on your Nellie. All those ghosts floating up and down the stairs . . .'

Pamela rolled her eyes. 'I'm not bothered about ghosts. You'll probably get plenty of those where *you're* going. No, it's my creature comforts. And I don't envisage much of those with Mr and Mrs Stone – aptly named, don't you think?'

Rosie swallowed hard and forced a smile as she joined the queue of Wrens, smartly dressed in their uniforms and chattering together, already bonding by simply being in the WRNS, as they waited to board the single-decker bus that was to take them to Woburn Abbey. Although it was grandly marked *Excursion,* it looked as though it was on its last legs, covered as it was by rust and dirt, the side nearest to her buckled in – probably from some ancient accident.

It was just as scruffy inside, Rosie noticed, as she looked

for a space. She appeared to be the only civilian apart from one man who had taken a seat at the back. It looked as though she'd have to keep herself to herself at Woburn Abbey as well as Station X. The first sniff of a Wren finding out she'd also been one for a short time could easily lead to embarrassing questions.

She needn't have worried. No one spoke to her on the bus. It was as though she didn't exist. Surrounded by chattering and laughter she felt a stab of hurt that they should ignore her. But she was the odd one out and if she didn't like it, then it was up to her to be the first person to speak. She turned to the girl sitting by her side on the hard wooden seat, looking out of the window at another grey day. The girl still wore her rating's hat.

'Hello.' She touched the girl's arm lightly. 'I'm Rosemary Frost.'

The girl didn't move a muscle. It was as though Rosie had spoken to a stranger's shoulder.

Maybe she didn't realise I was speaking to her. Or maybe she's a bit deaf.

She tried again. This time the girl looked round and to Rosie's shock she noticed there was a flicker of hostility in those pale-blue eyes.

'Really?' she said in a bored tone. 'How interesting,' and went back to staring out of the window.

Well, that's me being put in my place by a mere rating – the lowest rank of all.

She pressed her lips together to stop herself coming back with a sarcastic retort. She'd been down for officer training and if it had taken place this girl wouldn't have dared be so rude.

Lost in her thoughts she realised the bus had slowed and they were deep into the countryside. She looked over the

144

sulky girl's shoulder to see the bus swing up a wide drive, passing by a deer park. Several dozen pairs of curious brown eyes, standing stock still, watched the bus pass two lakes and woodland as it proceeded slowly down the long drive. She calculated it must be well over a mile before the house came into view.

She gasped. Up until now she'd only ever seen pictures of country houses in her schoolbooks, but Woburn Abbey in reality caught her by the throat. She didn't think she'd ever seen anything so elegant and perfect with its grace and symmetry, its columns and pediments, reminding her of the pictures she'd seen of Italian Renaissance palaces. Since it was going to be her new home, this kind of house was bound to have a library where she could find out more of its history. Surreptitiously, she pinched her arm, wishing her mother could see her now.

The bus finally came to a rattling halt. The girl who'd been sitting so sullenly beside her in the window seat stood up. Rosie took her cue and retrieved her suitcase. The driver opened the door and the Wrens, the one man at the back and Rosie stepped down from the bus.

Rosie breathed in a lungful of crisp country air. The atmosphere already felt different from anything she'd ever experienced. A Wren with rank badge on her sleeve and a tricorn hat stood by the bus with a clipboard.

'Good morning, girls,' she said. 'I'm Petty Officer Morris in charge of all of you.' She looked round and spotted the solitary man. 'And you must be Bill, our new maintenance man come to fix the tiles back on the dairy.'

He raised his cap. 'That's right, ma'am.'

'Jeff, our head gardener, will see to you. Ah, here's the man himself.'

The two men nodded a greeting and went off together.

'Come this way, girls.' PO Morris led them into a magnificent hall, reminding Rosie of the one in the Foreign Office at Whitehall. 'I'll register you right here where you can leave your suitcases, and then I'll give you a tour of the part of the house you're allowed to use.' After calling out the names she looked up. 'Right, I believe that's everyone.'

'Not quite,' Rosie called out. All the Wrens turned round, curious to see who it was.

'You are . . .?'

'Rosemary Frost.'

PO Morris furrowed her brow as she studied her list again. 'Yes, Miss Frost, I do have you down.' She looked across at her. 'I believe you're our only civilian quartered here. There may be others joining you, but in the meantime, you will take one of the servants' rooms. I'll show the others to their cabins and you can then take the back staircase to the attic.'

Several Wrens threw Rosie a sympathetic look, but she smiled back, at the same time breathing an inward sigh of relief. She was grateful she wasn't to be bundled with the Wrens, especially the surly one next to her on the bus. It was far safer away from them. And to be given a room of her own – even though it wouldn't be nearly so grand as the other girls' quarters – to *her* would be heaven.

PO Morris showed Rosie and the Wrens a drawing room where they were allowed to congregate on their time off, the library, where they could take a book providing they left their name and the title in the exercise book for that purpose, the kitchen, where two plump women in none-too-white aprons and caps announced they would be doing breakfast and suppers for everyone, and finally the bedrooms – or cabins, as PO Morris called them. She pointed out three rooms, ten bunks to a room, for the use of the Wrens. They'd obviously been beautiful bedrooms in their day when the family lived at the house.

Back on the second-floor landing, PO Morris opened a door to reveal a narrow, winding staircase.

'It leads to the attic,' she said. 'There are several cabins but you'll find three bunks in one of them, and that will be the one you will use. I don't think you need me to show you.'

'No, of course not.'

'Right. You may all go and collect your cases from the hall and get yourselves settled in. The Wrens will take the three rooms according to their names on the list pinned outside.'

'Will you be all right up there by yourself?' one of the Wrens asked Rosie.

'Oh, yes. I don't mind at all.'

'There's bound to be mice and spiders to keep her company,' the girl who'd sat next to her on the bus said with a hint of malice.

Whatever have I done to make her so obnoxious?

Rosie smiled sweetly at her. 'I'm sure it won't be long before I make friends with them.'

The girl simply sniffed and turned her back. One of the Wrens glanced at the girl and rolled her eyes at Rosie, making her want to giggle.

It was difficult manoeuvring the suitcase up the narrow stairs but she managed to push it round the last turn onto a cramped landing where there were four doors. The first one she opened was probably a servants' airing cupboard, but it was now empty. She opened another door, this time to a dark interior which must be one of the bedrooms. She found the light switch but all that lit up was one naked lightbulb dangling from the centre of the ceiling. It cast a shadow over three bunks, spaced no more than a couple of feet apart, taking up three-quarters of the floor area. She set her suitcase on the bare boards and blew out her cheeks.

A gloomy sight met her eyes. Drab dark green and brown wallpaper adorned the sloping walls and the bunks had similar dreary-coloured coverings. There was a shabby painted chest of drawers and several low eaves cupboards. She opened one to find four wooden coat hangers.

Rosie walked over to the two small windows, both with similar cheap dark curtains already pulled together as though it was night-time. They were threaded onto a piece of wire. She pulled them back, at least letting some light in, wrinkling her nose against the musty smell, and opened both windows. That was better. Everything was strange, but in a few days' time she was sure it would feel familiar and become her new home.

An hour later she was back on the bus to Bletchley Park. She was very early, but she'd have a walk to the town of Bletchley to get her bearings in daylight. She wouldn't admit she couldn't wait to get away from so many Wrens, every single one reminding her of her shattered career dreams.

Chapter Fifteen

The town of Bletchley was grim-looking under the dark clouds. Rosie wandered along the wide High Street, an avenue of trees dividing it in two. The trees were practically the only sign of life, save for a few figures dotted here and there. She walked up one side and down the other, peering into all the shop windows but they didn't seem to have much to offer especially if you needed any clothes or shoes, though her wages wouldn't stretch to any big purchase anyway. She wondered how the shop owners even existed. But then most towns were the same since the war started. A few men in Army uniform mooched around and it occurred to her that one or two of them might also work at Station X.

A gnawing feeling of hunger struck her. Breakfast had been unappetising to say the least. She decided to find a café where she could buy a sandwich. There were two to choose from and both, from what she could see through the grimy windows, looked packed. Decisively, she opened the door to the second one and immediately a swirl of smoke hit her nostrils. A quick glance showed only one small table for two with a spare seat. A golden-blonde woman about her own age sat in the other seat engrossed in a book. At that precise moment she looked up, smiled at Rosie and beckoned her over.

Rosie slid into the seat opposite.

'Thanks,' she said. 'The other café looked just as busy as this one, and I need a snack before I start work.'

'I'm Dale Treadwell,' the girl said.

'Rosemary Frost.'

A waitress came over and asked for her order. Rosie quickly scanned the few lunch items and asked for Welsh Rarebit and a pot of tea. When the waitress had disappeared, the golden-blonde woman said:

'Do you work in Bletchley, Miss Frost?'

Rosie hesitated. She needed to be very careful what she said. The girl looked friendly enough but that might not mean anything.

'Um, not right in the town.'

'What kind of work do you do?'

Rosie began to feel a little uncomfortable under those remarkable turquoise-blue eyes.

'Clerical.' She willed Dale Treadwell not to ask for any more details. 'For the war effort,' she added as an after-thought, not wanting the woman to think she wasn't doing her bit.

'Really?' Dale Treadwell looked at her with interest, her eyes narrowing as though weighing her up. 'Would that by any chance be for the Foreign Office?' She gave a wink.

Rosie thought quickly. She'd been told she was allowed to say 'for the war effort' but now she racked her brain as to whether she was allowed to mention the Foreign Office. This woman was asking far too many questions.

When she didn't reply, Miss Treadwell continued, 'I expect you're working up at the Park.'

Rosie shifted in her seat.

The golden-haired woman suddenly grinned.

'And you've only recently arrived as I've not seen you

150

around in the canteen or the café and I'm sure I'd remember that hair.'

Rosie gave an inward sigh of relief. Miss Treadwell obviously worked at Station X as well.

'Am I right?'

'Yes, you're right on both counts,' Rosie said, returning the grin.

'As we work at the same place, shall we use Christian names?'

'Oh, yes, I'm Rosie to my friends.'

'Well, let's hope *we* might become friends in time. Call me Dale. I'm Dulcie really, but I've always disliked it . . . except, well, until recently.' Her eyes looked away dreamily as though she were in another world.

Rosie thought she could smell romance with a capital 'R' and hid a smile. She couldn't help warming to her, as Dale chatted about the war situation, although nothing about her own job, and no more probing questions for which Rosie was thankful.

'Are you going to look around the town or are you going straight back to the Mansion?' Dale asked when they'd settled the bill.

'The Mansion?' Rosie said. 'Oh, yes, of course.' She gave Dale a rueful smile. '

Dale obviously didn't want to say 'Bletchley Park' in public.

'I'm due on the four o'clock shift,' Rosie said, 'so I think I'll make my way back.'

'Me, too,' Dale said. 'I'll walk with you . . . if you don't mind, that is.'

'That'd be nice.'

Dale was a mine of information, telling her about the plays and concerts and dances the Park put on, the ice-skating that had started since the lake had frozen over, the

Bletchley hairdresser who'd recently been allowed to come to the Park twice a week to give the girls a new hairstyle . . .

'He's not a bad cutter by the look of some of the styles he creates,' Dale said. 'Not that I've been to him, but some of the other girls have.' She looked at Rosie. 'Your hair is a glorious colour. Is it long?' Rosie nodded. 'Then I bet he'd love to get his hands on it.'

'Well, he won't,' Rosie said. For one thing she couldn't afford to go to a hairdresser. For another, she liked it long enough to put up.

Dale was pleasant company as they chatted.

'Do you know what Hut you're in?' she asked Rosie.

Was it all right to say?

'I'm in Hut 3,' Dale said. 'It's okay to say which Hut we're in as any one of us could see someone we know disappear into another Hut – but security is so tight we're never allowed to go into one which we don't work in – and of course we're not allowed to discuss or even hint at *anything* about the work we do to any of the other staff outside our own Hut.'

'I wouldn't dream of it,' Rosie said emphatically. 'I've had it well and truly drummed into me.'

'It won't be the last time,' Dale grinned. 'We're reminded of it at every turn with posters and notices in the canteen, library, the Huts . . . everywhere.'

'Well, as long as it's all right to say – I'm in Hut 4.'

Hut 4 ran alongside the Mansion. Like most of the Huts scattered around, Rosie noticed that the outside was shiplap boarding, painted a deep green, with an olive-green asbestos roof. She glanced at her watch. Ten to four.

She opened the door to the Hut, feeling as though she were trespassing. No one was about. A draught of cold air met her from the long narrow corridor, the top half of its walls painted mustard and the bottom half khaki. The brown linoleum floor was somewhat cheered by green doors placed at various intervals, the first one on her right marked 'Administration'. The corridor seemed to go on for ever and she was glad she was a few minutes early so she could locate the room she'd be working in. She could hear the noise of machinery through some of the rooms and occasional loud male voices. Doors marked 'Admissions', 'Intelligence Officers' Room', 'Duty Officer's Room', 'Teleprinter Room' . . .

And there was *her* room – 'Watch Room'.

Her heart quickened with excitement. She wanted to pinch herself. She was going to help with whatever tiny contribution she could make to win this war.

A murmuring of voices seeped from under the door. Without warning it swung open and she was face to face with several men, some in uniform, laughing and chattering.

'Well, who've we got here?' one of them said, his eyes appreciatively raking her from top to bottom.

For a second or two she was transfixed with nerves. Then she took a step back.

'I'm Rosemary Frost, and I'm to report here for the four o'clock shift.'

'Ah, yes, you're new.' A short wiry man, his glasses on top of his head, blinked as he peered at her. 'Do go in. Somebody will be with you shortly and show you the ropes.'

One or two others smiled at her and said hello and she heard one of them say as they turned into the corridor:

'Did you see that? What a looker.'

Rosie rolled her eyes as she walked into the room, much larger than she'd expected for a hut. Two other girls sat at a long U-shaped table. They both glanced up.

'You must be Rosemary Frost,' a plump woman, maybe

in her mid-twenties, with a mass of chestnut curls, exclaimed as she got to her feet and gave a welcoming smile.

'I am.'

'Good. I'm Nora Sedgewick and this is Alice Goodwin. Come and join us. We're early. There'll be some more coming in a few minutes.'

Alice put her pen down and stood. She was a tall, elegant brunette with a deep front wave, caught up by a tortoiseshell comb. Even though her hair hung loose, every shining strand was in place. But her eyes, a little too close together, looked hard at Rosie. She extended her hand.

'How do you do?'

'Very well, thank you,' Rosie said, taking the woman's cool thin hand in hers. Oh, why had she said something she'd had drummed into her not to say? What had Miss Little taught her in Speech class? The correct answer was to repeat the exact words, 'How do you do?' in reply, which always seemed rather silly to Rosie when you asked someone a question and they answered it by asking the same question.

Alice threw her a look. Rosie swallowed.

'Do sit down,' Nora said, 'and we'll try to explain what we can. Just don't think you're going to uncover war secrets straight-away,' she broke off with a smile, 'but whatever tiny snippet we reveal is apparently of deadly importance. Not that we're told the full picture, by any means.' She looked at Rosie. 'Have you any general questions we can answer beforehand?'

'Yes, loads,' Rosie began, as she took a seat opposite the two women, 'but I hardly know where to start.'

'Well,' Alice cut in, 'you're in the Watch where we do translations of Italian signals into English as well as many other jobs to do with checking.' She studied Rosie for a few moments. 'How's your Italian?'

'Reasonably fluent.'

'Good,' Nora said, looking relieved. 'And there's plenty of Italian books and dictionaries in the library in the main house so you can keep your Italian up.'

'I'll certainly do that,' Rosie said.

She felt a rush of air behind her as the door opened and a petite girl with blonde hair rushed in. She stopped short, her eyes fixed on Rosie.

'Hello. I'm Sonia Parsons. You're new.'

'Well done, Sonia, for stating the obvious,' Alice said.

Sonia giggled as she regarded Rosie. 'What's your name?'

'Rosemary Frost,' Rosie said, smiling. For some reason Sonia reminded her of Poppy. A bit excitable, outright, blunt, to the point. Her heart contracted. What was Poppy doing at this exact moment? What was her little girl thinking?

'Right,' Alice interrupted, her voice firm. 'It's gone four so let's get on with our job.' She turned to Rosie. 'I'm in charge of translations so you'd better come and sit with me and I can go through the sequence with you.'

At that moment three men appeared and glanced at the four women.

'Afternoon, ladies,' the first one said, his gaze falling on Rosie. 'Ah, you must be Rosemary Frost.' He paused. 'Paul Hodges.' He turned to the other two. 'Stuart McAllister and Jerzy Biskupski.'

The three men briefly smiled to her as though they had other more important things on their mind. Feeling overwhelmed, and trying to remember all the new names, Rosie shook hands with them.

'You're presumably one of the translators,' Paul Hodges said.

'I'm not sure what I'm doing yet,' Rosie admitted.

'Ah, well, you've got Alice here who'll explain,' he said, giving Alice a wink.

Rosie noticed Alice didn't react in any way.

'Right, better get on.' Paul clapped Stuart and Jerzy on the shoulders. 'We've got plenty to get through this afternoon.' He glanced at Rosie. 'It'll take you a while to learn the ropes, but you can always come to one of us if you get stuck. There's a lot to take in.' His eye fell on Alice. 'Don't be too hard on her, Alice.'

Ignoring him, Alice turned to Rosie.

'Right, I'll show you some of the stuff I'm working on, so you get the picture.'

Rosie sat next to her, breathing in the smell of expensive perfume. Alice passed her notebook over. Rosie gazed at the handwritten sentences in Italian but to her chagrin there were many words and acronyms in practically every sentence that she'd never come across in her brief period as a Wren. This was awful. She'd been over confident, but clearly she was in the wrong place. These people were all far more experienced than her – probably totally bi lingual and more than likely had been in the department for some time and were now used to specialised Italian naval language. Talk about being thrown in at the deep end. But this work was surely too important for a beginner like her.

'Well?' Alice broke into her stream of doubt.

'I'm sorry, but I'm not able to translate them in full.'

'Hmm.' Alice stared at her. 'Can you read *any* of it?'

'Some of it.' Rosie hesitated, her mind working fast. 'But the ones I can't understand look like they might be naval expressions I wouldn't be familiar with.' She peered again at the alien words. 'I know they're talking about ships and positions but obviously that's not the complete message.'

Alice gave a deep sigh. 'Well, I don't think we can allow you to do any translations from the Italian.'

Rosie waited. Her heart thumped as Alice tapped her pencil on her pad.

'I don't understand it,' Alice said, her forehead creased in an unbecoming frown. 'You came highly recommended for translation. We were told your Italian was excellent.' She kept her eyes fixed on Rosie. 'Well, that's not the word I'd have used to describe it.'

Rosie felt her cheeks flush with temper at the insulting tone.

'I think we'll put you on the messages that are already translated into English,' Alice went on. 'They're ones that might have gaps in them or typing errors or translation errors. Your job will be to correct them.' She looked directly at Rosie. 'That should be easier for you.'

It sounded just as difficult. How would she know what words were supposed to fill the gaps if the missing words were technical?

'It's Rosie's first day, Alice,' Nora said, cutting across the two women. 'She needs to be shown what to do. You can't just plunge her straight in. I didn't know which way was up when I first came, but I had some proper training.'

'That will come when we get the new boss,' Alice said.

'When will that be?' Rosie said.

'Should be within a fortnight,' Alice said casually, as though it didn't matter to her whether he turned up or not.

Rosie bit her lip. *A whole fortnight! What do I do in the meantime?*

'So until then,' Nora said, throwing Rosie a sympathetic smile, 'why not put her on the paraphrasing exercise? Get her a little used to the terminology.'

Alice appeared to give it some thought. 'You may be right,' she said at last, turning to Rosie. 'We also receive messages that have been translated from Italian into English and fully checked they are complete and accurate. Then we have to paraphrase them so they give the same meaning but are not word for word translated.'

Rosie's forehead puckered.

'I don't understand.'

Nora cut in. 'If the Italian message we've picked up and decoded is now translated into English, and we send it on word for word, and it gets into the wrong hands – the Italians or the Germans – and supposing we're passing on details of their troop movements or their ships – they'd know we've broken their codes. So we have to alter it but keep the same meaning, obviously.'

Clever. Rosie felt a shiver of excitement.

'Do you think you could manage that?' Alice's tone was on the verge of sarcastic.

She wasn't going to be an easy person to work with, Rosie thought. If only it was Nora in charge. But she wasn't going to muff this opportunity. She took in a deep breath.

'I'm sure I can.' Rosie paused and caught Alice's eye. She wouldn't be intimidated by the woman. 'Meantime, is there a glossary or something of technical words that I could copy and learn?'

'You'd better have a word with Paul,' came the curt reply. 'He borrowed it yesterday. Nora, can you give Rosemary that pile of translated messages and get her started?' Alice turned to Rosie. 'You can use this pad and I'll see how you get on. But don't be too long-winded as there's a lot to go through.'

Rosie studied the first translated message:

Cagni class submarine will attack merchant convoy heading Malta on 2 March.

She frowned. She had no idea what a 'cagni class' submarine was, but it probably didn't matter in this particular job. All she'd been asked to do was paraphrase the message and stick to the facts. She licked her lips and read it again, then picked up the pencil, aware of Alice's eyes boring into her from the other side of the table. How could she make the date any different? It was too vital a piece of information to muck about with. She racked her brain, then wrote:

Expect attack on merchant ships very early March en route to Malta by Cagni class sub.

'Let me look.' Alice's head bent over her notepad. 'Hmm. Not bad.'

The woman sounded surprised. Rosie hid a smile that held a tinge of triumph as she tackled the next message.

Chapter Sixteen

Rosie hated to admit it but she felt lonely, though it was only a week since she'd left home. She remembered having the same feeling when she'd become a Wren and had been made aware by a couple of the new recruits that she came from a working-class family who didn't have quite the right accent. It didn't help when there wasn't one person at Woburn Abbey she could relate to. Her room was far away from the dormitories on the first floor, and she felt awkward at mealtimes when she had to share a large dining table with several of them, by now all having formed friendships with other girls having similar backgrounds to them, and two or three of them seeming to make a point to ignore her.

Rosie shrugged. They were no better than she was, she told herself. But she wasn't wholly convinced. She missed her family – even the constant chatter of her siblings – and although she disliked the constant bickering at home, at least she wasn't made to feel inferior. She'd feel better when she'd heard from Mum. If it hadn't been for the friendly team of Paul Hodges, Stuart McAllister, and Jerzy Biskupski, who told her he was from Poland, Rosie would not have been able to keep her temper in check with Alice peering over her shoulder all too frequently and forever making comments as to how to improve her work. Yet Rosie noticed Alice never appeared to alter it.

But after several days of endless paraphrasing, and some help from Paul Hodges, Rosie began to feel a little frustrated. She was sure her Italian would be far more use than what she was doing, even though she realised this was an important part of the process. But she saw no sign of being given more responsibility. She decided to approach Alice.

'No, I'm leaving you to carry on with what you're doing until we have the new boss,' Alice said. 'He might have a different opinion, but personally I don't think you're up to it.'

'Alice, you made a judgement about me in the first five minutes of my first day,' Rosie said. Alice raised her eyebrows. Good. Frankly, she was getting tired of the woman's rudeness. 'I was expecting to have some training before being thrown in the deep end. Anyone would need it – not just me.'

'You can surely see how busy we are for training,' Alice snapped. 'But no doubt the new Lieutenant Commander will give you a formal briefing.'

'Have we got a date yet when he starts?'

'Not an exact one though it should be soon.' Alice studied the calendar. 'But for heaven's sake don't mention you want a transfer right away when you've only been here five minutes. He'll want a chance to settle in.'

'Surely if he's in charge he'll expect to deal with everything and anything at any time,' Rosie argued.

Alice let out an exaggerated sigh. 'Just settle down, Rosemary, and don't keep agitating,' she said, as though she were talking to some wayward puppy.

Rosie drew in her lips to stop herself from retorting something she'd regret later. She hadn't even been given the opportunity to start a list of technical words and phrases with the constant stream of messages laid on her desk. Something else to tell the new boss. She just hoped he would be more sympathetic than Alice.

Today, Saturday, was the afternoon to midnight shift. She was already mentally exhausted by just a few challenging days in the Watch. After she'd grabbed her coat and faced the cold night air, she saw the old bus standing just inside the gates ready to pick up a large group of Wrens and a handful of civilian men. The driver dropped off the men in the town and soon he was taking the country roads at quite a lick towards the magnificent estate that was Woburn.

Wrapped in her thoughts in the dark interior of the bus she wondered whether to ask if she could be sent to another billet. One where maybe she could share with one or two others that weren't hoity-toity. Well, she'd see how she fared on this new shift before deciding. It would obviously be more work for the accommodations people and they might be suspicious as to why she wasn't happy in such palatial surroundings. She could get tagged for being a fusspot, which could make her even more unpopular.

She drew in a breath. *For goodness' sake stop thinking like this. It's the work you need to concentrate on. Helping our boys.*

Ashamed of herself, she tried to think of something positive and taking her by surprise, John Palmer's image bobbed in front of her. She blinked and his face faded. She hoped she might see him again. For some reason she felt she could trust him. It was a good feeling to know she had one real friend.

Hanging behind the Wrens, Rosie climbed down from the bus which had dropped them at the bottom of the drive.

'Don't forget to wipe your feet in the straw before we go in,' one of the Wrens called out when they were almost at the house.

'What does she mean about wiping our feet in the straw?' Rosie asked the nearest girl.

'Oh, we're supposed to do it every time we come off our shift,' the girl answered, 'though most people either forget or don't bother. The straw's disinfected. It's so we don't spread foot and mouth to Woburn's precious herd of deer.' She put a hand on Rosie's arm. 'It's in one of the sheds near the back of the house. Come with me.'

Rosie did what she was told, wondering all the time if it would have any effect. She quickly moved her feet backwards and forwards and followed the others outside. It was too dark for her to catch her breath once again at the sheer splendour of the house and the most beautiful grounds, but the interior did not live up to it – not in her quarters, anyway. She was frozen cold in her attic room and most nights was losing sleep. Her eyes had gained dark circles and she sometimes felt quite shaky inside. She *had* to keep alert for her job. If something slipped, it could have devastating consequences.

Only stopping to brush her teeth and get into her pyjamas, Rosie climbed into her bed and dragged the blankets up closely to her face, then wished she hadn't. They smelt musty and dank. In the dark she screwed up her face. Maybe tomorrow she could air them outside. And ask someone if there was a hot water bottle anywhere.

The next morning she awoke to a thick frost that had coated her windows in a pattern like lace. It was so beautiful she wished she had a camera and could take a photograph of it. Her breath coming out through her nostrils in clouds like a

163

heavy smoker's, she went to the window and gazed out on the scene. She could see two girls, arm in arm, in the distance. Every tree glittered with frost, and although there was no snow, the sky had that grimy yellow look that indicated plenty was on its way.

She drew away from the window and picked up her watch she'd laid on the bedside table. She couldn't believe it. Nearly half-past eight. She didn't have to be on duty until four o'clock so she wasn't exactly late, but would the kitchen staff already be clearing up breakfast? She needed to get a move on. Her teeth chattering in the chilly room she went over to the sink and tried the hot tap but as usual there was not even a trickle of lukewarm water, let alone hot. She quickly splashed her legs and arms with stone-cold water, then dressed at top speed. With a rake through her hair and a dab of lipstick, she rushed downstairs. If she didn't soon have something hot to drink her insides would frieze.

Downstairs she heard girls' voices coming from the dining room but no sound from the kitchen although a strong smell of onions emanated from the crack below the kitchen door. She wrinkled her nose and opened the door to the dining room where the onion smell had permeated even that large space, then found an empty chair beside two Wrens who smiled in greeting. Many of the girls were picking at the food and pulling faces before they gave up and set their knives and forks neatly together on their plates.

'This is really too bad,' a thin fair-haired girl said, peering into a tureen on the side table. 'On the face of it, Woburn Abbey is supposed to be one of the grandest houses in the country, but I can't believe it when you see what the cooks have given us.' She turned to the others. 'How can you eat that? It looks like last night's dinner.'

'It is,' a girl with a bad skin piped up. 'Apparently, that's what they do on this shift. They heat up yesterday's leftovers from the evening meal and keep it hot in the oven for hours, then serve it up for breakfast.'

'It's downright disgusting,' a young girl in a beautifully fashioned uniform spoke up. 'I don't know what Mummy and Daddy would say, but I'm going to report it to our CO.'

'It won't do any good,' another Wren said. 'I tried that one and was told I was lucky to have food at all. When she told me people in places like Malta were starving as so many Merchant Navy ships carrying food have been torpedoed before they get anywhere near the port, I felt rather ashamed and shut up.'

Although Rosie completely agreed with the sentiment, the onion smell this early in the day quelled any appetite she'd had. There was more grumbling at the block of margarine under the butter dish lid, but to Rosie it reminded her of home and she spread it on the cold toast and ate it with no bother at all. Sometimes, she thought, giving a secret smile, it didn't pay to be too posh.

Back in her cold attic bedroom, Rosie settled to write a letter home. One letter would have to do for everyone, although she'd send a separate little note to Poppy. All she could say in the letter was that she was safe and well and she was working with a nice crowd of people (she wouldn't mention Alice) and getting to grips with the job. Should she mention she was living in a grand house? Better not. Any clue like that might be traced to the Park. She'd just say she was living with several girls in one house near where she worked. That would be vague enough. She ended by saying she hoped they would write to her separately as she did feel a bit homesick now and then and telling them how much she missed them.

Poppy most of all.
She'd feel better after she wrote to her.

DARLING POPPY,

  I HOPE YOU ARE BEING A GOOD GIRL AND DOING WELL AT SCHOOL. I ALSO HOPE YOU STILL HAVE YOUR NEW FRIEND. HOW IS YOUR READING? AM SURE HEATHER AND IVY WILL HELP YOU TO READ THIS LETTER IF YOU ASK THEM NICELY.

  I WOULD LOVE YOU TO SEND ME A PICTURE YOU HAVE PAINTED JUST FOR ME. CAN YOU DO THAT?

Rosie blinked back the tears. How she missed the child. Her green eyes, the colour of a blade of grass – the only one in the family with eyes that colour. But they were exactly like Hugo's. She swallowed and dipped her pen in the ink bottle.

  I LOVE YOU AND I'LL BE HOME BEFORE YOU KNOW IT.

  MOSEY XXXX

With her small box of crayons she drew some brightly coloured flowers around the edge of the half sheet of paper and on the bottom corners placed a brown dog on one and an orange cat on the other. Poppy had never stopped asking for a puppy or a kitten and didn't understand when Rosie had tried to explain that there wasn't enough money to feed an animal.

She popped the note into a separate envelope, smiling as she thought how thrilled the little girl would be to receive a letter with her name printed on the envelope. She only hoped Poppy would not keep her waiting too long before she sent a drawing back. As for now, she'd get the bus into town and have a wander round. She hadn't had much time to take it all in that first time when she'd met the blonde-haired girl called Dale. She fervently wished they'd bump into one another soon.

Chapter Seventeen

Strangely enough, that afternoon, she did spot Dale's golden-blonde head coming out of Hut 3 as Rosie was on her way to the café. Dale waved.

'How're you getting on?' she called.

'All right,' Rosie said, not really wanting to draw attention to herself with Alice walking towards her and frowning.

'You realise we don't talk to anyone outside our Hut,' she admonished as soon as she was close.

'I understood that only applied to talking about your work,' Rosie said, fighting a bubble of irritation.

Alice pulled her mouth tight. 'Well, just as long as you remember that.' She turned on her heel.

What was wrong with the woman? Rosie thought. Her mouth which was quite pretty when it was in repose, often had a sulky downturn. Rosie had crossed her fingers that being on a different shift might put her with different people, but no, Alice was still there, interfering, watching, nagging . . .

After her cup of tea, Rosie made her way slowly back to her Hut pondering as to why the woman treated her like an imbecile. When she entered the Watch Alice pounced on her.

'Oh, there you are,' she said.

As though I'm late, Rosie thought irritably.

'You're still rather slow with the paraphrasing,' Alice began. 'We need them done at a faster rate, so I've decided to let Sonia take over and put *you* in the Index Room.' She paused. 'They're desperate for help and you should be able to handle their simple procedure. Your training will take all of five minutes – that is, if you concentrate.'

Rosie flinched at the sarcasm. How many more different jobs was Alice going to mete out as though she were in charge? This one sounded very dull, like a filing clerk. It was exactly one of the replies she was allowed to use outside the Park when anyone, including family, asked why she hadn't joined up and if not, what work she was doing. Was Alice punishing her for something?

'I'll take you there now. You'll still be in this Hut,' Alice added, in a tone that said she wished it were otherwise.

She couldn't argue, Rosie told herself. She had to work where she was needed. But something didn't feel right. She thought she was making good progress on the message paraphrasing but obviously that wasn't Alice's opinion. She gritted her teeth. She wouldn't let the woman know she was unhappy with the decision. And the bonus was that she'd be out of Alice's vision. That would almost be worth the transfer.

The Index Room was only a couple of doors further along the corridor. Alice marched on ahead and without knocking opened the door. Three girls, two of them Wrens and one in civvies, raised their heads from a high table where they'd been bending over what looked like shoeboxes. The fourth girl, a WAAF, was using a narrow shelf to write on a small card. To Rosie's relief they all smiled.

'Oh, goody, you've brought someone to help,' a girl wearing thin rimless glasses on a chubby face spoke up.

'This is Rosemary,' Alice said. 'She's been with us a week or so but I think she'll be better suited at indexing.' She looked at Rosie. 'Well, I'll leave you to it.'

Rosie didn't know how to stop herself from saying 'good riddance'. She knew she was being childish, but really . . .

'Come and sit with us and we'll show you what we're doing,' a Wren with hair in a shining Victory Roll said. 'I'm Beryl, by the way, and this is Yvette – she's half French–' she winked at Rosie and gestured to the girl beside her who had dark brown wavy hair pulled up at the sides with tortoiseshell combs '– and sitting next to her is Vi, the only civilian so she's now got company.' Vi, her cherub face making her look the youngest in the room, had a mischievous twinkle in her eyes, even behind her glasses.

'And I'm last . . . as usual.' The WAAF stood up and grinned. 'But not least, I'm glad to say. I'm Diana. Pleased to meet you, Rosemary.'

'Oh, please call me Rosie,' Rosie said, stepping towards them.

'I bet you're glad to be out of Alice's clutches,' Beryl said with a chuckle, shifting along to make a space for her. 'God, she's a tartar. Far too big for her bossy boots. I did a fortnight with her once and it was enough for me.'

Rosie couldn't help it. 'Gosh, if only I'd been strong enough to have endured it that long,' she uttered in a bland tone.

The four girls broke into laughter and Rosie joined it. So it wasn't just *her* Alice had it in for. It looked as though the Index girls had Alice's number and suddenly her whole posture relaxed.

'Right, enough of the hilarity,' Beryl said. 'Everyone carry on and I'll show Rosie what to do.' She turned to Rosie. 'There's always tons more than we can get through in a day, but another pair of hands and eyes will make all the difference.' She paused and removed a piece of paper from one of the rectangular boxes. 'See this.' She pointed to the strips stuck onto the sheet. 'They come off a teleprinter. That's what all the noise in the Hut is mostly from – dozens of teleprinters bashing away. The messages have already been translated into English and we have to read them, then write down the main points on an index card like this –' she showed one to Rosie '– such as the person who sent the message which might name a captain or maybe a harbour master. That's vital. And where it's going. The name of the recipient, if it tells you. Then you want the name of the ship, and any other information that strikes you as important – any strategic movements . . . that sort of thing.' She looked at Rosie. 'Have you got that?'

'Yes – it makes sense.'

'Then you have to write all that down in a different order on another card with an appropriate heading and the date, then filed, so both cards can be cross-referenced.'

'How will I know what sort of heading to pick out?'

'We'll show you some samples. It really isn't difficult work but more important than some people give us credit.' She looked at Rosie with a wry smile. 'Sometimes someone from one of the other rooms – or occasionally from Hut 8 – asks if we've got any details of where a certain ship is heading, or they might only have the name of a captain or location – that's where the cross-referencing comes into its own. It builds up a picture for the cryptographers. You'll find when you get used to it that when someone gives you the name of a ship or person it will suddenly ring a bell and it won't take you more than a minute to find the card with the information they need. But if they ask to take the card out of the room, make sure they make a note in the book and sign for it. And keep an eye until it comes back – we don't like it out of our sight for more than 24 hours – then tick this column.' She showed Rosie a large, lined notebook with ruled pencilled columns. 'This book must be kept meticulously.' She glanced at Rosie. 'Now, let's get you started.'

The atmosphere in the Index Room was so different from the Watch. All four girls were cheerful and friendly, although Yvette was the shy one and quiet. She reminded Rosie a little of Ivy. Like her youngest sister, there was probably more to her than met the eye.

After two days Rosie began to get the measure of the work she was doing. It hadn't sounded particularly important the way Alice had described it – almost as though it was a comedown on the paraphrasing she had been doing, but she had a strong feeling she was cross-referencing information that few other people would see or know about. She hoped it would provide vital information to the person it was meant for. Yes, the work itself was monotonous in that there was no variation in the method of the cross-referencing, but when one of the cryptographers had just that morning poked his head through the hatch and asked if there was any information on the *Littorio*, Italy's lead battleship, she'd been able to quickly retrieve the two pertinent index cards, to include a previous signal from that same captain stating his position in the Mediterranean and asking for further orders.

He peered at them. 'These are just the ticket,' he said with a grin and a thumbs up as he'd hurried away.

I'm probably guessing, she thought, reaching for the next telex strip to note the important points on an index card, but these messages must have been originally sent in German or Italian code. And I bet the codes are being broken right here at the Park – maybe even in this Hut before they're translated into English. These could be important manoeuvres, which were obviously passed on to the Navy, and might even alter the course of the war. Her pulse quickened at the idea.

Oh, if only she knew for sure. She chewed her lip. Surely there was no harm in asking.

'Beryl, where do these messages originally come from?'

For once Beryl looked askance. 'Why do you want to know?'

'Well, I suppose I just like to understand things. I think if you know more about the job you're doing it makes it more interesting . . . don't you?'

Beryl raised her eyebrows. 'When you worked in the Watch, did Alice say anything about the rule of asking questions?'

'She wasn't particularly forthcoming about anything.'

'Mmm, sounds like her,' Beryl said, lighting a cigarette. 'I'd better warn you though, Rosie. The mantra at the Park is – do you need to know in order to do the job efficiently?' Before waiting for Rosie's reply, she went on, 'If not, don't ask.' She inhaled deeply and blew out a stream of smoke. 'I imagine Alice played down the importance of our job in the Index Room, but I reckon it helps the analysts no end in putting together all the information like a jigsaw puzzle and then making sense of it. Where it comes from, we're never told. Same as wondering how they use it. We'll never know that either, even though we'd dearly love to.'

Rosie had to be satisfied with that snippet of explanation.

'Time for a cuppa?' Beryl announced after Rosie and the others had been working silently for nearly three hours. 'Who's dying for one?'

'You obviously are,' Diana chuckled. 'Why don't you take Rosie and Vi and when you come back Yvette and I will go.'

Rosie gratefully got to her feet and stretched her back and neck. Doing such close work and keeping her handwriting as small and clear as possible, and not letting anything slip that ought to be registered on the cards, her eyes had begun to sting and then water. She dabbed them with her handkerchief and looked at her watch. Twenty to seven in the evening. A strange time for a tea break but they'd be eating supper at half-past nine. She wondered how long it would take her stomach to get used to it. Ah, well, it was only for a week. But the next shift was even worse, they said. Midnight until eight the following morning.

'Right-o, we shan't be long,' Beryl said, stubbing out one of her constant cigarettes. 'Come on, you two.'

The corridor was too narrow for more than two abreast, so Rosie stood back to let Beryl and Vi walk in front. Several of the workers probably had the same idea as they broke out of different doors to make their way to the entrance. There was much chatter and laughter and Rosie hoped it wouldn't be too long before she felt comfortable enough to relax with her co-workers in the same way. Beryl called out to Alice who was among one of the groups, but the woman just turned her head to nod and strode off. Rosie watched as Alice opened the front door, then stepped aside to let in a man in naval uniform.

He was a tall, broad-shouldered officer, his head bent, reading from a sheaf of papers, seemingly unaware of several people trying to get round him and outside. She saw Beryl and Vi give him a glance as they drew against the wall to allow him to pass. Seconds later he came into full view.

Every muscle in Rosie's body went tight. It was impossible. She was seeing things with all that eyestrain.

The top part of his face was hidden under the peak of his cap, bent over as he was, but she would stake her life on it – it was Hugo!

Chapter Eighteen

It couldn't be. But she knew she wasn't mistaken. She'd know that purposeful walk, the set of his chin, the long fingers holding his papers. She'd know him anywhere, however long ago she'd last seen him. In these few seconds there was no one between them. She wanted to flee – run anywhere – but she had to keep calm. Turn her face away. Her heart thumping sickeningly in her chest, she managed to open her handbag, pretending to look for something, so her own face would be hidden. But out of the corner of her eye she noticed him fractionally raise his head to glance at her as he passed by. She fancied she could smell the very scent of him. Feel the force of his personality.

Had his step faltered? It might have, but maybe only in her imagination. That meant he hadn't recognised her. And why should he? It was six years ago. She was no longer the schoolgirl madly in love with him but a twenty-three-year-old woman who had changed out of recognition. It had probably only been a schoolgirl crush anyway, she'd often told herself – the only consolation was that she'd had her darling Poppy. But if that was the case, then why had her heart banged so loudly just now? She supposed it was the sudden shock of seeing him. Her temper suddenly flared. What the hell was he doing here of all places? She knew she was being ridiculous. He had as much right to be here as she did. But after all these years . . . What on earth should she do?

With that glance, had he given any thought to the woman he'd just walked by? If only she could have seen his expression. Might he have thought she reminded him of someone? Probably not. Even her hair was different now. How he'd loved her red wavy hair. She remembered how he would bury his face in it. 'Never cut it,' he used to say. 'It's so beautiful and sexy . . . like the Pre-Raphaelites.' But in the factory she'd had to wear her hair up and under a white cap. She'd come to like the feel of it off her face and neck and had kept the style, at once feeling more grown-up. Poppy didn't like it, though, and was forever trying to pull out the pins.

Rosie swallowed hard, her chest tight, hardly able to breathe. It felt as if the corridor was closing in on her. She put her hand out and flattened it against the wall, desperate to steady herself, her brain zigzagging with fury. Was it possible she could bump into him again? If so, it might not be so easy to avoid him. Dear Lord, he was the last person she wanted to see and no doubt he'd feel the same about her. Plagued with guilt, I expect, she thought contemptuously. She could hear women's voices behind her and breathed out. There was no need to worry. This place was teeming with staff. She wouldn't come across him again.

Put him right out of your mind, she ordered. Beryl was holding the front door open for her.

'Come on, slowcoach,' Beryl said. 'They'll be out of tea at this rate. And we only have fifteen minutes.'

Rosie licked her dry lips. More than anything she was dying for a cup of tea after all that concentration this afternoon. She wouldn't admit it was Hugo who'd made her feel so shaken up. She glanced at her watch to clock the time.

176

But the watch only triggered her mind to replay the figure of Hugo striding towards her in the corridor. He'd filled out from the boy she remembered, though his face, the little she could see when he'd glanced at her, had looked drawn, as though he didn't sleep well.

Don't think like that, she told herself sharply. *His sleeping habits are nothing to do with you.*

She hoped against hope that he was merely a visitor at the Park and would soon be gone. But until she knew for sure where he was, she didn't think she'd have a moment's peace.

In the café she looked round wildly. There was no sign of him as far as she could tell in the fug of smoke. Thank God.

'Grab that table and I'll get the teas,' Beryl said. She looked at Rosie. 'Sugar?'

'I've given up.' Rosie unclasped her bag and took out her purse.

'I'm getting them.' Beryl vanished.

'You're ever so pale, Rosie,' Vi said when they sat down. 'As though you've seen a ghost.'

Rosie startled. 'What? Oh, sorry.'

'You were miles away,' Vi chuckled. 'I think the ghost was that tall naval officer. I'm talking about the one who just now came into our Hut,' she added when Rosie didn't reply.

Rosie gave a shudder. Vi would never know how very near the truth she was.

'Um, no, I didn't see anyone especially.'

'Hmm,' Vi said. 'I'm not sure I believe you. He was gorgeous.' She made a moue of her lips.

Oh, Vi, please don't keep on.

'Are you sure you're all right?' Vi put her own handbag on the empty seat beside her.

'Of course.' Desperate to change the subject she looked at Vi. 'Are you really a Violet?'

'Yes,' Vi laughed. 'And me mam calls me Violet when she's cross with me.'

'Parents always do that,' Rosie smiled.

'I was very nearly called Rose,' Vi went on. 'Aunt Rose wanted me to be named after her.'

Rose. That was the name Hugo always called her.

'But me mam loves violets. So me little sister got Rose instead, and I'm Violet, but I prefer Vi. Sounds more friendly.' She stared at Rosie. 'What about you?'

'I'm the eldest, Rosemary, known as Rosie, my next sister is Heather, the next one Ivy, and my baby sister –' she gulped '– is Poppy. So we're all plants and flowers, too – well, all except Roddy, my young brother.' She forced a smile. 'I don't think he'd have appreciated keeping up with the tradition.'

Vi giggled. 'I don't suppose he would.'

They chatted about their families until Beryl came back with a tray of tea.

'All the cakes had gone,' she said. 'But I managed to get us a bar of Kit Kat between us. We'll toss a coin for the last strip.'

No sooner had they put their empty cups down on the saucers than Beryl announced the quarter of an hour was up. They grabbed their bags and walked over to Hut 4 but as soon as they stepped into the corridor Rosie felt her stomach turn when she spotted two more naval officers walking towards her, deep in conversation. But neither of them was Hugo. She let out a jagged breath. This was a problem she'd never dreamt she'd have to face. She could only pray that if he wasn't a visitor, wherever he worked was the furthest possible point away from Hut 4.

'Okay, you two,' Beryl addressed Diana and Yvette. 'You

can buzz off.' She turned to Rosie, studying her. 'Rosie, you look quite peaky. You haven't had bad news or anything, have you?'

Only the worst shock ever.

'No, I'm fine. I think it's trying to adjust to this night shift. I'll be all right.'

'Hmm.' Beryl sounded as though she didn't believe her.

The three girls worked in silence, joined by Diana and Yvette, until it was suppertime.

'We can all go together.' Beryl stood up.

'I'll wait until you come back,' said Diana. 'I just want to finish this pile.'

'I'll wait with you,' Rosie quickly said.

'I don't like leaving just two of you on your own at night. It's against the rules, for one thing.'

'What on earth do you think is going to happen to us?' Diana said, grinning.

Beryl hesitated, then seemed to make her mind up. 'All right. We shan't be long.' She paused at the door. 'By the way, the new head of the Italian Naval Sub-Section is starting tomorrow so we'd better mind our p's and q's.'

'What's his name?' Diana asked.

'I'm not sure. It'll be on the door by now. Anyway, see you in a bit.'

Rosie thought she might sink through the floor. It would be the worst possible nightmare if Hugo Garfield was to be head of Hut 4 – overseeing everyone . . . overseeing her.

Her whole body trembled with the idea. How dare he walk calmly back into her life after all these years? Then she took hold of herself. He would have had no idea she'd be working here either. And anyway she was making assumptions before she knew for certain. The only thing was to check whose name was on the door. She forced

179

herself to concentrate on the index cards until the others came back.

'Ooh, I was getting hungry,' Diana said. 'Come on, Rosie.'

'You carry on,' Rosie said. 'I'm just going to spend a penny.'

She put the cards she'd been working on in a neat pile to file later, giving Diana a few moments to be outside. Then she picked up her bag and stepped into the corridor. There were a few people going in and out, but Rosie simply smiled as she walked towards the other end of the corridor, looking at the doors on either side. She'd never bothered before to look at other names at this end of the corridor.

She noticed Frank Birch, Head of Naval Section, and although she'd never met him, she knew his name and there'd been no rumour that he was leaving. She walked on. And there it was. Hugo . . . She swallowed hard, then blinked. No, it wasn't Hugo at all, it was Hugh. Hugh Gubbins, Head of Italian Naval Sub-Section. Same initials but not Hugo bloody Garfield, thank God. Pursing her lips to blow out her sigh of relief, and thoroughly annoyed with herself for over-reacting, she hurried to the canteen, her stomach rolling in protest that the strip of Kit Kat at seven had done a poor holding job.

Once in the canteen, warmth emanated from the ovens in the kitchen and although Rosie appreciated her limbs thawing out, she couldn't help scouring the room for any sign of Hugo. If she kept up this obsession with trying to locate his every movement from now on, she'd go barmy, she thought grimly as she picked up her tray of food. She'd see if she could spot Diana. Take her mind off him. But Diana was on a packed table deep in conversation with several men and women. She heard a voice close by.

'Rosie, do come and sit with me.'

She spun round and there was Dale beaming at her. Only

180

a morose-looking young man was sitting at her table, staring into space. Gladly Rosie slipped into an empty seat, deliberately picking the one with its back to the door, telling herself if he really did work at the Park she couldn't go being on edge the whole time.

'How nice to have a chance for a chat,' Dale said, 'though unfortunately I only have a few more minutes.' She took the last mouthful of food and set her knife and fork down. 'So tell me how you're getting on.'

'I've already been transferred,' Rosie said, a little shamefacedly. 'Apparently, I wasn't fast enough at the job.'

Dale raised an eyebrow. 'Are you still in the same Hut?'

'Yes, but doing something completely different with a very nice group of girls.'

'That makes all the difference if you get on with who you're working with,' Dale said with feeling.

Had Dale once had trouble with a member of staff here?

'Let's talk about something else,' Dale continued, her features relaxing. 'Do you ice-skate, by any chance?'

'No.' She wouldn't say there was no money at home for such luxuries.

'Well, they expect the lake to freeze over tonight, so people will be taking full advantage tomorrow.'

'Will you?'

'Oh, yes. I adore ice-skating.'

Rosie fought down a spike of envy. How wonderful to have the time and luxury for things like ice-skating. She wondered if there was any possibility she could learn in their time off. It did sound rather tempting. But where could she find some skates?

'They have a few pairs of skates here,' Dale said, seeming to read her thoughts, 'and I'm sure someone would be happy to teach you. *I* will if our shifts coincide one afternoon.'

At that moment the canteen door opened. Rosie couldn't help herself. Trying to appear casual, she twisted her neck round as several men and women entered. One man stood head and shoulders above the others. She snapped her head back to answer Dale. He mustn't recognise her.

'Oh, I-I'd love that,' she stuttered, her face feeling as though it were on fire.

Dale's eyes narrowed, then peered over to the canteen bar. But when she turned back, to Rosie's relief, she didn't make any comment, glancing instead at her watch.

'I'd better go. I'm already five minutes late. Thankfully, I work with a super team as well but I don't like to take advantage.' She jumped to her feet and at the same time the sad-looking young man rose, nodded to the two women and left.

Don't go yet, Dale. Don't leave me on my own with three spare seats.

'Perhaps the next time I see you I'll either be giving you a lesson or you'll be skating like a pro,' Dale said, smiling.

'I doubt that.'

But Dale had gone.

Rosie kept her head down and began to tackle the macaroni cheese and yellowing cabbage, but every mouthful felt as though she would choke, knowing Hugo was in the vast room. After a few pathetic attempts she put her knife and fork together. She couldn't help it. She glanced round. His tray in his hands, Hugo was staring straight at her.

Tension crackled between them, even from across the room.

Then he strode purposefully towards her now empty table.

'May I take this seat?'

His voice. She never thought she'd hear it again. It was only one of the things about him she adored – *had* adored, she quickly amended. His beautiful, modulated voice, which when amused would become full of laughter.

She wouldn't catch his eye – just in case he hadn't recognised her. But she knew he had.

'If you must,' she said.

'Yes, I must.'

He set the tray on the table and took the seat opposite her.

'Rose, it *was* you I passed in the corridor, wasn't it?'

She shot to her feet and grabbed her bag.

'Hugo, I don't want to make a scene –' she was gratified to see his eyes widen '– but I'd be grateful if you don't approach me any more. As far as I'm concerned, we don't know each other – we've never met.'

Feeling his eyes watching her, even though her back was turned, she stalked off, her head high.

She would never, ever let him know how much he'd hurt her . . . how much his very presence was like a knife piercing her heart.

Chapter Nineteen

Hugo watched her march away from him. She'd always been very pretty with her sensuous mouth and hazel eyes with those gold flecks that could spark with temper. Now she was stunning. She'd changed from an intelligent and delightful young girl on the brink of adulthood to a devastatingly attractive woman – in fact, the most beautiful woman he'd ever laid eyes on. But those eyes . . . deep hurt shone from them. She'd looked at him as if he were one of Hitler's Nazis. A familiar stab of guilt washed over him at the terrible way he'd treated her. But what more could he have done? He'd sent her a telegram on their wedding day to tell her about his father. She'd never answered. And he'd never heard from her again.

Hugo's fists tightened in frustration. He felt a strange pricking at the back of his eyes as the last six years melted away.

'You're making a serious mistake, my boy,' his father said as he entered his son's bedroom.

'Bit late for a lecture now a week before my wedding day,' Hugo replied.

'Are you absolutely certain you haven't got her into trouble? Because my offer still stands to take care of everything. I can arrange for her to see a physician and no one will be any the wiser. And give her a substantial sum of money. Her family could do with it, I'm sure. Or it would pay for her further education if she's as bright as you say she is. All you have to do is go and explain to her that you're calling off the wedding.'

Hugo could hardly contain his fury. His father could go to hell – Rose had far more pride than to take his blood money. He opened his mouth but his father put the palm of his hand up.

'Because, frankly, Hugo, your mother and I don't believe it. Her father would never let her marry at such a young age if she wasn't pregnant. I spoke to him about it when we all went out for supper that time. He said categorically he wouldn't allow his daughter to marry until she was at least nineteen and by then you'd be twenty-three and would have worked your way up in the business.'

'Well, he's changed his mind. And at least *Rose*'s family is attending. Which is a hell of a lot more than *my* family intend to do.' Hugo's lip curled. 'And if she is or she isn't having a baby – and I know categorically she's not – I still want to marry her. It makes no difference to me. I want her to be my wife. You keep going on about how young we are, but I don't see much love between you and Mother, and you were thirty and she was twenty-eight when you married. Maybe you were in love once but have since forgotten how it feels. Rose and I love each other, and we always will, no matter that you and Mother don't approve.'

Hugo noticed his father flush. 'Well, I just hope you know what you're doing. And whatever you hope for, I won't be changing my mind on the will. Marry this girl and you won't get another penny from me.'

Hugo spun round on his heel.

'I haven't forgotten – *Father*. And I don't hope for anything from you . . . or Mother.'

'You've broken your mother's heart – you know that, don't you?'

'I know nothing of the kind – only that Mother's always been too weak to stand up to your bullying. She'd come to the wedding if she could but she's helpless now she's in a wheelchair.'

'She feels the same as I do about this whole business.' He stared at Hugo. 'You've broken *my* heart, too, Hugo.'

'Don't make me laugh. You're as hard as nails.'

'Don't insult me. I *do* have a heart. Your brother isn't interested in the business so I longed for the day when *you'd* be old enough to take over and I could lessen my responsibilities. Take things a bit easy, for a change, since I had that scare last month.'

'Are you trying to make me feel guilty?'

He glared at Hugo. 'I've worked damned hard for you and your brother–'

'No one's saying you didn't.'

'–to give you both a good education and a tidy sum behind you,' Edmund Garfield said, ignoring him, 'but your brother just turned his nose up at it. But you, Hugo, were always interested in the business.'

'I wasn't . . . particularly. Since Lance told you years ago he wasn't going to join the company I knew it was what you expected of me once I finished university. I can't say in all truth that Garfield and Clarke's Insurance Services sets my soul alight. But I *was* willing to give it a go. Until I found that the girl I loved would never meet with your approval, so frankly I want no more to do with it.'

'What will you do? Where will you live?'

'That's none of your damned business. You've washed your hands of me.'

*   *   *

186

The trouble was, they hadn't had anywhere to live, Hugo thought, his food still untouched in Bletchley Park's canteen. But Rose's beloved Aunt Dot had said they could stay with her at least for a few weeks until they found some rooms to rent. But they hadn't been able to take up her kind offer. His father had managed to stop the wedding by having a major heart attack just ninety minutes before the wedding ceremony. And Hugo had only just squeezed in a telephone call to send Rose a telegram explaining the wedding would have to be postponed, due to a family emergency. Then the ambulance arrived and he and his mother followed in Hugo's car. Early the following morning his father died. By the time Hugo and his mother arrived home, he'd found the letter from Rose's father waiting on the mat that he or someone else had delivered by hand.

He could quote it word for word.

Rosemary asked me to tell you she never wants to hear from you again. She realises she is too young to know her own mind and intends to continue her studies and her mother and I agree. If you interfere with her education and her future you will have me to deal with, and I will have no hesitation in taking things further.

Nauseated by the congealing macaroni cheese, Hugo put his plate back on the tray and with a deep sigh stood. He slid the tray onto the rack, then turned and walked out of the warm canteen and into a blast of bitter cold air that felt like a slap in the face.

Chapter Twenty

Rosie made her way back to her Hut. She'd only just managed to keep up the front of being in control as far as Hugo was concerned. Her heart thudded in her ears with every step she took. She must keep calm. He wasn't going to be working in Hut 4. He wasn't Head of the Italian Section. That was a Hugh Gubbins. She didn't have to worry. All right, it looked as though he worked somewhere at the Park – but not here, she thought, as she pushed open the door to Hut 4. Diana had mentioned Hut 8 worked closely with Hut 4 so that's where he'd be. And if she did bump into him again she would simply look through him. She'd meant what she'd said. She didn't know him any more.

'Where did you get to?' Diana said. 'I'd saved you a seat. Didn't you see me?'

'The table looked packed,' she said. 'But I was fine. Someone I'd met once before in the café called me over. A really nice girl called Dale Treadwell. She works in Hut 3.'

'I know Dale slightly,' Beryl said. 'We sat next to each other at a concert last month. She's good company.' She looked round. 'Right, everyone, let's get our heads down and get this pile finished before we go off duty.' She paused. 'By the way, we now know who's taking over.' She looked at Rosie. 'We had Hugh Gubbins, Head of the Italian Sub-Section

– nice man, always kind and helpful, although we didn't see much of him – but he's been diagnosed with cancer, poor old chap, so he's been discharged. Funnily enough, this one's initials are the same – HG for Hugo Garfield . . . or rather Lieutenant Commander Hugo Garfield. He's in charge of Intelligence, and that includes our Index Room, so we must endeavour to look intelligent – '

From far away Rosie heard the others giggle, but her ears were roaring. Her worst fear was realised. She bit her lower lip so hard to stop herself from crying out, she tasted blood. She thought she was going to be sick.

'– when he comes in to introduce himself,' Beryl ran on. 'And, would you believe, Vi and I . . . oh, and Rosie, you were there, too . . . we three have already met him. Alice pointed him out.' She looked at Rosie, who was silent. 'He was the tall, dark and handsome naval officer who we all thought was gorgeous. You couldn't have forgotten *him*,' she persisted when Rosie didn't respond.

'So we've got that treat still to come,' Diana chuckled.

She was trapped. Trapped at Bletchley Park for the duration of the war. No one could save her. He would make her life a misery. Dear God. How was she going to stand it? She had to get out of the room, take some deep breaths and pull herself together before she broke down in front of everyone.

'Oh, yes, I remember,' she said, her voice shaking. 'Beryl, I've got an awful headache. Do you mind if I go and get a drink of water?'

'I *knew* something was the matter with you,' Beryl said. 'You just stay there. I'll get some water . . . and a couple of Aspros. Shan't be a jiffy.'

No, Beryl, not that way round. I need to get out of here for a few minutes.

But it was too late to say anything. Beryl had disappeared.

'What is wrong, Rosie?' It was Yvette looking concerned.

'Oh, nothing a couple of aspirin won't cure.' She tried to sound casual but her voice cracked.

Rosie took one of the index cards and looked at it but the words swam together. For heaven's sake, it was in English, she reprimanded herself. She forced herself to focus but by now the fictitious headache had turned into a real one, and she was relieved when Beryl appeared with a glass of water in her hand and a strip of Aspros.

'Take two,' she said, handing them to Rosie.

'Thanks.'

'Is anything at home worrying you?' Beryl asked as she watched Rosie swallow the tablets.

'I do worry about them – mostly Mum and my . . . youngest sister, Poppy. She's only five and I seem to be her favourite. Well, I looked after her full-time her first years because Mum wasn't in very good health.'

'I expect she thinks of you as a second mother with such a big age gap,' Vi said, overhearing. 'Like I used to be with my young'uns.'

Rosie swallowed hard. 'Perhaps you're right. Mum used to say Poppy missed me terribly when I went out to work and she hadn't started school, but now—' She broke off, tears filling her eyes, and blew her nose. 'It's just that I can't bear to think of her crying and asking where I am and when I'm coming home.'

'Well, you'll have to wait a few months before you get some leave,' Beryl said. 'Have you written to her?'

'Oh, yes. And I wanted her to draw me a picture, but she's not done so.'

'She *will* do,' Vi said. 'It's just at the beginning when you go. I think they're in shock, and when they're that young they don't understand how long or short time is when you try to explain when you'll be back.'

Vi seemed to speak out of experience. Maybe that was it. Maybe it was because she was missing Poppy so much that it was making her even more on edge than she might have been, and when she'd seen Hugo so unexpectedly it had been the final emotional straw.

'We're on the midnight shift tomorrow,' Beryl said. 'What say we go ice-skating on the lake tomorrow afternoon?'

'Not for me,' Diana said. 'I'm going to go for walks, then rest, and read and read until I go cross-eyed . . . though they're like that permanently from working in here.'

The others laughed.

'I will come,' Yvette said. 'The first time I did this was in France.' She shook her head. 'It was the last time. I was not very good. But I will try again.'

'Vi?' Beryl said.

'I'm game but I've never done it before. I'll probably fall over in the first few minutes.'

Beryl laughed and turned to Rosie. 'What about you, Rosie? Can you skate?'

'I've never tried, and I'm not sure I'd be any good.'

'Pity. The fresh air always helps to keep us awake for the night shifts.'

'I think I'll take a leaf out of Diana's book, literally, and have a good read, and write another letter to Poppy. Maybe go to the pictures.'

'If you fancy some company, I'll come with you,' Diana said.

'Before we all get carried away,' Beryl said, 'we'd better get on with some work. We don't want to present the new boss with an empty shoebox of index cards.'

There was silence in the room except for scratching of

pens and the occasional rattle of Vi's charm bracelet as her thin hand picked out another card. Rosie shook her head to try to clear the muddled thoughts that had collected since Beryl's announcement about Hugo. Taking the next sheet of paper with the teleprinted tape she began another monotonous session of filling in hundreds of blank index cards.

Every time someone lifted the hatch or came in the door for some information, Rosie's heart jumped to her throat. She willed herself not to look up when someone lifted the hatch just before the end of their shift. But it wasn't Hugo. Another man needing information on Italian ships in the Mediterranean. She breathed out. Hugo wouldn't look through the hatch; he'd come in. She had to stop this. She'd go crazy. But it would happen sooner or later, and she had to be prepared.

At the stroke of midnight, to Rosie's relief, Beryl said, 'Right, everyone. I'm tired. I think we all are. So we'll see one another on the midnight shift tomorrow.' She looked at Rosie. 'That's midnight to eight in the morning and I'm warning you it's a killer. Your stomach will be all over the place. So be prepared.'

It was as though Beryl had tapped right into her very thoughts. But it was nothing to do with working through, for the first time, the midnight-to-eight shift.

The bus taking Rosie and the usual crowd of Wrens to Woburn Abbey just after midnight was packed. Some of them nodded to her in recognition but they were soon chattering amongst themselves. She couldn't really blame them. They were in the military, and she wasn't. They would have completely ignored her if they found out she'd once been a Wren and then dismissed for lying. It was so unfair. Then she stopped herself. She mustn't moan. It was unfair that young men had to go and fight and lose their limbs and even their lives. She had it lucky. She had food and shelter – even though her room was freezing cold, she thought with a wry smile – and she had a job which was a small but apparently vital part of the war effort. When she considered the bigger picture, Hugo was just a minor irritation.

But with all that telling herself off, when she'd quickly cleaned her teeth and wearily got into bed, a feeling of unutterable loneliness swept over her.

Much as she tried to stop them, the tears flowed.

The next morning Rosie surveyed herself in the small, cracked mirror above the wash basin. Her eyes were still pink from her miserable night. She *had* to pull herself together, she told herself sternly. Or did she want to be shamefully dismissed from Bletchley Park? Because if so, that was where she was heading.

In the splendid dining room she picked at the unsplendid leftovers from what would have been the previous shift's supper, grimacing at the cold steak and kidney pudding – mostly kidneys – and cooked-to-death Brussels sprouts. There was muttering and noises of disgust around her and several girls put down their cutlery before they'd anywhere near finished. Suddenly her temper rose. Why should they all be made to eat this stuff at this time of day? She threw down her knife and fork and shot to her feet.

'You do realise the men wouldn't put up with this,' she said. All eyes swivelled to her. 'In fact, I'm going to report the cooks for giving us last night's leftovers for our breakfast.'

'Good for you,' someone said.

'It won't do any good.' It was the sulky girl she'd once sat next to on the bus. 'Some of us have tried already.'

'Well, *I* haven't,' Rosie retorted. 'I'll set up a petition and we'll all sign. Then I'll take it to someone who has the authority to change it to porridge and toast.' She looked round, seeing a new respect in the eyes of those closest to her. 'Anyone against it or have any other suggestions?' She looked round to see Miss Sulky smirking. It gave her even more determination to show them.

'We'll sign,' several chorused.

A girl she knew as Peggy stood up. 'And I'll make sure *everyone* signs.'

'Right. I'll start the petition and we'll get it circulated.'

There was a murmur of approval.

'Anyone have any notepaper to spare?' Rosie asked, looking round the table. 'No? Then I'll pinch some from work.'

A couple of girls clapped and a few others joined in.

'Don't clap yet,' Rosie said, smiling. 'It might not work, but I'm going to have a damned good try.'

A few cheers followed her as she left the room, her mood completely changed now she was about to do something positive. She would get the menu – if you could call it such – changed for breakfast if it was the last thing she did.

Chapter Twenty-One

While the Wrens were circulating the petition, Rosie decided it was pointless to speak to anyone at the Abbey when some of the Wrens had already tried and been unsuccessful. The only recourse was to go to the canteen and speak to someone in charge there. They might not have any jurisdiction over Woburn Abbey but surely they could point her in the right direction. And it was unlikely she'd bump into Hugo as he would surely have finished breakfast by now. Afterwards, she'd call in to the Post Room to see whether she had any letters.

A white-overalled woman who was busy wiping down the counters looked up.

'Sorry, love, you're too late.'

'Oh, no, I've already eaten breakfast at my billet.' Rosie gave her a smile even though her stomach curdled at the memory of the lukewarm kidney pie. 'But I wondered if I could speak to the person in charge of the canteen.'

'Hmm.' The woman stared at her. 'Are you wantin' to make a complaint?'

'Um, no—'

'Because if you are I shan't be best pleased. We work hard to put good grub on the table—'

'No, really, it's not that.'

'Good. Then I'll see if he's there.'

She was back in a couple of minutes with an older man wearing a worn suit, his tie skew-whiff.

'Yes, miss?' he said, looking her up and down. 'What can I do for you?'

The woman hovered but he merely turned to her. 'Thank you, Doreen.' She scuttled off.

'You may not be the right person to speak to,' Rosie began, 'but I'm billeted at Woburn Abbey, and on our shift that finishes at midnight, we're served leftovers from supper for our breakfast the following morning. It's lukewarm, dried up and frankly unappetising, especially that early in the day.' When he didn't comment, she said, 'I was wondering if you know who oversees the kitchen at Woburn Abbey.'

'They're all Wrens there, aren't they?'

'Yes.'

'Why don't you speak to your PO?'

'Because I'm not a . . . Wren.'

He squinted at her. 'Then you should get one of *them* to speak to their PO.'

'They already have – she says there's nothing she can do. It's the cooks who decide the menus.'

'Well, we can't waste food.' He lit a cigarette and frowned. 'I'm afraid it's a military matter. The cooks will be in the WRNS so there's nothing I can do. I'm sorry.' He looked at her. 'Why don't you speak to your boss? If he's in the Navy he might be able to put in a word.' With that he walked off.

Hugo? He'd be the last person she'd want to ask – and on such a petty matter. But it wasn't petty. They all needed their proper food in order to do a good job. Besides, she'd promised the Wrens she would see that it was altered. If she hadn't known Hugo, she wouldn't have hesitated. She scolded herself.

You'll have to face him sooner or later about something. He's here to stay – same as you.

But if he was on a different shift, she wouldn't know his whereabouts. Should she scrap the idea? Tell the girls she'd tried? But she so badly wanted to stick to her word. If it came to it, she could put a note under his door.

Rosie felt restless through the morning. She went for a walk to Fenny Stratford, a small village with some pretty buildings in the High Street. She had a wander, then walked back to the Park. Should she go to Woburn Abbey and have a nap? But she wasn't that tired. Maybe she'd go to the Park's library and see if they had any Italian books she could borrow. Her stomach rolled. She realised she'd only had a few mouthfuls of that revolting breakfast. Her watch said ten minutes to twelve. She'd have to brave the canteen again as there was no café that she could see in Fenny Stratford.

Her heart beat a little faster as she walked into the canteen, praying there would be no sign of Hugo. So far so good. She looked at the various pans. Sausages seemed to be the main dish on the menu. They looked greasy but maybe the mashed potato would help soak them up. She didn't recognise anyone, so she made her way to a table with several men and women, all in the Air Force, chatting away. They were polite and friendly but clearly had much to talk about amongst themselves. Really hungry by now, she managed one of the pair of sausages and her mashed potato and tinned peas, then quietly rose to her feet murmuring her goodbyes, and left.

Now for the library. She was about to turn into the main house, longing to be inside the warm, when the sound of laughter and shouts caught her attention. It was coming from the lake. She'd wander over and see close to what this ice-skating lark was all about.

About a dozen figures, all bundled up, scarves flying, were whizzing over the lake's icy surface. They looked as though they were having great fun. When was the last time she'd felt happy and carefree? She stopped to watch. One girl was skating like a ballet dancer. She wore a short pleated white skirt and what looked like a thick knitted jacket with woolly hat to match. Rosie stared. It was Pamela, the girl who'd been on the platform when she'd first arrived at Bletchley in the dark. It was the first time she'd had sight of her since that night. When Pamela spun round to face her, Rosie waved. Pamela smiled and waved back. But it wasn't to her she was waving, Rosie realised. Someone else had joined the skaters. A burning sensation gripped her stomach. He mustn't see her standing alone while he was having fun . . . with another woman.

Too late. He turned and saw her. He gave a slight shake of his head as the flying figure of Pamela skidded to a halt in front of him, did a spin and took his arm, waltzing him off, leaving Rosie, her teeth clenched, gazing after them.

She saw nothing more of Hugo that day. The following afternoon she heard the clatter of typewriters as she stepped into the impressive panelled hall of the Mansion. Walking a few feet, she opened a door on the left marked 'Library'. She recognised it as the room she'd registered in just a fortnight ago, with its massive fireplace, heavily plastered ceiling and dark panelled walls and the musty, dusty smell of second-hand books hiding their secrets. The noise was coming from the six desks, all occupied by women who were typing furiously. No one paid any attention to her as she moved towards the bookshelves.

It was what she preferred. Happy she could quietly wander round, taking down a book here and there, she eventually found a shelf full of books about Italy. Mostly they were on Italian history, more than one examining the masterpieces of the Renaissance, which immediately reminded her of Signorina Bonetti at school. But she needed books in the Italian language.

'Try this one,' a low voice behind her said.

She swung round and stared into Hugo's eyes. Was this how it was going to be from now on? Not being able to go anywhere without him popping up? He was clever. He knew she couldn't speak her mind in the hallowed room of a library.

He handed her a book. 'It's not easy reading but it's fascinating and will help keep up your Italian.'

So he remembered.

'Thank you,' she said in an icy tone, not giving him the satisfaction of even glancing at it. Instead, she forced herself to look him in the eye, willing her hand not to shake as she accepted the slim volume.

He looked so damned handsome in his uniform. She swallowed hard. She mustn't think like this.

'Rose, I need to talk to you,' he said quietly.

'Well, *I* don't need to talk to you.'

'Please, Rose.'

'No!' Her voice cracked.

'Shhhhh!' An older woman hissed as she looked up from her typewriter.

Rosie mouthed, 'I'm sorry' and took the book over to one of the other desks where a younger woman looked more sympathetic.

'Just sign for it in that book.' She gestured to a large open book on the empty desk. 'Make sure you put today's date in.'

Rosie did as she was told, hardly able to contain her fury

that Hugo made no attempt to leave. He'd cut her lovely library visit short before she'd even got the measure of where all the categories were. Blast and damn him! And then a thought occurred to her. This was the opportunity to tell him about Woburn Abbey's revolting breakfasts. At least it might lead to something positive, and at the same time not allow him a chance for any further personal comments or pleas to rehash the past.

Outside he said, 'Rose, whatever you're thinking, I must tell you—'

'Hugo,' she kept her voice neutral, 'I need to ask you something.'

'Anything,' he said quickly. 'What is it, darling?'

She flinched. How dare he use that endearment.

'We'll go somewhere private.'

'What I have to ask doesn't require privacy,' she said matter-of-factly.

'Anything we say to one another must be private,' he said, fixing his eyes on her. 'So we'll go to my office.'

Maybe that was a good idea. It would be in an official setting. And that's how she must keep it.

'All right.'

She certainly wasn't going to walk a couple of paces behind him, she thought, as she matched his long strides in the narrow corridor of Hut 4 to the end. There, he opened the same door she'd seen with Hugh Gubbins' name on the brass plaque. Only this time it read 'Lt. Cdr. Hugo Garfield, Head of Italian Naval Sub-Section'. She could kick herself for not double-checking. He stood aside to let her pass through the tight space, but not far enough, so she was forced to brush against him. It was deliberate, she knew, as she caught sight of the corners of his well-shaped lips twitching into a smile. She forced down the bubble of anger at his nerve.

Hugo gestured towards the visitor's chair and shut the door. She didn't want to sit down with him behind the desk lording it over her. She gritted her teeth as she took the seat. But she was no longer a Wren. As a civilian, she knew – and *he* knew – he couldn't pull rank on her. For the first time since her humiliation at being dismissed from the WRNS she was glad not to be in the uniform she'd been so proud to wear. On the other hand, she *must* control the conversation and keep it official. No deviating. She had a request to make and if anyone could get the cooks at Woburn Abbey to change the breakfast menu, he could. It was just so annoying that the figures of him and Pamela skating off together were still swirling in her head.

'What did you want to ask me?' Hugo said.

'It's to do with my billet,' she said, triumphantly watching a flicker of disappointment cross his face.

'What's wrong with it?' he said. 'You should be more than comfortable at Woburn Abbey. It's only the second largest estate in the whole country. I'd be delighted to be billeted there.'

How did he know that's where she lived?

'It's not as luxurious as it appears.'

He raised an eyebrow. 'Oh?'

'But it's not that.'

She briefly explained the problem.

'We're all going to sign a petition,' she finished.

'I see,' Hugo said, frowning slightly. 'And you say you've spoken to the canteen manager?'

'Yes, I already told you.'

He sighed. 'I just want to get it straight. So you want *me* to have a word with the head cook at Woburn Abbey?'

Did he consider himself too high up to do something so lowly?

'Yes . . . we'd all be very grateful.' She kept her voice even.

'All right. I'll see what I can do. In the meantime, don't worry about the petition. I'll ask for it if I need it.' He looked at her with those green eyes, exactly the same colour as Poppy's. 'And in return for the favour, will you please listen to my explanation as to what happened—'

She shot to her feet. 'You don't need to explain anything. It's all in the past, Hugo. You must understand I'm here to do a job and I want to do it to the very best of my ability. In my wildest nightmare I never thought I'd bump into you at Bletchley Park of all places. And *I'm* not asking for a personal favour – we're talking about dozens of Wrens who work hard and need to start the day with a proper meal inside them. And I refuse to be blackmailed—'

'What on earth are you talking about?' He stood and came round from the desk, towering over her. 'I'm not blackmailing you. I'm just asking for a few minutes of your time.'

'I don't have a few minutes to spare,' she snapped. 'And by the way, don't *ever* call me "darling" again.'

She slammed the door behind her as hard as she dared, not caring who heard, and oblivious to several curious stares in the corridor.

Chapter Twenty-Two

It was still only three o'clock. The hours stretched in front of Rosie, mocking her. She wouldn't be on duty for nine more hours. What on earth could she do with herself? Maybe she should try to have a nap so she'd keep alert tonight but her attic bedroom at Woburn Abbey was freezing. Besides, she was still smarting under the audacity of Hugo's calling her request a 'favour', then having the cheek to call her 'darling'. She'd never fall asleep with that conversation in her ears. And although she and the Wrens were allowed to gather in the morning room and one of the smaller sitting rooms, she always felt the outsider. Perhaps she'd catch the bus into Bletchley and see what was on at the cinema. If Diana was anywhere around, she might still be game to join her for the early evening show.

Rosie waited where the buses collected but one of the drivers said there wouldn't be one going into town until the evening. She blew out her cheeks. For something to do she stopped by the Post Room to see if there were any letters. So far she'd only had the one letter from her mother saying how busy she was, but that everyone was well. It had told her nothing.

To her delight the postmaster handed her two envelopes. One from her mother – thank goodness for some news – the other from Whitehall. Hmm. Were they checking up on her? She decided to read them in the ballroom that staff were allowed to use for their leisure now that the teleprinters had been relocated to one of the concrete buildings in the grounds.

Like the rest of the interior of the Mansion, the ballroom was extravagantly decorated with its gold and white plaster ceiling set in squares, and gold-swagged curtains at the window. It was heavily panelled and had carved wooden columns dividing the spaces. She chose a leather armchair, one of a group arranged around a small gilded table. There were a few other people in the room, all of them reading. She saw Diana with her nose in a book but decided not to disturb her.

At least it was reasonably warm, she thought, as she opened the official letter and glanced at the signature. John. Her heart lifted. Someone normal. Kind. Thoughtful.

She read:

My dear Rosemary,

I'm writing this from work as I think the postmark has some influence in getting to you!

I'd love to know how you're getting on and if you're using your Italian. Obviously you can't say in what way, but I hope the work is interesting and fulfilling. Whatever job you're doing, always remember, even if it doesn't appear so, that it's vital to the war effort.

I have a few days' leave coming up next week and wondered if you'd like to meet in London for a show or a concert if your day off coincides with one of mine next week. It would be so good to see you again, but I perfectly understand if you're too busy or it doesn't appeal.

You can write to me at my home address.

Fond wishes,

John

Rosie skimmed the letter again. He was such a thoroughly nice man. But why didn't her heart make any sign that she could think of him in any way other than as a friend? But going to London! To the theatre. Oh, it sounded so tempting. She just didn't want him to get the wrong idea. He more than liked her, she knew. And it wasn't just the 'My dear Rosemary' or the 'Fond wishes'. She also knew that he would behave impeccably. She'd have a think before answering his letter.

Sighing, she opened her mother's.

Dear Rosie,

I'm sorry not to have written for a while but haven't felt too good lately. Probably overdoing it. Ivy is doing all she can to help me when she's not at work but it's not the same as having you here, too. I'm afraid Poppy is getting out of hand. She is playing up at school and becoming a difficult child. She won't even obey Dad. She keeps asking when is Mosey coming home. I say soon, but she isn't satisfied. She asked yesterday how long is soon?

Anxiety crawled up Rosie's arms. She should be looking after her own child. She should have told the truth to the authorities so she wouldn't have been called up. But her father had made her promise never to tell anyone. Yet someone knew. The person who'd reported her to the WRNS knew. That mystery wasn't going to go away. She set her jaw.

She'd find out one day who it was who'd interfered with her life and sent her in another direction where the past had roared in to meet her.

She shuddered. She must stop this train of thought. It was too dangerous. She loved working at the Park, though admittedly her job was straightforward and mundane. She only hoped that Hugo would have the decency to let her alone. But she was not sure she could rely on him to do that.

Well, she had plenty of time left today before she started again at midnight. She'd write to Poppy and to her mother . . . and if she was given a day off and it coincided with one of John's, she'd say yes to his kind invitation. Meantime, she'd have a glance at the book Hugo had picked for her: *Il Principe* by Niccolò Machiavelli – *The Prince* – his indisputable masterpiece. She opened it and was soon immersed in the beautiful Italian language. It might take her a while to get used to the more formal style of the sixteenth century but if Hugo thought she was capable of mastering it, she would.

After an hour's concentration she could feel her eyelids drooping. She ought to have gone back to Woburn Abbey and had a proper sleep. How foolish to think she could occupy herself all day and still be able to do her work accurately throughout the night. It was her last thought as the book slid from her hands, and she fell asleep in the chair.

'C'mon, Sleepyhead. Wake up.'

Rosie awoke with a start, trying to focus on Vi, who was grinning down at her. She blinked as she glanced at her watch. Goodness, it was already gone six. She licked her lips.

'I was just off to the café for tea,' Vi said. 'Want to come?'

'Exactly what I could do with,' Rosie said fervently. 'And a bar of chocolate to go with it.'

'They only had one Mars bar left so we'll have to halve it.'

'That's much better than when I'm home,' Rosie laughed. 'Mum cuts it up very carefully into five exact-sized pieces.'

'Me mam does exactly the same for all us lot – only in six.' Vi took the knife and cut through the bar. She handed a perfect half portion to Rosie. 'It'll probably make us feel sick to suddenly eat such a big piece,' she said giggling.

There'd been too many hours to kill. Rosie had ended up in her attic room at Woburn Abbey after all. Although the tea with Vi had perked her up, and she was pleased to learn a little more about her colleague, who'd come from a background similar to her own, the evening had looked interminable. There were still four and a half hours to go. She would try to have a proper sleep and if she had time she'd write to John Palmer and accept his invitation. Now she had a plan in mind she pulled off her skirt but left on her thick sweater, then crawled under the bedcovers.

There was a loud bell ringing in her ears. She jerked up. Was it a fire engine? Then she realised it was her alarm clock. Oh, no. It was already quarter-past eleven. She'd overslept. She'd meant to set it to quarter to, not quarter past. The bus left for the Park promptly at eleven-thirty. She had ten minutes to finish dressing, grab her comb and rush downstairs and out of the door. To her horror she saw the last two Wrens boarding and the bus door close behind them. Then with a roar of the engine it moved off.

No, it mustn't.

She tore down the drive waving and shouting, oblivious to the daytime Wrens who would be asleep by now. To her relief the bus stopped.

'You want to give yourself more time, miss,' he growled as he pulled away again before Rosie could stumble to an empty seat, heart pounding, thankful she had a double seat to herself. The Wrens were quiet at this time of night, many of them asleep, but they still looked smart in their uniforms and she knew she looked a wreck beside them. She gave her hair a quick comb, thankful her mother wasn't there to see her do it in public.

By the time the bus reached Bletchley Park, Rosie's heartbeat had steadied from her panic. She was ready to tackle anything as she walked into Hut 4 and hurried to the Index Room. She heard a peal of girlish laughter as she opened the door and looked straight into the eyes of Hugo Garfield, sitting on the edge of an empty table, his arms folded across his chest, her co-workers looking up at him adoringly. She immediately straightened her back.

'Ah, there you are,' he said, in a tone which said: *where the devil have you been*? He pointedly studied his watch.

'The clock struck midnight just as the bus came into the drive,' Rosie said, her cheeks flushing, 'so I can't be more than two minutes off.' She wouldn't use the word 'late'.

He cocked his head. 'And you're billeted where?'

He knew damned well where she was billeted. Oh, how she wanted to wipe that smug look off his face.

'Woburn Abbey,' she answered coolly. 'The second largest house in the country, so I've been told . . . only just a few hours ago.'

Judging by his deflated expression, she'd caught him off-guard. Then he seemed to collect himself.

'Hmm. It might make sense to catch the earlier bus.'

Rosie was aware of the curious gaze of her fellow workers, particularly Beryl's raised eyebrows. She smothered a sigh and merely nodded in response.

'Right, then, now we're *all* here I'll introduce myself again for the benefit of Miss Frost –' he sent a quick glance to Rosie who pretended she didn't see it '– I'm Lieutenant

Commander Hugo Garfield, overseeing the various sectors of Intelligence in the Italian Section. The Index Room is part of it. I realise filling in cards all day long might seem a monotonous job, but it's a vital one for the war effort. You may have been told some very brief details, but for Miss Frost's sake, as I understand she's new –' another glance at Rosie '– I'll enlighten you as much as I can. The index cards are very important. If you can supply us here with the correct information of the enemy's whereabouts in the Med – usually entailing submarines and U-boats – that one card and its cross-reference could have a huge bearing on the outcome of that potential conflict, which in turn could have an impact on the eventual outcome of the war itself. It might only take that one card one of you has meticulously filled in.' He looked at everyone in turn, his eye resting on Rosie's a fraction longer. 'Anyone got any questions?'

'Yes,' Rosie said, aware of Hugo regarding her closely. 'What happens to the information when it leaves the Park?'

'It gets transferred to the respective Admiral.'

'How does it get transferred?' Rosie continued.

He gave her a sharp look.

'Sorry, but I can't say. You'll have to take my word for it. You don't need to know any more to do the work efficiently. The less you know – and that goes for *everybody* working here at the Park – the better it is for our security. You've signed the Official Secrets Act, but you need to remind yourself daily, hourly, what that means.'

'Thank you,' Rosie forced her voice to sound neutral. He didn't need to have spelt it out like that, as though she were still at school, in front of the others.

But you'd only recently left school when he last knew you. He doesn't know you as a woman.

'Any other questions?'

'No, sir,' they chorused – all except Rosie.

She could have asked him a dozen questions but they would be completely unrelated to her work at Bletchley Park.

'Miss Frost?'

'No,' was all she said.

'By the way, there's very little hierarchy at the Park. And you're all young women, so I doubt you call one another by your surnames.' He paused. 'So unless anyone has any objections, I'll call you by your Christian names so we all feel we're part of the team.'

'No objections, as long as you're Hugo to us,' Vi called out cheekily.

Hugo's mouth quirked at the corners. 'All right – that's a deal, but only in this room.'

When he'd left the room there was a buzz of excitement.

'Aw, that mouth – just made for kissing,' Vi giggled.

'And in that uniform! Phwoar!' Diana blew out her lips. 'A real live "tall dark and handsome" specimen.'

'Mmm. He's very charming but methinks too handsome for his own good,' Beryl put in.

Beryl had hit the nail on the head.

'You're being rather quiet,' Diana said, turning to Rosie. 'What do *you* think of our new boss?'

'He's all right, I suppose. Bit cocky for my liking,' Rosie said airily.

'Well, *I* think he's divine-looking.' Vi turned to Yvette. 'What about you, Yvette?'

'He did not treat Rosie very nicely,' the French girl said.

At least someone noticed.

'It's true,' Diana said. 'But do you know what *I* think?'

Rosie held her breath. What was coming now?'

'I think he couldn't take his eyes off Rosie. Didn't you see how many times he looked at her? He didn't do that with us. I think he's smitten and annoyed with himself because of it. And that's why he was a bit harsh with her. I don't believe he meant a word of it.' She turned to Rosie. 'What do you think, Rosie? Am I right?'

Was she? Was Hugo really putting on an act for the benefit of the others? But she must never ever let them, or anyone else, guess that she knew him from the past.

'Well, Rosie?' Diana said. 'You're blushing, so you *have* noticed him looking at you.'

'You're seeing things that aren't there,' Rosie smiled, trying to lighten the tone. 'It's probably his personality to pick on someone so he makes himself feel superior.'

'Hmm. I wonder,' Diana said with an irritating smirk.

'Well, now we've all given our opinions of Lieutenant Commander Hugo Garfield, we'd better get on,' Beryl said, her tone now business-like. 'As *Hugo* implied, the next card might just be the very one to change the course of the war!'

Chapter Twenty-Three

Rosie's stomach was playing havoc with the constant changing of shifts, but today was the first one on a normal 8 a.m. to 4 p.m. It seemed that happened once every three weeks, which meant she'd only been at the Park for a fortnight. It felt much longer. The war was not going in the Allies' favour and this morning the newspapers all carried the same story – Singapore had fallen to the Japanese. The devastated Winston Churchill described it as the worst disaster in British history, and there were even hints that he was losing his popularity since he'd promised Singapore would always be held.

Rosie was immersed in her thoughts of the suffering to come for the Allied prisoners when there was a knock at the Index Room door. But before anyone could jump up and open it, in walked Hugo followed by four civilians, casually dressed, making a contrast to Hugo's pristine naval uniform.

'Sorry to disturb you all,' Hugo began, as usual giving Rosie a quick glance before any of the others, 'but I'd like to show our American friends some of the things taking place here. They'd particularly like to see how we do our cross-referencing card system of information.' He paused. 'You can be perfectly open with them on anything they want to know.'

'Hi, I'm Gerry,' said the youngest and best looking of the four Americans, making a beeline for Rosie. He gave her a wide grin showing a set of perfect white teeth. 'Gerry Norton.'

Rosie was delighted that Hugo had his eye firmly fixed on Gerry. Taking no notice, she picked up one of the dozens of shoeboxes within reach, filled with index cards, divided by coloured partitions with the names of enemy ships and captains, locations and dates.

Gerry's eyes widened. 'You mean to say you keep all this top-secret information in *shoeboxes*?' His voice went up the scale.

Rosie kept her face straight, though she could hardly contain a burst of laughter at his expression.

'Yes,' she said. 'We have hundreds of shoeboxes filled with index cards.'

'Well, I'll be the son of a gun,' he said. 'Back home we'd have several shiny new filing cabinets for the job but they'd all be empty. But you Limeys use shoeboxes and they're all bursting with information.'

There were a few chuckles from the Index team.

This time Rosie smiled warmly at him, aware of Hugo staring at them.

Let him stare. Do him good.

She showed Gerry the telex tapes and took a clean index card. Methodically, she wrote down every detail of the tape's salient points, then copied it out again on another card, giving a different but appropriate heading and adding today's date, and popped each one in a shoebox under the correct section. Gerry shook his head in wonderment. The other three men looked equally bemused.

'Then when anyone asks for certain information, we have it at our fingertips,' she explained. 'Apparently, the cards can serve as a reference for solving something that might take place by the enemy in the future – a simple way to provide Naval Intelligence.'

'Well, I'll be darned,' one of the older men said. 'Just shows you don't need fancy equipment to get the job done.'

After ten minutes or so when Gerry's head came even closer to Rosie's, Hugo said, 'Right, then, we'll leave you all to carry on.'

'Sure good to meet you, Rosie,' Gerry said, throwing her another admiring look. 'I hope it won't be the last time.'

To Rosie's immense satisfaction, Hugo's stare had turned into a looks-could-kill glare. A minute later the five of them disappeared.

'Oo-er,' Vi said. 'Get you. Another conquest.'

'What are you on about now?' Rosie said, a little irritably.

'You know jolly well,' Diana said. 'Our American friend Gerry is well and truly smitten – like someone else I know.'

'That's as maybe, but it couldn't go anywhere even if I wanted it to – which I don't,' Rosie added hastily. Then she grinned. 'But he was rather sweet, wasn't he?'

'That's not the description Hugo would give him,' Beryl said, with a scream of laughter. 'He looked furious.'

The others joined in, and even though it was at Rosie's expense she couldn't help laughing with them. What a nice bunch they were. She loved being part of their camaraderie. Still chuckling at the thought of Hugo's expression, she reached for the next index card.

After a hurried lunch Rosie wandered over to the Post Room. Surely Poppy would have sent her one of her drawings with the new crayons she'd given her at Christmas.

'One for you, Miss Frost.' The tall skinny boy sorting the post handed her an envelope.

Rosie was surprised to see it was Heather's writing. She'd hoped to have heard from Ivy, but Heather – that was unlikely. They never seemed to get along. Heather was always quick to destroy any chance of closeness with her older sister. Rosie's heart gave a small swell of pleasure. Maybe Heather didn't dislike her as much as she thought.

She'd go back to her Hut. There was another ten minutes to go before the others would be back. She could sit quietly at her workstation and enjoy reading Heather's news. Maybe absence really did make the heart grow fonder.

As she expected, the Index Room was empty. She sat down and opened the envelope. A photograph fell out, face down. She bent to pick it up and turned it over. Someone had taken a photograph of Heather with a serious-looking Poppy sitting on her lap, Heather's arms wrapped possessively around her. And there was no denying it. Heather was looking straight at the camera with a triumphant smile.

Feeling churned up, Rosie fingered inside the envelope for the letter. There was nothing. No letter, no note, nothing. Heather couldn't have been more specific if she'd wanted to. The photograph said it all.

She was just about to put the envelope in her bag, barely aware of tears rolling down her cheeks, when the others stormed in. She looked up, then turned her head, furiously wiping her eyes with the sleeve of her jumper.

'Are you all right, Rosie?' Beryl demanded.

'Yes.'

Beryl's eyes flicked to the envelope in Rosie's hand.

'Not bad news, I hope.'

'Wh-why do you say that?'

'Because you're crying.'

The other girls gathered. Yvette put a hand on her arm.

'It's just that—' Rosie broke off. She couldn't be disloyal

215

to her family. How would she even begin to explain? They would think how thoughtful Heather was to send a photograph of Poppy.

'I'm a bit homesick for my family,' she said.

'We all get like that sometimes,' Diana said.

'Speak for yourself,' Vi put in. 'I couldn't wait to get away and have a bit of peace from mine.'

Rosie smiled. She knew they were trying to make her feel better, but she couldn't get rid of the lump now lodged in her throat. And if she ever tackled Heather about it, she could just picture her sister's wide innocent eyes.

'I thought you'd be pleased to see a photograph of us – especially your *favourite* sister, Poppy,' Rosie imagined Heather saying. 'I thought you'd *thank* me, not be horrible to me.'

Mum and Dad would agree, and think it was ungrateful of her not to appreciate such a thoughtful gesture, especially when they were aware of the constant strain between their two elder daughters.

Rosie couldn't get the photograph and Heather's intentions out of her mind. Getting ready for bed that night she couldn't bring herself to prop it up against her book on the bedside table even though she'd deliberately not brought a photograph of Poppy when she'd come to Bletchley Park for fear of anyone probing.

Her first instinct had been to get rid of it. Tear it into little pieces and throw them in the waste-paper basket. But she couldn't do it. Heather was her sister, like it or not, and Poppy was her precious daughter. She'd put the photograph back into the envelope, but not before she checked one more time, just in case there was a slip of paper tucked inside that she'd missed. But there was nothing. Thoroughly miserable, she slipped the envelope in her bag. Even though just looking at it clawed at her heart, she couldn't bear to put it in her suitcase and forget it. But it would be a long time before she mustered the courage to look at it again.

Now under the bedcovers she wondered if she'd been too hasty in thinking that Heather intended to make her jealous that Poppy's affections had been transferred. Maybe her sister's smile was simply a normal one in front of the camera, and not one of triumph. After tossing and turning for half an hour she stumbled out of bed and took the photograph from the envelope and studied it again. Now, thoroughly confused, she couldn't tell now what lay behind Heather's smile. She stuck the picture back into the envelope and put it into her handbag once more.

The following day Rosie was surprised to receive another envelope with Heather's handwriting.

Dear Rosie,
I hope you got the photograph of Poppy and me by now but I forgot to enclose this letter. Isn't it a nice one of Poppy?

So her sister hadn't been mean after all. Rosie swallowed, ashamed she'd been so quick to draw such a false conclusion. She'd write back and thank Heather at the first chance. The letter continued:

I hope you are enjoying your work. Mum and Dad have been talking and they have decided what must happen now when you get time off.

Rosie's eyes sharpened as she read on:

*They said if you come home every time you have leave
it would be too upsetting for poor Poppy now she's settled
back in school and we're all giving her special love and
attention. She doesn't ask when you are coming home any
more or cry, so if you care about her as you always say you
do, you will do what Mum and Dad want and <u>not come
home at all</u> until the war is over. Mum and Dad believe
it is for the best as far as Poppy is concerned.*

Rosie blinked, not taking in the words properly. She read
the paragraph again. It was true. Heather was telling her not
to show her face because it would upset Poppy. But why had
Mum let Heather say something this important? The war
could last for years yet, and until then she was being banned
from seeing her own beloved child. She tried to think
straight. It didn't make sense at all. Surely her mother would
have written and tried to explain if that's what they truly
thought was the best thing for Poppy. No, this was Heather's
doing. Rosie knew without any doubt that her parents had
never said anything of the kind. And she could bet they had
no idea Heather had written such a thing to her. At least
that gave her a shred of comfort. But it didn't take away the
most shocking realisation of all – that Heather didn't simply
dismiss her as having nothing in common with her. Heather
actively disliked her. But there was one thing Rosie knew
without any doubt. As far as Poppy was concerned, she was
not going to be told by anyone, including her parents,
whether she could go home on leave or not, and whether
she could see her own daughter.

No matter how Rosie tried to push Heather's letter out of
her mind, it stayed with her until her head throbbed, making
her nerves on edge. They'd never been close, but blood was

thicker than water and she would never have wished her sister any harm. On the contrary, she wanted the best for her. Heather wasn't a happy young woman. Even as a child she'd never stopped grizzling and grumbling, yet she'd quite cheerfully sat down and written that letter. She wondered if Ivy knew about this. They shared a bedroom and Heather liked to brag. Would Ivy have tried to dissuade her from sending such a letter if she'd known?

But for the time being she had to put it out of her mind or she would go crazy. She had to concentrate on the job she was brought to Bletchley Park to do. And as there was little chance of her having any leave in the near future anyway, when she'd only been at the Park for such a short time, there was really no point in mulling over it. The girls in the Index Room said they were lucky to get their day off in a busy week.

There'd been no further clashes with Hugo. Presumably Frank Birch, the head of Hut 4, was getting him settled into his new job. But if anything, it made Rosie even more on edge, thinking he would pop up when she least expected it. She occasionally saw him in the distance when she was having a walk in the grounds or in the canteen, and once he caught her eye but quickly looked away. Maybe he'd finally got the message not to pursue her any more.

'Right,' Beryl said to Rosie the day before the new shift from 4 p.m. until midnight, 'tomorrow we're all going ice-skating before the shift starts and you're coming with us.'

Rosie opened her mouth to protest but Beryl held up her hand.

'No excuses. I've found you a pair of ice skates. What are you – size five?'

'Six,' Rosie said, thanking her lucky stars she wouldn't have to make a fool of herself on the rink.

219

'They'll fit,' Beryl said gleefully. 'They always come up a bit big and they need to be snug.' She looked at Rosie. 'We're not taking no for an answer. We all need some fresh air after being cooped up in the Hut under artificial lights day and night. And you need a challenge, Rosie. Get you out of yourself. So make sure you're dressed warmly.'

She only had two jumpers and her old winter coat. The others would be wearing thick jackets with bobble hats and scarves to match. She wouldn't look the part.

'I'm afraid you'll have to count me out,' she said, fumbling for an excuse. 'I've got my monthlies so I'm not feeling on top at the moment.'

'So have I,' Diana said, 'but I'm going.'

'If you're worried about not having the right clothes, it doesn't matter a jot. I don't have the right ones. But it's having a laugh and some exercise that counts.'

Suddenly Rosie felt ashamed. She knew Vi came from a family where money was just as scarce as hers at home. If Vi could do it then so could she. She looked at the others who were waiting expectantly.

'All right, then. I'll come if you really want me to.'

Vi clapped. 'Even Yvette's going and she's only done it once.'

'Yes, it is true,' Yvette said, with a worried smile, 'but I will try my best.'

That's what *she'd* have to do, Rosie thought. Simply try her best.

Chapter Twenty-Four

Rosie's breath puffed out in cloudy circles as she sat on one of the chairs placed along the edge of the frozen lake and laced up the ice skates. Beryl was right. Although they were badly scuffed, they fitted as though they'd been made for her. A frisson of – well, not exactly excitement, but certainly anticipation, coursed through her. It did look fun. Maybe she wouldn't make such a spectacle of herself as she feared.

'Here, grab hold of me.' Beryl skated towards her extending her arm.

Rosie did as she was told, relieved to be supported by Beryl's sturdy figure.

'Where are the others?' Rosie asked.

'Don't worry about them. Diana's with Yvette and Vi's going to be a bit late.' She glanced at Rosie. 'Let your feet gently slide, one in front of the other.'

Tentatively, Rosie put out a foot and felt herself slide forward. She allowed the other foot to go in front.

'You're a natural,' Beryl laughed as the two of them skated several yards. 'How does it feel?'

'Nice,' Rosie said, surprised. 'But only because I've got you there to hold on to.'

'That's how we all start,' Beryl said. 'Do you think you can go a little faster? It will actually help keep a better balance.'

'I think so.'

At that moment someone shouted. Rosie automatically turned to see who it was. 'Yvette's fallen over,' she said.

'She'll be okay.' Beryl looked at Rosie. 'It happens to all of us some time or other.'

'She'll have a bruised bottom, I expect. I'd better go and check on her.'

Frustrated that she wasn't good enough to go to Yvette's side and help, Rosie hung on to Beryl's arm until they reached the edge and Beryl skated off. Rosie, managing by sheer willpower to stay upright, glanced around the lake at twenty figures or more, most of them looking as though it was second nature to them. One couple was holding hands, and two girls were arm in arm. She noticed one girl wearing a very short skirt twirling round and round on one skate in the centre of the lake. It was Pamela. Mesmerised, Rosie watched as Pamela stopped dead, then rapidly skated a few steps to suddenly crouch low, holding one leg, as she spun round like a top, and still spinning she gradually straightened up.

'She's good, isn't she?'

Rosie half turned to see Hugo's grin.

'Yes, very,' she responded coolly.

'Is this your first time?'

She remembered how he'd said those exact words the day she'd told him she wanted him to make love to her. Now, blushing at the thought, she wouldn't answer such a condescending question. But she'd show him. Gathering her courage, and not allowing herself to hesitate a moment longer, she skated off. It wasn't that difficult at all. Whatever had she worried about? All you had to do was stop being nervous and simply keep your balance.

The next thing she knew, her foot had slipped from under her and she landed on her back. She tried to struggle up but every time she tried, she slipped again.

'Rose.' It was Hugo, bending over her. 'Give me your hand and I'll help you up.'

She hadn't thought to wear gloves. Numbly, she took his warm hand in her own frozen one as he brought her to her feet. Strange how she remembered the feel of his hand. Did he remember, too?

'Are you all right?'

'I think so.'

'I was a bit worried the way you landed on your back. Are you sure you don't want to have it checked?'

'No, I'm fine.' Cross now because she was forced to keep hold of his hand, she felt her leg slide under yet again. He pulled her close.

'You're not fit to be let loose,' he said, chuckling. 'You'll have to hang on to me whether you like it or not.'

She wanted to wipe his grin off his face. Instead, she glared up at him.

'The last thing you need is a broken ankle, so swallow your pride and hold on, and I'll take you round so you get a proper feel of the ice beneath your boots and then you'll start to enjoy yourself.' When she didn't answer, he said, 'Don't you trust me?'

How dare he ask her that? How was she supposed to answer? If she did, everything would spill out of her. And she had far too much pride to allow that to happen.

'Rose?'

'Actually, I don't trust you,' she said, her voice matching the icy temperature.

At that moment Pamela skidded to a halt in front of them and for some inexplicable reason, Rosie was glad Hugo still had his arm firmly around her.

'Hello, Rosie. How's work going?' Before Rosie could draw breath, Pamela went on, 'Do you like it?'

Rosie was aware of Hugo's steady look, as though wondering how she might reply.

'Yes, I like it very much,' she said. 'And I'm working with a nice group of girls.'

'That's excellent,' Pamela said, taking her eyes off Rosie and instead staring at Hugo through flirty lashes. 'Do you fancy having an ice dance with me, Hugo?'

If she wasn't so irritated with him, Rosie would have laughed at his expression – not wanting to show his enthusiasm too much in front of her.

'Do go, *Lieutenant Commander*,' she said, emphasising his title.

To her surprise, he said, 'No, I need to see you safely back.'

Pamela gazed at him, her eyebrows raised.

'Maybe some other time,' she said as she waltzed off.

'Rose, just have one go round with me,' Hugo said. 'I think you'd really enjoy it. Please.'

She hesitated. It was tempting to join the others, some of whom were laughing and trying out different steps and turns in the cold crisp air. She'd love to know what it felt like. Even Yvette had recovered although she was holding on to Diana's arm for dear life as they kept to the edge of the lake. Rosie was about to say all right, she'd give it a go, when thankfully her brain took over.

'No, I wouldn't enjoy anything where you're concerned,' she said instead, looking directly up into his eyes. 'You of all people should understand that.'

A shadow passed across Hugo's face. He opened his

mouth. For a moment she thought he was about to say something personal – something about what had happened six years ago. But she wasn't interested in anything he had to say.

'Have it your own way,' he said crisply. 'But one day I hope you'll allow me to explain . . . just as a common courtesy,' he added.

Beryl was right about Yvette. The half-French girl had only suffered a bruise on her hip when she'd fallen over.

'But she picked herself up, dusted herself off and started all over again,' Diana chuckled when they were back in the Index Room. 'Just like Fred Astaire and Ginger Rogers did in *Swing Time*. You're a real trouper, Yvette.'

Rosie bit her lip. *She* certainly hadn't been a 'real trouper' and tried again. Hugo must have thought she was pathetic. But then what did she care what he thought? Or even what the others thought when she'd left the lake so quickly before she'd given ice-skating a chance.

'You okay, Rosie?' Vi asked.

'Yes, thanks.' Rosie looked at Yvette. 'Well done, you.'

'I loved it,' Yvette said enthusiastically. 'I was so busy not wanting to fall over again I didn't see how you got on.'

'It wasn't for me,' Rosie said shortly and picked up a card as a sign that she wanted to start work.

To stop thinking about what Hugo and the others thought of her, Rosie decided she would finally get down to answering John's letter when the others went off for a tea break at six-thirty. Until then, she would keep her head down.

Time crawled slowly by. Just before half-past six Beryl said, 'Right, ladies. Time for tea. Who wants to go first?'

'You can all go,' Rosie said. 'I'll stay behind.'

'You sure?'

'Yes. I want to write a letter.'

'Well,' Vi said, laughing, 'so long as it's to a boyfriend, we'll leave you to it.'

As soon as they'd disappeared, Rosie carefully tore a sheet of paper from her notebook. It was still jagged, so she took a pair of scissors and straightened the edge.

15th February, 1942

Dear John,

Thank you for your letter and I'm sorry I didn't answer straightaway. Work is keeping me very busy but I'm enjoying it and can't thank you enough for helping me get here. I would very much like to accept your kind invitation to see a show in London when I'm given a few hours off. At the moment I'm working nights but it changes every so often, so I will let you know when I might be free, if that's all right. I realise you might already be on leave but as you can see, it would have been impossible this week.

If you see Claire in the meantime, please give her my very best wishes.

Rosie chewed her pen, wondering how she should end it. He'd signed off *Fond wishes,* but she couldn't bring herself to do the same. She liked him. He was good company and her instincts told her he was a kind, thoughtful man. But she didn't want him to think she might become more than a friend especially as she was sure he more than liked her. The truth was, it had taken her several days to decide whether or not to go out with him, but was she being fair to him? If not, was this anything to do with seeing Hugo again?

She chewed her lip. Her reaction on seeing Hugo again was almost the same as when she was going out with him six years ago: heart beating too rapidly, her breathing shallow, excitement pouring through her veins – she could go on, because her reactions hadn't receded. But maybe this was because they were built on memories of their love. Maybe when she became more used to seeing him around the Park and in the Hut, she'd see him for what he was – a cad. Her mouth tightened.

She turned to her letter again. In the end she simply put *Rosie*.

Chapter Twenty-Five

'Rosemary, could you step into my office when you finish your shift today?' Hugo said, putting his head round the Index Room door one morning.

Five pairs of eyes, including Rosie's, curiously looked up.

It was already March and three weeks had passed since she'd seen Hugo. She guessed it was because he'd been busy getting to know the other departments and the staff. She gave an inward sigh. Her colleagues stopped what they were doing and waited. So far as she was aware, they didn't suspect she and Hugo knew one another before coming to the Park. But she was also aware they could feel the tension between the two of them.

They were on a normal daytime shift so she couldn't make any excuse not to see him. She couldn't have done anyway, Rosie thought bitterly. He was too high up to argue.

'Yes, all right,' she said curtly, then added for the others' benefit, 'Sir.'

He nodded and vanished.

'Oo-er,' Vi said, placing her latest filled-out card in the shoebox. 'Wonder what that's all about – just picking out our Rosie.'

I wonder, too. But she only said mildly, 'I expect he's pulling me up for something.'

'I doubt it,' Beryl put in. 'As far as I'm concerned, your work is exemplary, and you've proved yourself a great team member.'

'Thank you, Beryl.' Rosie gave a hard smile. 'I'll tell him what you said if he starts on me.'

For the rest of the day all Rosie could think about was the reason why he wanted to see her on her own, and not one of the others in the Index Room. If he brought up anything personal . . . She shook her head as though to bring her brain into line. It was no good guessing. All she could do was carry on with her work, hoping he hadn't found any fault with it.

For the last hour Rosie raised her eyes to the clock what seemed like every ten minutes. Then at last four o'clock came round.

'All right if I go, Beryl?'

'Yes, of course. And tell us what this is all about 'cos we're dying to know.'

Rosie bit her lip. She didn't feel at all in control when she knocked on Hugo's door.

'Come in,' he called.

She opened it to see Hugo at his desk scribbling some notes. He looked up with a serious expression.

Oh, blast.

'Have a seat.'

'I've just been reading your notes,' he said, 'and although you've only been here a short time, I understand you've already had a transfer from the Watch to the Index Room.'

'That's right.'

What was coming?

'What was the reason for the transfer?'

'Um . . .' For a few seconds she was taken unawares. Then she gathered her wits. She mustn't tittle-tattle at any cost where Alice was concerned. 'The first job Alice gave me was to translate Italian messages but there were gaps in my knowledge.' She looked directly at him, taking in his familiar face, now a little more filled out. She swallowed. 'So Alice thought the best thing to do with me was to transfer to the Index Room which wouldn't involve any Italian at all.'

Hugo was silent. She had to defend herself, so she gabbled on.

'I thought the words I didn't recognise must be technical ones – maybe even Italian naval jargon that I wouldn't have ever come across. But I didn't get a chance to see a list of their naval terminology and so many acronyms or ask anyone for help before I was transferred to the Index Room . . . where I'm perfectly happy,' she added quickly.

'Hmm.' Hugo took out a packet of cigarettes and offered her one.

Should she? She'd never smoked in front of him. She'd had her first cigarette behind the bike shed at school at fourteen but hadn't ever had enough pocket money to buy a packet herself. And there was no point in smoking if she had to beg and borrow for the habit. She had far too much pride.

Before she realised what she was doing, she stretched her arm out and took one that he'd half shaken out of the packet, willing her hand not to visibly tremble.

'Thank you.'

He lit it for her, his hand brushing hers as he flicked on his lighter. It took every ounce of effort not to snatch her hand away.

Keep calm, Rosie, she told herself. *Don't ever let him suspect he is having any kind of effect on you – good or bad.*

She inhaled and immediately coughed. Hugo raised one eyebrow, his lips quirking.

'Would you like some water?'

Furious with herself and with him, she said, 'No. It's just a tickle in my throat,' and promptly sneezed.

'Bless you,' he said, then added, 'You haven't got a cold coming, have you?'

She shook her head.

'I'll get you some water.' He stood and went to a filing cabinet where a jug of water and two glasses were laid out on a tray.

She balanced the offending cigarette on an ashtray, already containing several butts, and opened her bag for her handkerchief. But as she pulled out the soft piece of cotton, the photograph of Poppy and Heather fluttered to the floor almost at Hugo's feet, just as she took the glass of water from him.

It had landed face down, thank God. She bent to retrieve it, but Hugo was too quick for her. Rosie stretched out her hand, but he turned it over.

'Goodness, is that Heather?'

Rosie gulped. 'Yes.'

'She was just a kid when I last saw her. She's a young lady now.' He frowned. 'Who's the little girl?'

'The youngest,' Rosie said with a forced laugh. 'Mum can't seem to stop having babies.'

He looked at it again for several long seconds. It was as though they were the only two people in the world. All Rosie could hear was her heartbeat, thudding in her ears.

Finally, he handed it over. 'She's gorgeous,' he said, his gaze turning to Rosie. 'She looks the image of her big sister.'

Heat flew to Rosie's cheeks. What had he seen in the photograph? Had he emphasised the 'big sister' bit to see her reaction? Or was she imagining things? Keep calm, she told herself. Her hand trembling as she held the glass to her

231

lips, she downed half the water and set it on Hugo's desk. What should she do about the damned cigarette that was burning low in the ashtray? Pretend she'd forgotten about it? Oh, she couldn't take much more of this. She wanted to get out of his room. Away from Hugo's clever eyes that seemed to penetrate her mind and know exactly what she was thinking. She dreaded what he might say next about Poppy. But he wouldn't prise the truth from her, no matter what he'd guessed.

To her relief, he merely said, 'I'd like to transfer you to something that will tax you more.' He paused. 'Shall I go on, or would you rather stay in the Index Room? I don't want you to be embarrassed or unhappy, and I shan't think any the less of you.'

Rosie bristled. How badly she wanted to say she couldn't think any the less of *him* if she tried. But she swallowed her anger and merely said, 'Please go on.'

'Well, I want you back in the Watch on that same job you were supposed to be doing that first day – translating Italian into English.'

Rosie jerked up. 'No, please don't. Alice already told me my Italian wasn't up to it. And I love it where I am. The girls are a super bunch and we make a good team. As you said yourself, the index card work is vital.'

'It is,' Hugo agreed. 'But your Italian is even more so. There are very few of us who speak the language and frankly I don't want you wasting it.' He took in a drag of his cigarette. 'There is a glossary of the main Italian naval terms, but we also have a special department in our Hut with its own small library complete with dictionaries of naval terminology in German and Italian, and plenty of reference books – all sorts of information about equipment and types of ships et cetera which should give you everything you'll need. If you get any really tough translation problems you can go to a clever group known collectively as Research, where you'll find two English girls brought up in Italy who I'm told are expert in the field. Also, I'm here if you need me.'

At his last words, Rosie gulped.

'And if I know you,' he fixed his eyes on her, 'you'll pick it up quickly. Just a pity you never joined the WRNS as you'd have had a head start knowing some of the English terms.'

Rosie bit her lip to stop herself from blurting out she *had* been a Wren but had been unfairly dismissed. He'd want to know why. Even if she refused to tell him he could easily get to the bottom of it by his contacts. And then her secret would be blown apart. The very thought made her feel quite faint. She quickly swallowed the last of the water.

'Are you all right?' Hugo said.

How could she tell him she didn't get along with Alice. That the days under her malevolent eye were not happy ones. He'd say she wasn't here to be happy but to do her job, wherever she was needed. He'd be right. She straightened her spine.

'Yes, perfectly.'

'And by the way, I've spoken to Nora. She said Alice was rather impatient with you, not giving you a chance to get to grips with any of the jobs she gave you.' He paused. 'Alice is a member of the team, the same as you. I think she put herself in charge before I came as she'd been here the longest. But we're all adults, working for the same end and I like to keep a friendly, relaxed atmosphere. It's the best way for the job in hand. But *I* oversee this section.'

Rosie gave an inward sigh of relief. At least Alice couldn't lord it over her, though her pride would never let her go running to Hugo or anyone else if she had a complaint. She would deal with it herself if she possibly could.

'When do you want me to start?'

'Monday.' Hugo took a drag of his cigarette and blew the smoke over the top of her head. 'That will give Beryl and me a chance to see who will take your place. And I'll make sure you're given all the training and support you need.' He kept his eyes on her. 'That okay with you?'

'I don't have much option, do I?' she said churlishly, rising to her feet.

'Not really,' he admitted.

Then he smiled. That smile she'd so loved. It was enough to make any woman's heart melt. Dear God, she mustn't let it do the same to her.

'Before you go, I do have a piece of news which should cheer you up,' he went on. 'When you next come off a midnight shift to breakfast the next morning, you might notice a change in the menu.' She waited. 'Cornflakes, porridge, toast and marmalade,' he finished triumphantly.

'Thank you, Lieutenant Commander,' she said. 'The Wrens will be delighted.'

He stood and opened the door for her.

'I didn't do it for the Wrens,' he said, looking down at her. 'I did it for you.'

As soon as she came back to the room the girls surrounded her.

'What did the gorgeous Hugo want?' Diana demanded.

'Why was it just you he wanted to talk to?' Vi said.

'Give her a chance to speak.' Beryl got up from her desk and sat on the edge. 'Okay, Rosie, fire away.'

'I'm being transferred.'

'What!' Beryl jumped down. 'Where to?'

'Apparently back to the Watch.'

'Oh, I get it,' Diana said. 'You'll be closer to His Nibs.'

Was that it? Was that the real reason why Hugo wanted this transfer?

Rosie shrugged as though it made no difference to her one way or the other. Thank goodness they couldn't tell what was going on inside her. How her chest felt so tight. How her pulse raced at the thought of seeing him even more than she already did. The close contact with just the two of them – him coaching her. But her pulse wasn't beating so fast because she was still attracted to him, she told herself sternly. No, it was with frustration that there could be more uncomfortable encounters.

'Do you mind going?' Yvette broke into her thoughts.

'I don't want to leave this little team,' Rosie said truthfully. 'You've all made me so welcome.'

'What – more than Alice?' Beryl chuckled. 'Well, we'll all miss you like mad, but there's nothing we can do to change it, so we'd best get on with our cards, everyone.'

But Rosie couldn't stop thinking about the expression on Hugo's face. He really had sounded sincere. Was he trying to ask her forgiveness? Well, he wouldn't get it. But she had to admit she'd been rather ungracious after he'd been successful in carrying out her request, by deliberately calling him Lieutenant Commander and saying only the Wrens would be pleased. Sighing heavily, she picked up the next card ready to fill in the information from the telex strip.

That evening, Rosie was restless. Hugo was still on her mind. Those green eyes and the long dark curling lashes she'd always envied. She read some of Machiavelli's *Prince*, but it needed strict concentration to understand the formal sixteenth-century language and the controversial philosophy behind it. She just wasn't in the mood. Should she go downstairs to the drawing room? Perhaps there would be a Wren or two that she knew slightly and could chat to about something other than the Park. Yes, that's what she'd do. She needed a change.

She went down the two flights of stairs and could hear voices before she'd even opened the door. Inside, at least a dozen pairs of eyes looked up.

'Rosie, you did it! Three cheers for Rosie! Hip hip, hurrah!'

To her embarrassment the whole room cheered. Several girls called out.

'We're having a proper breakfast from tomorrow. Cereal and toast! What happened? Who did you speak to, to get this changed? We're dying to know.'

Rosie stopped in her tracks. There was no getting away from Hugo. He was there at every turn and would be so long as she worked at the Park.

'I spoke to our Lieutenant Commander who is in charge of my Hut.'

There were several gasps.

'What, Mr Handsome? The divine Hugo Garfield?' one of the Wrens called out.

How did these women know him when he'd only been at Bletchley Park a couple of weeks and as far as she knew, none of them worked in Hut 4?

'Yes, I think that's his name.' Rosie felt her cheeks flush. 'Hugo Garfield, I mean, not Mr Handsome.'

'You're blushing, Rosie,' a girl called Carole laughed. 'Methinks you've got a crush on him, just like we all do.'

'Well, *I* don't,' Rosie said crisply. Then she chuckled. 'But I *am* glad we won't have to eat lukewarm kidney pie for breakfast ever again.'

Chapter Twenty-Six

For several days the Wrens practically treated Rosie like a celebrity. Even Petty Officer Morris was delighted.

'I don't know what you did to get that awful breakfast changed, Rosie,' she said.

It wasn't lost on Rosie that it was the first time the petty officer had used her nickname.

'As you know, I already tried but didn't get anywhere,' Morris continued, 'but I understand it was the new Lieutenant Commander in your Hut who put in the right word.'

Rosie's cheeks warmed.

'Um, yes. I didn't have any luck with the canteen manager, so I thought I'd better go straight to the top man.'

'Good thinking, my dear.' Morris gave her a pat on the arm. 'We're all extremely grateful to you.' She paused. 'It must be quite lonely for you here, being the only civilian amongst all of us, especially up in the servants' quarters away from everyone.'

'It is a bit, sometimes,' Rosie admitted. 'But I have my Italian studies, and I do a lot of reading and letter writing. I'm all right, really.'

'Well, whenever you feel you'd like some company, just come down whenever you want. There's usually someone here to chat to. And I'd be pleased to have some Italian conversation now and again.'

'Really?' Rosie's face lit up. 'You speak Italian?'

'My grandmother's Italian. She came over here many years ago to be near her son, my father, but she refuses to learn more than the bare essentials of English. So she and I always converse in Italian. She's nearly ninety now but still has all her marbles.'

'Oh, that's wonderful,' Rosie beamed. 'And I'd love the opportunity to speak Italian with you.'

'Please call me Elizabeth – or Elisabetta, if we're speaking Italian.'

For the first time since she'd been at Woburn Abbey, a warm glow crept around Rosie's heart. It seemed she'd finally been accepted by the Wrens. She wouldn't feel lonely as soon as she walked through the Abbey's doors. Then her inner voice murmured:

Be careful, Rosie. If you get too carried away with the longing to make friends, you could let down your guard. And there lies danger that you'll blurt out something you shouldn't. You've been given a second chance. You won't get another.

This thought was still in her head two days later when Rosie, her jaw lifted slightly, walked into the Watch. The first person she saw was Alice, who looked up with tight lips.

'Oh, it's Rosemary Frost, here with us again.'

'Good morning, Alice,' Rosie said with a smile, determined to be polite.

There was no answering smile.

'I'm not sure why Lieutenant Commander Garfield has brought you back in here,' Alice said, coolly lighting a cigarette, 'especially as I had to be truthful with him and say your

Italian was severely lacking.' Suddenly her eyes became slits. 'Did you ask for this transfer?'

'No, I didn't,' Rosie said. 'I was very happy in the Index Room working with a lovely group of women.' *So different from you,* she badly wanted to add.

'I see.' Alice blew out a cloud of smoke.

'Can you please tell me where you'd like me to sit?' Rosie said, impatiently.

'I believe the new Lieutenant Commander is going to tell you where *he* wants you . . .'

Alice paused to let the emphasis sink in, but Rosie ignored her.

'. . . and everything else,' Alice snapped, looking towards the door. 'And talk of the devil, here's the man himself,' she muttered.

Hugo entered, immaculate in his uniform as usual. He smiled.

'Good morning, ladies.' He nodded to Alice, who treated him with what Rosie was sure was a rare smile reserved only for the men. 'Well, Rosemary, if you'd like to come to my office, I'll run through the system as I'm not sure how much Alice filled you in when you were first here.' He threw a glance at Alice who bent her head over her notepad.

'She's a bit of a tartar, isn't she?' Hugo said when he took his seat behind his desk.

'She's just doing her job,' Rosie said, non-committally. 'Can we just get on, so I don't waste any more of your time?'

He gave a start at her bluntness.

'Yes, of course.' His tone was brisk. 'I'm going to give you some background on how your new job fits in, so you know what you're looking for. Anything I tell you will not be divulged to anyone outside this section of the Watch. That goes for friends in the Index Room as well. Is that clear?'

'Yes, of course.' She had to say something. 'But I really don't want to be told any more than you would tell the others.' She looked directly at him. 'You *can* see that, can't you, if I knew secrets that people in my section didn't? It would be very awkward for me and not fair to them.'

Hugo lit a cigarette as though to give himself time to answer.

'Rose, you were a highly intelligent girl when I first met you,' he began, putting his hand up when she started to say something, 'and I'm sure you haven't changed in that respect. You and I used to talk about books and when I told you I was learning Italian you immediately wanted to do the same so we could practise together. I thought a lot of that. All I wanted—'

'Hugo, don't. Please don't talk about when we were young. Neither of us is the same person any more, so it has no bearing on my work here.'

Hugo shook his head. 'I'm sorry, but I'm trying to explain. I do know the Park's undisputed rule – and I quote, "Do you need to know the answer to your question to be able to do your job? If not, don't ask". But I trust you implicitly.' He gave her a half-smile. 'Having a fuller picture will give you a better understanding of the work we do in the Watch and where you fit in. That way, you'll be more use to us.' He took a drag of his cigarette. 'And don't worry – I won't be divulging any secrets. We've all signed the Official Secrets Act.'

So you keep reminding me. She bit back the retort.

He gazed at her for several seconds before continuing. 'I believe you're capable of working with the cryptanalysts.' He paused. 'You'll be working in a small team. For the first few days you'll simply be watching what they do and comparing the Italian messages with their English translations. Identifying who's sending it and to whom it's going – that

240

sort of crucial information. Over time, this builds up to an appreciation of enemy command structures which may well change in response to developments.' He stubbed out his half-smoked cigarette. 'You'll find they won't be translating them all smoothly and quickly. Often they'll be discussing a message and hopefully coming up with the right conclusion. I think you've met them when you first came – Stuart, Paul and Jerzy – all excellent chaps.'

She nodded.

'Alice and Nora will concentrate on doing a final check for accuracy and closing any gaps before the messages go off to the Admiralty.'

He cleared his throat.

'And you'll be working with me from time to time.' He kept his eyes fixed on her. 'How do you feel about that?'

'I don't feel anything.' She saw his eyes narrow a fraction. 'I'm sorry if that sounds rude but we're both here to do a job and as I said before, the past doesn't come into it.'

Hugo sighed. 'I hope in the not-too-distant future you might allow me to take you out for supper.'

'Why? It won't do any—'

'Not to talk about the past,' he interrupted, 'but just as a friend who would enjoy sharing a meal with you.' He stared at her, his green eyes unwavering. 'Would you do me the honour one day, Rose?'

She hadn't been prepared for this kind of question. Just the thought of going out with Hugo made her insides shake. She'd thought she was over being bitter and angry with him. They'd both been young. He'd changed his mind and had been too cowardly to tell her. It was as simple as that. But she hadn't known that one day she would be thrown together with him in a place where there was no escape. Once you got to Bletchley Park they didn't let you go lightly, because of security risks. He was putting her in an impossible situation she ought to be able to come to terms with now she was an adult. But how could she when every time she looked at him, she saw Poppy. Those same intelligent green eyes. She swallowed hard.

'You don't have to answer right now,' Hugo said. He came to sit on the edge of the desk. 'All right, let's get back to work. I'll explain the system so it starts to make sense.'

Rosie wished with all her heart he'd kept on his side. He was too close for comfort.

'First, the incoming enemy signals, obviously all in Italian code, have to be broken – a job which Hut 8 undertakes, staffed by a few brilliant mathematicians and usually very successfully. The Italians use numerals instead of letters so that's why we need mathematicians on the job. But the Italians have the annoying habit of changing the whole system of coding more often than we'd like, which can create a hiatus. That's bad news. It can hold up the system for weeks, even months, though we've had a good long run lately.'

He glanced at her.

'What we do here in Hut 4 is receive the incoming enemy signals, mostly from the Italian Navy, now decoded, and we translate them into English.' He looked at her. 'That's what you'll mainly be doing. At this point they're handwritten. They then go down to the typing room and when the typed messages come back, they get checked against the handwritten translations for any mistakes – even the typist's interpretation of the handwriting. Some of them are important enough to have a serious effect if they haven't been spotted. Then when the girls who work on them are satisfied they've meticulously checked every single detail to the letter, the messages are teleprinted to the NID.'

'What's that?'

'Stands for Naval Intelligence Division in the Admiralty. Unfortunately, they don't always arrive in time for them to take action, depending on how long it's taken for the original Italian codes to be broken, but when they do, Hut 3 Air Section sends intelligence to the Air Ministry. Fighter Command or Bomber Command or Coastal Command is then sent on the operation. A nice black cloud of British planes is quite a threat to stop the blighters from attacking our convoys. And when you have a stream of Merchant Navy ships carrying supplies of food, ammunition, petrol and so on, and losing possibly a thousand or so of the crew, it's a major disaster. On the other hand, we've had some terrific successes – more since we've recently reorganised our structure.'

Rosie raised her eyebrows but merely waited for him to continue.

'Hut 3, which used to deal mainly with Army and Air Force decrypts,' Hugo continued, 'is now working much more closely with the Naval section of this Hut and also Hut 8, who are breaking the Enigma codes in shipping intelligence.' He paused and drew on his cigarette. 'It's vital to have their cooperation as we haven't done too well in the Med lately and poor old Malta is nearly on its knees with the Luftwaffe attacking right, left and centre.' He shook his head and sighed, then brightened. 'But finally, the tide is turning in our favour with the Battle of the Atlantic, and that's hugely down to the codebreaking here at the Park.'

It all fitted together beautifully. A frisson of excitement that she'd be working close enough to feel part of the front-line chain of events rushed through Rosie's body.

'I think when you've got to grips with the jargon, you'll find the work very interesting and rewarding,' he said, blowing out a stream of smoke, then stubbing the butt into the ashtray.

'I'm even newer here than you, but I have some experience of Intelligence so the powers that be have taken a flyer with me. I'm determined they won't be disappointed.'

She was sure his last remarks were for her ears only.

The telephone rang. Hugo picked up the receiver. 'Oh, McAllister, can you give me a few moments?' He covered the mouthpiece. 'I think we've finished, Rose, unless you have any questions.'

Rose. His old pet name for her. She swallowed hard.

'No,' she said, standing up. 'If I do, I'll let you know.' She turned to go, then hesitated. Before she could change her mind, she half turned back and muttered, 'Thank you for having faith in me with all of this,' and swiftly left the room, immediately regretting she'd said something so personal to him. But he probably hadn't heard. He'd gone back to his telephone call.

Even as Hugo took the call he couldn't help watching as Rosie walked towards the door. Quickly, he answered McAllister's question about one of the Italian submarines, this time in the Atlantic, and put the phone down. He lit another cigarette. It unnerved him every time he set eyes on her. He blew out the smoke as a drawn-out sigh. At first he hadn't believed his luck that she was here at the Park when he arrived. It was as though fate had thrown them together. He'd been full of optimism, thinking she'd give him the chance to explain his father's heart attack on the very morning of what should have been their wedding day. After all, she only knew by his telegram there'd been a family emergency and the wedding would have to be postponed, which would have had to be after the funeral. It was Rosie who'd changed her mind by deciding to finish her education. Sighing, he took a drag of his cigarette. They needed to get

244

things straight, once and for all. But the fierce look in her eye and the way she'd snubbed even a hint of the past made him realise it was not going to be easy to get through to her. Still, he wasn't going to give up. Not ever. Something had gone badly wrong for her not to have responded to his telegram herself. Was her father the real one behind it? Had he persuaded Rose to have nothing more to do with him? Maybe worse. Maybe her father had taken events into his own hands. Maybe he'd written that terrible letter and Rose had known nothing about it. If that were the case, no wonder she was so dismissive. He frowned. All these questions had tossed around in his mind for the last six years and exploded immediately he'd set eyes on her only days ago.

Hugo grimaced. From his relations with his own father, he knew how powerful parents could be. Well, the only thing he could do was be patient. Perhaps he could win her trust in this new capacity. At least pulling her out of the Index Room and closer to both him and his team gave him more opportunity. Apart from that, he wanted to stretch that fine brain of hers and wondered not for the first time what the hell Alice had been thinking, not giving her a chance.

And what exactly was that last thing Rose had said when he was on the phone? It had been difficult to hear with McAllister on the end of the wire, but he was sure it was something about his having faith in her. If he'd got it right, it was the most positive thing he'd heard from her since he'd set eyes on her at Bletchley Park. His spirits rose. He'd have to hang on to that. Without realising he'd hardly touched his cigarette, he stubbed it out and strode over to Hut 2. It was all so complicated. What he wanted now was a simple cup of coffee.

Chapter Twenty-Seven

In the fortnight she'd been back in the Watch, Rosie had made significant progress on Italian naval terms, helped by a bulky glossary and a few extra books Hugo had added. He was cheerful, but professional, and she was grateful for that.

'The jargon is more difficult,' he'd said when he'd handed one to her. 'I think most of the terms are here but you might need the services of the two girls in Research that I was telling you about. They have all those off pat. Incredible, really. But because they were brought up in Italy, they learnt the language colloquially. And that's actually more important to us than hours spent studying grammar and structure, because it's how people talk and often how the enemy writes – particularly the Italians.'

'So I shouldn't take too much notice of Machiavelli,' Rosie said pointedly.

Hugo's mouth quirked. 'Machiavelli is to keep up your Italian with something more mind-stretching than most language books – but it's probably not the most help in translating enemy messages,' he added, with a grin.

She glanced at the first page.

'May I hang on to this?'

'Yes, it's for you. The other translators should have one, but they probably know them off by heart now.'

Rosie was immediately determined to do the same, just as fast as she could memorise them.

'The Italian Navy role is just as important as the German Navy when it comes to the Battle of the Mediterranean,' Hugo went on, 'so it's vital for the cryptologists to crack the codes as fast as possible so we can stop the invasion of Malta, which is strategically vital for the enemy. It would be a very dark day indeed if that happens. The islanders have suffered so much already and are practically starving as so many of our ships are being blown up before they reach the harbour. Then, of course, there's disease and a lack of ammunition for the islanders to defend themselves.' He looked at her. 'Did you know Malta has suffered twice as many bombs as London during the Blitz?'

'I didn't know that,' Rosie said, feeling ashamed she hadn't known, but glad she was gaining more understanding as to what was happening outside Britain. 'How awful. Poor people.'

'It's frightful, but they're a tough lot and incredibly brave. They just have to hang on a bit longer for the RAF and the Merchant Navy to gain power against such a siege – and that we *must* do . . . at all costs.'

Rosie was silent, taking it all in. She couldn't imagine what a desperate situation the people of Malta faced every day. How lucky she was to be here, far enough away from London to be relatively safe.

As though Hugo had read her mind, he said, 'Did you know that Bletchley Park took a bomb at the end of 1940?'

Rosie's eyes flew wide.

'Oh, my goodness. I thought we were safe in such an obscure place.' She looked at him. 'Did they suspect what goes on here?'

'I doubt it. It was more likely meant for the railway station, but it actually knocked *this* Hut completely off its feet.' Then he grinned. 'Frank Birch, who was in charge of the German Naval Section at the time, noted in the record book that our Hut was immediately winched back into place and the staff simply continued.'

'So no one was hurt?'

'Apparently not.' He took out a packet of cigarettes and offered her one, but she shook her head.

'Oh, my goodness. And was that the only bomb?'

'I believe so.' He regarded her seriously. 'But no one's safe until it's over, though we probably have a better chance here than most places.'

'What were you doing before you came to Bletchley?' Immediately she asked the question she wished she hadn't. It was too personal. And probably secret.

A shadow passed over his face. 'I was on a ship. Intelligence. Mostly chasing Italian submarines. It got pretty hairy sometimes.'

Rosie noticed there was a slight tremor in his voice. He cleared his throat noisily.

'Is there anything else I can help you with?' he said finally.

'No, I don't think so.'

'Any procedural questions, anyone in the team should be able to answer.'

'Thank you . . . Lieutenant Commander.'

'Why don't you call me "Hugo" if we're on our own?' he said, when she got up to go. 'You do sometimes when you forget yourself.' When she didn't answer he continued, 'You don't think it sounds odd with all that we've been to one another?'

She was spared making an answer as the room was plunged into complete darkness. 'Did you just switch off the light?' Her voice sounded suspicious to her ears.

'No. A fuse must have gone.'

She heard his footsteps on the lino moving towards her. He was so close she could smell the scent of him – was aware of his strength. Before she could utter a cry of protest, she felt herself swept up in his arms, his lips on hers. She struggled for a few seconds and then her body went limp and she was kissing him back, her arms snaking round his neck of their own accord. He pulled her closer as his kiss deepened. Oh, the familiar taste of him. What she'd craved . . . what she'd missed for so long. It felt so warm, so natural, so loving . . .

'Rose.' His voice was low and muffled against her hair. 'My beloved Rose. Oh, I've missed you so much. I've dreamed of this moment so often. I've never been able to forget you no matter how I've tried.' He kissed her again. 'Do you feel the same, my darling? Please say you do.'

My God, what was she doing? She angrily jerked free of his arms. Without thinking, she brought her hand up and soundly slapped him, catching his ear.

'Ouch! Why did you do that?'

'Because you had no right to do what *you* did.'

'You kissed me back. You can't deny it, Rose.'

She swallowed hard. 'I shouldn't have. I don't know what came over me. But never try it again or I'll report you.'

Shaken by the force of her rage she stepped towards what she hoped was the door.

Where's the doorknob? It must be here.

But her fingers caught in the blackout curtains on the window. All was silent save for Hugo's harsh breaths.

Then she heard him open a drawer and strike a match. The smell of wax filled the small space, but the candle he had lit only gave a weak light. Hugo walked across the room and opened the door into the corridor. It, too, was pitch black. Exclamations and curses were emanating from the Watch a few feet away.

'I'm not going to apologise, Rose,' he said softly, turning back to her, his eyes gleaming in the candlelight, 'because it was the best thing I've done in all these last years.'

The Watch door suddenly swung open and Alice's disembodied voice said, 'Anyone know where the fuse box is?'

A few people switched on torches and lit candles that produced small pools of light in the otherwise blackness. Rosie was glad of the dark. At least it hid her burning cheeks. She found her way into the Watch where there was much chattering and an occasional burst of laughter.

'Lucky you to get caught with the gorgeous Hugo in the dark,' Nora chuckled when Hugo strode past, now holding an oil lamp. When Rosie didn't answer, she said, 'I can't see you properly, Rosie, but are you all right?'

'Yes,' Rosie answered, her voice cracking.

'I wonder if the other Huts have had the same problem,' Paul Hodges said. 'I think I'll go and have a dekko.'

Rosie let the swirl of activity surround her. She felt numb one minute, then consumed with guilt for kissing him back the next. How could she have been so weak as to allow him to get so close and to respond with all her being? Because that's exactly what had happened. Her face burned again with the memory. How was she ever going to work in such proximity to him? But she had to. At all costs she must not let anyone suspect they'd had a relationship long ago. But how could she trust him when he clearly wasn't to be trusted never to put her in such a position again?

It was half an hour before the lights came back on. By that time Rosie felt a little calmer. Maybe she was making too much of it. Hugo had taken advantage of the situation as any man might in his position to grab a kiss. But then she remembered his words: *I've never been able to forget you no matter how I've tried.* And he hadn't grabbed her. He'd simply pulled her to him just the way he used to. Had she acted the way she did because she'd never had a boyfriend in these intervening years? Because she was starved of affection? She hardened her jaw. She had to prise Hugo out of her heart once and for all.

During the next two days Rosie caught sight of Hugo once in the canteen. She immediately averted her eyes. And once in the corridor she bumped into him when they both came out of their rooms at the same time.

'Sorry,' they said together.

He gave an imperceptible nod and walked on.

She began to relax. Maybe he'd decided he was losing the battle every time he tried to approach her. Or he didn't want to risk having his face slapped again, more like, she thought with a wry smile, as she went to the Post Room to see if she had any letters. To her delight, the post boy handed her two – one from her mother and one from *Roddy*! How wonderful. She couldn't wait to tear them open. Roddy's first, she thought. It was such a surprise as he hated writing even a thank you note at birthdays and Christmas when Aunt Dot sent the children presents without fail.

At the first opportunity she went to Hut 2's café and opened her brother's letter in his scrawling writing, a blob of ink blurring her name. He hadn't bothered to date it.

Hello Rosie,

Don't faint. Ma said I should write so here I am. I hope you like your job. Is it secret and thats why we dont have a proper adress for you? I bet its exsiting. Im doing ok at school. Ma and Pa gave me a little camera for my birthday. Did you like the one I took of Heather and Poppy. Heather said youd be pleased to know Poppy finaly stopped crying

when you left and she has taken over from you meeting her
from school. She said youd be pleased about that to.
Well thats all. WRITE BACK!
   Roddy

Tears pricked at the thought of Poppy crying at first, missing her, and then Heather stepping in, however sincerely, made her realise what a burden this lifetime lie was going to be. Heaving a sigh, she read her mother's letter.

Dear Rosie,

   I hope you are well and getting enough to eat where you are. I expect you've already made friends but I hope you haven't forgotten us! We are all well here. I know you will want news of Poppy. Well, it did take her some time to settle down as she was upset when you left, but we've all given her a lot of love and attention and she's much better. This is probably due to Heather stepping into your shoes. She explained to the manager at Woolworths that she had to help me with Poppy and could she leave work early enough to meet her from school. I was amazed he agreed. So you don't have to worry at all, dear. She said she sent you a photograph Roddy took with his new camera of her and Poppy and a letter but hasn't heard back. I do think you should write soon to thank her, dear. She's a good girl at heart.

   Ivy tells us titbits about what parts she has to make for the planes. Your dad and Roddy are very interested as you can imagine. She sent her love to you and will write soon.

   I'm knitting socks for the boys as well as the usual jobs in the house. Rations are getting worse but we manage so you mustn't worry about us.

   I think that's all.

   Love from Mum

Rosie sat numbly at the table shared by three Wrens she knew slightly from the Abbey. They were talking about the dance they were organising for the end of the week, but all she could think of was that Heather had stepped into her shoes where Poppy was concerned.

'We need to get cracking,' Louise said, 'before those four lovely Americans go back home.'

'Are you still seeing one of them?' a plump girl with a mischievous expression asked.

'Mmm.' Louise gave a sigh of contentment. 'Ralph's lovely. So generous. He gave me a pair of silk stockings. And treated me to the pictures and a box of chocolates.'

'You lucky thing.' The third Wren sprang to her feet. 'Well, we'd better go back.' She glanced at Rosie, who sat silently. 'Sorry we didn't bring you into the conversation but we thought you'd want to read your letters in peace.'

'Thank you.' Rosie tried to smile but her face felt stiff.

'Is anything wrong? Have you had bad news?'

'No,' Rosie answered. 'Just the usual family stuff.'

'And don't I know about that,' Louise said fervently. 'Are you a big family?'

'Seven of us with Mum and Dad.'

'Oh, that's quite a lot. They must miss you.'

Rosie gave a half-hearted smile and stood.

'Are you coming to the dance?' the plump Wren said.

'Um . . . I'm not sure.'

'Oh, do come. You're stuck in that attic room too much,' Louise said. 'It'll be fun.' When Rosie didn't reply, she said, 'I'll put a note up in the library at the Abbey with all the details.'

'Thanks,' Rosie said. 'I'll keep an eye open for it.'

She was being polite, but she wouldn't run the risk of seeing Hugo, though she didn't know whether it was because she didn't want to see him dancing with other women and not asking *her* for one, or because she was afraid he *would* ask her and she wouldn't know how to turn him down, especially in front of anyone else nearby who knew her.

'Don't forget it'll be this Saturday,' Louise carolled.

Chapter Twenty-Eight

Rosie studied the handwritten message and immediately noticed an Italian word she'd never come across. She ran her eyes over Hugo's long list but couldn't see anything that came close. The signal referred to something called 'Scrivello'. Would that be the name of a vessel? There was a date of 8th April. Might that be a sailing time? Frowning, she flicked the pages of *Jane's Fighting Ships*. But no, there was no vessel by the name of Scrivello.

Puzzled, her first instinct was to ask Hugo. She rose to her feet, then stopped. It would be just like him to imagine she was using it for an excuse to see him. No, it was time to pay the two English girls along the corridor a visit.

Rosie knocked on the door and entered. She glanced round. There was only half a wall lined with bookshelves, but these were crammed with all manner of books and what looked like manuals. Several men were sitting on chairs absorbed in reading piles of paperwork and scribbling, and the two girls, Bettina and Gioconda, were both quietly working at a desk. They looked up and gave Rosie a wide smile.

'Hello, what can we do for you?' the older one asked.

'I'm stuck.' Rosie showed her the handwritten message. 'I'm guessing this word means some kind of vessel, but it isn't listed in *Jane's*.'

The girl studied it. She raised her head. 'Bettina, do you know what this word pertains to?'

Bettina put her dark head close to her sister's. 'Never seen it before,' she said.

Rosie bit her lip. She'd have to ask Hugo after all.

'Enter!'

Hearing his voice made her toes curl. She gritted her teeth and opened the door. Hugo looked up and broke into a smile.

'This is nice,' he said.

She narrowed her eyes and detected a slight downturn at the corner of his mouth. After a few moments he cleared his throat.

'Have a seat.' This time he smiled. 'What can I do for you?'

She handed him the piece of paper.

'I know "*scrivere*" means "to write" but could it be a cover name for some existing ship?' She paused. 'I did check with the girls in Research first but they couldn't come up with anything.'

'I've not come across it as the name of a ship,' he said, after studying it for a few seconds. He looked up. '"*Scrivello*" means a small elephant's tusk they often use for making billiard balls but I can't see any connection there.' He furrowed his brow. 'It's possible it's something newly built though it's highly unlikely. The Eyeties –' he gave her a swift apologetic grimace '– I mean the Italians are so short of materials they haven't launched anything significant since hostilities broke out. As far as we can tell, whatever they do have is reserved for damage repair.' He paused. 'I'll have it checked anyway – someone else in Intelligence might have heard of it.'

He was silent, brow furrowed in concentration. She found it hard not to stare at him.

'But there could be something else,' he said at last. '"Scrivello" could be a surface task force, ready to strike east towards Egypt and hit our coastal supply line there. Or worse.'

'It sounds bad enough already.'

'I'm thinking aloud now,' he said. 'It might even be an invasion force. Not just ships but men as well. Maybe not just Italians. Germans too. And if it is, there can only be one target.' He looked directly at her.

Rosie felt her body tremble, though it was hard to know if it was from the ominousness of his words, or his gaze upon her.

'Do you mean Malta?'

'Yep. It just might be. And if it is, there's a damned good chance they could take it.' He shook his head. 'If we can't solve this "Scrivello" and my guess turns out to be true, we're as good as defeated in North Africa.'

'Don't forget we start the midnight shift tomorrow,' Alice announced when everyone was sitting at their desk at four o'clock, ready for the night shift. 'So be here promptly at midnight.'

There was a groan from Sonia. 'It really is a killer,' she said. 'And you know what it means, Alice. We won't be able to stay very late at the dance the Wrens are organising.'

'We're not here to dance,' Alice said sourly. 'We're here to work.'

'Yes, I know, but tomorrow's Saturday. We need some fun as well or we'll go crazy.'

Rosie drew in a sigh of relief. She didn't have to worry any more. Didn't have to make any decision about the dance. It was worth being on the midnight shift for that reason alone, and in the meantime try to think how to work out the Scrivello word.

'Well, I'm going to be like Cinderella,' Sonia said, her lips pouting. 'I don't care if I'm on the midnight shift. I shall go to the dance and come straight into work at midnight . . . before I turn into a pumpkin,' she added with a giggle, turning to Rosie. 'Are you going, Rosie?'

Before Rosie could answer, Alice said, 'I don't think she'll be doing anything of the kind.' She threw Rosie a glare. 'Rosie, being the newcomer, needs to pay attention to her work, not have her mind wandering with dancing partners.'

'We can have a nap in the afternoon,' Sonia said firmly. 'How about it, Rosie?'

Alice's challenging glare infuriated Rosie. There were no rules forbidding you to participate in, or watch any of the evening events some of the staff organised, if you had a shift coming up. It was your responsibility to make sure you were capable of a day or night's work, but it was strictly an individual's own decision. How dare Alice speak for her and in such a rude manner.

'Yes, I'll go. I could do with the exercise after sitting all day.'

Sonia's face broke into a beam. 'That's settled then. We'd better get our glad rags sorted.'

'If you wouldn't mind, both of you, we all have work to do,' Alice said coldly.

The next morning, Saturday, Rosie looked through her scant wardrobe that hung forlornly on a few coat hangers in the cupboard under the eaves. Why on earth had she said she'd go to the dance? If she were honest, it was only to get back at Alice, who thought she could still boss her around. The evening was bound to be a disaster. Sonia was obviously from a moneyed family and would have brought several evening dresses for just this kind of occasion. But she couldn't even ask Sonia if she could borrow anything – they were completely different sizes. She was much taller than the blonde girl and must be a size larger. Her eyes fell on her silky blouse and black skirt she and her mother had made. Even though the blouse was splashed with bright flowers it still wouldn't be right in comparison with all the others in their glamorous gowns.

Rosie bit her lip. She'd have to tell Sonia she'd changed her mind. She glanced at her watch. Just gone nine. A long day stretched in front of her. She might as well go to the Park and see if she had any post, and then maybe walk into town for a change. Perhaps even see a film, then come back to her room for a nap so she'd be alert for the night ahead. That should pass the time.

She picked up the letters she'd written to her parents, enclosing one to Poppy, and a separate one to Roddy. After much thought, she'd decided to write a combined letter to Heather and Ivy. It would be easier than writing one just to Heather when she really didn't know how to respond.

In the Post Room the clerk handed her two letters – one from Ivy and another one from John.

As she turned to leave, she almost knocked into Dale.

'Hello, Rosie. Not seen you around for a while. You must be on a different shift. I'm on the morning one, just having a coffee break. And you?'

'We start the midnight shift tonight,' Rosie said.

Dale wrinkled her nose. 'The graveyard shift . . . the worst one.' She paused. 'Look, why don't we have a walk into town when I finish at four and have tea there for a change. I've got to be there for a dentist appointment anyway.'

'Oh, I'd like that,' Rosie said.

'Then it's a date,' Dale grinned.

*   *   *

Rosie thought Dale looked a little drawn when her friend emerged from Hut 3, though she had a ready smile when she saw her.

'It's so good to be out in the fresh air,' she said, briefly taking Rosie's arm. 'These Huts are not the healthiest place to spend so much time in, so let's hope what we're doing will go some way towards bringing this awful war to an end.'

'At least it should start to turn in our favour now the Americans are in,' Rosie commented, then saw a faint shadow pass over Dale's fair complexion.

'Mmm, it's what we've all been waiting for – especially Winston Churchill,' Dale said, then changed the subject, saying how wonderful it was to see the beginnings of spring. 'Look at the magnolia tree, ready to burst with flowers. It gives one hope, doesn't it?'

In the café Dale ordered a pot of tea and two buttered crumpets.

'You do have real butter, don't you?' she asked the waitress.

'I'll have to check.'

Dale turned to Rosie when the waitress disappeared. 'Before I went to live at Langton Hall, a pile not on the scale of Woburn Abbey, but very grand all the same, I had digs in a cottage in Bletchley. I was stuck in a tiny attic where I kept bashing my head against the rafters. Anyway, even though I gave the landlords my ration book, the woman served her husband with superior food and more of it, and we were left with scraps. And he had his own butter dish with real butter and she and I weren't allowed to touch it. We had marg. I stole some one morning when he wasn't there and had just spread it on my toast when he appeared. I thought he was going to have a heart attack.' She chuckled.

'What a horrid man,' Rosie said. 'So what's it like where you are now?'

'It was very cold this winter,' Dale said, 'but Lord and Lady Langton are delightful. They treat me almost like a daughter.'

'Oh, how wonderful.'

'And you?'

'I'm with all Wrens, but not being part of their group it can be a bit lonely.' Rosie swallowed. 'They live in dormitories and I'm up in the servants' quarters. It was strange at first, being a civilian, but they're a nice bunch now I've got to know them better. Like your place, we've had a bitter cold winter. There're no extra blankets and the Wrens tell me they're frozen at night in their dorms as well. And yesterday we were told our water is contaminated and it now has to be brought in from Bletchley. We're not even allowed to boil it to make a cup of tea. So it's not at all luxurious living there, though I expect money was no object in its heyday.'

Dale's expressive eyes opened wide. 'Good gracious. It just shows, doesn't it, that these places can sound very grand but underneath the grandeur . . .' She broke off and grimaced.

It was pleasant chatting as they ate their hot buttered crumpets and drank their tea. Rosie could tell Dale had had a good upbringing by the way she spoke and her table manners, but she wasn't what Rosie would call 'hoity-toity' with her nose in the air. Though her next question took Rosie by surprise.

'What do you think about the gorgeous new chap in your Hut? Hugo somebody.'

Rosie couldn't stop the heat rising to her cheeks.

'You mean Lieutenant Commander Hugo Garfield, to give him his full title,' she managed, trying not to let Dale know how her insides trembled just to speak his name. 'He's all right, I suppose. We don't see that much of him.'

'Well, he's got all the girls a-flutter, and not just in *your* Hut,' Dale said, her unusual turquoise eyes gleaming. She stared at Rosie. 'Forgive me if I'm getting too personal, but do you have a boyfriend at home?' She chuckled. 'I'm saying "at home" because you probably haven't been here long enough to have one – though with that divine red hair of yours, you won't have much trouble.'

It would be too pathetic for words to simply say 'No, I don't have anyone'. And she needed to put Dale off the scent of Hugo Garfield.

'There is someone,' she said, thinking of John and feeling a little guilty she was using his name. 'But it's very early days.'

'Oh, how romantic,' Dale said immediately. 'Do tell me about him.'

'There's nothing to tell,' Rosie said, then smiled. 'But when there is, I promise you'll be the first to know.'

The two girls laughed as though they'd been friends for years. It was what she'd missed so much, having to be at home to care for Poppy and the others for five years, and then Caley's where she and the factory girls had had little in common except wanting to do their bit for the war. Though to be fair, quite a bit of this conversation with Dale had been taken up talking of boys. In fact, she'd continue it.

'What about you, Dale?' she asked. 'Do you have anyone?'

Dale's expression immediately became dreamy.

'Yes. He's an American called Glenn.'

'Ah, that's why you looked rather thoughtful when I mentioned things will be better now the Americans are in.'

Dale gave an enigmatic smile.

'Where did you meet him?'

'On Westminster Bridge. The very night London went into blackout.'

'Now who's being romantic?' Rosie chuckled. 'It must have been quite something to witness.'

'It was. We had supper afterwards and I—' She gave Rosie a rueful smile. 'Well, let's just say it was love at first sight – for both of us.'

'How wonderful.' Rosie's smile widened. 'Does he work in London?'

'No, he's all over the place. He's a broadcaster. But I'm not allowed to say more than that. And of course I can't tell him where *I* work, but he gathers it must be a top-secret place doing war work.' She looked at Rosie. 'By the way, are you going to the dance tonight?'

Rosie hesitated. 'I wasn't. It's going to be too difficult when I'll be working immediately afterwards.'

'That won't stop most people,' Dale smiled. 'They'll just go straight into work when the clock strikes twelve – in their uniforms if they wear one, or still in their evening finery if they can't break away earlier.'

'The thing is, I've had very little practice on the dance floor and I don't want to embarrass myself – or my partner – that is, if anyone asks me.'

'If you have a good partner *anyone* can dance.' Dale wiped the last of the crumbs away on her napkin. 'And with your face and that fabulous hair, I doubt you'll be short of partners.' She gave Rosie a sharp look. 'You don't seem terribly enthusiastic. Are you worried about having fun when your boyfriend can't be here?'

'Not exactly.'

'Because it doesn't mean you can't enjoy yourself sometimes,' Dale continued. 'It's what *they're* doing if they get the opportunity. And it doesn't mean they're being unfaithful to us, it's just a break in this awful time we're going through. Everyone's under the same strain.' She touched Rosie's hand. 'So don't worry about it.'

How could she confess to Dale it was the possibility of seeing Hugo that was still worrying her? And he *was* very much here. But he might not go. And if he *did* and asked her to dance, all she had to say very politely was 'No, thank you'. She set her jaw.

'I'm not going to give it another thought,' she said. 'I'll be there.'

Dale beamed. 'Good. That's settled.' She glanced at her watch. 'I've got a dentist appointment in fifteen minutes so I'd better get going. And *you* –' she gave Rosie's hand a light squeeze before letting it drop '– need to have a nap before all the excitement to come.' She stood and made to pick up the bill.

Rosie grabbed it. 'I'm paying this time, and no arguments.'

'Okay, you win,' Dale laughed. 'See you this evening – unless you're whisked away by a tall dark handsome stranger.'

Hugo. Rosie bit her lip hard.

Chapter Twenty-Nine

In the end Rosie chose the black wool skirt and the red short-sleeved jumper she'd worn for the Christmas party at Caley's. It had been perfectly in keeping after everyone had finished their shift for the day. But it wasn't an evening outfit. She'd knitted the top when she'd first met Hugo and he'd taken her out for supper or to the pictures at weekends. But it wasn't right for this evening. And she had nothing else suitable. She sat on her narrow bunk bed ready to burst into tears, then gave herself a good talking to. She was placing far too much importance on a casual evening. If they didn't like the way she dressed they could jolly well lump it.

Should she take Dale's advice and try to have a nap now? But she was much too awake to drift off. She was wasting time trying. Pulling Machiavelli's book from the little shelf by the side of her bed, she opened it. Maybe this time she'd have better luck in concentrating.

She soon became absorbed, following Machiavelli's *Prince* without having to resort to translating the Italian into English in her head. Maybe it was because it was her third reading of this particular piece. To her surprise, the next time she glanced at her watch it was time to go to the Abbey's dining room for supper. There was a loud chattering emanating through the doors when Rosie walked in.

'Evening, Rosie,' PO Morris called out. 'There's a spare chair over here. We haven't had a chance for a chat since you managed to get our breakfast menu changed so spectacularly.' Rosie took the seat by the petty officer. 'And are you going to the dance this evening?'

'I've been persuaded.' Rosie gave a rueful smile.

'Good. It's not healthy for young people to be cooped up day and night without having a break sometimes.'

'What about you?' Rosie lifted an eyebrow. 'Are *you* going?'

'Try to stop me,' Elizabeth Morris grinned. 'The Wrens' dance is the highlight of the month.'

Without the right clothes, she'd have to be extra careful with her hair and make-up this evening, Rosie thought, as she took her brown eyebrow pencil and expertly drew a line down the centre of her calves to represent stocking seams. If she had an American boyfriend like Louise she'd be slipping on some proper nylons, she thought ruefully, as she adjusted the black skirt and buttoned it at the waist, then slipped the red jumper over her head. Her mother had suggested green wool so it didn't clash with her hair, but Rosie had stubbornly chosen the cherry red. It *did* clash, but tonight as she pulled the hairbrush firmly through her long hair, brushing it until it glowed, she decided at least people wouldn't pass by without noticing her. She tossed her head one way and then the other, allowing the red waves to tumble about her shoulders. She'd leave it loose tonight as a change from always being tied back at work. She dragged up a hank of hair on one side and fixed a fake tortoiseshell comb in it. Next, she dabbed a little spot of cold cream on her face and smoothed it in and finished with a touch of her precious powder for her nose.

She noticed that in spite of the havoc caused by the

constant changing of shifts to her sleep and digestion, her eyes were bright with only faint shadows underneath, and her complexion still creamy clear.

'You'll have to do,' she told the small mirror, then picked up her bag and coat and left to catch the bus back to Bletchley Park.

The dance was scheduled to begin at eight o'clock. As soon as she stepped through the entrance to the Mansion she could hear the band. Goodness, it sounded almost as loud as a full orchestra. For a moment she stood frozen. What on earth was she doing here? She must have been mad. She couldn't go in and face everyone. She turned to go and immediately bumped into a young man.

'Oh, sorry,' she said immediately.

'Hey, you're not leaving already, are you?' He looked at her. 'Say, aren't you the English gal who was in what they call the Index Room when me and the guys paid you a visit? Rosie, I seem to recall.' He grinned. 'D'ya remember me? Gerry Norton.'

'Of course,' Rosie said smiling. Somehow his clear open expression put her a little more at ease.

'You weren't really about to leave, were you, Rosie?'

'Um, well, I—'

'Because I won't let you, even if you didn't bring your dancing shoes.' Gerry winked. 'In fact, I insist upon having the first dance.'

'How can I resist.' Rosie's smile widened.

He crooked his arm for her. 'Ma'am.'

'Thank you, sir,' she said, taking it.

'Would you mind stepping aside,' a voice came from behind. 'No one can get by.'

It was Alice. Rosie grimaced. Really, the way the woman

267

had sneered when the girls had been discussing the dance, Rosie was surprised Alice had bothered to come. Well, she wouldn't give her the satisfaction of acknowledging her. Before Gerry had the chance to turn round and apologise, she gripped his arm, steering him towards the ballroom.

'I need to go to the cloakroom to take my coat off,' she said.

'Okay. I'll wait for you.'

Minutes later she was back, acutely conscious of her lack of evening attire, but to her relief she noticed several Wrens in their uniform coming through the entrance. Maybe she wouldn't stand out as not being able to afford a more appropriate dress after all. Her heart calmed down a little.

'You look like a million dollars,' Gerry said, gazing at her appreciatively.

She felt her cheeks warm. It had been a very long time since she'd had such an extravagant compliment from a man. Nervously, she licked her lips, then smiled.

He held out his arm. 'Shall we go in?'

She nodded and he led her through the open door where the band was playing. Couples were already on the floor dancing. Her heart beating a little too fast, she quickly glanced round. If Hugo was here, she'd spot him and avoid him, but there were too many people crowded in front of her to see everyone clearly. She couldn't see Sonia, but Dale was already on the dance floor and waved at her.

'This is the first time I've been in the ballroom.' There was a note of awe in Gerry's voice. 'What a place.' He looked up. 'I've never in my life seen such a ceiling.'

'It is rather grand, isn't it,' Rosie said with a chuckle. 'Talk about how the other half live – or did before we came here. The good thing is that we're allowed to use this room in our leisure time.'

'And when you're not at leisure are you still working on those cards?'

Careful, Rosie thought. Gerry was a genuine person, she was sure, but being sure wasn't good enough. Best to play safe.

'They sometimes give me other things to do,' she answered cagily.

He grinned. 'I'm not about to question you, if that's what you're thinking. We've been told loud and clear about the security here, but I still can't get over those cards in a *shoebox*, of all things.'

'The English are quite eccentric,' Rosie grinned, 'and you have to admit the shoeboxes work.'

'They sure do.' He looked at her. 'I hope you'll come and sit with me and my buddies. They're saving me a table. You already met them that time.'

She hesitated, then took a breath.

'That would be nice. I'd like to say hello to them again.'

At least if she was sitting at a table with Gerry and his friends, Hugo wouldn't have the nerve to approach her – if he was here.

The three Americans stood as she and Gerry approached their table.

'You remember Rosie from when the lieutenant commander took us into the Index Room,' Gerry said.

At the mention of Hugo, Rosie took a furtive look round but could see no sign of his tall figure. She breathed out.

'Hi, Rosie,' they said in turn, shaking her hand. 'Good to see you again.'

They scraped their chairs to make room for her and Gerry went to a nearby table to ask if he could have a spare chair. One of them offered her a cigarette but she shook her head. The atmosphere was smoky and she didn't want to disgrace herself by having a coughing fit.

One by one the three men stood up and sauntered over to a group of Wrens huddled together near the makeshift bar.

'Ralph's hoping to see Louise if she's not working,' Gerry said. His gaze settled on her. 'Would you care to dance, Rosie?'

Her stomach fluttered. It had been years since she'd been to a dance at the Samson & Hercules, but her partners had mostly been awkward boys – that was, all except Hugo. He'd been different. He was far more sophisticated and knew his way round the dance floor. But this was Gerry and she didn't want to make a fool of herself or make him wish he'd never asked. She swallowed. What had one of the girls said? Something about only following your partner. And if he's good then so will you be.

'All right. But I'm not used to dancing.'

'Don't worry – you're with me.' Gerry took her hand and led her onto the floor.

He put his arm around her waist and with his other hand folded her right one to his chest. Without thinking, she gently took it from his chest and stretched their entwined hands to the side as she'd been taught. He raised an eyebrow but didn't say anything.

He was a little jerky in his movements but she didn't have any difficulty following him and after a minute or two she relaxed enough to enjoy it.

'Where do you live when you're not here?' he asked.

'Near Norwich.'

'That's in Norfolk, isn't it?'

She was surprised. 'Do you know it?'

'There's a big US base near there. I haven't been but a friend of mine is based there and tells me Norwich is a beautiful city.'

270

'It is, though we live in the suburbs.'

'What did you do before you came here?'

'I worked in a chocolate factory.'

He raised both eyebrows. 'But you have a perfect figure.'

She laughed. 'I didn't eat chocolates all day long, as people seem to think. I packed them to be sent all over the country . . . and all over the world. They even sent them to the troops in the Great War.'

'That sure is something.' He twirled her and they bumped into another couple. 'Sorry about that,' he said. 'Where were we? Oh, yes, what make are they so I can look out for them?'

'The factory where I worked – Caley's – also made Mackintosh. They're very famous here – especially their Rolos.'

'Rolos?'

'They're little cone-shaped chocolates with a soft toffee centre – and delicious. But rationed now with all the other chocolates.'

'I'll get you some Hershey bars from the base before we leave here and see what you think of American chocolate.'

He chatted a little more about England and how he wasn't ready to leave in a few days' time.

'I could almost live in England if it wasn't for all the rain you guys have. Yet you don't seem to take any notice but carry on – even outside. I've even seen folk having a picnic in an automobile.' He chuckled. 'If that doesn't beat all.'

Rosie laughed. 'If we stopped doing things just because of our weather we wouldn't ever leave home.'

Gerry, Tucker and Bob took turns asking her to dance. Ralph hadn't returned. He must have found Louise, Rosie thought, as she concentrated on Bob, who was an excellent dancer. She followed easily until he tried to hold her too closely, pressing his cheek against hers.

271

'Please don't,' she said, pulling away.

He gazed at her with raised eyebrows.

'I didn't mean to offend you, Rosie. We're just having fun.'

'I know. And that's all I want this evening. Just to have fun. Nothing more.'

'Okay. When the music changes, I'll show you a dance we're crazy about in the States – it's called the jitterbug.' He grinned, showing even white teeth. 'Then you'll *really* have some fun.'

'Hmm. I've seen it done once on Pathé News and I definitely wouldn't want to be tossed around like they were doing.'

'I won't do that, I promise.'

Although she hoped the music *wouldn't* change and she'd have to say no to him, Rosie found she was enjoying herself more with the friendly group of Americans than she had done with anyone for a long time. To her relief they didn't discuss work, not even the war.

'I can't dance another dance,' she said, laughing as she sat down.

'We didn't know what you drank so we thought you might like a cocktail,' Tucker, a wiry man with intelligent eyes, told her.

'That's kind. Thank you.' Rosie took the delicate saucer-shaped glass to her lips and sipped. 'Delicious,' she told them. 'What's in it?'

'Oh, some fruit juice. A little vodka.'

She'd never had anything like it before. Finishing the fruity drink, she watched as the bandleader walked up to the microphone.

'Ladies and gentlemen – it's swing time. Everyone on the floor for "In the Mood".'

Gerry sprang up. 'My favourite.' He grabbed her hand.

272

'C'mon, Rosie, your chance to do the jitterbug. You'll love it. I'll do most of the work. You'll soon pick it up.'

'Hey,' Bob said. '*I* promised to teach her.'

'Too late, *old chap* – as they say in England,' Gerry grinned.

Whether it was the cocktail that had gone straight to her head, or Glenn Miller's pulsating rhythm urging her feet to tap, Rosie couldn't decide, as he pulled her onto the dance floor.

He took both her hands. 'I'll keep hold of you all the time. It's just quick quick, slow slow, quick quick, hold on the fourth beat and the sixth. Then repeat. You start by stepping back with your right leg. Small steps. Just sway with the music.'

She noticed out of the corner of her eye some of the more experienced dancers were doing dangerous-looking acrobatics. What on earth had she let herself in for? She was on the verge of saying she was going to sit it out, but Gerry pushed her back, then brought her towards him, keeping hold of her as he twirled her like an ice-skater, making her dizzy, then the other way, until she was laughing and gasping for breath. The beat vibrated through the very heart of her and she felt a strange freedom as she turned and twisted, Gerry's face now a blur.

All too soon it was over. Gerry kept his arm round her waist as he led her back to the table.

'Phew,' was all she could manage as she took her seat.

'Did you enjoy it?' Gerry's smile was one of smug satisfaction as he poured them both a glass of water.

She noted his forehead was shiny with sweat. Oh, dear. Hers must be looking the same.

'I did – very much – so thanks for risking untold embarrassment.'

'What, with you?' he grinned. 'You looked like a pro. We'll grab another when you've recovered.'

Rosie asked the little group what they thought of England.

'Everything's small,' Tucker said. 'The roads, the shops, the automobiles . . . everything.'

'Except here at the Mansion,' Rosie smiled.

'Yeah, this is different,' Tucker agreed as he glanced up at the ceiling. 'We've got nothing like this at home.' He looked at her. 'Few Americans have ever been out of our country until now – me included.'

She gave a wry smile. 'When you Yanks finally came into the war in January.'

'We came to save you Brits last December,' he corrected her, then chuckled. 'I do apologise. That sounded a bit – how do you say over here? – cocky. It's my humour. Don't take any notice of me.'

'I'm as bad,' she laughed. 'But thanks for the warning.'

'We'll continue with more Glenn Miller,' the bandleader announced a few minutes later, 'a medley of favourites, especially for our American friends here in the Park, who I'm sure you've all made most welcome.'

There were several cries of 'Hear, hear.' Gerry took Rosie's hand and gave it a light squeeze before letting go of it.

Rosie smiled as she joined in with the clapping. There were a few whistles from several other tables.

The bandleader beamed. 'And we assure our American guests that we love Glenn Miller every bit as much as you do in the United States. So grab your partners and dance the night away.'

'Now you're gonna be in for a treat,' Tucker said.

'And this is the chance to take your opportunity, gentlemen –' the bandleader went on '– because the next number, "I'd Know You Anywhere", will be the Gentlemen's Excuse Me.'

There was a loud cheer.

'Rosie,' Gerry said, putting out his hand.

They'd hardly been on the floor two minutes before a tall man appeared from the shadows and tapped Gerry on the shoulder.

'Excuse me – I believe this one's mine.'

Chapter Thirty

Rosie smothered a gasp. In her enjoyment of chatting and dancing with Gerry and his friends, she'd practically forgotten about Hugo. Now, here he was, towering above them with a smile she wanted to dash from his face. But she mustn't show any emotion.

'Okay, as long as it's only the boss and not any real competition,' Gerry grinned, stepping back and treading on some woman's toe. 'Oh, sorry, ma'am.' He turned to Rosie. 'I'll come and claim you for the next one.' He disappeared in the crowd as the singer crooned:

'I'd know you anywhere . . .'

Oh, it was too bad. She tried to block out the romantic words that echoed their present situation. She didn't dare look at Hugo, who she could have sworn had given her hand a tiny squeeze. In the end she couldn't help herself and quickly glanced up. He gave her a smile, holding her firmly as he waltzed her through the dancing couples, never allowing anyone to bump into them, then expertly negotiating the corners. But to her embarrassment her feet caught his several times.

'It's a very long time since we've danced together, isn't it?' he murmured in her ear. 'Just relax. Pretend you don't know me, and I don't know you. Then there's nothing awkward between us. Just follow me. Don't even think. Can you do that?'

She gave a small nod. It was as though her throat had closed for good. She was too aware of the scent of his skin, her right hand enclosed in his left, his other hand on her back. She could almost feel the shape of his fingers through her jumper – just a few strands of wool between his skin and hers – and gave an involuntary shiver. Had he felt it, too? He held her a fraction away and looked down into her eyes, his expression in the low light unfathomable.

The song finished. She had to get away before the next one started. She turned but he was too quick for her.

'I'd like another dance with you, Rose,' he said quietly, staying her with his hand on her arm. Before she could protest, he'd taken her into his arms again and another vocalist began to sing 'The Nearness of You' in a beautiful rich voice, the words echoing Rosie's dreamy thoughts – she was in Hugo's arms, feeling so close to him.

He must feel the same, she thought, as she felt him pull her body even closer – felt him brush the top of her head with his lips.

She closed her eyes, her mind numb except to follow this man, allowing her feet to match his steps. Expertly, he twirled her into the corner of the dance floor, then back again, then swung her over his arm and pulled her up, holding her even tighter. She could feel his heart beating against her chest. She hadn't been this close to anyone since her love affair with him. And now, here he was as though he'd never left. She felt lightheaded. That was just it. She must keep her head. Simply follow him. They were to enjoy the dance for what it was – merely a dance. Nothing more. But she never wanted the music to stop. Wanted to hear him all night humming softly to the words:

'. . . *the nearness of you.*'

'That was perfect,' Hugo whispered as the dying notes faded. 'As though the words were written especially for us.' He paused. 'Did you think the same, my love?'

She jerked back to reality. How dare he call her his love? He'd said they should forget they ever knew each other so she would relax. Forget everything. But how could she when he'd used such an endearment? More likely he'd said it to take her off her guard because now he was saying the song was made for them. She bit her lip in anger. He'd gone back on his word. The old Hugo. Letting her down once again. And she'd almost been tempted to think he'd changed into a nicer person. What a fool she was.

'I thought nothing, Hugo.' Her voice was cool. 'I simply enjoyed the dance – just as you suggested.'

He didn't answer, but she knew his mouth had hardened as it used to when he was confronted with something he didn't like.

'I have to go,' she said, peering at her watch. 'It must be nearly midnight and I'm on duty.'

'I see you've kept it,' he said softly, gesturing towards her wrist.

Furious with herself that she'd brought the watch to his attention, she said, 'I couldn't afford to buy another.'

'Are you sure that's the reason?' Without waiting for a reply, he said, 'I'll see you back to your American friends.' His voice matched hers in ice as he guided her over to the table.

'Thank you for the dance, Lieutenant Commander,' she said pointedly in front of the others. He nodded and she watched him walk away. 'I'm on duty now so I'll have to say goodbye,' she told Gerry, then glanced at his colleagues. 'Thank you for a lovely evening. I can't tell you how much

278

I've enjoyed it. And if I don't see you again before you go, have a safe journey back to America.'

'I'm sure we'll see you before then,' Gerry said, jumping up. 'Let me see you to your Hut.'

'No, please stay with your friends.' She paused. 'Good-night, everyone, and thank you again.'

They all stood up, smiling and pumping her hand.

'We enjoyed your company, Rosie,' Bob said. 'You made our evening.'

Rosie nodded and picked up her handbag. What nice polite men these Americans were. She was just leaving the room, thinking how different they were from Hugo, when she saw him dancing with Pamela, laughing at something she must have said to him. Rosie had to admit the girl looked absolutely stunning in a mid-calf pale yellow evening gown, her blonde hair pulled back into a gleaming Victory Roll.

Rosie abruptly turned her gaze away, but it was too late. Hugo had already caught her eye over the heads of the other dancers. She gave an inward shrug. As far as she was concerned, he could take a running jump in Bletchley Park's lake. It was only a great pity the ice had long melted.

Back at the long table where she worked, Rosie heaved a sigh. Hugo had managed to spoil the best evening she'd spent in ages. Then she scolded herself. Why should she allow him the power to do that? She'd had a lovely evening in spite of Hugo's arrogance that she would easily fall into his arms. But wasn't that exactly what she'd done?

Paul Hodges glanced at her.

'Are you all right, Rosie?'

It seemed as though everyone lately was asking her if she was all right. She pasted on a smile.

'I am at this minute, but I think I'll pay for it tomorrow having a night's dancing and then straight into eight hours working.' She grimaced. 'Just give me a shove in the ribs if you see my head drooping.'

Paul chuckled. 'It will be my pleasure.'

She was grateful Alice wasn't working on the midnight shift this week. Paul and Nora were easy colleagues, but she hadn't been entirely truthful with Paul. Seeing Hugo for the first time not on duty – being held closer than a stranger ought to hold her on the dance floor – had made her even more aware of him, just like the heady days when they'd first met, and now she felt completely drained.

Every sinew in her body begged her to put her head on the table and let it go to sleep. Rosie blinked, trying to focus on the job in hand. Maybe if she splashed some cold water over her face . . . But she'd only just sat down. She had to get on with it.

Thankfully, the first messages were quite straightforward in that they mainly said where certain Italian submarines were located in the Mediterranean, though the word 'Scrivello' still haunted her. As she methodically translated a stack of messages into English, she imagined the relief for the Royal Navy knowing where the subs were and avoiding them or confronting them with their own ships. It gave her a profound sense of satisfaction watching the pile of completed messages mount up to be whizzed off to the Admiralty by one of the despatch riders. Time sped by until she yawned and stretched her arms up in the air. Ah, that was better. She rolled back her shoulders, then twisted her neck this way and that. It felt stiff from the intense concentration of two solid hours. It was at that moment something struck her. 'Scrivello' might not be a vessel at all. Or any of the other things Hugo had mentioned. It might be the code name for some very important military person. Her thoughts flew. But how could she find out? And then she tapped the side of her head.

Of course! The Index Room! Home of cross-referencing. If anyone could find the information, those girls could. She scolded herself for not having thought of this before.

'I need to stretch my legs,' Nora said, catching Rosie's yawn. She got up and blew out her cheeks. 'Let's go and have a cup of cocoa.'

'Sorry, Nora, but I need to check on something urgently.'

Nora raised an eyebrow, but Rosie decided not to expound in case she was wrong.

'Well, come if you still have time,' Nora said. 'The cold night air will do you good after all that dancing in a smoky atmosphere.' She gave a knowing grin. 'By the way, did I see you dancing with our very charming Lieutenant Commander?'

'Yes, but most of the time with the Americans I was sitting with,' Rosie retorted.

'Maybe, but it was Hugo Garfield who you were with the longest.'

'Look, Nora, you're making something out of nothing. He's our boss. He asked me to dance. I accepted. He's a much better dancer than the Americans – but what of it?'

'All right, keep your hair on,' Nora said with a chuckle. 'It's just that he looks at you whenever he comes into the room as though he would like to know you better.' She gave Rosie a sly smile. 'You must have noticed.'

'Well, I haven't. I'm trying to translate incomplete Italian messages, not worrying about where Lieutenant Commander Hugo Garfield's eyes are roaming.'

Nora snorted. 'You are funny, Rosie. It's good having you back with us. Cheers us up although Alice doesn't always get your humour.'

'No, she never does,' Rosie laughed. But inside, she didn't feel much like laughing.

Nora disappeared and Rosie went straight to the Index Room. Diana and Yvette, the only ones there, both looked up.

'Hello, stranger,' Diana grinned. 'Have you come to make us green with envy about all the handsome men you've been dancing with?'

'Hardly.' Rosie forced a smile. 'I'm puzzled by a name – "Scrivello" with a capital "S". Could you look it up for me?'

'I'm sure I came across that name yesterday,' Yvette said, furrowing her brow. She rose and went to one of the shoe-boxes and rifled through, then shook her head. 'It's not in here. Maybe it was the day before.' She took another box and swiftly checked the first dozen or so cards, then pulled one out with a triumphant smile. 'Ah, this is what I think you're looking for.'

Her eyes stinging from lack of sleep, Rosie peered at it. There it was. Scrivello. Her heart raced with excitement. Scrivello was indeed a person – the code name for an Italian General called Curio Barbasetti di Prun. And by the looks of the information on the card, he was a new chief of staff being sent to North Africa. Her heart jumped.

Hugo had mentioned North Africa.

'This is exactly what I want, Yvette,' Rosie said, smiling broadly, hardly able to hide her elation. 'I'll bring it back as soon as I've shown Hu—' She could have bitten her tongue out. 'Lieutenant Commander Garfield.'

'Known to us as Hugo,' Diana chortled.

Heat flew to Rosie's cheeks. She muttered her thanks and spun on her heel.

'You haven't signed the book,' Diana called.

Diana's shout of laughter followed Rosie out of the door.

She couldn't face Diana's innocent teasing. She'd sign for it when she returned it.

Rosie knocked on Hugo's office door, her heart beating hard as it always did when she knew she was about to see him. But there was no answering voice. She knocked again, then tried the door, not surprised that it was locked. She'd have to track him down. Solving the Scrivello puzzle could have important implications.

But no one had seen him. All she could do was slip the index card under his door.

At 4 a.m. Rosie was in the canteen having a mug of cocoa and a round of toast at a table tucked away from the main chatter, her brain numb as she tried to think where on earth Hugo was, when she glanced up and saw him walk in. Immediately, he caught her eye and strode over.

'Ah, there you are,' he said. 'I've been looking for you. Let me just get a cup of tea.'

'You look dead beat,' he said when he came back to the table and sat down opposite her. He took a swallow of tea. 'Dancing 'til midnight and then straight to working an eight-hour shift is pretty gruelling.' Then he smiled. 'Though I'm glad you went. I wouldn't have missed dancing with you for anything in the world.'

She was silent. She wanted to tell him she felt the same. *You're at work, and don't forget it.*

He took the index card from his pocket.

'I imagine this came from you.' When she nodded, he said, 'I might not have guessed, had we not had the conversation about Scrivello, because you hadn't signed for it.'

'I know. I'm sorry. I just rushed out without thinking.' She quickly said, 'It seems as if Scrivello is to be a replacement for someone.'

'Yes, this Barbasetti di Prun, code name Scrivello, is replacing someone. At a guess I'd say it's General Gambara, who from some recent Enigma decoding seems to have fallen out with Rommel. And as Rommel is top dog, he's not going to be having any nonsense from one of his Italian generals. Let's hope this new one will prove just as difficult for Rommel to deal with.' He looked at her. 'Forewarned is forearmed, Rose. So well done.'

'I didn't do anything that much.'

'You did. All these seemingly inconsequential pieces of information fit into a gigantic jigsaw puzzle.' He paused. 'Thank the Lord it's not so dramatic as me thinking it could be the code name for an actual invasion force ready to attack who knows where.'

'You know, I wouldn't have thought about index cards if I hadn't worked in the Index Room,' Rosie said. 'That's why it seems to me important to be allowed to liaise with the other departments as well as the Index Room.'

'You may be right.' Hugo drained his cup. 'But our secrecy depends upon the principle that the fewer people who know exactly what goes on in each Hut, the better.' He stood up and put the card back in his pocket. '*I'll* take this back to Diana.' With an annoying grin he added, 'Saves you getting into trouble for not having signed for it.'

Chapter Thirty-One

End of April 1942
Sprowston, Norwich

Rosie peered out of the train window, clean for once. Though still cool, it was a beautiful spring day. How she wished everyone could enjoy it. Her thoughts turned to the people in Malta and what Hugo had said they'd been through – and still no end to the bombing and devastation. But it hadn't broken the people's spirit. And now that King George had granted the whole island the George Cross for their heroism, the recognition had apparently made them all the more determined not to go under. If they can persevere under such terrible conditions, Rosie thought with a grimace, then so can we.

In a few minutes the train would be pulling into Norwich, more than an hour late after two delays, both between stations, with no explanation. She smothered a yawn from working the midnight shift and only a couple of hours' sleep that morning. Her heart quickened at the thought of seeing her little girl . . . and everyone else, she hastily told herself. It had been three months. She pinched herself. She'd been given four days, then back Monday morning first thing, ready for the four o'clock shift. It was a shame Poppy would be at school but she'd go and meet her just as she always had and spend as much time with her as she possibly could. At least her time off included the weekend so Poppy wouldn't have to be in school.

Then she grimaced. Heather would be none too pleased to have her nose put out of joint. Well, that was too bad. She reached up to retrieve her small case as the train began to slow down. Hardly able to contain her excitement she pulled on her hat, picked up her handbag and slid open the carriage door before the other passengers had even moved. In the corridor she pushed down the window of the train door and stuck her head out. Immediately, a smut flew in her eye and she winced, trying to blink it out. But nothing could mar the thrill of approaching the city she loved and the anticipation of seeing her family . . . of hugging her darling Poppy. Her heart somersaulted with the thought. Now the smut had dislodged from her eye, she could see the spire of the cathedral. Almost there. They were pulling into the station. If a bus came along soon, she reckoned she'd be home in forty-five minutes.

'Hello, love.' Her mother's smile was wide as she hugged Rosie. 'Did you have a good journey?' Without waiting for a reply, she said, 'Put your bag in your room and I'll get the kettle on.'

Rosie opened the bedroom door to a draught of cold air. She looked round in amazement. She'd never seen it so neat and tidy. Had her mother told Heather to clear her things to give her elder sister some space? Or had Ivy finally spoken up and nagged her? But maybe Heather had turned over a new leaf. Then Rosie remembered the curt words in Heather's letter, advising her not to come home and upset Poppy all over again. She blew out her cheeks.

It looked as though Ivy had taken her bed this time, so she picked up the book from the bedside table and Ivy's little clock and set them on the shelf by the other bed. Heather was not going to like it, not having the bed to herself. Well, she'd have to put up with it. It was only for four nights.

She looked at her watch. Time for a quick cup of tea with her mother and then go to meet Poppy. She ran down the stairs, her heart full of joy at the thought of seeing her darling's little face.

'Do you mind if I rush off to meet Poppy from school, Mum?' she asked as she took a deep swallow of her tea.

Her mother's brow creased.

'What is it, Mum?'

'Well, um, you know it's Heather's job now. She took it upon herself and frankly it's a relief to me.'

'And then I come back and elbow her out of the way – is that it?' Rosie couldn't stop the edge to her voice.

'Don't say that, dear.'

'But she knew I was coming today, didn't she?'

'Oh, yes, but you know Heather – she doesn't like anyone to upset something she's organised.'

'Well, I'm sorry, but I'm going to meet my daughter from school.'

Her mother bit her lip. 'Don't use that word, love. It's too risky. If someone heard—'

'But that's what she is,' Rosie flashed. 'My daughter. And whatever lies I have to tell, or however Dad thinks otherwise, nothing will change a biological fact.'

'But that was your dad's bargain. He'd take Poppy as full responsibility, just as if she were his own child, so no one would think the worse of you.'

'That's not exactly it, if you remember,' Rosie said bitterly. 'I was just lucky – if you can call it that – that he took to Poppy immediately, and even named her. But I'm getting sick and tired of this charade.'

'I know it's difficult, dear, but I think it's best we all stick to what we agreed.'

'Mum, will you answer me truthfully? Has Heather tried to turn Poppy against me?'

Her mother was busying her hands stirring a tip end of sugar into her cup. Round and round went the spoon, scraping against the bottom of the cup until Rosie thought she would scream.

'Mum?'

Her mother finally opened her mouth. 'Where did you get that idea from?'

'Something she said in the letter which came the day after she sent the photo of Poppy sitting on her knee made me wonder what was in that conniving mind of hers.'

'Don't talk like that about your sister,' Shirley said. 'She told me she was sending the photograph which Roddy took with his new camera. I thought what a kind girl to think of you like that. You know, Rosie, you always seem to have a bad word for her. She's not the easiest, I admit, but she's changed since you've been away. I think she's finally maturing. Haven't you noticed the bedroom?' She looked straight at Rosie. 'I don't know what I would have done without her.'

So it was true. Heather had found a way to hurt her, though why, she couldn't imagine. But all it had needed was to take over Poppy, and now Mum, too, by the looks of things. Rosie drew in a sharp breath. She'd be damned if she was going to let that happen.

'I thought the girl from the village – Eileen – was helping you.'

'She didn't really fit in. Poppy didn't take to her.'

'Hmm. I wonder if it was someone else who didn't take to her.' Rosie couldn't help the remark. She drained her cup and got up from the table. 'I'm going to meet Poppy, Mum,

288

whatever Heather says. So do you need anything while I'm out?'

'You could bring a tin of peas,' her mother said. 'I've only got half a small cabbage, so that will help eke it out. I've made your favourite dish.'

It was only a ten-minute walk to Poppy's school, but Rosie hurried along the road so as to be in good time. But as she rounded the corner where the mothers congregated, the first person she saw was Heather bending low over a pram, her face hidden under the canopy, talking to the baby who was propped up by the pillow, staring up at her. There was a sudden howl and Heather stepped back sharply. Rosie recognised the mother and quickly hurried towards them.

'Oh, dear, I didn't mean to make it cry,' she heard Heather say.

Joan Francis made cooing noises to her baby. 'I expect he's hungry.' She looked up.

'Oh, here's your sister. Hello, Rosie. I haven't seen you for quite some time.'

Heather swung round. 'It's all right, Rosie. I'm seeing to Poppy so you can go home and be with Mum. I don't suppose you're here for very long and she's been looking forward to seeing you.'

Something snapped inside Rosie.

'I've just had tea with her and told her I was meeting Poppy.' She looked at Joan. 'I work quite a long way from Norwich but I'm home on a short leave.'

'That's nice to be with your family.' She gazed at Rosie with innocent eyes. 'Did you just fancy a change to another factory?'

Rosie was aware of Heather's curious eyes fixed on her.

'No, nothing like that. I'm in the War Office – clerical work.'

'Well, I hope it helps win the war,' Joan said fervently.

'You hear dreadful things about bombing in London.' Her anxious eyes looked at Rosie. 'Oh, I hope I haven't said the wrong thing. You're not in London, are you?'

'Nowhere near.'

'That must be a great comfort to your parents to know you're out of harm's way.'

Rosie smiled. 'I don't think anywhere is particularly safe at the moment.'

'Mmm. You might be right,' Joan agreed. 'I just hope they don't start on Norwich.'

'Ma!' a young boy shouted and began to run, his face beaming.

'Ah, there's my Bobby –' Joan turned to greet her son '– and your little sister's with him.'

Heather opened her arms wide and bellowed, 'Over here, Poppy, darling.'

Poppy looked up and suddenly stopped dead.

'Mosey! Mosey!'

Her little legs flew as she ran straight to Rosie and flung herself against her.

'Hevver didn't tell me you were coming today,' Poppy cried out.

'Well, here I am.' Ignoring Heather's glare, Rosie bent to kiss the little girl, who tugged at her hand.

'I'm the bestest reader in my class now. Teacher says so.'

'That's wonderful, darling. You can read *me* a story while I'm here.'

Heather sulkily dragged behind as Poppy held Rosie's hand and rambled on about school. As soon as they were home Poppy ran round to the back and flung open the scullery door.

'Mummy, Mosey's back!'

Rosie followed Poppy into the kitchen where her mother was making supper.

'Hello, love.' Shirley bent and kissed Poppy's cheek.

'You didn't tell me Mosey was coming today,' Poppy accused.

'We weren't sure, love.' Shirley took Poppy's jacket. 'Go and hang this by your bed.'

'It's not a bed, it's a stupid cot,' Poppy whined. 'I hate it. No one at school sleeps in a *cot* like *a baby.*'

'It's all we can afford, dear,' Shirley said calmly. 'Do what I say and then I'll make you a piece of bread and jam while we wait for supper.'

Poppy disappeared upstairs.

'It's cold in the bedrooms, Mum, for the end of April. Is Poppy warm enough at night?'

Her mother hesitated. 'She has her own hot water bottle. The girls share, but since the coal rationin' *and* the gas and electricity last month, it's been hard. If the government don't sort it out soon we'll be in for a very hard winter. I daren't light the fire in the dinin' room until just before your dad's home.'

Rosie felt a spike of guilt. Even though her attic room at Woburn Abbey was as chilly, she knew on the whole she had a better diet and more of it to keep warm.

This damn war has affected everything.

'Where's Heather?' Shirley asked. 'Wasn't she there?'

'Yes, I was there,' Heather said as she marched in. 'But Rosie wouldn't let me near Poppy. And to think *I'm* the one who's been looking after her.'

'That wasn't very nice of you, Rosemary,' her mother said mildly.

'It wasn't like that at all, Mum. Poppy was excited to see me and wouldn't let me go.'

'Well, you must sort it out between the pair of you,' Shirley said, 'and leave me to get on with supper – that is, unless either of you like to give me a hand.'

Heather stormed out and Rosie heard her stamping up the stairs.

'That leaves me, then,' Rosie smiled. 'What do you want me to do?'

'You can shred the cabbage. Oh, and open the tin of peas.'

'Oh, sorry, Mum, I forgot them.'

Her mother clicked her tongue. 'That was all I asked for.'

'I know. I'm sorry.'

As soon as Heather sat down to supper she began complaining about how she'd had to clean all the glass counters at work besides sweeping the entire floor. Dad would have soon told her to be quiet and get on with her meal, Rosie thought. But he was on the afternoon shift and wouldn't be home until midnight. Her mother didn't say a word but slowly ate her meagre helping of corned beef and cabbage. Suddenly, Heather turned on Roddy.

'I saw that!'

'What?'

'Putting your knife in your mouth. You've got the manners of a pig.'

'And you act like one,' Roddy shot back.

'Stop it, you two,' Rosie said. 'I'd like just one meal without an argument.'

'Will you read me a bedtime story, Mosey?' Poppy said when Rosie had cleared the table.

'Yes, darling. Then tomorrow it'll be your turn to read *me* one. Can you be a big girl and get into your nightie and clean your teeth, then I'll be up.' She looked at her mother. 'Mum, you go and put your feet up while I do the washing up.'

'I'll help,' Ivy said.

* * *

In bed that night, Rosie thought how much she loved reading Poppy a bedtime story. This evening, she'd assured her how much she loved her and missed her when she was away. She'd even told Poppy she couldn't stay long because she was needed at work to help win the war, but she'd come and see her as often as she could.

'Are you going to kill the nasty men?' Poppy said, her green eyes wide.

Rosie hid a smile. 'No, darling. Ladies aren't allowed to do that. But we can do other things to help.'

'When are you going back to work?' Poppy's voice held a note of despair.

'Not yet, my love. And we're going to spend as much time together as possible. I've asked Mummy –' Rosie swallowed on the word as she always did '– if she'll write a note to excuse you from school tomorrow and then we can spend it together. After that we've got the whole weekend to do things.'

'Goody.' Poppy threw her arms round Rosie's neck and kissed her cheek, leaving a wet mark. 'What shall we do tomorrow?'

'What would *you* like to do?'

'I don't know.' She raised her head. 'Can we go to the libe-berry?'

'Yes, but not all day. Maybe afterwards we'll go to the rec.'

'Just me and you?'

'Yes, darling. Just you and me.'

'Can I go on the swings?'

'That's why we're going.'

Poppy beamed. 'And the roundabout?'

'Yes.' Rosie grinned at the eager little face. 'That's what we'll do then. And the sooner you go to sleep, the sooner tomorrow will come.'

Chapter Thirty-Two

Rosie's mother had written a note for her to take to Miss Andrews, Poppy's teacher, to ask permission for Poppy to be absent from school, just for today. Miss Andrews had read it and nodded. The fine weather held and after the visit to the library, where Poppy chose two books but insisted they were too heavy for her to carry and made 'Mosey' carry them, they walked to Sprowston Recreation Grounds. By the time Poppy had tried all the swings several times over, pushed her feet through the climbing frame, performed a few somersaults on the grass and become dizzy on the roundabout when two older girls spun it hard, Rosie could tell by the way she was wobbling on her thin little legs that her daughter was tired out. Thankfully, she spotted a stall selling tea and cakes where Poppy chose a cupcake and a glass of orange squash, and Rosie downed two cups of tea and a currant bun.

It was time to go home. Rosie decided they should get the bus back.

'Can we sit on top?' Poppy asked, when the bus came in view.

'Yes, if you hold the stair rail very tightly as you go up.'

* * *

'Did you have a lovely day?' Shirley said when Rosie and Poppy took off their jackets and went into the kitchen to find her.

'I've got two new books from the libe-berry,' Poppy said.

'Oh, let me have a look.' Shirley wiped her hands on the small kitchen towel.

'Mosey's got them.'

Rosie handed them to her mother who glanced at the titles then flicked a couple of pages of one of them. She frowned.

'They look a bit old for you, love. I think Mosey will have to help you.'

'I can read them myself.' Poppy's lip quivered.

'I'm sure you can.' Shirley glanced at Rosie. 'Can you lay the table for me, dear?'

'Yes, of course, but don't forget I've been invited out for supper tonight.'

As the bus trundled its way towards Norwich, Rosie couldn't stop thinking about Heather's attempt to turn Poppy against her. On the face of it, it didn't appear to have had a lasting effect, but who knew what was going on in the child's mind. She wasn't yet six and that was a perfect age to believe everything adults told you. And Heather, now taller than her mother, would, in Poppy's eyes, be a figure of authority. It was all very well whilst Rosie was at home giving her love and attention, but what would happen as soon as her back was turned? Heather would start putting wrong ideas into Poppy's head again.

Hugo sprang into her mind. If he knew he had a daughter and what Heather had been up to, she dreaded to think how he'd respond. For a few moments a feeling of guilt spread through her. She should tell him he had a child. It wasn't fair, no matter how angry and let down by him she'd been.

Seeing him in a different light at work had given her a new perspective. He took his responsibilities seriously, he worked hard, he kept the team in the Watch not only inspired but mostly harmonious. His quick intelligence had obviously led to his being picked for the job he was doing at the Park. Also, at the start of the war he'd been on a ship and had probably not come out unscathed, though he'd never hinted at any conflict with the enemy in those two years. But then he wouldn't. He was sworn to secrecy the same as she was.

Rosie shook herself. She mustn't become too soft as far as Hugo was concerned. He'd let her down in the cruellest way and she must never forget it.

But he keeps trying to explain what happened, the little voice inside her insisted. *Don't you think you should at least give him that opportunity?*

'No, definitely not,' she muttered, then caught the curious stare of a woman sitting across from her. The woman would probably think she was funny in the head. She sent the woman a rueful smile, and the woman gave her a nod then quickly turned away.

Think about John. Where does he fit in?

He'd been writing to her regularly every week. She hadn't always answered immediately, worried that he might be getting the wrong idea. But there was no denying that his letters had become steadily warmer. She ran his last one over in her mind.

Happy to report I've got a three-day pass at the same time as you, so I'll be staying with Claire as usual. I'm hoping to see as much of you as I can while you're home. I know it's only a few days, and you'll want to spend time with your family, but I'm hoping you might fit me in as well.

I can't wait to see you again, dearest Rosemary.

'Dearest Rosemary', he'd written. Did she mind? Or was it just his way? He was rather a dear himself. Well, she'd be seeing him in less than half an hour. Briefly, she closed her eyes, trying to work out how she felt about him. He was a thoroughly decent person with a lovely aunt. They were the only friends who knew about Poppy and hadn't judged her. That was what was so relaxing about being in their company. Yes, she told herself, she was looking forward to seeing him again.

'Norwich Castle,' the conductor called up the stairs.

Rosie grabbed her bag and held on to the handrail as the bus swayed to a stop. She thanked the conductor and stepped onto the pavement. John had suggested the Castle Hotel in Castle Meadow which apparently had a decent menu, even in wartime. She'd just answered that it would be lovely but hadn't added that she'd never been to a restaurant in Norwich. Even when she'd met Hugo, he'd always taken her to country inns. Anything Hugo suggested had always been wonderful to her. Now, she wondered if he'd been worried that someone would see them and report it to their parents.

Stop thinking about Hugo, she told herself sternly. *You're seeing John this evening.*

John was sitting on one of the comfortable armchairs in the foyer waiting for her. As soon as he saw her walk through the door he sprang up.

'There you are,' he said, kissing her cheek.

She smiled at him as he helped her off with her jacket. Immediately, a uniformed man came forward and took it.

'And your hat,' John said.

She took it off and handed it to him, then smoothed her hair.

'Do I look as though I've been dragged through a hedge backwards?'

'You look like one of those Pre-Raphaelite women in the National Portrait Gallery,' John said, admiration shining from his eyes. 'Your hair is beautiful. And so are you – a sight for sore eyes.'

Her stomach pinched. Hugo used to say the same about her hair.

Mustn't think of him. I'm here with John.

'Thank you, kind sir.' She laughed a little self-consciously, not having expected such an extravagant compliment from him quite so soon.

A waiter came forward. 'May I take you to your table?' When they were settled, he handed them each a menu. 'And here's the wine list, sir. I'll be back shortly to take your order.'

'Thank you.' John opened the menu and Rosie did the same.

'There aren't any prices,' she said. 'Is that because it's terribly expensive?'

'No. It's because all main meals are capped by the government, so they're not allowed to charge more than £5 a head. Unless it's something extra or very special, which most restaurants can't normally offer nowadays. But I want you to choose whatever you fancy.'

Rosie skimmed the handful of main meals that all looked heaps more appetising than the canteen.

'I'd like the fish, if that's all right.'

'Of course it's all right,' John said, closing the menu. 'It's only boiled cod, so nothing really special, but I'll join you.' He studied the wine menu. 'Would you like a white wine to go with it?'

'Not if it's going to make my head spin like it did the last time at your aunt's.' Rosie's smile was rueful.

They were discussing Claire's training as an ARP warden when the waiter came to pour their wine.

'To Claire in her latest venture, and to you, Rosemary.' John clinked his glass with hers. 'You look well. The new job must be agreeing with you.'

'It does,' Rosie said. 'It's really interesting and I feel I'm doing my bit.'

'That's excellent.' He leaned forward. 'I don't even know where you live, let alone the precise work you're engaged in, but I do know you'll have signed the Official Secrets Act so I'm not going to grill you.' He touched her hand. 'I just want to say how delighted I am that things have turned out so well for you.'

'It was all your doing,' Rosie said. 'If you hadn't had faith in me, I wouldn't be where I am now, so I can't thank you enough.' She hesitated. 'You know I wouldn't have been able to get another decent job as soon as they saw I was dismissed from the WRNS.'

'It wasn't any fault of yours – something unfortunate that happened all those years ago. I didn't want that clever mind of yours to go to waste.'

'I don't know about being clever,' Rosie said, 'but I'm more fulfilled when I use my brain.'

John looked directly at her. 'I expect your little girl was thrilled to see you – Poppy, isn't it?'

'Yes, she was very excited.'

Should she say anything more? About Heather? It felt so disloyal to speak badly about any of her family. Thankfully the waiter appeared with their meals.

'Sir, madam,' he said, setting down the two plates. 'Be careful – they're very hot.'

When he'd disappeared, John took her hand.

'I think there's something worrying you. But let's eat first.'

They chatted about John's parents. They had moved to Scotland when they'd married during the Great War, and

299

although he'd grown to love it, he preferred to live and work in England.

'It's bitter up there in the winter,' he said.

'Have you sisters and brothers?'

'A sister . . . Laura. She's younger – still at school.'

'Have you ever been married?' As soon as she spoke the words, Rosie wished she hadn't. A faint flush rose on his cheeks. He finished the last bite and put his knife and fork together.

'No. I was engaged once but I broke it off. We were too young and didn't know our own minds. There's been no one really serious since then.' He took her hand again. 'But we're not talking about me. It's *you* I'm worried about.' His warm grey eyes were full of concern. 'You know you can tell me anything and it will go no further than this table. I might not be able to help but you know what they say – a problem shared is a problem halved.' She stayed silent. 'But don't if you'd rather not,' he added.

'Heather's trying to turn Poppy against me,' she blurted.

John's eyes widened but he just said quietly, 'In what way?'

'Telling her I've gone away and won't be back. Apparently, Poppy was terribly upset. Well, of course she was.' Rosie's eyes blazed. 'She's too young to understand. But I'd wondered why she didn't send me one of her drawings as she'd promised. I only found out through Heather sending me this photograph.'

She took it out of her bag and pushed it along the table towards him. He picked it up and studied it.

'I don't understand. Surely sending this was to let you know Poppy was well and happy.'

Rosie shook her head. 'The following day I got a letter from her telling me Poppy was so upset that it had been difficult to cope with her tears and tantrums and that I shouldn't come home when I had any leave as it would stir her up again.'

'Hmm. I don't like the sound of that.' He hesitated. 'I'd like to meet your little girl. Do you think that would be possible tomorrow sometime? Maybe I could take you both for lunch – or a picnic in one of the parks if the weather's fine.'

Rosie drew in a sharp breath. Was John merely being a genuinely good friend who liked children, or did it mean something more serious was developing in their relationship? And if that was the case, did she mind? She shook herself. He was just being the nice decent man she'd first met. The trouble was, Hugo had made her mistrust other men – not that she'd become remotely close to anyone since him. That was probably the reason why she'd made no attempt to bother about meeting anyone new. She chewed her lip. John was waiting for her answer.

'Um . . . well, I think Poppy hopes to have me to herself while I'm home.' She looked directly at him. 'That sounds horrid, doesn't it?'

'No, it's entirely understandable.'

Rosie thought quickly. She could still spend the whole morning with Poppy. 'I think she'd like a picnic,' she said.

'Then that's settled.' He smiled. 'Have you ever been to Eaton Park?'

She shook her head, relieved he hadn't mentioned Waterloo Park, where she and Hugo had often gone when they were courting. Hugo had found a bench a little further apart from the others, the tree branches dropping down to give them some privacy. That was where he'd first kissed her, where he'd first told her he'd fallen in love with her, and only weeks later asked her if she would marry him . . .

Desperately she tried to concentrate on what John was saying.

'It's had pots of money spent on it since the Great War and there's plenty to do for children. They have their own play area and there's a wildlife section as well as a duckpond. I think Poppy would love it.'

'And can we make it Sunday?' Rosie said. 'Then she'll probably be tired of me and happy to have you along.'

John smiled. 'Of course. I shall look forward to it. Shall we say twelve noon? I'll pick you both up . . . and bring a picnic hamper.' He paused. 'In the meantime, Claire has invited you for supper Sunday night. She suggests around seven-thirty.' He paused. 'I know it'll be your last night but she'd love to see you while you're here.'

Rosie hesitated, her mind racing. If she said yes she'd feel guilty not spending the evening with her family. But then her mother usually had the meal on the table by half-past five at her father's request when he was on the day shift. She'd still have time to put Poppy to bed, read her a story, and catch the bus to Claire's. It would be so good to share an evening meal with people who didn't keep arguing all the time, and being constantly grilled by her father.

'Tell Claire I'd love to,' she said.

Chapter Thirty-Three

It was Saturday evening, and Sid Frost, sitting at the head of the table staring at his plate, suddenly looked across at Rosie and said:

'What have you been doin' today then, girl?'

Rosie breathed out her relief, sure he'd been going to ask her about last night.

'Poppy and I went to the swimming pool. She's getting on really well.'

'I can nearly swim, Daddy,' Poppy piped up.

'That's marvellous, poppet.' He turned back to Rosie.

'And where were you yesterday evenin', girl?'

Here it comes.

Rosie felt the warmth rush to her cheeks and was acutely aware of Heather's eyes on her. Roddy and the girls were busy eating. Her mother hadn't touched hers.

'I told Mum I'd been invited out for supper.'

'By that posh bloke from London?'

'If you mean John, he's not posh,' Rosie said. 'He's perfectly normal.'

'Hmm. I don't remember you having that good a judgement – particularly where boys are concerned.'

'John's hardly a boy,' Rosie retorted, knowing she should

keep silent in front of Roddy and the girls, but not able to help herself.

'What does he do?'

'He's in the Navy. And if you must know, his aunt Claire has asked me to dinner tomorrow evening.'

'And he'll be there, too, I suppose,' he said, staring at her. He put an overflowing forkful of food in his mouth. 'You want to mind what you say to him, Miss.'

He's terrified I'll find someone who likes me enough . . . She wouldn't allow herself to take the thought any further *. . . and I'll take Poppy away from him.* She watched as he ate fast, hardly chewing before he swallowed the next mouthful. He'd told her once it was because they never had much chance to enjoy their food at the fire station, always being on the alert. How did she truly feel about him? Well, she loved him because he was her father, but she didn't always like him or agree with him. *Could* he have been the one to have written to the WRNS about her so it would get her dismissed? So that she wouldn't be mixing with any men and in his eyes put Poppy in danger? Her mother had categorically said no, but she wouldn't put it past him. He didn't like anyone going against him. But if it wasn't him, who could have done such a mean trick?

The question refused to go away.

When Rosie tucked Poppy up in bed that evening, she said:

'I'm thinking about what we're going to do tomorrow, darling.'

'I want to do the same as today.'

'No, darling, we should do something different. And you won't have read your books by then so there won't be any point going back to the library.'

'But I want to go back and swim,' Poppy whined.

'Wouldn't you like to go to a big park where they have a pond and ducks?'

'Can I feed them?'

'Yes. They'd be pleased to see you if you bring them some bread.'

'Can I sit on top of the bus again?'

Rosie hesitated. Might as well come out with it.

'We're not going on the bus. A friend of mine is going to come for us in his motorcar.' She shut the book she'd been reading to Poppy. 'You'd like that, wouldn't you – having a ride in a motorcar?'

'No, I want it just me and you.' Poppy screwed up her face and squeezed out a tear.

'He's a very nice friend, darling, and he said he wants to meet you. He doesn't have any children of his own and I think he's sad.'

'Why doesn't he got children?'

'Because he doesn't have a wife.'

'Why doesn't he?'

'I don't think he's found anyone to love enough to marry.' *Please, Poppy, stop asking so many questions.*

'Does he love *you* enough to marry?'

Rosie startled at the child's probing. How on earth had she put *that* together?

'No, sweetheart, he's just a nice friend.'

'I *hate* him!' Poppy stuck out her lower lip. 'You want to be with *him* and not me.'

'Darling, it's not true. I thought you'd like to have a lovely day out. He's going to bring a picnic.'

'I don't want a picnic. I just want me and you.'

'You're tired, Poppy. We'll talk about it tomorrow.'

* * *

In bed that night Rosie couldn't sleep. Heather, after much grumbling that she had to give up her bed *again*, was snoring as usual, and Ivy was doing her heavy breathing. What was she going to do about John tomorrow? The last thing she wanted was to upset Poppy when their time together was so precious, but she'd thought – wrongly, it seemed – that her little girl would enjoy something different. Maybe things would right themselves in the morning.

But she was disappointed. Poppy clung on to the idea of having her Mosey all to herself.

'The trouble is, darling, that we can't let him know. It's quite a long walk to the nearest telephone box and he might not even be there to answer it. He's not coming until lunchtime so we can have the whole morning to ourselves.' She tried to give Poppy a hug but she shrugged her off.

'I want ALL DAY!' Poppy shouted.

She had to put a stop to this. Poppy was behaving like a spoilt child.

'We'll have the morning together,' Rosie said firmly, 'then when Mr Palmer comes to collect us, you can decide what to do.' Then something struck her. 'Poppy, do you remember the Christmas tree someone left on the doorstep on Christmas morning?'

Poppy's smooth little forehead furrowed as if she couldn't follow the sudden change of subject. Then her eyes brightened as she remembered.

'Father Christmas left it for us with a box of pretty balls to hang on it.'

'No, darling, it wasn't Father Christmas, it was Mr Palmer.'

Poppy's eyes flashed. 'It wasn't your stupid friend – it was Father Christmas. You said it was.'

'I thought it was at the time,' Rosie said, 'but I found out it was Mr Palmer. His name is John and he's not stupid – he's a very kind man.' She gazed down at Poppy. 'But if you still don't want to come, I shall go because I said I would, and it would be very rude of us to send him away on a wasted journey. So what would you like to do this morning?'

Poppy was silent.

'All right. I'll decide,' Rosie said. 'Shall we go and buy a penny's worth of aniseed balls from the Kandy Kabin?'

'Can I have a sherbet with a lickish stick?'

Rosie hid a smile. 'I think you mean a sherbet with a liquorice stick.'

Poppy frowned. 'That's what I said.'

'All right. We'll get you dressed and maybe see Bonzo out for a walk with Mrs Day.'

'Oh, yes.' Poppy looked up at Rosie with eager eyes. 'Mosey, can *we* have a puppy?'

'One day, darling.'

'When?'

'When the time is right.'

'When will it be right?'

'When the nasty men stop fighting us.'

'Do you promise?'

'I promise,' Rosie said, swallowing hard.

One day, when she had her own home and could claim Poppy as her daughter, she would take her to choose a puppy. Please God, don't let it be too long.

When John Palmer drew up outside the cottage, she still didn't know if Poppy would go with them. And if she wouldn't, Rosie still hadn't decided if she really would leave her behind. As she heard him knock, she pulled in a deep breath and crossed her fingers. She opened the door and he stood there smiling, his fair hair catching a beam of sunlight.

'Hello, Rosemary,' he said. 'Are you both ready?'

'I am but I think Poppy's still upstairs. Can you wait a minute?' Rosie turned and shouted up the staircase. 'Poppy, Mr Palmer's here. We're ready to go.'

There was no reply. Rosie bounded up the stairs, her heart thudding. She went into her parents' bedroom. Poppy was on their bed, face down and sobbing.

'Poppy – what's the matter?'

'You're going away again. And you won't come back.'

So that was it. Poppy was already thinking ahead. 'Not today, darling. I'm not going until tomorrow. And when I do, of course I'll come back – as often as I can. But Mr Palmer's waiting for us outside and then we're off to the park in his motorcar. We're going to have a lovely afternoon in the sunshine feeding the ducks and having a picnic. Here, blow your nose.'

She handed Poppy a handkerchief.

'Are you ready?'

Poppy shook her head and sniffed.

'We'll wait for you five minutes,' Rosie said, making up her mind. 'If you don't come, then Mr Palmer and I will have to feed the ducks and have a lovely picnic on our own.'

She closed the bedroom door quietly behind her and hurried downstairs to find her mother.

'Mum, John's here. I don't think Poppy's coming with us. We're going to wait a few minutes in case she changes her mind.'

'Do you want me to have a word with her?'

'No. She's old enough to make her own decision.'

She gave her mother a peck on the cheek and went to open the front door. John was standing outside his car looking serious.

'Where's Poppy?'

'I don't think she's coming,' Rosie said. 'She's upset that she's not having me to herself for the rest of the day. But we've been together all day yesterday and this morning and I've told her what a nice afternoon we've planned.'

'I don't like to take you away from her,' John said. 'It isn't fair to either of you.'

'She has to learn she can't always have everything her way.' Rosie chewed her lower lip. 'Let's get in the car. I've given her five minutes.'

'All right.' He opened the passenger door for her and made sure she was comfortable before shutting it. Then he went round to his side. Ten minutes slipped by.

'I think we should go,' Rosie said. 'She's obviously not coming.'

'If you're sure.' John put the key in the starter and switched on the engine. He had just looked in the mirror to pull away when Rosie heard a shout.

'Wait for me! Wait for me, Mosey!'

John immediately turned off the ignition and Rosie sprang out while Poppy ran towards the car, pigtails flying.

'Can I sit in the front?' she said.

'Yes, darling, you can sit on my lap.' She turned to John. 'This is my friend, Mr Palmer. Can you say hello to him?'

'Hello, Mr Palmer. Are you going to marry Mosey?'

Chapter Thirty-Four

'Someone at the station is sick so Claire's had to rush off,' John said, as he opened the door to Rosie that same evening. He ushered her inside. 'It's her first night on duty after her training so she couldn't get out of it and sends her profound apologies. She didn't have time to leave us anything so I'm afraid it's going to be scrambled eggs on toast.' He gave a rueful smile. 'I'm not much of a cook.' He took Rosie's hat and coat.

'We've had that lovely picnic you brought,' Rosie said, 'so I'm not ever so hungry. Scrambled eggs would be perfect.'

After the light supper, Rosie said, 'Is Claire enjoying her volunteer work?'

'She took to the training like a duck to water. She's that sort of person. Reliable, calm in an emergency, already has some basic First Aid, and remembers people's names – jolly useful for an ARP warden, I'd say.'

'I think she's marvellous,' Rosie said. 'I don't think I could do it. I'm too squeamish with blood.'

'Let's hope she doesn't see too much of that,' John said, taking out his pipe. He began to light it, then looked contrite. 'Oh, sorry, Rosemary, I didn't ask if you minded.'

'No, go ahead. I quite like the smell of tobacco.'

'Do you think Poppy enjoyed her afternoon with us?'

'I think she did. She loved feeding the ducks. That was her favourite although she was fascinated with the fountain. It was the first one she'd ever seen.'

Please don't say anything about Poppy's bombshell question.

John smiled. 'I know what you're thinking. And I think Poppy's adorable.'

'She's a precocious little girl, as you can tell. She thinks because you're a man and a friend that . . .' She broke off, the warmth rushing to her cheeks.

'That I might be a contender for your hand,' John grinned. 'She's very perceptive for a child of that age.' He looked at her, his eyes twinkling. 'It's not such a bad idea, is it?'

Rosie gave a start. Was he serious?

'You know, Rosemary, I've become awfully fond of you.' He took her hand. 'And I think you like me.'

'I do, but—'

'Let me finish, dearest.' He brought her hand to his lips and kissed it. 'I don't need to tell you how dangerous this war could still get. The worst seems to be over in London but Liverpool and poor Coventry as well as many other towns have taken a beating. I know you're in Buckinghamshire somewhere, and I pray you keep safe, but you never know when Jerry will strike next. If we married, you'd have your own home and could finally claim Poppy as your daughter. And I think Poppy would grow to like me. I don't have children – part of the reason I broke off my engagement . . . well, she didn't want them. So you'd be doing me a huge favour by allowing me to be Poppy's father.' He took her gently by both arms. 'And if anything should happen to me, you'd have a widow's pension to provide for you both.' He paused, his grey eyes looking deeply into hers. 'What do you say, my dearest?'

He hasn't mentioned my work. Almost taking it for granted

311

that I'd automatically give it up. For that matter he hasn't even mentioned love.

'I-I don't know. You've taken me completely by surprise. We hardly know one another.'

'I know all I need to know, and that I want to take care of you. You've had a rotten start as a young girl with a baby, having to cover it up like some dirty secret, and then that business about being dismissed from the WRNS . . . I just want to be there for you.'

'Can I think about it?'

'Of course.' He kissed her forehead. 'But don't keep me waiting too long.'

'It's getting late, John. I think I'd better go.'

He glanced at the clock. 'Claire thought she'd be home by now. She'll be sorry she's missed you.'

There was a sudden loud crack. Rosie jumped as the room was plunged into blackness.

'Whatever's happening?'

'Must be a storm coming and it's fused the electricity. I'll go and check.'

She felt rather than heard him get up, then stumble on something.

'Damn! I need to find a torch and I'm not sure where Claire would keep one.'

And then a blood-curdling sound ripped through the darkness. Starting low, it crescendoed to a high whine that sounded like a thousand people screaming; then the note dropped down the scale. Dear God, it was the air-raid siren. She'd only ever heard it the day war was declared – just a practice to alert people to the sound – and on Pathé News. The howling started again, then the whine. It kept repeating, sending shudders through her body every time. She held her breath. Was this it? Was an enemy bomb at this moment hurtling towards them? Even overhead? Were they about to die?

'Damn! I didn't expect that tonight.' John's voice was urgent. 'We're given about five minutes. There's an air-raid shelter in the garden but I don't want to risk going out in the dark. I think we'll be better off in the cellar. If only I could bloody see what I'm doing.' He flicked his lighter which did very little.

'There's some candles in the candelabra on the dining room table.'

'Right. I'll grab a couple. You stay where you are.' John's voice was calmer now, but it didn't stop Rosie's legs from shaking as she managed to stand.

'I've found the candles,' John called. 'Where are you?'

She heard him open the drawing room door. It was so black she couldn't see her own outstretched hand. 'By the sofa.'

'All right.' There was a soft pool of light from the candle John was holding. 'The cellar door is near the end of the hall.'

The siren went off again, and this time it sounded like hysterical shrieking, shredding her nerves, until it sank into a low-pitched gurgle. She was aware of John lifting a trapdoor and then the thud of the lid as he let it back.

'They don't sound far away,' he said. 'Keep close to me. I'll go down first so you can see where you're going. Just take it slowly.'

He turned and backed down.

'All right, Rosemary. Come down backwards.'

She turned round and took hold of the edges of two wooden rails supporting what didn't feel any more substantial than a ladder, when there was a sudden deafening bang. Instinctively, she put her hands to her ears and would have toppled backwards if John hadn't shot back up the steps and held her steady. She twisted her neck round.

'I'm sorry, John, I can't go down that ladder. I don't want to be buried alive.'

She scrambled back up the ladder, when there was a sudden flash of light illuminating every detail of the hall, then instantly she was plunged into darkness with the force of an explosion. The house seemed to totter, knocking her off her feet and sending her crashing onto the marble-slabbed floor.

She heard John shout her name.

Then everything went black.

'Rosemary, wake up. It's me, John. Come on, dearest. Please wake up.'

She couldn't pull herself out of the black tunnel. She heard a voice calling from afar and she was vaguely aware of something burning. But it was nothing to do with her. All she wanted was to be left to sleep. For ever. She sank back into oblivion.

Rosie's eyelids fluttered. What were those strange swirling shadows? Where was she? She tried to move her legs but they were too heavy. It was too much of an effort to think about what had happened to them. One of the shadows was bending over her. She could feel warm breath on her cheek. Why didn't they leave her alone? All she wanted to do was . . . Her eyelids drooped down. She felt herself slipping back . . .

'Rosemary, my dear. Don't worry. You're quite safe.'

A woman's voice. She recognised it. Warm and concerned. This time she opened her eyes.

'Mrs Edgerton – Claire?' Rosie's voice came out in a croak.

'Yes, my dear.'

And then she remembered. Dear God. That bang. She'd thought her eardrums had burst. She wanted to shake her head to dislodge the jumble inside.

She tried to pull herself up in the bed.

'John . . .' Panic made her voice rise. 'Is he—?'

'He's fine. Don't try to speak.' Gentle hands set her slowly back onto the pillow. 'Have a few sips of water.' She held out a glass and Rosie took it with trembling hands.

'H-how long have I been here?'

'A few hours. I've only just got back. But John stayed with you until I came. It's been quite a night while you've been sleeping.'

'The house – was it hit?'

'Mostly on the far end – it could have been a lot worse. But we still don't have electricity. Thankfully, we've plenty of oil lamps.'

'I heard bells.' Rosie licked a drop of water from her lips.

'It was the fire brigade,' Claire said. 'They were very efficient and soon put out the fire.' She shook her head. 'It must have been a terrible shock for you.'

Rosie couldn't think clearly. Then she pulled herself up.

'What's the time?'

'Nearly three.'

'In the morning?'

'Yes.'

'Oh, no. Mum . . . Dad – they'll be worried.'

'I know. John says they're not on the telephone. But now you're awake he's going to drive over and let them know you're safe.'

Claire plumped a pillow behind her head and Rosie sank back, then remembered it had been her friend's first night as an ARP warden.

'You must have had a dreadful night if we felt the raid out here.'

'It *was* grim. I've only just got in. Someone told me our road had been hit so they let me come back early. I was so worried about you both.' Rosie heard her take in a jagged breath. 'They're still trying to find people who are missing.'

There was a knock at the door and John walked in carrying an oil lamp. He hurried to her bedside.

'Oh, good. You're awake. I've made a pot of tea. I think we could all do with one, but I'll bring yours on a tray.'

'No, I want to get up,' Rosie said, throwing back the covers. 'I'm perfectly all right.' She looked at him. 'Were you hurt at all?'

'No, but I would have been if you hadn't changed your mind about going down the ladder. I would have been halfway and the explosion would probably have blown me backwards and smashed my head in. As it was, I immediately followed you up the ladder, to find you'd been sent flying. Bloody Jerry.' He gave her a rueful smile. 'Excuse my French.'

'You're excused,' Rosie smiled weakly as she sat on the edge of the bed, feeling her feet on the floor.

'Here, let me help.' John held her arm as she got to her feet.

Her head swam but she wasn't going to tell these two dear people that. They would insist she stay at least a few more hours. But Mum and Dad were her greatest priority.

'I'll just have that cup of tea and then I'd be grateful if you'd take me home,' she said.

John pulled up outside her house, now silent and black like all the other houses in the row.

'Are you sure you'll be all right?' he said.

'Quite sure.'

'I'll wait until you're in.' He turned to her. 'I meant what I said about us getting married.' He kissed her swiftly on her lips – so swiftly and lightly it was hardly noticeable. 'Don't keep me waiting too long, will you?'

'I won't.'

'May I come over later when you've rested to see how you are?'

'If you can face my dad.' Rosie hesitated. 'John, I'm due at work this afternoon, on the four o'clock shift. I have to catch a train in good time in case there are any hold-ups.'

'If you're well enough to travel—'

'I will be,' she interrupted.

'If you're well enough to travel,' he repeated, 'I'll run you to the station. And if you have any symptoms of concussion, I shall run you to the hospital instead.'

He made to get out of the car to open her door, but she stopped him. 'You go on.' She hesitated, then gave him the same brief kiss he'd given her. 'Thank you for all you've done, John.'

She unlocked the front door and was on the first tread of the staircase when her father's voice came from the parlour.

'Where the devil have you been? No, don't tell me . . . you've spent the night with your fancy boyfriend.'

She stopped in her tracks, her heart thumping. Was he insinuating what she thought he was?

'Come in here, Rosemary,' he ordered. 'I want to talk to you.'

Rosie hovered in the doorway.

'I'm sorry, Dad, it'll have to wait till morning. Then I'll explain. But I'm too tired now.'

'*You're* tired.' He bolted up. 'I've been sittin' up all braddy night waitin' for you. We heard the sirens go off in the city. Your mother's been worried to death that you might've

317

been caught in the air-raid. I happen to know different. You've not learnt your lesson, have you, girl? It weren't enough that you got yourself up the duff when you were only seventeen.' He glared at her. 'Look at you. Your hair's a mess . . . your eyes all red. And this time you're old enough to know *exactly* what you're doin'. There's no excuse. And if you find yourself with another kid, I won't be bailin' you out this time.' He paused. 'So what do you have to say for yourself?'

Fury surged through her. Bailing her out? How dare her father speak to her like that without hearing what had happened. Her eyes must be red from the explosion, but why should she stand here listening to him making these shocking accusations.

Before she could stop herself, she blurted in a tone laden with sarcasm:

'What I have to say for myself is that John has asked me to marry him. I told him I would think about it. But you've just now persuaded me that it's the right thing to do.'

His eyebrows shot up.

'He has, has he? And have you mentioned you have a child already?' her father said as though he were playing his trump card. 'A child by some bounder who jilted you. Refused to make an honest woman of you. Because when you *do* tell him about Poppy, I think you'll find he'll change his mind. No man wants to take on another man's child, particularly an illegitimate one.'

The words cut through her like a knife. She stepped into the room. Her father was still in his chair, looking up at her, his eyes gleaming.

'Yes, you've told me that once before,' she said quietly. 'And I believed you. But not any more.' She watched as his eyes narrowed. 'Be prepared to give up Poppy. You will no longer be her daddy. John knows about Poppy and he wants to give us *both* a home. He's proposed marriage to me. I'm going to tell him yes – and the sooner, the better.'

She marched out, slamming the door behind her.

Chapter Thirty-Five

'Where were *you* last night then?' Heather demanded as she sat up in bed the following morning – Rosie's last. Ivy was still asleep beside her.

'You probably snored your way right through the air-raid,' Rosie retorted.

'What air-raid? I didn't hear nothing.'

'In Norwich. Late last night.'

'Where were you then? With your boyfriend?' Her tone was mocking.

'If you mean John, yes, I was with him at his aunt's. Then as he was about to take me home, a bomb exploded on the house.'

Heather's eyes widened.

'Oo-er. How exciting.'

'No, it wasn't,' Rosie said curtly as she attempted to get out of bed. The room swam. She sat on the edge, taking in deep breaths, willing the dizzy spell to subside. She put her hand to her forehead, feeling nauseous. If she were honest, she hardly felt any better than when she'd first come round at Claire's. John had been worried she had concussion. Well, she'd get up and wash and have something to eat. Maybe she'd feel more like it with some porridge inside her.

'You look terrible,' Heather said with a smirk. 'I expect it's a hangover.'

'Well, it isn't,' Rosie snapped. 'For your information the explosion caused me to have an accident, but of course you wouldn't be interested in that simple explanation, would you?'

She pulled herself upright and put on her dressing gown.

'Well, what happened then?' Heather's tone was peevish.

'I don't think you'd be interested to hear the details, Heather,' Rosie tossed over her shoulder as she left the bedroom.

'I couldn't sleep 'til I heard you come in last night,' her mother said when Rosie entered the kitchen.

'I'm sorry, Mum.'

'We heard the air-raid sirens go off. I was worried to death. Where were you?'

'I told you – at Claire Edgerton's.'

'With her nephew?'

'Yes, John was there, too. I did tell you.'

'Well, your father and I are not pleased, him keeping you out late like that with an air-raid going on.'

'Mum, please let me explain. Claire invited me for supper but she'd had to leave before I got there. She's now an ARP warden and was filling in for someone who was ill. John and I were just chatting when we heard the sirens go off. We tried to take shelter but there was no warning. The planes were already overhead and one of them dropped a bomb and hit the house. I was thrown to the floor and hit my head and was knocked out. I don't know what happened after that. When I woke up Claire was there. Whatever Dad has accused me of didn't happen. Nothing happened between John and me. That's the truth. I'm hurt that you've both jumped to the wrong conclusion.'

Her mother let out a long sigh.

'All right, I believe you, love, but your father takes a lot of convincin'.' She stirred the saucepan of porridge, her back towards Rosie. 'He's very upset. He said this man has asked you to marry him and you've said yes.' She turned round. 'It that true?'

'Yes, it's true.' She stared at her mother. 'I thought you'd be pleased for me.'

'Do you love him?'

'I'm very fond of him. He's kind and thoughtful. He helped get me my job after I was dismissed from the Wrens. He's a good man. I think Poppy liked him and he wants to give both of us a proper home.'

'But you don't love him.' Her mother gave her a sharp look. 'Does he love you?'

'He doesn't wear his heart on his sleeve. But I know he does.' She looked at her mother directly. 'Mum, I can't stay with you for ever. And I want Poppy to know she's my daughter. You and Dad don't seem to understand how it's affected me all these years pretending she's my young sister.'

'I know it's been hard for you, love. But you must think of Poppy. What a shock it would be for her to be torn away from us, from Dad who adores her, and live with a stranger.'

'John won't be a stranger. He'll be her new daddy.'

Poppy's new daddy. She bit her lip hard. It should have been Hugo. He wouldn't have been her new daddy but her *real* daddy. But he didn't know of Poppy's existence, though what was the point of dragging this up when it wouldn't lead anywhere. John was a decent man. She knew he would keep to his word and take Poppy as his daughter and would likely officially adopt her. But she might as well admit – even if only to herself – that she wasn't in love with him.

Heather stormed into the kitchen.

'What's the matter with Poppy? She was crying her eyes out just now.'

'She knows I'm leaving today,' Rosie said, then wished she hadn't said the words. This was exactly what her sister had warned her would happen.

Heather looked stonily at her. 'I'd better go up and see her as I'm the only one she'll listen to. The only one that can stop her tears.'

But minutes later she came down saying that Poppy was inconsolable.

By the time John drew up, Rosie still wasn't feeling right. She heard the motorcar and went outside. The last thing she needed was another member of the family saying disparaging things to a person they'd never met.

'Right. The Norfolk and Norwich Hospital for you,' John said when he saw her pale face. 'I think you've still got concussion.'

'I'll have to let my mother know.'

Rosie was back in two minutes.

'Oh, dear. She's going to worry about me now until I'm home,' she said as she settled into the passenger seat.

On the way to the hospital John told her that apparently there had been well over a hundred bombs landing in the city, though they hadn't yet been given the official figures.

'You can see the difference in the traffic this morning,' he said, 'but the milkman and postman and paperboy came at their usual time. The postman said he's seen whole streets obliterated.' He turned to her. 'Didn't you say your sister Heather works at Woolworths?'

'Yes.' She felt a sliver of fear.

'That's been hit as well as Curls department store – but not badly, I don't think.' He gave her a quick glance. 'You know I could hear them while you were out of it. Thank

323

God it was over in an hour and, by the time you came round, the Luftwaffe was on its way back to Germany.'

'I just hope it was a solitary raid,' Rosie said, feeling sick as John suddenly braked as he almost missed the turning into the hospital car park. But it was full.

'Must be from injuries or worse last night,' he said grimly. 'I'll have to find somewhere outside the gates. You go in and tell them what's happened at Reception.'

Rosie walked into a packed waiting room and registered.

'Someone will be with you shortly,' the receptionist told her.

Rosie looked at her watch. It was already coming up to eleven. If she didn't get in until eleven and they had to run tests and wait for results, there was no way she'd be back at Bletchley Park to start her afternoon shift. She began to be agitated, then scolded herself. It wouldn't help matters so she might as well calm down. She'd have to find a phone box, that's all.

'Miss Frost.' A smiling nurse called her name.

'That's me.' Rosie shot up.

She followed the nurse, who showed her into a small room off the corridor.

'Mr Hawkins, Miss Frost for you.'

The man sitting at the desk in his white coat remained seated. He gestured to the chair.

'Please take a seat and tell me what happened before we examine you.'

She quickly explained.

'Do you still feel dizzy?'

'Not now. I did this morning.'

'Any nausea?'

'A bit.'

'Headache?'

'It just feels dull.'

'What day was yesterday?' he suddenly barked.

She startled. 'Um . . . Monday.'

'And the date?'

'Twenty-seventh of April.'

'And who is our Prime Minister?'

'Winston Churchill.'

He nodded. 'Good. It doesn't look as though your memory is impaired. But you might feel inordinately tired for a few days – even a couple of weeks or so. You need to rest. Have some quiet time. Reading, writing letters, listening to some music – not too jazzy.' He smiled for the first time, and she gave him a tremulous smile back. 'Do you work, Miss Frost?'

'Yes.'

'In Norwich?'

'No. I work for the Foreign Office.' He raised an eyebrow. 'Clerical work,' she added.

'In London?'

'No.' She hesitated. 'I'm sorry, doctor, I've signed the Official Secrets Act so I can't say more.'

His eyes widened a fraction. He looked at her directly with what seemed like new respect.

'Then let them know you won't be back for at least a fortnight. After that, so long as you feel much better, you can go in.'

'B-but I can't be away that long.'

'I'm afraid you'll have to. You probably have a mild case of concussion, but on rare occasions it can become complicated and you could end up needing to go to hospital. But if you rest, I'm sure you'll be fine. Your brain has been jolted. You just have to allow it to settle down. Any headaches, take a couple of aspirin. No alcohol at all. Drink water and get plenty of sleep and you'll be right as rain.' He stood. 'And don't hesitate to come back to us if you have any worry whatsoever.'

'Thank you, doctor.' This time he raised both eyebrows. 'I'm sorry,' Rosie corrected herself, 'I meant *Mr* Hawkins.'

He nodded. 'That will be all. And good luck. I don't expect to see you in my consultancy room again.' He gave a flash of his teeth and looked at his list to see who his next patient was.

Rosie's head threatened to swim again with the thought of being off work for the next fortnight, as she walked back to the waiting room. What would Hugo say? He'd think she was a weakling. Really, she was perfectly all right. She should at least go back tomorrow.

John stood as soon as he spotted her.

'How did you get on?'

She told him, playing down the rest and quiet, not mentioning it would be impossible to have that at home with all the comings and goings, sharing a room with her two sisters and her dad on shift work.

'Didn't he say you ought not to be going back to work just yet?' John said with more perception than she'd given him credit for.

'He mentioned something about having a few days off,' Rosie muttered.

'Why don't I talk to Claire? You could stay with her. It would be a lot quieter for you.'

'Oh, please don't,' she said. 'It's a really kind thought but—'

'No buts,' he interrupted. 'Claire already told me on the q.t. that if the doctor says you are not to return to work straightaway, then she'd love to have you – for as long as necessary. And she means it.'

It was too tempting. But she'd feel disloyal to her family.

'I'll see how I get on and if it doesn't work, I'll ring Claire,' she said.

'Promise?'

'Yes.'

'Let's get out of here.' He opened the hospital entrance door for her to pass through.

'I need to make that phone call to let them know at work,' Rosie said, 'and then I'll be perfectly all right to get the bus home. You've used up enough petrol on me already.'

'I'm lucky and get a supply.' He looked at her. 'And I'm taking you home.'

He didn't say anything further until they were sitting in his car. Then he turned to her.

'I'd like to meet your mother if she's there.' He smiled. 'I'm hoping she's going to be my mother-in-law.' He smiled. 'That is, if you give me the answer I'm longing to hear. Will you say yes, Rosemary?'

He seemed to think it was a foregone conclusion. She took a deep breath. 'You know I'm fond of you, don't you?'

'I should hope so,' John chuckled.

'But that's not enough for marriage.'

He studied her. 'Listen, Rosemary, I once loved someone desperately. It didn't work. I think that kind of love is over-rated, so I'll settle for fond. I just want to take care of you and Poppy.' He smiled, his warm grey eyes lighting up. 'And one day, I hope we'll have more children.'

What a thoroughly nice man. Honest. Kind. Loving. Not saying he hoped they'd have children of their own but simply hoping they'd have more. Maybe she would never have such an opportunity again . . .

'If you're really sure,' she said shakily.

'I'm sure.'

This time he kissed her fully on the mouth, his lips lingering on hers. His breath was fresh. It was a warm kiss. Gentle, tender, sweet. But he didn't kiss like Hugo. No one ever would.

Chapter Thirty-Six

That evening had been fraught, to say the least. Heather had looked none too pleased to hear that Rosie was not going back to work for another day or two and Ivy was grumbling that they'd been told by the foreman they all had to step up their work.

'"We can't go no harder," I told him,' Ivy said, looking round the table, her glasses slipping down her nose. 'And everyone clapped.'

'Good for you,' Rosie said, pleased her sister, who was usually so quiet, had stuck up for the other girls. Maybe going out to work would be the making of her.

'At least your place weren't hit,' Heather joined in. 'How do you think I felt when I went into Woolies and found half the store smashed to bits? We were told to save what we could and they're going to turn some buses into shops and serve from there.' She looked round the table. 'That should be a laugh. I don't know if I've even got a job.'

Dad, who had not said a word at supper, and barely glanced at Rosie, got up to leave the table and prepare for the night shift.

'I hope there won't be any bombing like last night, Sid,' Shirley told him.

'You never know. We just have to expect anything nowa-days.'

'Have you got your spectacles?'

'Yes, I've got everything.' He gave her a quick kiss on her cheek. 'Well, cheerio, m'duck.' He turned to the children. 'Behave yourselves, kids.'

For a fleeting moment his glance fell on Rosie. Then he was gone.

'I do worry about Dad,' Shirley said, looking after his retreating figure. She looked at Rosie. 'I know you two don't always see eye-to-eye, but he means well.' She momentarily closed her eyes. 'He's a brave man to do the job he does.'

'I know, Mum, and I really respect him for that. But I just can't stand some of the hurtful things he comes out with to me.'

Rosie awoke with a jerk. What was that? Please don't say it was another air-raid. No, it wasn't that. Someone was knocking on the front door. Who on earth . . .? Oh, it'd be Dad – forgotten his key again. Whatever time was it? It was too dark to see and she didn't want to put her bedside light on for fear of waking her sisters. She couldn't hear any sound from her parents' bedroom. Puffing with irritation she flung on her dressing gown and hurried downstairs. She unlocked the door and stepped aside to let him in. But it wasn't her father.

Two policemen were standing on the step, their expressions grim.

'Sorry, to disturb you, miss. We'd like to have a word with Mrs Frost.'

Rosie stood transfixed, her heart pounding in her ears.

'I'm Miss Frost.' She looked at the older officer. 'It's my father, isn't it?'

She caught the glance between them. Without answering, the same officer stepped forward.

'May we come in, miss, and have a word with your mother?'

'The last thing he said to me was "Cheerio, duck".' Shirley Frost blew her nose soundly. 'I don't know what we're all going to do.'

'Go and put the kettle on, Ivy. Make a large pot,' Rosie called after her.

For once Heather sat mute, her face white with shock.

'I didn't hear the sirens going off in Norwich,' Rosie said. 'Was it a very bad air-raid?'

'We don't know the full story yet, miss,' the older one said, 'but your father was right in the middle of it. He was one of the firemen trying to quell the flames at Caley's. I'm afraid that's another factory completely destroyed.'

Caley's. Where she used to work. Her insides shivered and her limbs felt as though all the energy had been sucked from them. Dad was dead. She'd never see him again. Her last memory was their argument and the way he'd ignored her this evening. She felt the nausea rise in her throat.

'Was anyone else killed?' she finally asked, her voice jagged.

'No. The only thing in our favour is that Jerry comes at night. At least he has for the last two nights. Unfortunately, the night porter had both his legs blown off.'

'Oh, goodness, poor man,' Ivy murmured.

'The men in his team said he was exceptionally brave,' the younger policeman said.

'Did my husband . . .?' Shirley trailed off.

'They said he died instantly.' The older man threw her a sympathetic glance. 'He wouldn't have had time to know what was happening.'

You're wrong, Rosie thought. *He would have known exactly what was happening.*

'If you could sign here, Mrs Frost, just to let the station know we've seen you, we'll be on our way and let you all get some sleep.' He paused. 'Someone from the fire brigade will be round very soon to give you support.'

The officer handed Shirley Frost a fountain pen and sheet of paper on a clipboard. Rosie noticed her mother's hand shake as she formed the letters. Poor Mum. No Dad to lean on. Suddenly, a thought struck her. Would this mean she'd have to leave Bletchley Park to come back and look after them all? Her mother was still not that robust.

Dear God, she couldn't bear it if that were the case. Not using her brain doing work she really enjoyed, feeling she was contributing to winning the war, no matter how small her effort was in the grand scheme of things. She briefly closed her eyes and Hugo's image came into the forefront of her mind. Not seeing him again.

Stop that! *Hugo means nothing to you any more.*

Roddy didn't say a word the next morning when Shirley told him before breakfast that their dad had been killed trying to put out a fire in the city. He blinked several times, his face white, as he stared up at his mother. Without asking permission to leave the table he jumped down and rushed out of the scullery door.

'Oh, dear.' Shirley shook her tear-stained face. 'Poor little chap.' She stared at Rosie. 'I don't think I can break the news to Poppy, Rosie. Would you do it?'

Rosie nodded. She'd had no sleep at all since she'd crept back into bed a half-hour after Heather and Ivy had gone back upstairs. Her eyes were stinging and her head felt every bit as bad as it had when she'd first come round in one of

Claire's bedrooms. It already seemed a year ago instead of just yesterday.

'I'll take her for a walk,' she said. 'It might be better away from the house.'

'You do what you think, love.'

'I'll go and get her dressed,' Rosie said.

'Can I stay with you today, Mosey?' Poppy said when Rosie gently woke her. 'I don't want to go to school now you're here.'

'You don't have to. Not today anyway. We'll get you ready for a walk after you've had your porridge.'

'I don't like porridge.'

'Would you like a piece of toast and jam?'

The little girl beamed. 'That means a treat.' She gazed up at Rosie. 'Is today a treat day, Mosey?'

If only . . .

'Not exactly, darling.'

Rosie and Poppy sat in the garden of the Lazar House library. Poppy had wanted to change her book so Rosie hoped it might be a diversion after the news she was about to give the little girl. The sun warmed her face as Poppy chattered away and giggled about another new friend, Tommy, and how they'd played a trick on Miss at school. She couldn't bear the thought of watching her daughter's face crumple. And worse, not being able to say that Daddy was really her grandpa. That would have to come later. Rosie took a deep breath.

'Poppy, darling, I have something very sad to tell you about Daddy.'

Poppy stopped in her tracks.

'You know he has to help put out big fires?'

The little girl nodded, her eyes wide.

'Last night there was a very big fire.'

'Was it a 'splosion?'

'Yes, darling, the fire was caused by a big explosion and Daddy got badly burnt.'

'Is he in hospital?'

'No,' Rosie said. 'Poor Daddy was too poorly to go.' She took Poppy in her arms. 'Poppy, you know about the angels, don't you?'

'Yes.' Poppy's voice was like a kitten's mew.

'Well, the angels came and fetched Daddy and took him to heaven and they're looking after him.'

'Will he come back when it's supper?'

'No, darling.' Rosie drew her little body close. 'We won't be able to see him again. But he can still see you.'

Poppy strained her neck upwards.

'Miss says heaven is in the sky. Is that where Daddy is?'

Rosie followed her gaze.

'I expect so. But the angels will know the safest place to keep him.'

Poppy nodded, her auburn curls bouncing.

'Can we change my libe-berry book now?'

Rosie hugged her. 'Of course we can, darling,' she said.

To Rosie's surprise Heather opened the door to them. Poppy skipped ahead.

'Have you told her?' Heather asked.

'Yes.'

'And?'

Rosie closed the front door behind her.

'She obviously doesn't realise she won't ever see him again, but I told her Daddy's with the angels in heaven.'

'Didn't you say he was dead?'

'I told her in the kindest way a five-year-old would under-stand.' Rosie fought to keep her temper. 'She accepted it as much as she was able.' She looked at Heather. 'Shouldn't you be reporting for work today?'

'I told you last night, but no one listened.' Heather's voice was harsh. 'We can't open until the building's been cleared and made safe. You should have seen it.'

'I thought you said they were going to operate from buses.'

'Well, they haven't organised them yet,' Heather returned. 'And who knows when that will be.'

Rosie frowned. 'Won't they need you to help set them up?'

'Maybe. But for the time being I'm taking full responsi-bility for Poppy and you can go back to your precious job,' she smirked. 'I'll be here at home to help Mum.'

Rosie stared at her. 'You don't need to stay at home. You'll be bored sick. And anyway, Poppy goes to school all day.'

'Is that you, Rosemary?' Shirley called. 'I'm in the kitchen.'

'Coming, Mum.' Rosie glared at Heather. 'I want to speak to Mum . . . alone.'

Poppy was sitting on one of the kitchen chairs drinking a small cup of milk.

'I told Mummy Daddy's gone to heaven,' she said proudly, making a gurgling noise with her last swallow of milk.

'Poppy, can you play with Dolly for a little while?'

'But I can't hear what you're saying.' Poppy pouted as she slid down from the chair.

'Exactly,' Rosie said. 'I need to talk to Mum without you hovering.'

'What's *hovering*?'

'Go and play, Poppy, there's a good girl.'

Rosie told her mother briefly about her conversation with Heather.

'I'm not allowing that,' Shirley said firmly. 'I can't have her moochin' around under my feet all day. Your Aunt Dot is comin' down for a few weeks to give me a bit of support. She'll be here tomorrow. And Heather can get herself back to work. I've found out Woolies in't been hit nearly as bad as some of the stores. It's Curls that's goin' to use buses. The postman told me Woolies are still open for business as usual.' She looked directly at Rosie. 'So, love, you can go back to your work – I know it must be important war work because you can't tell me even where you are, let alone what you do. But if they can spare you to help me with Dad's funeral arrangements, I'd really appreciate it.'

Chapter Thirty-Seven

It will hit Poppy hard when it sinks in that she's never going to see her beloved daddy again, Rosie thought, as she stood in the phone box, the smell of stale cigarette smoke finding its way into the back of her throat.

And to make things worse, I'll be gone, too.

'Number, please,' came the nasal twang of the operator.

She was put through quickly to the Park's internal switchboard.

'. . . so I'd be really grateful if you could put that message through to Lieutenant Commander Garfield,' Rosie finished.

'Would you hold the line a moment, please.'

There was a crackling sound over the wires. Then a man's voice.

'Rose, is that you?'

Dear God, she hadn't expected to speak to Hugo. Just the sound of his voice . . .

'Rose?'

'Yes, it's me.'

'I'm sorry to learn you're still not recovered enough to come back to work.'

What was he talking about? Then she realised the operator must have only told him she wanted an extension to her sick time.

'My father's died,' she said in a flat voice.

'Oh, Rose, I *am* sorry. And on top of the accident.' There was a pause. 'How's your mother coping?'

'Not too badly, surprisingly.'

'And your sisters? Especially the little one – Poppy, isn't it? She's going to miss him but she's probably too young to understand he's never coming back.'

Rosie tried to answer but her mouth had dried up.

It was strange hearing the very words she'd been thinking only moments before – and from Hugo of all people.

When she didn't reply he said, 'Children are surprisingly resilient, but I'm worried about *you*.'

'I'm all right.' Rosie closed her eyes to stop the threatening tears. Why did he sound so concerned? Was it all part of his charm?

'Have you a date for the funeral?'

'Yes. Tuesday the twelfth. I'll be back the following day if that's all right with you.'

There was such a long pause she wondered if the connection was broken. Then she heard him clear his throat.

'Listen, Rose. Take as long as you need. But just to let you know, we all miss you.' This time the silence felt full.

Then she heard him say, very softly, 'Me, especially.'

'I don't see why I'm not allowed to go to Dad's funeral.' Roddy kicked the dining room chair leg. 'I'm twelve but everyone treats me as if I'm a baby like Poppy.'

'I'm not a baby,' Poppy piped up.

'You are.'

'Stop arguing, you two,' Rosie said. She looked at her brother. 'You can't miss school. You've got a test today. And you know it's a really important one.' She handed him his cap. 'Have you done your revision for it?'

337

'Course I have.' He snatched up his satchel and slammed out of the door.

Rosie sighed. Her mother was still upstairs with Aunt Dot, who was sharing the double bed. Roddy had begun to behave badly ever since Aunt Dot, well-meaning but sometimes a little too sharp, had arrived. Poppy repeatedly asked when her daddy was coming back and Aunt Dot had told the child bluntly that her daddy was going into a big hole in the ground today.

'It's not true.' Poppy stamped her feet. 'The angels will bring him back.'

'The sooner she learns reality the better,' Aunt Dot said when Rosie had tried to distract Poppy. 'I think you should let her attend so she has the chance to say goodbye to him – same as everyone else – except Roddy,' she added with a grimace, 'though he should be going as well.'

Maybe her aunt was right, Rosie mused. The trouble was, Aunt Dot had never had children. She liked to remind people that she called a spade a spade, but sometimes, Rosie thought, her aunt went too far. She'd better have a word with her mother. But when she broached the subject, all Shirley said was, 'I'll leave it to your judgement, dear.'

'I think I've changed my mind, Mum,' Rosie said. 'We'll let her come with us. Then she'll remember she said goodbye to him when I tell her that her daddy was really her grandpa.'

Shirley gave a start. 'When will you do that?'

'Before John and I are married. But that won't be just yet.'

Rosie brushed her hair, then swept it up the way she did when she was getting ready for work. She glanced at her watch. Coming up to nine. Although she was ready, wearing her only smart dress in navy blue her mother had made her three years ago, they hadn't allowed much time to get to the service arranged for ten o'clock in St Cuthbert's Church. Her mother, Aunt Dot and Ivy had been busy early that morning making the sandwiches in the dining room where there was more space. There'd been a whip-round in the street to pay for drinks, the modest reception to be held in the church hall. Rosie had helped Poppy wash and dress and had made breakfast for everyone, and afterwards had kept the sandwich-making team supplied with more bread and fillings. Heather had gone to their bedroom saying she had a headache and didn't feel at all well but would be down in time to leave for church.

To Rosie's surprise the church filled quickly. She recognised several firemen, but there were many she didn't know. Her father would have been pleased with such a turnout. She'd introduced John to her mother and Aunt Dot, who had both nodded their approval. Rosie breathed a sigh of relief. Now they took their places in the front pew, Poppy sitting between Heather and Rosie, with John on Rosie's other side.

The service was short, as Shirley had requested, and after they had sung 'Abide with Me', John stood aside for Rosie to leave the pew in front of him, ready to congregate for the burial. Rosie walked slowly down the aisle holding Poppy's hand as she glanced both ways at the several dozen people in attendance. Some of them nodded but every face was a blur. She was almost at the church door where the vicar stood waiting to shake hands with everyone, when a figure jumped out of the shadowy corner.

'Roddy!' she hissed. 'You're supposed to be at school.'

'Miss told me I could be excused. She said I should be allowed to go to Dad's funeral, and I can do the test tomorrow.'

'Can everyone please move forward,' one of the ushers

said, his arm guiding Rosie forward as though she were a wayward sheep.

'I'm sorry we insisted you should go to school today,' she told Roddy when they were under the outside porch. 'It wasn't fair to you.' She smiled at him and ruffled his hair. 'But I wish you'd come and found us and not had to sit alone at the back of the church.'

'Oh, I wasn't alone,' Roddy shot back. 'I sat next to an officer in the Navy. If the war's still on when I'm seventeen, that's the one I'm going to join.' He raced off.

Rosie's heart missed a beat. She spun round to see John walking behind all her family. He caught her eye and gave her a reassuring smile over the tops of their heads.

She gave a wan smile back, her mind in such a turmoil that she forgot there was a step down to the gravel driveway. She was about to lose her balance when she felt a pair of strong arms around her.

Strong, familiar arms.

'All right. I've got you.'

She looked round and into Hugo's grass-green eyes.

Rosie did her utmost not even to glance at Hugo, who stood well behind some of her father's colleagues on the other side of the coffin, but he was too tall to go unnoticed. Poppy clutched her hand tightly as though she would never let it go, and John had Rosie's other firmly in his. It should have felt comforting, but she felt trapped. She quaked at the thought of the two men meeting. Gently extracting her hand from John's, pretending she was looking for her handkerchief, she prayed Hugo would quietly slip away.

After hearing sombre words about the dearly departed, the crowd turned to make for the church hall. Although the day was sunny and mild, Rosie felt a chill at the back of her neck. She would have to invite him to stay for refreshments. But her mother would be furious and might even say something to cause embarrassment. The last thing Rosie wanted was for sparks to fly. All her mother knew of Hugo was that he'd jilted her daughter on their wedding day and it was good riddance that she'd never heard from him again.

'John, I'm just going to have a word with Mum.'

'Of course, dearest.' He wandered towards the church hall.

Poppy still clinging to her hand, Rosie caught up with Heather and Ivy, who for once appeared to be in deep conversation.

'Can you both keep an eye on Poppy for a few minutes?'

'Come to me, poppet,' Heather said immediately, clawing Poppy's hand from Rosie's.

Poppy let out a wail. Ivy fished a sweet from her pocket and unwrapped it, but Poppy shook her head, tears swimming in her eyes, and grabbed Rosie's hand again.

'All right, you can stay with me if you keep hold of my hand and don't butt in when the grown-ups are trying to talk.' Rosie glanced down at her. 'Can you do that?'

Poppy made her mouth disappear. Then she said, 'Yes.'

'Come on, then. We need to catch up with Mummy and Auntie Dot.'

The two women were about to enter the church hall when Rosie called out.

'Mum, stop a minute. I—'

Shirley and Dot stopped in their tracks, waiting for the two of them to catch up. When her mother spoke, Rosie saw her eyes were fierce.

'I know what you're goin' to say, Rosie. I've just seen Hugo. What's he doin' here after all this time? Your father would turn over in his grave if he knew.'

'I see him quite often,' Rosie said quietly. Shirley and Dot stared at her. 'I've never told you because I knew Dad would go barmy . . . but Hugo's my boss.'

'Well, get rid of him,' Dot snapped. 'We don't need him here. He's caused you enough hurt.'

Rosie blinked. Aunt Dot's words cut into her, even though Hugo deserved it.

How could she get him on her own? He was already making his way towards them. Then out of the corner of her eye she noticed Heather standing stock still, her eyes fixed on Hugo, watching his every step as though she were tracking the movements of a ghost. For a reason she couldn't explain, Rosie felt her scalp prickle.

'Hello, Rose,' Hugo said as he sauntered up to the group, then turned to Shirley. 'Hello, Mrs Frost. I'd like to offer my condolences for the loss of your husband.'

'Thank you, I'm sure,' Shirley said, her mouth in a grim line as though she were forcing out the platitude.

'May I have a word with you, Rose?' Hugo said the words to Rosie but his gaze fell on the little girl by her side. 'Hello, Poppy.'

'How do you know my name?' Poppy demanded, her neck stretched up as far as it would go.

'Because I've seen a picture of you,' Hugo said, smiling.

'Where did you see it?'

Hugo hesitated. 'Your sister, Rosie, showed it to me. But it's much nicer to see you in real life. I can see your lovely red hair like your sister Rosie's and—' He broke off. Seconds went by. And then he looked directly at Rosie, a question in his eyes.

What had he been about to say?

She felt her heart hammering so hard she thought her chest would burst. Had he been about to mention Poppy's unusual green eyes? That they were exactly the same shade as his own?

'I'm five and three-quarters.' Poppy threw her arms and legs out in a star shape.

'Well, you're a big girl – nearly six,' he grinned, though to Rosie his eyes were alert.

Please don't go on any further, Hugo.

A lump formed in her throat. Would he work out Poppy's age? Her eyes. Put two and two together? Or was she imagining things because of her guilt? It was almost a relief when she spotted John striding towards them. She braced herself to introduce them.

'Well, I don't believe it! If it's not old Garfield.' John's smile widened as he extended his hand to Hugo. 'What are *you* doing here?'

'I could say the same to you, Palmer,' Hugo grinned, enthusiastically shaking John's hand.

'You two know each other?' Rosie glanced from John to Hugo.

'Oh, yes,' Hugo told her. 'The Navy's a small world.' He turned to John. 'So what brings you here, old boy?'

'He's a—' She'd been about to say a good friend when John interrupted her.

'I'm the luckiest man in the world, Garfield. Rosemary and I are engaged to be married!'

Chapter Thirty-Eight

There was a deathly silence. Poppy gazed curiously up at the two men.

'Well, that *is* a piece of news,' Hugo finally said. 'I must congratulate you.' He looked at Rosie. 'When is the happy day?'

'We haven't set a date yet,' she gulped.

'The sooner the better as far as I'm concerned,' John said, taking Rosie's hand. 'She only has to name the day.'

'That man's Mr Palmer,' Poppy said, her little heart-shaped face upturned to Hugo. 'What's *your* name of the day?'

Hugo chuckled. 'My name of the day is Hugo.'

Poppy's eyes widened. She tried it out. 'Hoogo? That's a funny name.' She gazed at him, then hopped up and down, chanting, 'Hoogo, Hoogo, where do you go, Hoogo?' She squealed with laughter.

'You can't call grown-ups by their Christian names,' Rosie put in quickly. 'It's rude.'

'She can if I give her permission,' Hugo said. 'She looks very grown-up for her age.' His eyes crinkled as he gazed down at Poppy. 'I hereby give you permission to call me Hoogo.' Poppy giggled. 'Shall we shake hands on it?'

Poppy let go of Rosie's hand and held it out to him. Rosie thought her heart would break as Hugo took the little girl's hand – his daughter's hand – in his own.

'Hoogo can come with us, can't he, Mosey?' Poppy said, turning back to Hugo to give him a beaming smile.

Rosie's eyes flickered to John who was standing by silently. Feeling a spike of guilt that she'd not exactly forgotten about the man who was now her fiancé, but had certainly been distracted by Hugo, she took his arm.

'I'm sure we could all do with something to eat,' she said. 'I know I'm longing for a cup of tea.'

Poppy had already skipped ahead without waiting for permission. Rosie looked round, ready to include Hugo in the invitation – but he was nowhere in sight.

Shirley was very quiet when they were home again after the reception in the church hall.

'Thanks for coming, Aunt Dot,' Rosie said when she and Dot were in the kitchen and her mother had gone upstairs to have a rest. 'You don't know how grateful I am.'

'I'll stay as long as she needs me,' Dot said gruffly. 'After all, I don't have my Eric to wait on and kow-tow to his every demand.' Then her plain face broke into a grin. 'I haven't the heart to tell her yet,' she confided, 'but it in't all bad news to be able to make your own decisions.'

Rosie hid a smile. As far as she was aware, her Aunt Dot had always worn the trousers.

'Thanks, Aunt Dot. At least I know you're here when I'm back at work.'

'I expect they miss you.' She paused. 'What do you do, love?' Dot's eyes were wide with curiosity. 'Your mum don't seem to know exactly.'

'That's because I'm not allowed to say.'

Dot straightened in the kitchen chair. 'Ooh. It's secret war stuff, is it, duck?'

'Um, yes, sort of. I had to sign the Official Secrets Act.'

'You don't have to say no more to me, dear. I weren't born yesterday. Don't forget I drove an ambulance in the last war. *And* I was trained to repair the engine.'

Rosie smiled. She'd heard the story many times, but it didn't dilute the pride she felt in her aunt. She told her so.

Dot grinned. 'Best years of my life. Gave me my independence.' She cocked her ear. 'Do I hear the kettle boiling?'

There would be another tearful parting with Poppy, Rosie thought, her heart enclosed in a ring of pain as she took the little girl to school the next day. The day John Palmer was taking her to the station to catch her train to London.

'I don't want you to go, Mosey,' Poppy said, her lower lip trembling.

'You have to help Mummy and Auntie Dot, darling.'

'Won't Daddy come back ever?' she asked plaintively.

'Not that daddy,' Rosie said, swallowing the lump in her throat. 'But one day I hope you'll have a new daddy.'

'I don't want a new daddy – I want my old daddy.' She looked at Rosie, her green eyes dark with tears. 'Why didn't Hoogo stay?'

Rosie's heart somersaulted.

'He had to go back to work.' They were almost at the school gate.

'I like Hoogo. He makes me laugh.' Poppy looked up at Rosie. 'Do you like him, Mosey?'

Rosie gulped. 'Yes, Poppy. I like him very much.'

'Nice chap, Garfield,' John said, his eyes fixed on the road ahead as he drove Rosie to the station. 'He did me a bit of a favour once. Funny bumping into him after all this time.'

Hugo was the last person she wanted to hear about as she

leant back in the car seat and closed her eyes, trying to sort out her jumbled thoughts.

John filled in what might have been an awkward journey by switching subjects and talking about Hitler.

'He's changing tactics now he's done his worst with bombing London to smithereens, even though it hasn't destroyed the Londoners' morale as he'd planned,' John explained. 'So now he's using the German Baedeker guidebooks.' He briefly took his eyes off the road. 'Have you heard of them?'

She shook her head.

'They are an excellent set of guidebooks showing what Britain considers some of its most historical places of interest – and cultural. I've got a couple somewhere. Anyway, Hitler's ordered the Luftwaffe to rain bombs on these major cities, and poor old Norwich happens to be one of them.' He paused to let an elderly woman cross the road. 'They got Exeter and Bath a few nights ago and they'll methodically carry on trying to obliterate more.'

What an evil man. She couldn't help a shudder as she thought of Poppy. *Please keep her safe . . . and my family,* she muttered.

'We haven't been all clean and white ourselves,' John continued. 'The RAF bombed the hell out of Lübeck in March and these Baedeker raids are seen by Jerry as a reprisal.' Before she could comment he said, 'Oh, God, look the other way, Rosemary.'

But she didn't. Her head swivelled to where he was looking.

A row of houses in a street to their right was almost completely razed to the ground. They had been Victorian cottages, not dissimilar to her own home. People who must have lived there were wandering about in the debris, some of them calling out names.

'They're probably still looking for their pets,' John said with a grimace, 'and any belongings, poor things.'

Was anyone looking for a member of the family?

Rosie felt the nausea rise to the back of her throat. She mustn't be sick. She was made of sterner stuff. But the sight of those people wandering amongst the rubble of what had once been their prized possessions, looking dazed, gripped her stomach.

She turned to him. 'Oh, John, when is this madness ever going to end?'

He lifted his shoulders. 'Only when the Germans come to their senses and realise their wonderful leader has led them into poverty and misery and the contempt of most of the world.'

He pulled up at the railway station and helped her out with her case. They walked onto the platform where her train was pulling in, belching steam, and they could hear the sharp shrill sound of the brakes bringing the iron beast to a halt.

She thought she'd got away with it until he said, 'So you work with Hugo Garfield.' It was a statement.

Rosie gave a start. 'Um, yes. He's my boss.'

'Hmm. He seemed to know your family as well.' He was studying her. 'Quite a coincidence.'

'I was surprised to see him there,' she said truthfully.

'But you knew him before.' It was not a question.

Oh, why doesn't he just kiss me goodbye and go?

'Yes, a long time ago. I can hardly remember. He's the brother of one of my schoolfriends.' She had to give him a better explanation, the way he was staring at her. 'I had a bit of a crush on him at the time,' she added lamely, hoping the steam from the train swirling around them would disguise the fire that rushed to her cheeks.

'Hmm,' he said again, his eyes shadowing. 'It looked to me as though you still might . . . and I'd say it's reciprocated.'

She willed her voice not to shake.

'Nonsense. He's my boss and nothing more. He was just here to support me.'

'And you're sure you still want to marry me?'

'Of course I do. Why would anything have changed?'

She shouldn't have asked that question. The last thing she wanted was for him to think he had some kind of competition.

But he didn't answer. Instead, he bent and kissed her swiftly on the lips. 'You'd better board,' he said. 'Write to me, won't you, dearest?'

'Yes, of course.' She kissed his cheek. 'And thank you for everything, John. You were wonderful.' He gave her a quizzical look. 'You *are* wonderful,' she corrected hastily.

He smiled and nodded and moments later he strode away – leaving her in a state of confusion.

Chapter Thirty-Nine

Bletchley Park
May 1942

It was a relief in a way to be back at work, Rosie thought, as she settled into her night shift in the Hut. Everyone had been so kind. Even Alice said she was sorry to hear about her father. But lurking in the back of her mind was Hugo. He was bound to say something after John's announcement. Fancy the two of them knowing one another. Oh, it was too bad, though why it made her feel so uncomfortable she couldn't say. She'd seen nothing at all of Hugo but she knew he was on her shift that week as he so often was. She could only pray he would leave her to carry on with her job. Heaven knew, it needed every bit of her concentration.

Most evenings she continued reading *The Prince* to sharpen up her Italian and occasionally chatted in Italian with Elizabeth Morris in the Wrens' drawing room of Woburn Abbey. To Rosie's delight, they were becoming good friends.

She glimpsed Hugo at odd intervals in the corridor and the canteen, and once she was forced to pass by him when she was walking round the lake. He was looking thoughtful. Her heart began to thump but he merely nodded and moved on. So far he hadn't asked for a private meeting and her tension began to ease. Maybe he'd finally accepted that she didn't want any personal discussions about what happened more than six years ago. She'd been having headaches since her accident, but these had now subsided. John had written a loving letter and not mentioned Hugo. Maybe she'd overstated his reaction in her mind and he'd forgotten it. She'd written immediately back as she'd promised, feeling better about everything. Except her father.

She sighed heavily. He'd been furious about her coming in so late on the night of the first raid in Norwich and had tried to make her feel cheap, but there was something more behind that. He'd been terrified that John was a decent man who was quite prepared to take Poppy on as his daughter. His precious Poppy who looked upon him as her daddy. But for him to have barely acknowledged her when he'd said goodbye to his other children after supper that evening had been quite a shock. It wasn't made any easier to realise he hadn't known it was going to be his last day. She was sure if he'd lived, she'd have had a fight with him every day until the wedding and possibly even beyond. He had been the most stubborn man.

She briefly closed her eyes. It was hard to grieve for a man who'd changed her life inexorably without her having had any say in the matter. And yet she knew it had probably been for the best, rather than be a single woman with a baby, living in God knew what awful place to bring up a young child. Tears rolled down her face and she angrily brushed them away as she tried to fathom the latest message. This particular handwriting was always the most difficult to decipher, and what made it worse was that if she interpreted a word wrongly, it could have unforetold – even tragic – consequences.

'Let's all take a break,' Alice said. 'I need a cuppa.'

'I'd like to finish this pile,' Rosie said. 'You all go – I'll follow in a few minutes.'

But the next message flummoxed her. It was that pesky technical jargon again. Something she hadn't come across before. She rubbed her neck and scribbled a couple of things in her notebook, but she knew she was only guessing.

A shadow fell across the table and her heart stood still. Hugo.

'Can I help at all?' he said as he pointedly looked over her shoulder to read what she'd written. 'No, that's not right.'

She forced down a bubble of irritation.

'I know,' she snapped. 'I was just trying things out. It's an art of doing something and marina is the sea, but I can't work out what the connection is.'

'*Arte marinaresca* means marlinspike seamanship,' he said calmly.

'I still don't know what that means,' Rosie said, feeling utterly foolish. She'd never heard the term during the short time she was in the WRNS.

'It's the art of working with rope and cables and wires – tying knots, splicing, maintenance – all that sort of thing.'

'Thanks,' she said coolly. 'I'll add it to the list.'

'You probably need to leave it for a few minutes.' He paused. 'Why didn't you go with the others?'

'I wasn't ready to.'

'Will you come with me to the café? I could do with a cup of tea . . . though it's a pity they don't serve beer there,' he added, smiling.

Rosie hesitated. If she said no, he would give it more importance. He would think he'd really got under her skin. After all, he wasn't inviting her to dinner or anything. Just a cup of tea – at work.

'Maybe I do need a drink after all,' she said.

The café was quieter than usual, most people having gone to the canteen. Hugo picked a table in the corner away from anyone else.

'What would you like with your tea?' he asked.

'Oh, nothing.'

He was soon back with a tray of sandwiches and tea, and a small plate of biscuits. She watched as he set the mugs and plates on the table, remembering the touch of his hands when he caressed her.

Stop it! she admonished herself. *You're treading in dangerous waters.*

Hugo sat opposite, watching her with those unnerving eyes, just like Poppy's. When he spoke she gave a start.

'I want to ask you a serious question,' he said, not taking his eyes off her. 'I want you to answer it truthfully. I mean it.'

Rosie felt her chest tighten. This was it. He'd put two and two together about Poppy.

'Do you love him?'

Several seconds ticked by on the café clock. In the background she heard soft chatter, a clang of a teaspoon on the saucer, the lady serving saying there were no more sandwiches left. He was staring at her. She had to say something to stop him thinking she still had feelings for him.

'Of course I do, or I wouldn't be marrying him.'

He took her hand. The warmth of his touch seeped through her. Furious that he still had such an effect on her, she snatched it away, but he took hold of it again, this time tighter.

'Answer me, Rose. I'll say it again. Do you love John Palmer? A simple yes or no.'

She stared back at him.

'You can't answer, can you?'

353

'I've told you. I wouldn't be marrying him unless I did.'

'That means nothing when I look in your eyes.' He let her hand drop. 'All right, let's try it another way. As you now love John and you're perfectly happy and contented with him – and in my opinion you couldn't be engaged to a nicer chap – then you won't have any problem allowing me to explain what happened on the day *we* were to be married.' He gazed at her. 'Because I don't think you know anything like the whole story, or I'd have heard from you.'

She was silent.

'If someone wants . . . *needs* to apologise,' he went on, 'it's a rotten trick if the other person won't allow it.' He paused. 'So I say again, if you love John as you say you do, you'll let me tell you what happened. And I'd like to hear your version as well. I think there are gaps that neither of us knows about.'

He'd trapped her. And he knew it. If she stubbornly clung on to her decision not to drag up the past without giving him the courtesy of telling his side, he'd take it that she wasn't in love with John. That she might still have feelings for himself. At least if she agreed to listen to him he might realise once and for all that she'd finally found happiness with someone else. Someone he even approved of.

'All right,' she said. 'I'll listen.'

Did his eyes narrow a fraction? As though her willingness to listen told him she did love John after all? Feeling uncomfortable under his gaze, she drained her mug of tea.

'Good,' he said, glancing at his watch. 'But we need to get back to work now. I'll take you out to supper one night when we're on the day shift which I believe will be next week. We can relax off duty. Maybe even manage to enjoy one another's company and lay the past finally to rest.'

Chapter Forty

The following week, on the coveted day shift, Rosie opened the small brown envelope on her desk marked 'Personal'.

Supper booked for tomorrow night. Will pick you up from WA at 7.
Hugo

Had she done the right thing by agreeing to have supper with him, knowing they'd be raking up the past?

That evening she looked at her scant wardrobe. She sighed. She'd have to wear her flowered silky blouse with the black skirt as a change from the red jumper. She didn't remind herself she'd kept the blouse for a special occasion. It wasn't that she was out to impress him, she told herself crossly. She was only going because she'd finally agreed to give him the chance to tell her what had happened that fateful day.

The first person she saw the next morning in the corridor was Hugo coming out of his office. He gave her a wink and mouthed, 'See you tonight,' grinning as he strode by, making for Hut 4's outer door.

355

Trouble was, he was so damned attractive – and he knew it.

Rosie stepped down from the tired bus that had managed to drop her and forty Wrens outside Woburn Abbey. She usually admired the beautiful grounds, the deer park and the house itself, but this evening all she could think of was what Hugo might say. He seemed so determined to relive that day, whereas she would be quite happy to let it go. But why would she think that? Was she worried he might say something that would put him in a different light? That all her bitterness for all these years had been for nothing? She gave an angry shrug. No. Whatever he had to say would never alter the fact that he hadn't let her know. He'd changed his mind and been too cowardly to tell her in person. She breathed out a long sigh. Hugo was right – she *was* happy now with John, so there was no reason why she shouldn't forgive and forget. She'd feel better and she imagined Hugo would, too.

She was outside waiting for him when he drew up in a smart red MG with the hood down. Leaving the engine running, he sprang out and opened the door for her. She didn't miss his glance when the straight skirt rose above her knees as she settled herself in the passenger seat.

'Off we go, then,' he said, smiling at her before he put the motor into gear and roared off, sending the gravel flying on both sides, and Rosie's hair flying into her face. He pulled up, ready to turn into the road.

'Can you wait a moment?' she said. 'I need to put my scarf on.' She removed the spotted scarf from her neck and tied it round her head. 'Where are we going?' she asked as Hugo put his foot on the accelerator again.

'To a quiet restaurant in the country, away from prying

eyes, I hope. It's called The Inn on the Lake. It used to be a pub but it's got a good reputation – even in wartime.' He glanced at her. 'So just settle back and relax.'

The inn was just as Hugo had described. Even though it was officially spring, being the middle of May, there was a log fire burning in an inglenook with a few people sitting round having a drink. The waiter took their hats and jackets and escorted them to a quiet table in the corner. He was soon back with their menus.

'I want to make this a special occasion – we might never have the chance to do it again,' Hugo said.

What was he saying?

'We'll have a bottle of champagne,' he told the hovering waiter. 'A decent one. I'll leave it to you.'

'I think you'll find it's nicely chilled, sir,' the waiter said as he brought a champagne bucket and set it at the side of their table. He opened the bottle with a pleasing pop.

'Thank you.' Hugo watched as the waiter poured the two glasses, then disappeared. Hugo picked up his glass and Rosie did the same. He clinked it with hers.

'I meant what I said the other day,' he said, 'about John being a good chap. So this is to toast your engagement to him and to wish you both every happiness.'

'Thank you, Hugo,' Rosie said, not quite meeting his eye, her stomach fluttering. 'It's very kind of you.' In her confusion she took too large a swallow of champagne, causing the bubbles to go up her nose and making her cough. Hugo immediately handed her a white handkerchief.

'I'm not used to this sort of luxury,' she said, still spluttering.

'I can see that,' Hugo chuckled.

She laughed, and somehow it broke the tension between them.

Hugo opened the menu. 'I say we eat first and talk later over a coffee – all right?' She nodded. 'What are you going to have?'

They settled on plaice cooked in breadcrumbs and garnished with horseradish sauce, accompanied by new potatoes, greens and a small crisp salad.

'Better than the Abbey?' Hugo asked, an amused smile playing on his lips as he nodded towards Rosie's plate.

'Heaps better.' She couldn't help smiling back. 'It's delicious.' She hesitated. 'And so are the breakfasts since you intervened.'

Hugo was good company, as he always had been. She sometimes saw a flash of that younger Hugo, but mostly she was beginning to enjoy this more worldly version. She sensed by the way his eyes sometimes looked melancholic when he thought she wasn't looking that he hadn't had an easy time when on active duty on his ship before he came to Bletchley Park.

They finished with a small bowl of tinned peaches – with apologies from the waiter that fresh fruit had been difficult to get hold of lately – and a good scoop of vanilla ice-cream.

'If you'd like to take a seat over by the fire, I'll bring the rest of your champagne,' the waiter told them.

'Thank you. And two coffees, please.'

'Coming up, sir.'

Rosie felt her head swimming as it had the night she'd been concussed. But this was different. She put it down to the champagne she wasn't used to, but she'd only had one and a half glasses. Feeling Hugo's hand under her elbow she allowed him to lead her into the lounge where the fire was burning.

'It's going to be too hot right by the fire,' Hugo said. 'Let's take the sofa over there where we can be more private.'

When they were seated side by side, Hugo turned to her and briefly touched her jaw with his fingertips. Her skin tingled.

'Will you let me tell you what happened that day without interrupting, Rose?'

She took in a deep shaky breath.

'All right,' she said. 'Go ahead.'

'Where to start?' he muttered.

'Our so-called wedding day would be a good place,' Rosie said, not able to hide the sarcasm that rushed to her throat.

'Yes, our wedding day,' he repeated. 'The day I'd been longing for – the day you'd be my beautiful bride. My parents, you'll remember, weren't any more enthusiastic about our wedding than yours. But I'd just turned twenty-one and didn't need their permission.'

He reached for her hand, but she drew it away. This was too important for any distractions. He caught her eye, then cleared his throat.

'It didn't turn out as I . . . as *we* planned.'

You're telling me. But she kept silent and waited for him to carry on.

Here in the restaurant it seemed to Rosie as though it was the young Hugo telling her what happened. He talked about how his father had begged him not to marry her. How if he went ahead, he'd cut his son out of his will. Then his father's heart attack on the very morning of the wedding.

'My mother went to pieces,' he said. 'She felt helpless, not being able to get about. But I sent you a telegram letting you know there was a family emergency and that we'd have to delay the wedding.'

'I didn't receive any telegram,' Rosie put in sharply.

'Well, I can assure you I sent one.' He paused. 'Anyway,

let me continue. My father died in the early hours of the following morning before Lance could even get a flight from India. I had to take care of everything. By the time I'd finished the funeral arrangements and could come and see you to explain everything, I had a letter from your father.'

'From *Dad*?' Rosie squeaked. 'Why would *he* write?'

'He never liked me.' Hugo pulled out a packet of cigarettes and offered her one, but she shook her head. 'I wonder now if he was the one who intercepted the telegram.' He lit the cigarette and took his time to inhale deeply. 'Anyway, he told me you had specifically asked him to write—'

'I did no such thing,' she said through gritted teeth.

Hugo held up his hand.

'You said you wouldn't interrupt so let me finish,' he said. 'This is hard enough.'

Rosie slumped back in the sofa. She could hardly take it in. Her father writing to Hugo saying she'd asked him to. One of them was lying.

'He said you'd changed your mind. That you were too young and wanted to finish your education. And he warned me never to contact you again or I wouldn't hear the last of him – or words to that effect.'

'I didn't tell him I'd changed my mind,' Rosie said stiffly, stifling the fact that she'd said just that to his best man, William, outside the church that terrible day.

'Well, I wasn't sure if you had or hadn't, so I wrote to you.'
'I didn't get it.'

'It wasn't just the one letter, Rose.' He looked straight at her. 'I wrote you many at the beginning telling you where I was, what I was doing, and that I still loved you. I must have written you at least two dozen altogether. And then I gave up after about three years. It was too upsetting never to receive an answer. I realised I wasn't being fair to you – you'd probably met someone by then and were happy and married – maybe even with a child. I had to give up all hope.'

Rosie swallowed hard. *Was he lying? If not, and he'd written so many, why had she never received them? Not even one.*

She watched, mesmerised, as Hugo traced his finger round the rim of his glass, then swallowed the rest of the champagne. He looked up. 'You can imagine how it hit me when I passed you in the corridor of the Hut. I thought fate might be giving me a second chance.' He paused. 'Too bad I was too late.'

What did he mean? That up until finding out she was engaged to another man he'd genuinely thought he might have another chance with her?

Her hands clenched. She felt a pounding in her ears. Her own heartbeat. How *dare* he think like that? After she'd been on her own for six whole years living a lie with her own child, her siblings, and everyone else she happened to meet.

'Rose, what's the matter?'

She threw her hands up. 'I'm ready to go home, Hugo.'

'What have I said? I—'

'You're *lying* to me.' Her voice was too loud. She was barely aware of the curious stares from the other couples nearby. 'Maybe I could see a letter or two going astray,' she went on, her eyes blazing. 'Even three or four, but not *two dozen* over three years. And I doubt very much that a telegram would be lost when the post office is responsible for something so important.' She glared at him as he sat looking up at her, his jaw slack. 'But to give it the benefit of the doubt, maybe *one* of those could possibly have got lost. Not both. Not *all* the letters you say you sent *and* the telegram disappearing from the face of the earth!'

She could feel herself working into a frenzy.

'If that's how you want it,' Hugo said, standing up.

'It's *not* how I want it. But I never expected after all this time you would lie to me.'

Hugo's eyes were flint. He caught the arm of a passing waiter.

'May I have the bill, please?'

Hugo put the hood up on his sports car and made sure she was settled, then without saying a further word drove her back to Woburn Abbey. She was glad. She had nothing more to say to him. A quick sidelong glance showed her that Hugo's mouth was drawn in a tight line, his jaw hard, as he stared ahead. He'd hardly stopped outside the Abbey when she opened the passenger door and scrambled out.

Trembling with a mixture of anger and misery, she said through the still open door, 'Don't get out.'

With that, she slammed the car door shut and half ran to the tradesmen's entrance at the side which she knew would still be open. The last sound in her ear was a furious crackling and crunching as Hugo spun the car, causing gravel to fly up from beneath the wheels, and roared back up the drive.

Hugo clenched his jaw as he sped along the narrow roads towards his digs in Bletchley. For the second time, he'd let the girl he loved with all his heart slip through his fingers. Why hadn't he been able to convince her? Was there something more that lay behind her anger? She'd obviously had a rough time since that terrible day, even though she'd told him virtually nothing about her life throughout those years. Being the older sister with a mother not in the best of health, it had probably fallen upon Rose to take on most of the responsibility. Yet her mother kept on having children. He shook his head. That little one, Poppy, was a darling. But precocious. She reminded him so much of his Rose. Except she wasn't his Rose and never would be. Yet he was sure she still felt the same attraction to him as he did to her. But it was too late. He could think of nothing more to make her believe that everything he'd said was true. He hadn't given up trying and hoping for all those years. But now he had to resign himself that he'd failed.

He felt a strange pricking at the back of his eyes. Rose was happy with someone else and was planning to marry him. Who would have thought she'd choose old John Palmer? Yes, he was a decent bloke. Dependable, loyal . . . all the right qualities in a husband. He'd make a good father, too. But maybe just a bit too stolid. John had been sent to Whitehall before the war started and was still there in relative safety – no doubt doing an important job – while *he'd* come face to face with the German Navy on more than one occasion. Not to mention their blasted U-boats. It was a miracle he'd survived that last attack. So many of the crew hadn't. And if they'd plucked him from the sea only half an hour later . . . He shuddered at the thought and forced his mind back to Rose.

Maybe that's what Rose craved. Stability. Well, John Palmer was certainly a lucky sod.

He needed a drink. He needed to get well and truly plastered to blot out the black tunnel of a future without Rose.

Chapter Forty-One

That night in bed Rosie replayed the scene in the restaurant over and over. What a fool she'd been. To think she'd begun to actually like seeing Hugo again. Enjoy being in his company. She'd even admitted she was still attracted to him. More than once she'd tossed the idea around that maybe she'd never completely stopped loving him. It was certainly better for her peace of mind to think of him in a more generous way than allowing the bitterness of years to fester, especially as she now had a future with John. But this evening he'd ruined everything. If only she'd been firm enough to tell him it was time to let the past rest. That explanations were no longer important. But she knew he wouldn't have taken any notice. He was ready with his pack of lies. If he'd convinced her he was telling the truth then maybe he'd have thought he could win her over in other ways. All that 'darling' nonsense. Well, she was not going to be manipulated by him or any man.

She turned over in the bed, trying to get a more comfortable position. One thing good had come of this. She could finally lay him to rest and look forward to her life with dearest John, who, contrary to what her father had warned her, had assured her he would take Poppy into the marriage and bring her up as his own flesh and blood. On that, she never doubted him. And one day, when the war was over, they would have children of their own. And then something struck her. Something PO Robins had said about Hugo when she'd just been dismissed from the WRNS. 'After all, he is the father,' she'd told the tearful Rosie. 'It doesn't seem quite right that he doesn't know he has a child.'

She cried herself into a restless sleep.

A fortnight passed by. May had slipped into June and the Hut began to get stuffy. The Park's stunning magnolia tree had been in bloom for several weeks and the gardens were alive with colourful flower borders. People were enjoying tennis on the new court Winston Churchill had ordered for the workers, and occasionally Rosie had made up a foursome. Hugo had kept well out of sight, and when he saw her, he would merely nod and stride by. He rarely came into the room where she worked, and if he did, he treated her as politely and indifferently as he did everyone else.

A numbness formed itself around Rosie's heart. She threw herself into her work and to her relief found that most of the messages were much easier to translate and fill in the gaps. Her technical Italian was improving rapidly, as was her fluency, thanks to Elizabeth. They'd spent some pleasant evenings talking in Italian and she enjoyed the sound of the language rolling off her tongue. But one evening it brought with it memories of years ago when she was first learning and Hugo would make her practise. They would sit on their special bench in the park and, taking her workbook, he would fire questions at her in Italian and she would have to answer. They would mostly end up giggling and falling into one another's arms, the laughter turning to passion as they kissed.

After one of these episodes he drew away, still holding her.

'Darling Rose, I love you.'

It was the first time he'd said it. The words were the sweetest she had ever heard.

'I love you, too,' she'd almost choked out the words she'd been bottling up for what seemed for ever.

'I know we haven't known one another very long, but I also know my own mind. You're the only girl for me.' He quickly kissed her lips again. 'Will you marry me one day? One day soon?'

She'd said yes immediately. There'd never been a second's doubt in her mind that he was the only man for her.

Rosie swallowed hard at the memory as she looked at the next message to translate. The sooner she and John were married, the better. He'd said he didn't want to wait too long.

That afternoon, after a tea break with Nora, she wandered over to the main house to see if there was any post. Her heart lifted when she saw one from Roddy in his spiky writing. She knew what an effort it was for him to sit down and write to her. She bet that Ivy had reminded him, as there was one from her as well – a thick brown envelope. There was no time to read them now. She'd have to wait until she was back at the Abbey just after midnight where she could savour them, then sleep in a little later in the morning.

After what seemed to be a longer journey than usual, the bus dropped the full load of Wrens and Rosie.

'Coming for a cocoa, Rosie?' one of them called.

'Not tonight, thanks. I'm exhausted. I can't wait to get into my bed.'

'Goodnight, then.'

Rosie hadn't exaggerated. She was drained but she knew it wasn't all from work. She quickly undressed and hopped

366

into bed, taking her precious letters to read. Propping herself against the one mean pillow with her jacket stuffed behind it to support her, she opened Roddy's first.

Dear Rosie, I expect you will be surprized to recieve this letter. There int much news but yesterday what do you think? You wont guess. The yanks have arived!!! They dont half look smart. Heather goes on and on about them. I saw two today when I came out of school.

Got any gum chum? I said. I knew that was the thing to say from my Beano. The yank threw a hole packet at me and my friend. We was the envy of all the class next day.

I came 13 in class from all them tests we had to take. Mum said I could do better if I put my mind to it. Hope you are geting on with your secret work. I hope the war is still on by the time Im old enouf to join up.

Roddy

PS Sorry about sp mistakes!!

Rosie smiled as she tucked the letter back into the envelope. He wasn't a bad boy. She reached for Ivy's. Dear Ivy. She wrote religiously every week without fail. Even their mother didn't manage that. She ripped open the envelope, wondering why it was so thick? There were two full sides of Ivy's neat handwriting on the sheet of paper she drew out. Good. Ivy would tell her how they were all coping without Dad, especially Poppy. And whether Aunt Dot was still there. There was another envelope inside Ivy's addressed to Rosemary Frost, typed and marked 'Strictly Private & Confidential' in the top left-hand corner. Strange. But longing for news of home, she settled back on the makeshift pillow to read her sister's first.

Dear Rosie,

I hope you are well. We are all well here though Heather is in a bad mood and refuses to speak to me. But this time I'm standing my ground.

Rosie sighed. What was Heather up to now?

We were clearing out Dad's drawer and came across this letter addressed to you. Heather was very curious and thought it might be to do with Dad's will and we all had a right to know, but it had Private and Confidential written on it and I said it was dishonest to open it. She didn't like that one bit. She's also in a bad mood because now Poppy's seen you again she's asking when you're coming back. I keep telling her as soon as they give you some time off. She's doing well at school and has 2 friends, and she and Aunt Dot get on really well which probably makes Heather jealous. Just as she's jealous that you are Poppy's favourite sister.

Are you really going to marry that naval officer? He seemed very nice though rather quiet. Did you feel strange seeing Hugo again at Dad's funeral? He hasn't changed much – in appearance, anyway! I recognised him imme-diately. I always wondered what happened on that awful day. Anyway, now he's your boss I expect he's told you why he called off the wedding and you've forgiven him.

If you only knew, Rosie thought.

Aunt Dot sends love and Mum's going to write to you tomorrow. Hope it won't be long before we see you.

Love from your sister Ivy XX

Rosie grimaced. So Heather was up to her old tricks again. But this time it didn't appear that Poppy was quite so attached to her. Rosie slit open the typed envelope and removed a sheet of paper handwritten on both sides. It was her father's handwriting, dated Saturday, 18th April 1942, barely a week before he died. Not quite certain why her heart began to pound, she read:

Dear Rosie,

Your mother says you'll be here Thurs for a few days, but there's something I should have told you a long time ago and keep putting off. So I have decided to write this letter and let you have it when you're on the train going back to work. It's best if you read it on your own. If I try to explain it while you're here you will get all upset.

When you were 17 I had to resign myself that you were going to marry Hugo Garfield come what may.

Rosie's heart lurched. Instinctively, she braced herself.

On the day of your wedding a telegram was delivered a few minutes before you must have set out. Mum found it unopened in Heather's coat pocket when she was sewing on a button a few days later. It seems Heather had forgotten to give it to you on the day. As several days had gone by Mum was reluctant to give it to you as it would be a reminder about Hugo not turning up. We thought it would be just another congratulations message. But we were shocked to learn it was from Hugo to say there was a family emergency and the wedding would have to be delayed. I made your mother swear not to give it to you — to leave things as they were. It was for the best.

Every muscle stiffened. Scarcely able to take the smallest breath, Rosie read on:

But because Mum and I thought he'd jilted you at the altar I'd already written to him the day after telling him you'd said for me to write that you'd changed your mind about marrying. You were too young and wanted to finish your education and he mustn't ever contact you again.

'I don't believe this,' Rosie choked the words aloud in the attic room, fury with her father threatening to swamp her. He'd deliberately ruined her life – and Poppy's and Hugo's. Sick at heart she forced herself to finish reading.

Hugo wrote to you over the years but I got hold of them before you had a chance. The last one he wrote was three or four years ago and nothing since, so he must have given up. I know you will be upset with what you will call my interference but I did it for your sake – and Poppy's. Please believe me when I say I didn't want you to be hurt <u>again</u>. I never opened any of them and nor did your mother. She thought I was keeping them until I decided the time was right to explain this to you but I destroyed them all. I still hope you never set eyes on him again but I thought I owed it to you to come clean.

Rosie took some deep breaths. *Yes you bloody did owe it to me, Dad.* She bit back the nausea. He hadn't mentioned the real reason at the back of all this.

She turned the second sheet of paper over.

But there's one thing I'm not guilty of, Rosie. Whatever you might think I didn't inform the WRNS about Poppy.

All I can think of is that it was someone from the baby home. But why they should do that is a mystery to me.

Don't blame your mother for any of this. It was all my doing.

You've had a rough time and we're now in a world war so anything can happen. I hope you won't think too badly of me. I'm glad this is now out in the open and we can put it behind us when you come home next time. I know you're a good girl at heart.

Love Dad

Rosie felt a stinging at the back of her eyes. So Hugo *had* sent the telegram. And written regularly over the years, just as he'd said. He hadn't lied the other night. Dear God, she'd been so horrible to him in front of those people in the restaurant. Her cheeks burned. She hadn't believed him.

It was impossible to imagine how he must have felt at the time, never receiving an answer from the telegram. Never being able to explain what happened. Maybe still declaring his love for her. And the way she'd treated him at Bletchley Park – offhanded, curt, rude . . . How she must have hurt him.

She read the letter more slowly. And then she remembered. She'd been getting ready on her wedding morning and she'd told Heather to tell the driver they'd be down in a few minutes. When Heather had come back upstairs she'd mentioned the telegram boy had been and there was one for her. But she'd thought it was just another congratulation and told Heather she'd read it later. She'd forgotten all about it. Oh, if only she'd read it there and then, how her life would have changed. She would have read that Hugo had a family emergency. There was no doubt now that he would have contacted her as soon as he was able.

Something niggled in the back of Rosie's mind. She reread Ivy's letter. Heather had wanted to open the brown envelope marked 'Confidential', but Ivy had stopped her. And then a sick wave of realisation struck her. She clung on to the edge of the bed, perspiration breaking out on her forehead. It wasn't Mum or Dad, or someone from the home, who had betrayed her – it was Heather. Somehow Heather had found out she was Poppy's mother and had actually written to the WRNS to tell them, deliberately to get her sister into serious trouble.

But how could she prove it? And even if she did, what good would it do? But worse was the burning question – *why* had Heather, her own sister, wished her harm?

Rosie sat where she was, her father's letter strewn on the counterpane, trying to work it all out. Thank goodness he'd finally decided to tell her the truth. But it would be a very long time before she could begin to forgive him. What he'd done to Hugo was even worse than saying Poppy would have to be adopted because she would have scrubbed floors before she'd have allowed that to happen. But he'd sounded sorry even though he hadn't said the words, but hoped all would be better between them when she came home next time. But there'd never been a next time for him.

For the first time since his death, she flung herself on the bed and sobbed her heart out.

Over the next few days the questions tumbled through Rosie's mind every time she was on her own, usually when she was in her attic room getting ready for bed, and they were the first thing that sprang to her mind when she awoke. It had to stop. She either had to confront Heather – force the truth out of her – or lay it to rest. But even that she couldn't decide. It was beginning to play havoc with her sleep.

Her work colleagues were beginning to notice.

Beryl from the Index Room plonked down next to her on one of the easy chairs in the ballroom while Rosie was continuing her efforts with *The Prince*. Beryl's smile faded when she studied Rosie.

'Don't say anything,' Rosie pre-empted her, closing the book. 'I know I look like a worn-out dishrag.'

'If only you looked that attractive,' Beryl quipped. 'Seriously, you had such a worried look on your face when I saw you sitting there staring into space.'

'Family problems,' Rosie said.

'Do you want to tell me?'

Beryl was a dear. She'd made her feel so welcome on the first day. But she wasn't going to confide in her or anyone.

'It's too complicated. They'll probably resolve themselves.' Rosie gave her a rueful smile. 'Anyway, how are you and the other girls? Did you find anyone to replace me?'

'Yes . . . unfortunately.'

'Oh – why unfortunately?'

'Because Miss Pamela Perriman-Hale has taken your place. And woe betide if we ever forget what an important family she comes from.' Beryl pulled a face. 'It's completely altered our little group.' Then she gave a wicked grin. 'But she does give us some entertainment, though she doesn't know it. She's set her sights on our gorgeous lieutenant commander, but the more she eyes him the more he ignores her.' The grin was now a smirk. 'There's no yearning in his eyes like he used to have when *you* were with us.'

For a few brief moments Beryl's remarks cheered her.

Chapter Forty-Two

How would she ever be able to apologise to Hugo for not believing him? She pictured those green eyes, hard as marbles.

'Bit late for that, aren't you?' he'd say.

And she'd shrivel under his glare.

She was in a nightmare mostly of her own making. Her work was beginning to suffer. She didn't always finish a translation, or worse, she'd get it wrong. She struggled to fill in the gaps. The night shift moved into the midnight shift. She started getting headaches again and had difficulty sleeping for even a few hours at a time. She couldn't face food. Everything made her feel nauseous. It was almost like being pregnant with Poppy. She knew she couldn't carry on like this. Then she would tell herself it wouldn't make a scrap of difference if she told him she'd found out that he'd been speaking the truth.

'So you needed proof, did you?' he'd say. 'You couldn't trust my word.'

She shuddered from his imagined look of contempt. No, it was best to let the matter drop. Concentrate on John and a new life. She couldn't let *him* down and hurt him the way she'd carried the hurt from Hugo.

Alice was the first to draw her attention to her work.

'You look done in,' she said, after Rosie had had three

nights in a row of little sleep. 'Whatever's the matter, it's affecting your work.'

Alice wasn't the only one to comment.

After supper at the canteen, when Rosie was about to begin working and dreading it, Hugo put his head in the door of the Watch. This time he looked straight at her. She couldn't bear to meet his gaze. Her eyes ached and her head throbbed unmercifully. At this rate she'd have to go and see the dreaded Nurse Bull for a couple of aspirins.

'Rosemary, would you step into my office.' It wasn't a question.

He looked even grimmer than usual. Shakily, Rosie stood and followed him out of the door. He opened it and stood back to let her go in front. He jerked his head to the chair opposite his seat at the desk.

'Sit down.' He studied her for a full minute.

She began to feel uncomfortable under his gaze and shifted in her seat. What was he about to say? Was he about to get rid of her?

'I'm afraid –'

Oh, God, here it comes.

'– I'm going to have to –'

She grasped the edges of her seat, the skin thinning and tightening over her knuckles.

'– send you home—'

'No!' She sprang from her chair. 'Don't get rid of me. I promise—'

'Sit down,' he ordered. 'I'm not doing anything of the kind . . . you're going home on a month's sick leave.' He kept his eyes fixed on hers. 'You're too pale and you've got dark circles under your eyes.' He paused. 'I understand you've been taking tablets most days. Have you been having headaches?'

'Yes,' she answered in a small voice.

375

Who had told him about taking aspirin? She chewed her lip. *Probably Alice.*

He nodded. 'I think you're still feeling the aftermath of the concussion.'

'But that was ages ago.'

'Some symptoms can last for months. You came back too early after your accident, and your father's funeral. You didn't give yourself a chance. Thing is, this is no ordinary work. It's intense concentration every minute with huge responsibility attached to it. All that plus the punishing night shifts have knocked you for six. You need to rest. You'll feel a whole lot better when you come back.'

She breathed out. She wasn't being fired. But there'd be little peace and quiet at home.

'Will anyone be there to look after you besides your mother? I know she used to suffer from ill health.'

'My aunt's helping out.' She hesitated. 'But I can't be away a month. I'll forget my It—'

'You won't forget your Italian, if that's what you're worrying about.' His mouth held the glimmer of a smile. 'I hereby order you to finish *The Prince* and I shall ask questions later to make sure you've carried out my instructions.'

He's not lecturing me. He's being kind, even though I don't deserve it after what I called him.

Heat rushed to her cheeks.

Come on, Rosie, now's the time to apologise for acting so despicably in the restaurant.

She licked her dry lips and drew in a deep breath to steady herself.

'Hugo, I want to—'

'No need to thank me,' he said brusquely. 'Just get well and come back when you're ready. Go now. I've got a taxi waiting outside to take you back to the Abbey to collect your things – he'll wait and take you to the station. No need to give him anything. He's paid up.' He picked up a slip of paper. 'Here's your railway warrant.'

Biting her lip she took the voucher. She couldn't speak if she'd wanted to.

'Good. Then off you go . . . but mind you come back to us,' he added softly.

He turned to a file on his desk. She was dismissed.

'Straight to bed for you, my girl,' Aunt Dot said firmly when Rosie had told her and her mother that she'd been ordered to take some time off work and rest.

Rosie had refrained from telling them about her father's letter. That would come later.

'I think your boss is right for once,' Aunt Dot went on. 'It's the after-effects of the concussion. You might have to go and be checked again at the hospital.'

'I'm sure I won't need to do that.' Rosie gave a feeble smile.

'I'll bring you a cup of tea when you're in,' her mother added.

'Thanks, Mum.' She rose to kiss them both and went upstairs wishing she had her own room.

As it was, she never heard her mother enter the room and leave a cup of tea on the bedside table. Nor did she hear Heather and Ivy come in. She slept right through the evening until nine o'clock the following morning without stirring. Then a little heart-shaped face peered round the doorframe.

'Mosey,' Poppy whispered. 'Can I come in?'

'Of course you can, my love.' Rosie held out her arms and Poppy ran into them.

'Are you here for ever?'

'Maybe not for ever, but for quite a long time.'

'Are you poorly?'

'Not really – just very tired.'

'Are you too tired to play with me?' Poppy pulled back the bed covers and climbed in beside her.

'I'm never too tired for you, poppet.' Rosie felt a tear run down her cheek – then another.

'Why are you crying, Mosey?'

'People don't always cry when they're sad,' Rosie said, hugging her. 'Sometimes they cry tears of joy. That's what I'm doing because I'm so happy to see you.'

'So'm I,' Poppy said. 'Did you see Hoogo?'

Rosie couldn't help smiling at Poppy's sudden change of subject. 'Yes, darling, I've seen Hoogo. He sent you his very best.'

'What's his very best?'

Rosie swallowed. 'I expect he meant he's sending his love to you.'

Poppy put her head on one side. 'He's funny – better than Mr Palmer.'

'That's not very nice, Poppy.'

'But it's true.' She stared at Rosie with Hugo's eyes. 'You said I always have to tell the truth. And now I did, you're cross.'

'I'm not cross at all.'

Dear God, was she ever going to get anything right?

But after that one precious night of uninterrupted sleep she was back to her sisters' voices, Heather's upstaging Ivy's as she tried to pick an argument.

'For heaven's sake, Heather, shut up,' Rosie said. 'Some of us want to go to sleep.'

She pulled the blanket over her head, thinking she would have been better off in her attic room in the Abbey. At least there was no one to disturb her. But she wouldn't have had Poppy, and that was the best thing about being at home.

The next morning, leaving Heather snoring and Ivy snuffling in their bed, she came downstairs and into the hall where she heard her mother and Aunt Dot talking.

'I hate to say this, Shirl, but Rosie needs rest and quiet and she in't gettin' that here in this noisy crowd.'

Rosie stopped. She'd had a clip round the ear from her father the only time she'd ever eavesdropped when she was a child, but she was curious as to how her mother would answer.

'I know it in't perfect, but do you have a better suggestion?'

'Yes. I was goin' home tomorrow as I need to see to things, but I'd be glad for Rosie to come with me. Some sea air would bring the roses back to her cheeks. I think it would do her the world of good.'

'You may be right,' her mother's voice came more slowly. 'But Poppy will be upset all over again. It don't seem fair to the child, all this unsettlin'.'

'It don't seem fair not to tell her who her real mother is.' Dot's voice was dry.

Rosie froze.

'Now Sid's gone Rosie should be allowed to tell the child the truth,' Dot went on.

Rosie needed to be part of this conversation. She marched into the kitchen. Her mother and Dot looked up, guilt written all over their faces.

'I'm sorry I've intruded on a private conversation, but it seems to be about *me*. So can we please discuss it together?'

'Sit down, love. There's tea in the pot.' Aunt Dot poured a cup and handed it to Rosie. 'Poppy's old enough to know who her real mother is and you'll feel a lot better knowin' she knows.' She studied Rosie. 'That's half your trouble. It in't no good nursin' secrets. I never did think it was the right thing to do.'

'I think maybe Dot's right,' her mother said slowly, her eyes anxious. 'It's time to tell her.'

'I don't need anyone's permission to tell my own child,' Rosie said, her temper bubbling. What was it with her family forever interfering with her life? 'I will tell her in my own time. Just as in my own time I will tell her who her real father is.'

She was satisfied to see both sisters' jaws drop.

'But aren't you going to marry John?' Her mother's eyes were wide.

'Yes, I'm going to marry John. I'm not saying when I'll tell her, but when *I* decide the time is right.' She hesitated. She'd have to have it out with her mother. 'You know Hugo is now my boss?'

'Y-yes.' Her mother's voice faltered as though she knew what was coming.

'He's been very kind to me, though at first I refused to let him explain what happened on what was supposed to be my wedding day.' She caught a glance between her aunt and mother. 'But the other evening when he told me he'd sent a telegram to say there'd been a family emergency – it turned out his father had had a heart attack an hour before Hugo was due to leave for the church – I said I never got it. He told me he'd had a letter from Dad the following day saying I'd changed my mind and wanted to go back to school and he was not to contact me again.' She looked at her mother. 'Did you know about this letter, Mum?'

Her mother shook her head. 'I didn't even know about the telegram until a few days later, when I found it in Heather's pocket.'

'But you *did* know, Mum, that Hugo wrote me dozens of letters over several years. You knew that, didn't you, because Dad must have told you to make sure you picked up the post before I did. You were always up before me and when I used to take Poppy to the park when she was a baby, you were conveniently at home making lunch to pick up the second post. Isn't that right?'

'Yes.' Her mother's voice was a whisper.

'Oh, the poor boy,' Dot, who had been silent up until now, burst out. 'And to think I couldn't forgive him for jiltin' you at the altar.' She shook her head at Rosie.

'I called Hugo a liar.' Rosie stared at her mother. 'All the time Dad let me believe what a bounder he was.'

Her mother gave a sharp intake of breath at the word. Rosie couldn't care less. It had to come out now.

'How could you not have told me, Mum?' Her voice shook with misery. 'All those wasted years when I could have been happy, and Poppy would have had both her natural parents.'

'It's no use cryin' over spilt milk,' Dot said. 'Sid persuaded your mum he were doin' the right thing.' She touched Rosie's arm. 'Don't fall out with your mum, love. We all make mistakes – even you, love, if I may say so.'

Rosie's mouth went dry. She tried to speak but the words wouldn't come. She didn't know how to answer.

'Maybe I do need to get away for a bit,' she said to no one, then turned to her aunt. 'If you're really sure, Aunt Dot, I'd love to take up your offer –' she paused '– but may I please bring Poppy with me?'

There was one more thing Rosie needed to do before she and Poppy accompanied Aunt Dot to her home by the sea the next day. If she didn't do it she'd never be able to settle. All the lovely sea air and her joy at being with Poppy would

381

count for little because the question burning in her head would never go away. She had to have it out with Heather.

Her chance came that evening when the young ones were in bed. Ivy and her mother and Dot had gone to the pictures to see the latest Barbara Stanwyck film.

'Heather, we must talk,' Rosie said urgently as her sister, a magazine under her arm, opened the door to the parlour,

'There's nothing to say,' Heather tossed over her shoulder, slamming the door behind her.

Rosie took a few deep breaths, then opened it to find her sister on the sofa buried behind *Woman's Own*. There was an illustration on the cover of a couple kissing. Something stirred within her. What was it? Surprise that Heather was reading something so romantic when she always insisted she hadn't got time for all that soppy stuff? Sadness because she didn't really know her sister? Or was it guilt for not attempting to?

'Heather, please put that down and let's have a talk. I don't want to go to Aunt Dot's with so much unresolved between us.'

'Just go,' Heather said flatly. 'You're Aunt Dot's favourite, so go. I'm sure you and Poppy will have a wonderful time.'

Rosie went to sit next to her.

'Heather, why do you dislike me so much?'

Heather threw the magazine on the floor, and turned on her.

'It's always about *you*, isn't it? Rosie, the beauty with the flaming hair. Rosie passing the scholarship with flying colours. Rosie with the exciting life, Rosie nabbing the only man I'll ever love—' She broke down, sobbing.

'Oh, Heather, please don't.' She wrapped her arms around her sister and for the merest moment Heather went limp against her. Then she pulled herself up and looked at Rosie, her grey eyes wet with tears.

'I've loved Hugo since I was thirteen,' Heather burst out. But he only ever had eyes for you. And when you were going to marry him that day I wanted to kill myself.'

So that's what it was. Old-fashioned jealousy and resentment.

'Hush,' Rosie said, holding her close. 'Don't say such things. No one's worth that. You'll find someone of your own one day.' She held Heather a little away. 'You know, I forgot to ask you for the telegram on my wedding day. If I had, things would have been so different.'

'You might not believe me but I forgot it. It was only when Mum—'

'I know,' Rosie cut in.

'She must have shown it to Dad. I didn't know what happened to it afterwards.'

Rosie's eyes stung. 'He kept it from me.'

'I didn't have nothin' to do with that.'

'I know that, too.' Rosie paused. 'Look at me, Heather.'

Heather turned to face her.

'You have a beautiful complexion, a lovely smile that we don't see often enough, and you're good at your job or they wouldn't keep you—'

'I hate working at Woolies,' Heather burst out.

'You don't have to stay there for ever.' She stroked Heather's hair. 'Why don't you join up? Maybe in the ATS to train as an ambulance driver like Aunt Dot in the Great War. You don't panic at the sight of blood.' She looked directly at her sister. 'You know, Heather, I loved being a Wren for that short time.'

Get it out in the open, Rosie.

'It *was* you, wasn't it, who told them I'd had an illegitimate child?'

Heather looked away and nodded.

'How did you find out?'

'I had the curse and needed a Kotex. I didn't have any so I looked in your drawer and there it was, hidden inside the packet – a photo of you holding a new-born baby. I could tell straightaway it was Poppy. I turned it over and there was the date of Poppy's birth. It was easy to put two and two together.'

'But why did you want to get me thrown out?'

'I didn't realise they'd do that. I just thought you'd get told off,' Heather said miserably. 'And if you ask me why I did it, it's because you had everything I ever wanted. You even had Poppy. And I loved her more than anyone else in the world – even more than Hugo.'

Rosie's heart squeezed. 'Do you know, Heather, that's the best thing I've ever heard you say. Because I thought you just *pretended* to love her to get at me.'

'I did to start with,' Heather admitted, drying her eyes on the back of her hand. 'But Dad was right – she's such a poppet – and the only one who can make me laugh.' She sniffed. 'I'm sorry, Rosie. It was a horrible thing to do.'

'Well, I'm sorry I didn't spend more time with you – been a more understanding big sister.' She kissed Heather's forehead. 'Shall we try to be like proper sisters from now on?'

Heather nodded.

'And do you think you could be a proper auntie to Poppy?' Rosie said.

'I'd like that more than anything – if she's not too confused.'

'She's a bright child. Takes after her mother – and her auntie, of course,' Rosie grinned.

And at last Heather smiled back.

Chapter Forty-Three

Although Aunt Dot hardly ever stopped talking, Rosie had relaxed into a quieter rhythm at her aunt's cottage at Caister-on-Sea. There was no sea view, but it was only a five-minute walk to the beach, where the sun shone almost every day. Her aunt was no cook and after Rosie had watched her struggle for the first day or two cooking for three, she asked if she could take over the kitchen.

'It'd be a way of paying you for Poppy and me to have such an unexpected holiday.'

'You're family, love. I don't want no payment. But yes, you can gladly have the kitchen. And on Friday nights we'll stroll into town and have fish and chips . . . on me.'

'Can I go?' shouted Poppy, dancing up and down.

'Yes, you, too, poppet,' Rosie said.

'Daddy used to call me that.'

For a long second Rosie's eyelids fluttered down.

'I know, darling.'

'Mosey, do you miss Daddy?'

Poppy's upturned questioning little face clawed at her insides.

'Yes, darling, we *all* do.'

'Me more than anyone else in the world,' Poppy said seriously.

Rosie's aunt encouraged her and Poppy to go for walks by the sea although she never joined them.

'I've done enough walkin' by the sea to last for the rest of my life,' she said, when Rosie would invite her. 'Eric always dragged me along in all weathers. And anyway,' she said with a knowing smile, 'you and Poppy need time on your own.'

Three weeks had already passed. The war seemed a long way away from Caister-on-Sea although one evening she'd seen enemy aircraft roaring towards nearby Yarmouth. There were some signs of the war when she walked into town and saw sandbags piled against some of the shops, and women queued for food the same as they did at home, some grumbling, but mostly they were cheerful and gossiping with their neighbours.

Rosie wished she could stay longer, but she knew she must leave Aunt Dot's in the next day or two and prepare to go back to work. But she dreaded it. Facing Hugo every day. She'd had plenty of time to think about him. She'd been an utter coward. How could she have left her job without apologising to Hugo? Telling him how sorry she was that she hadn't believed him. And where on earth did it leave John? She'd had three whole weeks to decide what to do about John. He didn't deserve to be dangled like this. But why was she indecisive? Was it because she wasn't sure he was the right man for her after all? She admitted she didn't have that magical being-in-love feeling she'd had with Hugo – but did she love John enough to marry him? Spend the rest of her life with him? If so, surely she wouldn't keep questioning herself.

Today on the beach she sat upright on one of Aunt Dot's old towels reading, with one eye on Poppy, who was paddling at the edge of the foamy waves.

'Don't go in any further,' Rosie called.

'I won't.'

She doesn't cling to me so much or throw herself into a tantrum like she often used to when she didn't get her own way, Rosie thought. Perhaps she's growing up. And her little cheeks are rosy with being out in the sun making sandcastles and collecting shells. Everything she saw and picked up was a wonder and a treasure. Even a piece of seaweed or a bit of bark.

Contentment crept around Rosie's heart. She was here with her little girl by the sea – something she could never have imagined. It was perfect weather – the sun warming her face and limbs as she sat in her bathing costume, but not too hot in a cloudless blue sky. There were some families nearby and a man walking along the beach throwing sticks for his dog, but nothing disturbed her. A sudden wave rushed at Poppy's ankles. She ran giggling towards Rosie as another flock of seagulls swooped over their heads diving and screeching.

'Don't the seagulls sound happy, Mosey?' Poppy shouted.

'They do, darling. They're having fun playing and calling to one another.'

'How do they know what they're saying?' Poppy threw over her shoulder as she bent to pick up the stick the dog had dropped. She tossed it back to the dog who caught it in his mouth.

Rosie looked up from her book, not sure what sort of answer to give her. A shadow fell across her.

'Because they talk in seagull,' a familiar voice said. 'They understand exactly what the other seagulls are saying.'

Rosie jerked round at the same time as Poppy screamed, 'Hoogo!'

Hugo bent and swung the little girl up in his arms, Poppy squealing in delight.

Dear God, what is he doing here? How did he find me? Did he go to the house? Did Mum tell him I was staying with Aunt Dot? If so, Aunt Dot must have told him we'd gone to the beach . . .

She couldn't think any more. Hardly breathing, she watched the pair of them, mesmerised, her heart seeming to pound in time with the waves breaking on the shore.

For goodness' sake, woman, pull yourself together.

The clear salty air felt clean and refreshing as she drew in some deep slow breaths. She only hoped she was looking composed by the time he'd set the little girl down.

'Hello, Rose. Mind if I sit with you?' Hugo said with a smile in his eyes as well as on his lips.

'Come and play sandcastles with me, Hoogo,' Poppy demanded.

'I will very soon. Can you start building one? I'll come and have a look at it in a few minutes and help.'

Poppy tilted her head as if making a decision.

'Promise, Hoogo?'

'I promise.'

'It isn't hard,' Poppy said, having the last word as usual. 'I can do it by myself.' She skipped off, kicking little piles of sand in front of her.

Hugo grinned as he watched Poppy run off. Then he turned to Rosie and his smile faded.

'She's ours, isn't she?'

This was it. After all these years. And now he knew.

Numbness crept over her.

When Rosie didn't answer, he took her hand. 'It's obvious.

She's got your hair and my eyes.' He gave her hand a little squeeze.

'When did you realise?' Rosie managed.

'I was almost certain when I saw that photo of her with Heather but I didn't like to confront you at the time because you were always so prickly. Then at your dad's funeral she told me her exact age and that was proof enough.' He put her hand to his lips and kissed the palm, then folded her fingers over, just as he used to. He looked deep into her eyes. 'Oh, darling Rose, why didn't you tell me?'

She ran her tongue over her lips. 'I didn't know I was expecting at the time.' Her voice sounded thick in her ears. 'I didn't have any idea on our wedding day.'

Hugo shook his head. 'I'll never forgive myself for believing your father when he said you didn't want anything more to do with me. You were just so young, I didn't want to ruin your life if you'd made up your mind.' His eyes strayed to Poppy, a determined look on her face as she emptied out a small bucket to form part of the new castle. 'Oh, Rose, she's perfect.' He twisted round to her. 'She calls you "Mosey". Does that mean she doesn't know you're her mother?'

'Yes. Dad would never let me tell her. If he'd had his way, she would have been adopted.'

'My God!'

'Don't worry. I wouldn't have let it happen. This was before Poppy was born. And the minute he set eyes on her he made a bargain with me. He and Mum would look after her and love her as if she were their own. If I didn't agree, I was not allowed home again.' Her voice was flat. 'I didn't have any money to look after a baby. I wouldn't have known where to go. As it was, I had to go to the Mother and Baby Home in King's Lynn.' She looked at him. 'They're terrible places.'

389

Her voice shook with the memory of the cruel barbs that never ceased.

'Dear God, how could he do that to his own daughter?' Without waiting for a reply he said, 'What about your mother? Didn't she have anything to say about her grandchild?' He didn't bother to disguise the bitterness in his tone.

Rosie swallowed. 'Mum was the one who persuaded him not to make me put the baby up for adoption. It was her idea to pretend she was pregnant and would be the baby's mother. All to stop the scandal I would have caused.' She looked at him. 'The only good thing was that he kept his promise. He adored Poppy.'

Hugo was silent. Eventually he said, 'When are you planning to tell her the truth?'

Rosie swallowed hard. 'Before John and I are married.'

'Oh, I see.' He gave a deep sigh. Then he brightened. 'Well, if that's the case, this is "before you and John are married", so why don't we tell her together that we're her real Mummy and Daddy.'

'I have to tell her when it's the right time.' She forced herself look at him. 'It's going to be a lot for her to take in.'

'But she seems to like me already,' Hugo said, 'and anyone can see she adores you.'

'This is not the time,' she said, desperate to change the subject. 'Did Mum tell you where I was?'

'No, it was Heather.' He smiled. 'You know, I always thought she had a bit of a schoolgirl crush on me.'

'She did.' Rosie hesitated. 'You knew I was chucked out of the Wrens, didn't you?'

'I knew there was a bit of trouble there but I didn't know the reason, though I realise now.'

'Well, Heather found a photograph one of the nurses took of me holding Poppy when she was only two days old. She

390

realised I was Poppy's mother and wrote to the WRNS telling them I'd lied on my application form. They got rid of me immediately.' She sighed. 'I was lucky to be allowed to work at Bletchley Park.' She wouldn't mention it was John who'd brought it about.

Hugo's eyes strayed to Poppy, happily building her sand-castle. He turned back to Rosie.

'Do you have any proof it was Heather?'

Quickly she told him Heather's confession and her father's decision not to hand over the telegram. Hugo took a deep breath.

'And then he intercepted all your letters because he was terrified you and I would get together and Poppy would be taken from him.' Rosie briefly shut her eyes. 'I'll never forgive him for that. But at least he had the decency to write to me explaining why he'd acted the way he did, though I didn't get the letter until after he died. Ivy found it and sent it on to me at the Park. When I read it I was so upset and tried to tell you the day I thought you were getting rid of me – when you sent me home for a month.' She looked directly at him. 'Hugo, I feel so dreadful I doubted you. Please believe how sorry I am.'

Hugo raised his eyebrows. 'Our fathers have a lot to answer for.' He held her gaze. 'Did you make it up with Heather?'

'Yes.' Rosie traced her fingers in the sand. 'It was partly my fault. I haven't been a very understanding or loving sister. She was going through a bad time but we're much closer now. And she truly loves Poppy – her saying that made everything better.'

'I'm glad.' He smiled. 'You know something, Rose. If she hadn't reported you, you'd still be in the WRNS, and it's unlikely you'd have been sent to BP. So really she brought us back together.'

391

Rosie was silent for a few moments. Did he consider things might now work out between them?

'Rose?'

She looked at him.

'Are you absolutely certain that you still intend to marry John Palmer?'

'Why are you still asking that question?'

'Because if you are, and you don't love him, it will be the biggest mistake of your life.'

Aunt Dot insisted Hugo stay for the night, giving Rosie a mischievous wink behind his back, adding: 'It won't be the first time I've slept on the sofa.'

Poppy was wildly excited at the idea.

'Will you read me a story, Hoogo?'

'Course I will, my love.' He looked over the top of her head to Rosie. 'If that's okay with your mummy.'

Rosie stared at him, her body rigid with shock.

'Oh, my God. I'm so sorry.' Hugo's face looked stricken. 'It just slipped out. I promise I didn't mean to.'

'She's not my mummy, she's my big sister,' Poppy piped, gazing up at Rosie. 'Aren't you, Mosey?'

Dizzy with confusion, Rosie bent down. 'Yes, darling, I'm Mosey but—' She gulped.

Should she say Hugo had made a mistake? But this would make things even worse when she finally had to own up. And she'd always instilled into Poppy that she should tell the truth no matter how painful it was. Maybe this was the right moment to tell her child at least one truth about her real parents.

Poppy stared up at Hugo.

'I've already got a mummy.'

Rosie looked up to see Hugo watching her. She put her

arms round her daughter. 'Darling, I've got something important to tell you and now you're a big girl, I think this is the right time.'

Poppy's green eyes, so like Hugo's, fixed on hers. Rosie glanced at him and he nodded. She swallowed hard.

'Poppy, darling, I'm not really your sister. I'm your mummy. Your *real* mummy.'

Poppy stared wide-eyed. Rosie kissed her forehead.

'My mummy's at home,' Poppy said in a tiny voice.

'You're very lucky, poppet. You have *two* mummies to love you.'

'Oh.' Poppy chewed her lip. 'Does Auntie Dot know?'

'Yes.'

'Does my mummy at home know?'

'Yes, she knows, too.'

'Is she pleased?'

'Yes, darling, she and Auntie Dot are both very pleased.'

'Are you still Mosey?'

'Of course I am, my love.'

Please let her one day call me Mummy. Rosie blinked back the tears.

'Why are you crying, Mosey?'

'Because I'm so happy.' She hugged Poppy tightly and kissed the top of her head.

It seemed to satisfy the little girl and she ran off.

Hugo looked directly at her, a question in his eyes. She knew what he wanted her to add.

'You know, love, the more I've seen of Hugo, the more I like him,' Aunt Dot said as they laid the table for supper. 'He's suffered enough. He should be allowed to get to know his own daughter. And he's crazy about you.' Dot paused and gazed at Rosie. 'Just as you are about him, dear. And the sooner you come clean with that John and call off that engagement, the better.'

'I can't do that, Aunt Dot. I made my decision and I'm not altering it. I won't hurt John. I'm going to marry him, and I don't want to hear anything more about it.'

Are you sure this is really what you want?

'That's all I needed to know.' Hugo came into the dining room, his face dark.

Rosie spun round.

'I'm sorry, Hugo. I—'

He held up his hand.

'No, Rose. You don't need to say anything more.' His eyes never left hers. 'I'll just ask for one thing – the photograph of you and Poppy as a baby. You've deprived me of being her father for the first six years of her life, so I think that's the least you can give me – don't you?'

Chapter Forty-Four

Poppy and Aunt Dot carried the conversation at supper with Hugo half-heartedly joining in. Rosie was glad when she could clear the things away in the kitchen.

Keep busy. Don't be left alone with him. It will only stir up old hopes and dreams.

Aunt Dot bustled into the kitchen.

'Poppy wants to know if Hugo can put her to bed. She's already told him she knows what to do.'

Rosie's heart turned over.

'What do you think, Aunt Dot?'

'She's his daughter, love. But you must make the decision.'

'Yes, all right. Tell her it's all right.'

Tears stung her eyes. What was she getting into? Things had been going perfectly well. John was fully prepared to take Poppy as his own. And if Hugo had been completely out of the picture, she would have been perfectly happy. But Hugo was now very much *in* the picture. So how could she deny him spending time with his own daughter?

The cottage was small and Rosie could hear Hugo's deep tones interspersed with Poppy's squeals of laughter. It was quite a while before it died down and Hugo finally came into the sitting room where Rosie sat on the small sofa reading.

'Where's Dot?' Hugo asked.

'She's gone to the neighbour's to ask her about a pattern she's knitting,' Rosie said, a flush rising to her cheeks, desperately wishing her aunt hadn't been so obvious.

'That's tactful of her.' Hugo sat on the chair opposite. He gazed at her. 'Rose, I'm really sorry I was so nasty to you earlier on. It's just that I can't bear to think you're going to marry John – just when I know I have a daughter.' He kept his eyes fixed upon her. 'You sounded so firm when you said you didn't want to hurt John but it didn't seem to occur to you that you'd be hurting *me*.' He sighed. 'But if it's really what you want – if you *really* love him and he promises to be a good father—' Hugo broke off, his voice breaking. He went to sit by Rosie's side, then took her hands in both of his. 'Can you forgive me?'

Rosie felt her eyes prick with tears. 'I'm sorry, too,' she whispered. 'I felt terrible when I realised you'd overheard me. As soon as I'd said the words, I regretted them.'

He gave her a penetrating look.

'Are you saying you said the words about marrying John but in your heart you didn't believe them?'

'I-I think so . . . yes, that's what I meant,' Rosie stuttered, not able to meet his eyes.

'We both said things we ought not to have done.' Hugo sighed. 'Do you know, Rose, that our daughter's adorable?'

'Yes, I know.'

'But there's something you *don't* know. And I need to tell you now.' He paused. 'Look at me.' She raised her eyes to his. 'I've never stopped loving you – not for one single moment. And if I never say another word to you, I want you to know that you are – always have been – the love of my life. And before you ask – yes, I've had girlfriends. I wouldn't be normal if I hadn't in all these years. But no one has ever come close to you. And no one ever will. Nothing has changed in my mind as far as *you're* concerned.'

She felt the physical masculinity of him. The familiar scent of him. Oh, it was too much. It was . . .

He put his finger under her jaw and gently turned her head towards him.

'Kiss me,' he whispered.

Without waiting for an answer, he put his lips to hers. She let herself melt into the magic of his mouth on hers. She heard him groan. His hand moved to her breast over the top of her blouse and she quivered with longing. She felt him undo the buttons and slide his hand inside and round to her back, where he deftly undid her bra, then his hand enclosed her bare flesh. It was as though a flame leapt from the core of her.

He stood, pulling her up and holding her close against his chest. He kissed her again and again, his kisses growing more intense, and she found herself responding – just as she always had.

'Rose, I want to make love to you.' His voice was husky. 'Will you let me?'

She couldn't speak. What was he thinking of in someone else's house? But she knew Aunt Dot had left them alone on purpose. Arguments were swirling in her mind until Hugo left a necklace of little kisses around her neck.

'Come upstairs with me, darling.'

He took her hand. She followed him.

'In *my* room,' she whispered.

It was as though they'd never been apart, was Rosie's last thought.

*   *   *

Aunt Dot was pouring out a cup of tea from her large brown pot when Rosie walked into the kitchen the next morning.

'Well,' she said, staring at Rosie, 'you certainly look a different girl from how you came back from wherever you work. You were in a right state. But now . . . look at you. All flushed and happy.' She put her head on one side as if puzzling the transformation. 'Anything to do with a certain gentleman who happens to still be upstairs?'

'Stop teasing, Aunt Dot. You're too clever for your own good.'

Dot snorted. 'A good thing too. I nearly gave your bottom a tannin' yesterday when you said you were still goin' to marry John. Nice gentleman though he is, he in't right for you.'

'Any tea left?' Rosie asked.

'And it's no use tryin' to change the subject, my girl,' Aunt Dot said as she poured her one. 'You're in love with Hugo. Don't deny it. It's written all over your face.'

Rosie sighed. 'I know. But I don't know what to do about John. I'll have to tell him but I'm dreading it.'

'The sooner you do it, the sooner it's done,' Aunt Dot said briskly. 'And I'll even let you use my telephone, which I don't normally let anyone have unless it's an emergency.' She fixed her eyes on Rosie. 'But I should say this is one of them times.'

'John Palmer speaking.'

'John, it's me.'

'Rosemary! How lovely to hear your voice. Where are you?'

He sounded so cheerful. She bit her lip.

'I'm with Aunt Dot . . . in Caister-on-Sea.'

'I'm delighted. The sea air will do you the world of good after all you've been through lately. I hope you're managing to get plenty of rest.'

'I am – I mean I have. Aunt Dot's looked after me really well.'

'When are you going back to work?'

'Tomorrow.'

'Would you like me to come and pick you up?'

Rosie swallowed. *Now, Rosie.*

'It's awfully kind of you b-but Hugo's here. He's offered to take me back.'

'Oh. I see.' There was a dead silence. Then he said, 'He's still in love with you, isn't he?'

'Yes.' Her voice was small.

'I knew it. I only had to look at the two of you. I just kept hoping . . .'

'It's more than that, John. He's Poppy's father.' She heard his sharp intake of breath. 'I never told him but he worked it out when Poppy told him her age at Dad's funeral, and I think he could see the resemblance to himself. He came to tell me.'

'I see,' John said again. 'And you're breaking off our engagement.' It wasn't a question.

'John, I'm so very sorry.'

She heard him sigh. 'Well, that's the second broken engagement. I did it last time, so I suppose it serves me right.'

'Don't say that, John. You're the kindest, loveliest man. I'll never forget how you offered to take Poppy as your own. Most men wouldn't be prepared for that—'

'Don't tell me any more or I'll wonder why I couldn't keep you.' He paused. 'And it's right that Poppy has her real father. I'm just sorry I never had the opportunity.'

She heard the flick of his cigarette lighter.

'Hugo's a lucky blighter and you can tell him I said so.' There was a pause. 'There is one thing, Rosie. With both of you working at the same place, if you marry him – which I presume you will – you realise you'll have to give up the job you love.'

Rosie blinked. It had never occurred to her. But he was right. Very few companies allowed married couples to work in the same organisation. And government was the same. Then she brightened. Bletchley Park was a very different, very special, organisation. They'd allowed her to work there even though she was sure someone there knew she'd been turned out of the WRNS for not declaring she had an illegitimate child. No, surely John was wrong. Besides, Hugo hadn't mentioned anything about marriage. And if he did, she'd fight to the end to keep her job.

But supposing they said she had to go? She couldn't risk being dismissed from a job she loved – again.

'Rosemary?'

She took in a breath. 'If that's the case, I shan't marry until the war is over.'

'You might have a long wait.'

Hugo had insisted upon taking Rosie and Poppy home. Then Rosie would collect her things and say her goodbyes, and the two of them would be back at Bletchley Park by evening.

'Thank you for everything, Aunt Dot,' Rosie said, hugging her aunt. 'I'll never forget how you've looked after me twice now when I most needed it.'

'Well, it's now up to your young man to take over,' Dot said, then lowered her voice. 'Has he popped the question yet?'

'No. And I don't want him to. I want to get to know him again. This time I'm not going to rush into anything.'

She didn't mention she didn't want to risk losing her job before the war was over.

* * *

It was more difficult saying goodbye to her mother.

'Can you ever forgive me?' Her mother's eyes were anxious. 'Your father persuaded me he was doing the right thing by you.'

'That was always his excuse, Mum. The moment he set eyes on Poppy, he adored her. But instead of allowing me to be honest and come home with her as her mother, where he would have still seen her every day, he wasn't going to have neighbours wagging their tongues. He put them before his own daughter.'

'That was to protect *me* as well as you,' her mother said. 'Mrs Blake in the next road told me when her girl had an illegitimate baby, the neighbours wouldn't speak to her or any of the family. In fact, one of them crossed the street whenever they saw Lily pushin' the pram with her baby.'

Rosie stared at her. 'And yet Mr and Mrs Blake didn't turn her out – or make Lily pretend it wasn't hers.' She let that sink in. 'Well, I don't care a toss about neighbours. But I *do* care that I've lived a lie for so long. And deprived Poppy of her real parents.' Then she softened. 'I know you persuaded Dad to allow Poppy to be brought up as part of the family. But you took the "love, honour and obey" in your wedding vows too literally. Well, it's done now and Dad's no longer here, so we must put it in the past where it belongs.'

'What are you going to do about John?'

'I've told him I can't marry him. He was understanding. I didn't really deserve him to be.'

'What about Hugo?'

'He knows Poppy is his daughter. Poppy doesn't know, but we'll tell her in good time. But she *does* know I'm her mother.'

Shirley gave a gasp of surprise. 'What did she say?'

'She mentioned you. But I told her she was lucky. She had two mummies, and she seemed perfectly satisfied.'

Her mother smiled. 'I'm glad she knows, dear.'

'I'm going to leave it to you to tell the others because Hugo wants to get going right away. He has a long drive in front of him.' She paused. 'Mum, Heather told me she was the one who wrote to the WRNS.'

'You know, I did wonder. I was goin' to ask her but your dad said it would stir things up again.'

Rosie sighed. 'Well, things are finally settled between us. It wasn't all her fault. I should have seen the signs. But at least we have a proper understanding now.'

'I know, dear. She told me. I couldn't be more pleased.' She kissed Rosie's cheek. 'I told you she wasn't a bad girl at heart.'

'You did.' Rosie looked at her mother. 'Why don't you go with her to meet Poppy out of school? The weather's so lovely now and the walk will do you good.'

'Good idea.' She looked at Rosie. 'Do you know, I'm feelin' better in myself since I got over the shock of Dad. He did keep me under his thumb. It was my own fault. I should have spoke up more for myself. Dot being here has made me look at things different. I've joined a Make Do and Mend group, showin' other women, especially the youngsters, how to sew and, more importantly, how to do repairs now that clothes rationin' has really hit us. We're goin' to meet in each other's homes.'

'That's marvellous. Do you good to get out and meet other people. You've been stuck in the house too long.' Rosie hesitated. 'Talking of sewing, do you still have my wedding dress?'

Her mother shook her head. 'I gave it away when you started your new secret job. And Elsie's promised it to a friend afterwards. I think it's going to do the rounds.'

'I probably couldn't get into it now anyway,' Rosie said. 'I've put on a good few pounds since I've been working for the Foreign Office where there's always plenty to eat.'

Her mother smiled knowingly. 'I thought you weren't interested in getting married now you've given up John.'

'That's true,' Rosie grinned back. 'But I do know one thing – *if* I ever get married, I am *not* having the word "obey" anywhere in the service!'

Chapter Forty-Five

'I'm worried about all this petrol you're using up,' Rosie said, when they were approaching Cambridge.

'I get a special allowance.' Hugo braked hard behind a car that had cut in front of him while approaching a corner. 'Silly bugger. Good way to get killed.' He turned to her. 'When is Poppy's birthday?'

'Next month. Sixth of August. She loves it, being six on the six, as she says it.'

Hugo chuckled, staring ahead. 'I love her to bits, Rose. I'm sure you were just like her when you were her age.'

'Incorrigible, do you mean?' Rosie kept her face straight.

'Yep. That's about right.' He glanced at her. 'Can we tell her on her birthday that I'm her father? I'll make sure we get a couple of days off to see her.'

'All right.'

'Good.' He paused. 'But for now, I think it's time to stop for something to eat.'

It was late in the afternoon before they arrived at Woburn Abbey. Rosie's legs had practically gone to sleep by the time she scrambled from the car. Hugo removed her case and walked with her to the back entrance.

She only hoped they wouldn't bump into Elizabeth. But

all was quiet except a murmuring of voices from the drawing room. Well, if anyone 'caught' them, Hugo outranked every one of them, Rosie thought, as they mounted the main staircase and then the creaking set of stairs to the servants' quarters. She unlocked the door to her room and Hugo entered and set down her case. He looked round.

'Hmm. I see what you mean about being billeted in a country pile. Not much luxury here.'

'It suits me very well,' she said.

There was an awkward silence. Neither of them moved. She didn't know if she was supposed to say goodbye this minute or not. She only knew that once his back was turned and he was gone, the room would feel lifeless and unwelcoming, just as he had obviously thought when he'd come in.

He made up her mind by taking her into his arms.

'Dear Rose.' He briefly kissed her mouth. 'I don't know what to say.'

'Nor do I.'

'There's been so much to take in since yesterday.' He looked at her. 'Do you regret last night?'

'No,' she said softly. 'I wanted it as much as you.'

'Impossible! If you only knew how much I've missed you all these years, my darling, you'd have felt quite sorry for me. Though last night I believe you went some way in making up for lost time,' he added with a grin, 'but it's going to take many more times before I tell you we're even.'

She laughed. 'I'll have to see what I can do. But I have a feeling you're not going to tell me anything of the kind.'

'Not for years anyway,' he chuckled.

It's what she'd missed as much as anything. All their silly banter.

'But I know one thing. I won't rest until you answer my question.' He gazed down at her. 'Rose, darling, will you give

405

us a chance to get to know one another with the idea in mind that we'll be together one day . . . have our own home . . . you, me and Poppy?'

'*I* have a question.' She looked up at him, her hazel eyes intense. 'I have to know that if I hadn't had your child and you'd met me again at the Park, you'd still want to be with me.' Unconsciously, she tugged at his lapels. 'In other words, it's not just because I have Poppy and you quite rightly want to be part of her life.'

'I'd want you if you were on your own or if you'd had a dozen children . . . as long as *most* of them were mine,' he grinned. Then he became serious. 'I love you, Rose. I always have, I always will. And Poppy is part of you, so I love her, too. But I also love her for her own independent personality. She's a joy to be around. I only wish I hadn't missed all those years. I feel so upset sometimes.' His eyes were bright with unshed tears. 'She does like me, you know.'

Rosie touched his cheek. 'She adores you. It's as though she senses the strong connection between the two of you. It's wonderful to see.' She played with his hair, pushing it back off his forehead. 'But you understand what I'm saying.'

'I do.' He hesitated. 'I haven't told you this, but I nearly got engaged once to a very nice girl who loved me. Mother wanted me to marry her, because in her eyes she was the right class who Father would have approved. A match made in heaven, she said.' Hugo sighed. 'I tried to love her back. I'd almost convinced myself I did.' He looked at her. 'Probably a bit like you with John. But when she talked about marriage, I suddenly couldn't bring myself to ask her to be my wife. I knew it would be a disastrous mistake. I felt such a heel but there was only one girl for me, and I'd given up hope of ever seeing her again. When you walked past me that time in the corridor, I thought I was hallucinating. I was so used to rushing after every girl about your height with red hair ... and there were a few embarrassing moments, I can tell you.' He gave a rueful smile. 'But this time there was no doubt it was you. And I thought fate had sent us to the Park to give us a second chance.'

Rosie blinked. 'Hugo, if you're asking me to marry you—'

'I am, dearest Rose.' He looked at her, his face crestfallen. 'What's the matter?' he said urgently. 'What is it?'

'I can't marry you.'

'What!'

'Not right now. I'd have to give up my job – the one thing that I believed in, the first day I arrived. I was with people who wanted to do their bit in the war effort – and I wanted to be part of it. Use my brain. If we marry I doubt they'd let me stay at the Park so I'd just be a housewife. Yes, I'd have Poppy but I wouldn't be contributing in any way. I'd lose my sense of purpose. Can you understand?'

Hugo rubbed the back of his neck. 'Yes, I think so. I wouldn't expect you to stop working – I know how much you love it and you're damned good at your job – but I admit I hadn't thought of that.' He looked at her. 'So what do we do in the meantime?'

'Even *you* said for us to get to know one another and that's important to me. And it will be an easier transition for Poppy when she knows you're her father.'

'But when the war is over – and I hope to God it's not going to drag on, for everyone's sake—'

'Then I'll speed fate on its way and *I'll* be the one to pop the question!'

Rosie smothered a yawn as she rolled back her shoulders after being hunched over piles of messages for three hours on the trot. It had been a long night. She looked up as the door opened.

'Rosemary, can you pop into the office when you're ready for a break?'

'Go on, Rosie,' Sonia giggled. 'I expect he wants to give you a sneaky kiss.'

Rosie grinned back. It was no good trying to pretend. Everyone in the Watch knew that the two of them were in love and there'd been plenty of good-natured teasing.

When she was seated, Hugo beamed at her.

'I've got some excellent news,' he said. 'I've had a word with the boss.' Rosie raised an eyebrow. 'Yes, Commander Travis himself. After I explained about us he said there are several married couples in the Park. One couple even bumped into each other in the corridor – just like we did – and neither of them knew the other one worked here even though they'd had breakfast together that morning.'

'Unbelievable.'

'I know.' Hugo grinned. 'We weren't unique after all. But it does mean we're allowed to get married and still be here doing exactly the same job.'

'I don't want to rush into anything.'

'What about if we set it for January the twenty-third? The same date as last time? It just happens to be seven years later. That's six months from now.' He gave her a smile that melted her. 'Would that be long enough for us to get to know one another again, my darling?'

What was the point of waiting for this interminable war to end? The question rushed through her mind. She loved Hugo with all her heart and she knew he loved her. They could keep Poppy in her school where she was now doing well and making friends, and visit her as often as they could. She'd spoken to at least three women at the Park who'd left their children with their parents so they could contribute to the war effort. Most important of all, Poppy would be safe with her mother until the war ended.

Rosie drew in a breath. 'Well, I said I'd pop the question when the time was right.' She couldn't help laughing at his stunned expression. 'But I refuse to go down on one knee to you or any man.' She became serious. This was the moment. 'Hugo, will you marry me?' She kissed him soundly on the lips. 'But before you answer . . . if it's a "yes", there'll be one condition.'

Hugo frowned. 'What's that?'

'You'd damn well better turn up next time!'

After . . .

The war showed no signs of coming to an end. Since November, Germany and Italy had occupied Vichy France, but at least the Russians appeared to be pushing back the Germans in Stalingrad, Rosie reminded herself.

There was one major problem. She didn't have a wedding dress. Even if she'd had the money – which she didn't – rationing on clothing was becoming even more severe. Besides, even if she had managed to save up enough coupons, there was no guarantee there'd be a dress for her anyway. She was determined that Hugo wasn't going to hear about her problem, but the wedding was getting near. Her mother had mentioned it was almost impossible to find any suitable material.

'You might be able to hire one,' Dale said, when they were having lunch together one day in the canteen. 'That is, if you don't mind wearing a dress that's been worn by others.'

'I don't mind at all,' Rosie said. She wouldn't say she was used to hand-me-downs. 'But if I don't find something soon, I'll be walking down the aisle in my trusty black skirt and red jumper!'

It was Elizabeth who came up with a possible solution.

'Have you ever heard of Barbara Cartland?'

'The author?' Rosie said. Elizabeth nodded. 'I've never read any of her books, though my mother has.' She looked at her friend. 'They're a bit soppy, aren't they?'

'They might be soppy,' Elizabeth said with a knowing grin, 'but that's because Miss Cartland is an extremely romantic lady. Did you know she always dresses in pink, and not only her dress but everything else – stoles, shoes . . . and wouldn't be seen dead without her fuchsia-pink lipstick.'

'What's that got to do with finding a wedding dress?'

'Well, because she's so romantic, and has a good heart, she knows material and dresses are scarce now, but brides still want to look the part. She collects dresses like some people collect books. She has hundreds.' She looked at Rosie. 'Rosie, if I say something, please don't be offended.'

'I won't. I've grown a thick skin over the years.'

'She doesn't charge to hire out a dress so long as the girl can prove she can't afford to buy one.'

Rosie felt her cheeks flush.

'Oh, dear, I knew I shouldn't have been so blunt.'

'No, it's all right. I can't afford one even if the perfect dress was dangling in front of me.'

'Well, I think she'd be able to help. I'll find out how you can get in touch with her.'

A few days later Rosie saw Elizabeth walking into the dining room at Woburn Abbey.

'Just the girl I'm looking for,' Elizabeth said, smiling broadly. She plumped down by the side of her and fiddled in her bag. 'I've found out Miss Cartland's address. Ah, here it is.'

She handed a slip of paper to Rosie who glanced at it. It

411

was a London address. Where was her pride if she had to beg an unknown woman – and a famous one at that – to borrow a wedding dress? No, she couldn't do it.

'So you'll write to her,' Elizabeth persisted.

'Um, oh, yes.'

'She loves weddings. Maybe you should invite her to yours!' Elizabeth went off chuckling.

Rosie changed her mind many times over, and then vanity won. She did want to look like a proper bride – go down the aisle in a traditional wedding dress – for Hugo's sake as much as her own. What would be the harm? But what proof did Miss Cartland want to convince her that her plight was genuine? She decided to keep the letter simple and to the point, that she was doing special war work that didn't require a uniform so she had nothing appropriate to wear and very few coupons. Was there any way Miss Cartland could kindly help? She remembered to include her measurements and height and that she had red hair. She finished the letter by saying, *I must mention that my mother reads your books and is a big fan.* Two days later she was amazed to receive a typed answer.

3rd January 1943
Dear Miss Frost,

Thank you for your letter and the background to your request. Your work sounds very mysterious and anything we can do to bring this terrible war to an end is of paramount importance.

You say you are getting married on Saturday, 23rd January, so I will have your dress delivered at the beginning of that week to make sure it fits. My secretary is very good at matching the dress to the young lady, so I am sure you will be pleased with whatever she chooses.

Please make sure you don't allow anything to get spilt on it or come to harm in any way, and after the event I would appreciate it if you could arrange for it to be returned to me the Monday after the wedding so it's ready for the next bride!

Good luck, my dear, and I wish you a long and happy marriage.

Yours sincerely,

Barbara Cartland

P.S. Please give my kind regards to your mother. Tell her she has impeccable taste in books!

Rosie chuckled. What a nice lady. She must let Elizabeth know straightaway. But on the Thursday morning at breakfast, just two days before the wedding, Rosie changed her mind. Miss Cartland seemed totally unreliable.

'I'm sure it will come today,' Elizabeth said. 'I don't think she'll let you down.'

'But if it doesn't, I've got no other option,' Rosie said, annoyed with herself for putting her trust into a person she'd never met, just because she was famous.

Calling into the Post Room later that day, she was once again disappointed. Thoroughly dejected, Rosie mooched back to her Hut. It would have to be the navy dress she'd worn at her father's funeral. At least it was simple and smart.

But hardly the colour a bride would wear.

She shrugged the thought away. She was allowing the

wedding itself to override the joy of finally becoming Hugo's wife. Well, he'd have to take her as he found her. She wouldn't allow her mind to drift to that first wedding day when her mother had made her such a beautiful dress that Hugo had never set eyes on.

The following morning she walked over to the Post Room yet again.

'I'm expecting a parcel,' she told the clerk.

'Sorry, miss. Oh, hang on. I believe there *is* a parcel.'

Her heart leapt. Miss Cartland hadn't let her down after all.

The clerk was back in a trice. 'Sorry, miss. I must have muddled it with someone else's. But this came this morning.' He handed her a thickish white envelope with her mother's handwriting.

Curbing her disappointment that Miss Barbara Cartland had let her down, she hurried into the Mansion to find a quiet seat. She pulled a greetings card from the envelope with a picture of a prayer book on the front and the words: *A WEDDING WISH FOR YOU.* Inside, was a letter from her mother, but before she opened it, Rosie read the messages.

Thinking of you, dear Rosie and Hugo on your special day, love Mum xx

Rosie's eyes pricked to see her mother had included Hugo in her good wishes.

Wish I could have been your bridesmaid when you and Hugo get married. Have a lovely day. Ivy xx

Dear Ivy. Rosie hoped her youngest sister would meet someone nice one day. After all, she was nineteen and deserved to begin her own life away from the family.

Good luck Sis. Say hello to Hugo. Tell him I approve! Roddy

Roddy was growing up. She couldn't help grinning at his cheeky approval.

to Mosey lov from Poppy XXX

Darling Poppy, Rosie thought, smiling at the image of her daughter painstakingly writing it out. She wondered if Poppy would ever stop calling her 'Mosey'. In a way she hoped not. She glanced at the last entry.

To Rosie and Hugo, I wish you a happy day, Love Heather X

A warmth stole round Rosie's heart. Having a more sisterly understanding between them was something she'd never dared to hope for. She opened her mother's letter.

My dear Rosie,

I have something important to tell you. Poppy kept asking when Daddy in heaven was coming back so in the end I felt I had to say something. I hope you will not be too upset but I've told her gently on her own that her beloved Hoogo is her real daddy. I told her Daddy in heaven loved her very much and was taking Daddy Hoogo's place until Daddy Hoogo could come back and marry Mummy Mosey. Then one day you will all live together in a house. She's taken it in her stride and hasn't stopped skipping and dancing and singing at the top of her voice that she has the best Mummy Mosey and Daddy Hoogo in the world. She's made you this little picture for your wedding present.

I hope I haven't done the wrong thing, dear. Ideally, it should have been you and Hugo to break it to her, but it seemed the right thing to do and she's so happy.

Thinking of you on your special day,

Love from Mum XX

So Poppy knew. Rosie blinked back the tears. Hugo would be terribly disappointed not to have been there but he would understand – there was a war on and they might not have any leave at the same time for months. She couldn't blame her mother. After all, she had full responsibility now for Poppy. But it was overwhelming to take in the fact that after all this time, her daughter now knew who both her real parents were. But where was Poppy's drawing? It wasn't in the card. Don't say Mum had forgotten to put it in. She stuck her fingers in the envelope and pulled out a thin slip of folded paper shaped like a card. And there was Poppy's work of art – a smiling stick-limbed couple outside their house, a little girl in pigtails standing between them. They were all holding hands. The woman was wearing a long dress, her hair crayoned bright red, the man's crayoned black.

Poppy had written 'Mummy Mosey' and 'Daddy Hoogo' underneath them, and POPPY underneath the little girl. Rosie swallowed hard. It was the most wonderful wedding present she could ever wish for. She opened the paper card, then broke into a broad grin as she read underneath:

Evry day I like to stay and play.
 do you like my pome Mummy Mosey?
 from Poppy XXX

Yes, my darling Poppy, I like your 'pome' very much, Rosie thought. If only her little girl could come to her wedding. She would have made a gorgeous little bridesmaid. And the family would have enjoyed it, too. But Hugo had warned her that even if they made the long journey from Norwich for the actual wedding, taking into account the usual train delays, they would have to leave immediately after the church service, because the strict security wouldn't allow them to attend the reception at the Park.

Hugo wasn't bothered. His brother was abroad and

416

his mother would have difficulty travelling when in a wheelchair.

'Ours is a war wedding,' Hugo had said, 'and it feels right to celebrate with our friends and colleagues at the Park.' He kissed the tip of her nose when she'd been alone in his office one day. 'We're all in the same boat doing everything in our power to help shorten it.'

No, Rosie thought now as she sat smiling at Poppy's drawing, she didn't need any fancy wedding dress to broadcast her love for Hugo.

23rd January 1943

Rosie awoke early and lay huddled beneath the worn blanket, a smile curving her lips. Today she was finally going to marry the only man she had ever loved. It was hard to believe it was seven years to the day. Something struck her. She cocked an ear – not to any sound but to the strange sense of peace. Hopping out of bed she pulled back the curtains of the attic window and gasped. Only the sky was still dark. Everywhere else was covered in a white blanket of snow. It clung on to every branch, every twig, every roof, the greenhouses were buried under it, the drive had disappeared . . . All was perfectly silent.

It was as though she was looking out onto a fairyland.

Yes, it was beautiful, she admitted, but she was going to look like a poor relation in her old coat and hat. She was not going to look like a bride on her big day. But this was wartime and instinctively she knew Hugo wouldn't care how she was dressed. All he'd asked was that she let her hair loose. That was simple enough. But she would pay special attention to her face.

Yesterday evening in the drawing room the Wrens had

presented her with an enamelled powder compact and a scarlet lipstick. 'To clash nicely with that mane of titian locks,' one of them had called out, laughing. It had quite shaken her to see their grins when she'd given a squeal of delight. She'd never owned a powder compact with its own little mirror and powder puff, though she wouldn't let on to them. Most of them, Rosie could tell, came from good homes and would never know what a treat it was to have something so pretty.

This morning, on her wedding day, she took her time in the bathroom located on the floor below, careful not to fill the bath beyond the wartime rule of five inches. It wasn't difficult to judge as someone had painted a black line round the inside of the bath to denote the measurement. Back in her room she put on the new underwear her mother had made her from part of a silk parachute. It felt so luxurious against her skin, and her mother had even trimmed the brassiere with lace – something else hard to come by these days. At least she was wearing something beautiful underneath, Rosie thought wryly, then grinned. Hugo was sure to appreciate it, especially knowing only *he* would ever see it.

The service in the church was to start at eleven. She might as well go down to breakfast in her modest wedding outfit. She glanced at her watch, happy that she'd never sold it as her father had once suggested.

She went downstairs, wondering what all the noise and laughter seeping through the door of the dining room was about. As soon as she entered everyone at the long table stood up and cheered, then burst into song:

For she's a jolly good fe-e-llow – and so say all of us!'

'Happy wedding day, Rosie,' someone shouted.

'Hip hip, hurray! Hip hip, hurray! Hip hip, HURRAY!'

'Thank you so much, everyone,' Rosie said, her words

swallowed up in the enthusiastic clapping. She felt quite overwhelmed. What a grand bunch these Wrens had turned out to be. Somehow it had made up for the humiliation she'd suffered when she'd been stripped of her Wren's uniform. So much had happened in the meantime.

'Is PO Morris on nights?' she asked, not seeing her friend Elizabeth.

'Yes,' one of the Wrens answered. 'She said she hoped to see you before you leave to wish you luck. She's going to try to keep awake to see you in church.'

Rosie wouldn't hold her breath. She knew only too well how gruelling the midnight-until-eight shift was on the body. But it would be lovely to see her friend there.

Back in her attic room, Rosie was brushing her hair, allowing the soft waves to fall around her face when there was a knock at the door. She opened it to find a beaming Elizabeth holding a large bulky parcel. She put it in Rosie's astonished arms.

'It's addressed to you,' Elizabeth said. 'If it's what I think it is . . .'

Rosie could hardly breathe as she turned the parcel over. *From Barbara Cartland.*

She hadn't let her down after all.

'Shall I stay and watch you open it?' Elizabeth said, chuckling. 'Looking at the state you're in, I think you could do with some help.'

Rosie set the parcel on top of her bed. The string was secured with red sealing wax. She looked round at Elizabeth.

'I haven't got a knife.'

'I took the liberty of borrowing one from Cook,' Elizabeth said, grinning, and dug into her pocket. Cook had tied some newspaper round the blade for extra safety and secured it with a rubber band.

Rosie's hand shook as she took the knife, then handed it back to her friend.

'Will *you* do it? I think I'd be dangerous wielding a knife today.'

Elizabeth deftly cut the seal and untied the string, which she wound into a ball for reuse.

'Over to you,' she said.

The brown paper crackled as Rosie unfolded it to find the contents wrapped in tissue paper. She put a hand to her heart as though to still it.

'Oh, Elizabeth, I daren't look in case it doesn't fit . . . or it doesn't suit me.'

'Let *me* take it out then.'

In the car park outside the Norman church of St Mary's in Bletchley, the chauffeur helped Rosie out of the private motorcar Hugo had sent for her and escorted her to the church entrance. A verger stood at the door and smiled at her.

'Good morning to you.' He held open the heavy door and she swept through the entrance and into the nave.

A sea of faces, some she recognised from the Park, together with many curious locals, turned to watch her begin her deliberately slow walk up the aisle in her cream velvet full-length dress and cape, carrying an artificial posy that Ivy had sent. On her flame-coloured hair was a wide band of the same dress material, the veil fluttering at the back of her neck from a sudden cold draught caused by a band of latecomers opening the main door.

Just as the organist began to play 'Here Comes the Bride', Hugo turned. His expression was exactly how she'd dreamed this day seven years ago – eyes wide with surprise at the transformation, and then a slow smile lighting up his face.

She looked back at him and grinned, keeping her studied pace, letting the music of Mendelssohn's 'Wedding March' seep through her until it stopped at the precise moment she reached Hugo.

'You look beautiful,' he mouthed.

'Thank you,' she whispered back.

The vicar began the service. Hugo held her hand as they made their vows to one another.

'And do you, Rosemary Margaret, promise to love, honour and o—' the vicar abruptly stopped. 'That is, to love, honour and *cherish* him.'

Rosie stifled a giggle at the slightly disapproving emphasis on the word 'cherish'.

'I do,' she said firmly, her eyes not leaving Hugo's.

Moments later Hugo sealed their love by kissing her in front of the congregation. Rosie thought she would burst with happiness.

Back at the Park, the Wrens had organised with the canteen cooks a special wedding reception buffet. In the ballroom they had jammed together trestle tables and spread white sheets over the top, ready for the cooks to bring in the dishes. They'd also been hard at work stringing festive bunting down the elegant columns, with Union Jacks making more than one appearance. There was already a happy buzz when Rosie and Hugo entered the elegant room.

She felt a tap on her shoulder and spun round to see Pamela Perriman-Hale.

'You look stunning,' Pamela said, turning her gaze full onto Rosie, 'but a bit dazed, if you don't mind my saying so – as if you can't quite believe you've ensnared the enigmatic Hugo Garfield.'

Out of the corner of her eye, Rosie caught Hugo's grin.

'Actually, I think it's the other way round,' she said, not allowing Pamela to get under her skin today of all days. 'I think he can't believe *his* luck.'

'She's right, Pamela,' Hugo put in, his grin widening even further as his arm went firmly around Rosie's waist. 'I can't believe it.'

'In that case, congratulations,' Pamela said, staring up at him, then turning back to Rosie. With that she smiled, then made her way deliberately, so it seemed to Rosie, to the second best-looking officer at the Park.

Hugo led Rosie over to the buffet, where the wedding cake – two tiers, beautifully iced – took pride of place.

'I'm amazed they managed to do all this,' he said, 'when sugar is so hard to come by. Did the cooks here make it?' Rosie nodded. 'Well, I can't wait to try it.'

'We'll cut it when everyone has a glass in their hands,' Rosie said, hiding a smile. Hugo had always had a sweet tooth.

'Ladies and Gentlemen,' Jerzy Biskupski said, 'would you please raise your glasses to the happy couple, Rosie and Hugo.'

There were some whistles and cheers and shouts of 'Speech!'

Hugo caught Rosie's eye. She nodded and he stood.

'Rose and I want to thank you all for sharing this day with us. Few people probably know what I'm going to tell you.' There was a hushed silence. 'On this exact day, seven years ago, Rose and I had set the wedding day. For reasons I won't go into, it didn't happen, and so today is extra special as we lost contact and never dreamt we would ever meet again. But fate threw us together here at Bletchley Park and we realised we still loved one another.' He grinned. '*I* realised it immediately but Rose took a bit of convincing.'

422

There was a ripple of laughter and Hugo waited for it to die down. 'I'm told this is the first time the Park has allowed a wedding to take place on the premises – or perhaps I should say a reception – but it just shows that if you dream hard enough, it's possible to make anything happen. But you have to be prepared to give fate a bit of a heave-ho.' There were more chuckles. Hugo raised his glass. 'So please will you join me in the toast to my beloved wife, Rose, *and* –' he paused dramatically '– our darling daughter, Poppy, now six years old.'

There was a collective intake of breath. Then cheers rang out to the clinking of glasses.

'To Rosie and Hugo . . . and Poppy.'

'And –' Rosie stood up to link her arm through her husband's '– may Jerry do the decent thing and give up so we can all get on with our lives. But until that happens, we shall carry on with our secret work at Bletchley Park until the cows come home!'

'We'll drink to that.'

'Time to cut the cake,' Hugo announced in a loud voice, picking up the special cake knife. His gaze went to every corner of the room. 'Three cheers to the cooks who made the wedding cake.'

To the sounds of 'Hip hip, hurrah', Hugo put the point of the knife into the icing. Nothing happened. Rosie saw his slight frown as he pressed a little harder, then looked at her as though not knowing what to do next. She gently took the knife from his hand and laid it on the table, then put both hands around the second tier and lifted off the cardboard cut-out, waving it in the air. There were shrieks of laughter, Rosie's louder than anyone's as she watched Hugo's dumbfounded expression. Then, keeping a straight face, he picked up the plate to let everyone admire the diminutive and unassuming fruit cake that had been hiding underneath.

'I'm sure you'll agree the cooks have done a first-rate job,' he said, then could no longer contain his guffaws, amidst enthusiastic clapping and shouts of 'Hear, hear'.

Rosie glanced round at the crowd and spotted several friends and close colleagues: there was Elizabeth in her smart petty officer's uniform sending her a salute, Dale from Hut 6, grinning at her with raised glass, Beryl, Vi, Diana and Yvette from the Index Room, Nora, Paul, Stuart and Jerzy the Pole, Sonia – and, goodness, was that Alice actually smiling? There were many others she now recognised, making the most of a welcome break from the unceasing concentration and stifling atmosphere in the Huts to share their colleagues' happy occasion. But after the wedding reception was over, she knew they'd be back at their desks, buried in their work, doing their bit to beat Hitler.

She looked up at Hugo, who was still chuckling.

'What are you thinking, darling wife of mine?'

'I was thinking it would be nice to have a honeymoon planned.'

'I know, my love, but all I could wangle was three days. So it looks like we'll only be going as far as Bletchley – to my digs at the Shoulder of Mutton. Not the most romantic venue in the world but it will have to do for now. All I can say is to promise you a proper honeymoon one day – in Italy, as I once promised you. But that might have to wait until the war's over.'

'I was also thinking of Aunt Dot.'

His eyebrows shot up. 'Why Aunt Dot?'

'She happens to be visiting Mum at the moment.' Rosie sent him a wicked smile. 'She wondered if we could find any use for her empty cottage by the sea after the wedding. I said I couldn't think we'd find any sort of use for it at all.'

Hugo's eyes gleamed. 'You little minx. I hope you said "yes" immediately.'

Without answering, Rosie peered at the silver watch Hugo had given her seven years ago.

'Goodness, is that the time? We'll need to start off in the next hour so we're there before dark.' She looked directly at him. 'And on the way, there's a certain little person we have to pick up.'

Hugo's face split in two. 'We're taking Poppy?'

Rosie nodded. 'She's beside herself with excitement and already packed her bucket and spade, though heaven knows how she thinks she's going on the beach in this freezing weather.'

Hugo gazed at her, his green eyes shining with tears.

'I let you go once,' he said. 'I'll never let it happen again. But there's one thing I haven't told you properly yet.' He kissed her swiftly on her lips. 'How very beautiful you look today, darling Rose. And your dress – it's just gorgeous. I couldn't believe my eyes when you walked into the church. My beautiful bride. It hugs your figure in exactly the right places,' he added admiringly. 'Where did you manage to find it? I thought it was impossible these days with the rationing and getting all the coupons. I kept thinking you'd warn me you wouldn't be getting married in a wedding dress and I was going to tell you I didn't care if you turned up in a boiler suit.' He lightly stroked the velvet pile on one of the sleeves. 'This must have cost a fortune.'

'It cost me nothing,' Rosie grinned as his eyebrows lifted. 'Just don't be surprised if you notice I've swapped Machiavelli's *Prince* for soppy romantic novels.'

She laughed delightedly at the puzzled expression on Hugo's face. One day she'd let him into the secret. But not here at Bletchley Park on their wedding day.

Acknowledgements

As a writer, I'm often asked where I get my ideas from. I had in mind a completely different subject for a wartime story, but as soon as my editor of Avon HarperCollins asked if I would consider doing a series on Bletchley Park, I felt a tingle of excitement. I knew I would love to do it! But could I ever come to grips with even the *methodology* of deciphering the myriad codes let alone crack them? I began to read so many books about Bletchley Park and the people who worked there in several of the fascinating departments, deciphering the apparently undecipherable codes and signals, I sometimes thought my head would explode. And yet I loved every minute of the journey! Somehow, with expert help, the first one of the new Bletchley Park Girls series, called *Summer Secrets at Bletchley Park*, went out into the world in April 2022. And yes, all the codes my heroine, Dale, cracked are original – created by me but based on real samples.

Writing this second book in the series has opened my eyes yet again to the thousands of amazing people who worked at this most secret (they always used the term 'most secret' rather than our modern 'top secret') location. For this second novel I wanted to concentrate on the Italian Naval Section. In many ways this proved more difficult as there was less information available and most of it was highly technical in naval terminology as well as the Italians often using numbers instead of letters when they encoded their messages. I needed to find someone who was interested in naval history who could explain things to me in simple terms. To my relief, Alison Morton (more of Alison later) introduced me via email to one of her writing pals, Antoine Vanner. What a super chap he is! He's the author of a long-standing, naval-based series: The Dawlish Chronicles, and although he rarely sets them in my era, i.e. the Second World War, he turned out to be exactly the right person to help me gain a glimmer of understanding of some of the secret Italian naval signals – although probably not enough for the Park to have recruited me! And 'Scrivello' was his suggestion when I was badly stuck on one of the secret messages I was trying to create. Thank you for coming to my rescue, Antoine.

Back to Alison Morton, author of the successful Roma Nova series and lately a pair of contemporary thrillers. She and I have been each other's critique writing partners since we were casual business friends (both owning our own businesses). It was in that capacity we discovered we had just finished the first draft of our very first novel some ten years ago, never realising what a journey we were undertaking until some ten novels apiece later. We joke about using up the ink in our red pens as we meticulously go through each other's manuscripts with beady eyes, but we support each other unfailingly and have become close friends over the years.

I make up the fourth person of two writing groups, the Diamonds and the Vestas – we're all published writers and supportive friends who work in very different genres. Now we've come through the other side of lockdown, the

Diamonds – that's Terri Fleming, Sue Mackender and Tessa Spencer – have gone back to monthly meetings in person with belly laughs mixed in with sound advice and welcome suggestions for plot holes (my computer insists on changing this to 'potholes' but it's not much different!). Sadly, the Vestas – Gail Aldwin, Suzanne Goldring and Carol McGrath – are spread over the country so we are continuing with Zoom sessions until we meet in person, usually twice a year for a writer's retreat in one of their delightful holiday homes. There's little retreating but plenty of writing.

Thank you, Ladies. I treasure you all.

I must mention the publishing professionals who have helped in the creation of this novel and its journey to publication and beyond. I couldn't wish for a better agent than Heather Holden Brown of HHB Agency. Not only is she a great source of information with solid years of publishing experience as well as agency, but we gelled right from the start, and quickly became firm friends.

When I was a struggling writer, I always dreamed that one day I'd be picked up by HarperCollins. I set the bar high, and because of a massive stroke of luck by an author I'd never met introducing me to her Avon editor, Helen Huthwaite, it worked! Avon, an imprint of HC, keeps winning 'Imprint of the Year', and I can quite see why. The team is second to none. My delightful editor, Lucy Frederick, clicks into my stories and characters with huge enthusiasm, but suggests how to make them even better, and with her sharp eye spots things I've overlooked. Then there's the graphic art, digital, PR and marketing, and sales teams – all who make my stories into a beautiful book which you, dear reader, have been kind enough to read. I thank you all.

But I still hope Avon will one day let me write a series on that special wartime subject I mentioned at the beginning and to my knowledge, don't think any novelist has ever tackled!

A small request – if you've enjoyed this story, would you please consider leaving a short review on Amazon? They are like gold dust to authors and we love to hear from you.

Historical Note

For any interested readers, I'd like to mention a few people who appear in this novel and who were real.

Bettina and Gioconda Hansford were sisters, English but born and brought up in Italy, whose job in the small reference library in the Watch Room at Bletchley Park was exactly as I described in this novel. They and a small group of talented people were known simply as 'Research' and were enormously respected for their linguistic ability and efficiency in producing vital information for the Royal Navy.

A married couple (who shall remain nameless!) both worked at Bletchley Park. They had breakfast together one morning, said their goodbyes and went their separate ways to work. Later that day, to their astonishment, they bumped into one another in the corridor of one of the Huts, neither of them having had any inkling that their spouse also worked at Bletchley Park. Many of the men and women who worked at the Park went to their graves decades later, still not telling their families what they did in the war. Can you imagine keeping that kind of secret in our social media-obsessed world nowadays? But for a novelist, it was a demonstration of the power of having signed the Official Secrets Act, and was such an amazing coincidence, I knew it would be the perfect place and way for my heroine and hero to spot one another after so many years apart.

Barbara Cartland, the romantic novelist, really did collect wedding dresses during the war and loan them to brides who didn't have enough coupons to buy a wedding dress or even the material to make one, or because of rationing there simply wasn't anything suitable that was available. In the end she had hundreds of dresses in her collection. I came across this charming and generous gesture quite by accident and immediately realised it would perfectly fit my story. Also, I discovered that Miss Cartland had served in the ATS (Auxiliary Territorial Service) from 1941 until well after the war ended, so there was more to her than met the eye. And for the record she wrote 723 novels and sold over 750 million copies!

Reading List for *A Winter Wedding at Bletchley Park*

Codebreakers: The Inside Story of Bletchley Park by F H Hinsley & Alan Stripp
The Road to Station X by Sarah Baring (A memoir)
The Codebreakers of Bletchley Park by Dermot Turing (Alan Turing's nephew)
Bletchley Park People: Churchill's Geese That Never Cackled by Marion Hill
The Bletchley Girls by Tessa Dunlop
The Secret Life of Bletchley Park by Sinclair McKay
The Lost World of Bletchley Park by Sinclair McKay
Norfolk at War 1939-45 by Stephen Browning

Now you've finished Rosie's story, don't
miss Dale's adventures in the first
Bletchley Park Girls novel . . .

Available in paperback, eBook and audiobook now.

And why not check out Raine's wartime tale of hope and friendship in the Victory Sisters series?

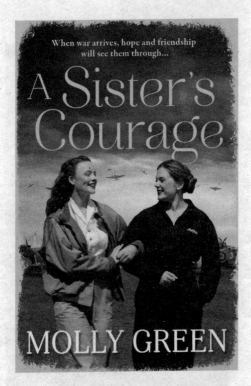

In the darkest days of war, Suzanne's duty is
to keep smiling through . . .

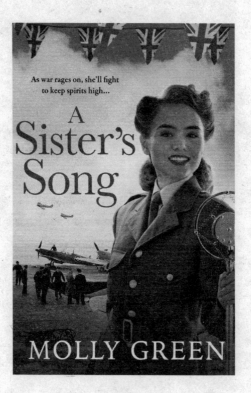

Available in paperback, eBook and audiobook now.

Ronnie Linfoot may be the youngest sister, but she's determined to do her bit . . .

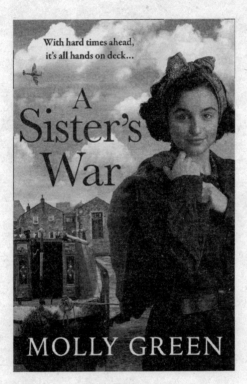

Available in paperback, eBook and audiobook now.

Or why not curl up with Molly Green's heart-warming Orphans series?

Available in paperback, eBook and audiobook now.

War rages on, but the women and children of Liverpool's Dr Barnardo's Home cannot give up hope . . .

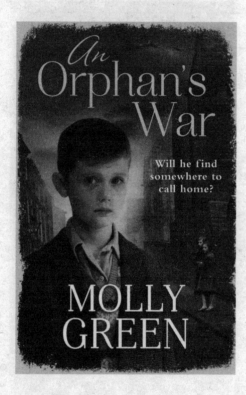

Available in paperback, eBook and audiobook now.

Even when all seems lost at Dr Barnardo's orphanage, there is always a glimmer of hope to be found . . .

Available in paperback, eBook and audiobook now.